## In the House of the Wicked

"Remy and his human friends are engagingly believable characters in a series noted for flashes of humor despite its overall serious tone. Series fans and followers of Jim Butcher's Dresden Files will enjoy this urban fantasy."
—*Library Journal*

"A fun . . . thought-provoking book." —Innsmouth Free Press

"Sniegoski ups his game in this most recent Remy adventure, and we begin to see some of the grand scheme he is setting up for us. The conflict and situations within this novel are refreshingly personal, bringing the forefront of activity back to the Boston area. The characters are varied and very well developed, bringing life and humanity into this novel largely centered around the angelic pantheon. With *In the House of the Wicked*, Sniegoski has crafted a very powerful, very personal tale that is equal parts gut-wrenching, heart-warming, and awe-inspiring." —The Ranting Dragon

"An excellent read and part of an excellent series that gets better and better."
—Fangs for the Fantasy

## A Hundred Words for Hate

"Sniegoski nicely juggles a large cast and throws in some touching moments (Remy's conversations with his late wife, Madeline, are especially sweet) and humor (as always, provided by Remy's dog, Marlowe) to balance the epic violence. There's more than enough nonintrusive exposition to let new readers jump into the story, while longtime fans will appreciate the development of recurring characters." —*Publishers Weekly*

"A fun, fast ride that takes advantage of a strong setting and interesting characters. And when a book combines that with serious angel smackdowns, really, what else do you need?" —The Green Man Review

## Where Angels Fear to Tread

"This strong, fast-paced noir fantasy is a treat. Remy is a compelling character, as he constantly struggles to hold on to the shred of humanity he forged for himself by suppressing the Seraphim. . . . Sniegoski adds a creative new spin to the good vs. evil scenario while bringing in some biblical characters that are decidedly different [from] what you read about in Sunday school. This is one of the better noir fantasy meets gumshoe detective series on the market today." —Monsters and Critics

*continued . . .*

## Dancing on the Head of a Pin

"[Sniegoski] nicely blends action, mystery, and fantasy into a well-paced story . . . a very emotional read with the hero's grief overshadowing his every move. An intense battle is fought, new secondary characters are introduced, and readers should gain a more solid picture of the hero's past."

—Darque Reviews

"Equal measures heartbreaking and honorable, Sniegoski has created a warm, genuine character struggling with his identity and destiny. Although this innovative urban noir draws heavily on Christian beliefs, the author's deft touch keeps it from being preachy. The fast pace, gratifying character development, and a sufficiently complex plot to hold your interest from start to finish make this one a winner."

—Monsters and Critics

"A fun read. The pace of the book is excellent, and it never has a dull moment. . . . The tale is definitely something that you would read out of a 1930s crime noir novel, and it is engaging, tightly written, and moves along at a rapid pace."

—*Sacramento Book Review*

"*Dancing on the Head of a Pin* is the second novel in the Remy Chandler series and a wonderful addition it is. . . . Remy has this twisted sense of humor that lightens whatever situation and makes the story even more delightful to read. The plot of the stolen weapons is tight and very focused. Along with the great characters, including the secondary ones, and the action-packed plot, *Dancing on the Head of a Pin* is an entertaining and smart detective story."

—Night Owl Reviews

"A powerful urban fantasy."

—Genre Go Round Reviews

## A Kiss Before the Apocalypse

"The most inventive novel you'll buy this year . . . a hard-boiled noir fantasy by turns funny, unsettling, and heartbreaking. This is the story Sniegoski was born to write, and a character I can't wait to see again."

—Christopher Golden, bestselling author of *Waking Nightmares*

"Tightly focused and deftly handled, [*A Kiss Before the Apocalypse*] covers familiar ground in entertaining new ways. . . . Fans of urban fantasy and classic detective stories will enjoy this smart and playful story." —*Publishers Weekly*

"This reviewer prays there will be more novels starring Remy. . . . The audience will believe he is on earth for a reason as he does great things for humanity. This heart-wrenching, beautiful urban fantasy will grip readers with its potent emotional fervor."
—*Midwest Book Review*

"It's kind of refreshing to see the holy side represented. . . . Fans of urban fantasy with a new twist are likely to enjoy Sniegoski's latest venture into that realm between humanity and angels."
—SFRevu

"Blurring the lines between good and evil, *A Kiss Before the Apocalypse* will keep readers riveted until the very end. This is an emotional journey that's sometimes filled with sadness, but once it begins you won't want to walk away. Mr. Sniegoski defines the hero in a way that makes him very real and thoroughly human. . . . Fast moving, well written, and wonderfully enchanting, this is one that fantasy readers won't want to miss."
—Darque Reviews

"A fascinating look at religion and humanity from a different point of view. Mr. Sniegoski has written a compelling story of what emotion can do to even the most divine creatures. *A Kiss Before the Apocalypse* is not a book that one can pick up and put down easily. Once you start, you will not want to put it down until you are finished."
—Fresh Fiction

"An exciting, page-turning mystery with the bonus of the popular paranormal aspects as well. This author has created a compelling central character with both human and angelic features, which allows the reader to become completely immersed in the story and the tension as it builds. The suspense alone leaves the reader anxious to come back for more. The story builds to a thrilling, edge-of-your-seat, nail-biting conclusion and will leave you wanting to read more of this character and certainly more of this author."
—*Affaire de Coeur*

"An intriguing, amazing story about a person torn between trying to live as a human while hiding his angel side as well. Remy was a very interesting, complex main character . . . a funny yet sometimes heartbreaking story and I had a wonderful time reading it."
—Night Owl Reviews

ALSO BY THOMAS E. SNIEGOSKI

*A Kiss Before the Apocalypse*

*Dancing on the Head of a Pin*

*Where Angels Fear to Tread*

*A Hundred Words for Hate*

*In the House of the Wicked*

# WALKING IN THE MIDST OF FIRE

## A REMY CHANDLER NOVEL

### THOMAS E. SNIEGOSKI

A ROC BOOK

ROC
Published by the Penguin Group
Penguin Group (USA) Inc., 375 Hudson Street,
New York, New York 10014, USA

USA I Canada I UK I Ireland I Australia I New Zealand I India I South Africa I China

Penguin Books Ltd., Registered Offices: 80 Strand, London WC2R 0RL, England
For more information about the Penguin Group visit penguin.com.

First published by Roc, an imprint of New American Library,
a division of Penguin Group (USA) Inc.

First Printing, August 2013
10   9   8   7   6   5   4   3   2   1

 REGISTERED TRADEMARK—MARCA REGISTRADA

LIBRARY OF CONGRESS CATALOGING-IN-PUBLICATION DATA:

Sniegoski, Tom.
  Walking in the midst of fire: a Remy Chandler novel/Thomas E. Sniegoski.
    p. cm.
  "A ROC book."
  ISBN 978-0-451-46511-5
  1. Chandler, Remy (Fictitious character)—Fiction. 2. Private investigators—Fiction. 3. Angels—Fiction.
4. Boston (Mass.)—Fiction. I. Title.
  PS3619.N537W35 2013
  813'.6—dc23      2012050860

Set in Adobe Garamond
Designed by Alissa Amell

Printed in the United States of America

PUBLISHER'S NOTE
This is a work of fiction. Names, characters, places, and incidents either are the product of the author's imagination
or are used fictitiously, and any resemblance to actual persons, living or dead, business establishments, events, or
locales is entirely coincidental.
  The publisher does not have any control over and does not assume any responsibility for author or third-party
Web sites or their content.

*For Brian Kozicki—*
*Gone far too soon, but never ever forgotten*

# ACKNOWLEDGMENTS

With love, and gratitude, to my lovely wife, LeeAnne, and to Kirby for sharing with me some of his best ideas.

Thanks also to Christopher Golden, Ginjer Buchanan, Katherine Sherbo, Rosanne Romanello, Liesa & James Mignogna, Scrawny Johnny Morrison, Kathy & Dave "thing from another world" Kraus, Pam Daley, Erek Vaehne, Garrett Jones, Mom & Dad Sniegoski, Paul Deane, Mom & Dad Fogg, Pat & Bob, Kenn Gold, and Timothy Cole and the Walking Dead down at Cole's Comics in Lynn.

By the prickling in my thumbs . . .

# WALKING IN THE MIDST OF FIRE

# PROLOGUE

*Jericho*
*26 AD*

Simeon was dead.

He was not aware of the length of time he had been lying within the cold embrace of the ground, wrapped in a shroud of burlap, for he had transcended such mundane, physical concerns, his spirit destined to unite with the other life energies that comprised the stuff of creation.

These energies . . . these *souls* as they were sometimes called, were the clay of the Almighty, and Simeon was joining them, experiencing the unimaginable joy of being one with the Creator as all that Simeon once was gradually melded with the whole that was God's glory.

Simeon had believed that he'd known bliss in his lifetime: the love and devotion of a good woman, three healthy children to carry on his bloodline, strong hands that allowed him a craft to support his family's lifestyle. It was all that one such as he could have hoped for in life, but it was nothing compared to the euphoria he experienced as he gave freely of himself, merging his own love with the love of all who had lived, and died, and would live again in another of the myriad forms of existence.

*This is what it was for,* Simeon thought as he was about to surrender his identity.

About to experience the completion of the cycle of life.

About to become one with God and creation.

One moment he was there, and the next . . .

Simeon was suddenly confused by the absence of joy and the sensation of pain.

He'd thought himself beyond the torment of the physical, but it appeared that he was wrong.

Simeon could feel the tether around his spirit, dragging him inexorably back to the corporeal world. He tried to fight it, begging the Creator to take notice of his dilemma.

But God did not see, or He chose not to.

Powerless, Simeon was pulled back through the veil of death, each level of his reemerging physical existence adding another dimension to his agony.

To have come so close to rapture, only to have it ripped away.

Deep within the cold darkness, Simeon was screaming, the pain unlike anything he'd ever experienced, worse even than it had been before his passing.

And no matter how much he begged to be released, nothing changed.

Nobody was listening.

He thrashed in the embrace of burlap, his fingers now claws tearing through the sack that had held his corpse. His once-dead lungs screamed for air as he pulled himself up through the dirt and rock meant to be his final resting place. And in a perversion of the rite of birth, he emerged, hands snaking out from the sand, the gentle touch of the hot desert breeze sending waves of sheer agony through his body.

Through a haze of anguish, he pulled himself from the ground and collapsed atop his burial mound. Everything hurt: his joints, muscles and skin, even the hair upon his head and the beard that sprouted from his face.

Simeon had no idea how long he'd lain there, immersed in a cocoon of suffering, before he realized that he was not alone. Even though it felt worse than any injury he had ever experienced, he lifted his eyes to the form that stood before him.

The figure was tall, with a kind face that bore a look of absolute shock. But its dismay soon transformed into the warmth of a smile.

Simeon gazed up at the youth, and as he looked upon him, he suddenly knew that this boy was responsible for his misery.

That this young stranger had somehow stolen Simeon from the vast comfort of the Lord God's embrace.

A single croaking word managed to break free from Simeon's throat, along with a cluster of hard-shelled insects that had made their nest in the rigid flesh of his trachea. "Who?"

The young man continued to smile as he bent to one knee beside Simeon. "I am Jesus of Nazareth," he said. "The Son of God. And I have raised you up."

Those words were even more painful than the agony his body was enduring. This boy—this child—had dragged him back from the euphoria of death and the promise of eternal union with the Creator of All Things.

"Why?" Simeon asked. "Why would you do this?"

The youth smiled all the wider, reaching down to touch Simeon's pale, dirt-covered face. "To see if I could," he said simply.

The words attacked Simeon, burrowing deep into his flesh, squirming their way into his heart and mind. The pain was so great that he began to scream.

And he did not know if he would ever be able to stop.

# CHAPTER ONE

Remy Chandler's eyes wandered to the television hanging above the crowded bar.

He didn't want to watch, but he couldn't help himself. There was always a nervous trepidation these days, a fear that he would see something that might compel him to act. Things were different in Boston—in the world, really—since a tear had been rent in the fabric of reality. It had swallowed up the top floors of the Hermes Building in Back Bay before Remy was able to close it.

And thanks to the media, millions of people throughout the world had caught a glimpse of something that had, until then, managed to remain in the shadows.

The news tonight was more mundane—tornadoes in the west, a school shooting in California, more sanctions about to be imposed upon a hostile Middle Eastern nation, and an eighty-nine-year-old woman who had hit the lottery for two hundred and fifty million dollars.

No more holes in the fabric of time and space spilling nightmare creatures into this reality . . . at least not in this news cycle. Maybe they were saving that one until the eleven o'clock broadcast.

"Are you gonna eat that last one?" Linda asked, pulling his attention back to his dinner companion.

"I'm sorry," Remy said, tearing his eyes from the television and gazing at the attractive, dark-haired woman sitting across from him. "Something caught my eye."

"Whatever," she replied. "Do you want that or not?" Her fork hovered over the last cube of fried manchego cheese on the plate in the center of the table.

"No, go ahead," he told her.

"I was hoping you'd say that." Linda grinned as she speared the cheese, dipped it in a red sauce, and popped it into her mouth.

Remy picked up his drink, watching as she closed her eyes in ecstasy while she chewed. She opened them and giggled when she saw him staring at her.

"I feel like such a pig," she said, swallowing and wiping her mouth with a red linen napkin, "but I could eat a hundred of those things."

They were at Loco, a tapas and wine bar located thirty minutes southwest of the city. Linda had mentioned wanting to try it once or twice and, feeling as though he had been neglecting his lady friend of late, Remy had made reservations for a special night out.

The waitress, a lovely girl by the name of Jessica, brought out their next selection, a flatbread pizza covered in Gorgonzola cheese, sprinkled with pine nuts and basil, and drizzled with a balsamic glaze. Remy wasn't quite sure how he was going to feel about this one, but he was put at ease with the first bite.

"This is pretty good," he said, nodding slowly.

"You seem surprised." Linda laughed.

"Guess I just didn't know what to expect," he said as he took another bite.

"Kinda like how it was with me." She winked at him over her slice of pizza.

Remy smiled warmly, feeling her hold upon him growing even stronger. "I got more than I bargained for with you," he said, swirling his drink in the glass, the melting ice cubes tinkling like wind chimes.

"And is that more in a good way or more in a bad way?" she asked, with a lovely tilt of her head.

He suddenly thought of Madeline. She was the love of his life and always would be. But there was definitely something about this woman sitting across the table from him, this Linda Somerset, that made Remy happy he hadn't abandoned his human visage when Maddy had passed away.

"I think you already know the answer to that," he told Linda as he helped himself to another piece of the flatbread.

"I know what I think," she said, once again helping herself to the last piece. "But I'm not sure you'd agree."

Linda kept her eyes on him as she took a large bite of the bread.

As an angel of the host Seraphim, Remy Chandler had fought for Heaven against the forces of Lucifer Morningstar. What he had seen, and done, during the Great War had soured him to the ways of Heaven, and so he had sought refuge on the world of the Almighty's most cherished creations. Remy, then Remiel, had come to the Earth to lose himself, crafting a human persona of his very own, suppressing his true angelic nature.

After thousands of years, it was Madeline who had solidified his mask of humanity, and made it something so much more. Her love for him had made him human, and now she was gone. The fabric of his humanity had begun to fray, and he'd had little hope that it would last—until he'd met Linda Somerset. Remy was beginning to believe that there just might be some hope for him after all.

"I knew you were trouble the minute I saw you," he said, looking at her, taking in the sight of her.

"So, is that good trouble or—," she started to ask, holding back her laughter as he interrupted.

"Knock it off. You're the best kind of trouble I know." He reached across the table to take her hand in his.

He'd been fighting his feelings for her since he'd met her, that annoying voice in the back of his brain reminding him how devastatingly painful it was to lose such love.

And no matter how human Remy believed he was, he faced a harsh reality. He was immortal: destined to watch anything he came to love wither and pass from life, always leaving him alone.

"Suddenly so serious, Mr. Chandler," she said, and he could see the beginnings of concern in her eyes. "Is everything all right?"

He smiled, but didn't release her hand. It felt good in his, and he wanted to keep it there for a little while longer. "Everything's fine," he said. "No worries."

But he was worried. Things had been getting progressively worse since the Apocalypse had been so narrowly averted just a couple of short years ago.

Remy remembered the prophetic dream he'd had just after the Hermes Building incident, when he'd spoken with a very familiar old man on a Cape Cod beach about a coming war.

Linda looked at him as if trying to see more than what he was willing to show her. "Okay, so why do you look the opposite?"

Jessica brought them their entrees—braised short ribs for Linda, a filet mignon with lobster for him; she then left to refill their drink order—another glass of Cabernet for her and a whiskey and ginger for him.

Linda continued to watch him. "Hello?" she asked.

Remy picked up the steak knife from the corner of his plate. "I've just been feeling a little bit guilty," he said with a shrug as he cut into his steak. It was so tender, he could have sliced it with his fork.

"Guilty about what?" Linda asked, tasting a bit of her own meal.

"I don't think I've been such a great boyfriend lately," he said, placing the meat in his mouth and chewing. It tasted as good as it looked.

Linda laughed out loud.

"What's so funny?" Remy asked.

"You said you're my boyfriend."

"Yeah? And that's funny because . . . ?"

"You've never said it before," Linda answered, looking down at her plate and suppressing a smile. "I liked hearing you say it."

She turned her dark eyes up to him, and he just about melted.

He used to feel a nasty twinge of guilt when she looked at him like that, as if he was somehow cheating on the memory of his departed Madeline.

But Remy had come to an understanding with these feelings, an understanding that this was just another aspect of being human: that it was nearly impossible to stop loving, for without love, there really wasn't much of a point.

Especially for him.

Without love he would be forced to return to what he really was; a warrior with the blood of his brothers on his hands, an angel that had lost faith in Heaven and its Creator.

Remy needed to love, and needed the love of another to truly live.

And really, wasn't that the truth for just about everyone?

"I would like to think of myself more as your Lambykins, or Snugglebunny," he said without cracking a smile as he stabbed a piece of beef and lobster with the end of his fork and popped it into his mouth.

"Interesting. I was thinking more along the lines of Honeybunny," Linda said slyly, scrutinizing him with a careful eye from across the table. "Yeah, you're most definitely a Honeybunny."

Sarah, who was tending bar at Loco that night, brought them their new drinks just in time.

"Honeybunny it is," he said, lifting his glass in a toast.

"To Honeybunny," Linda replied, picking up her wineglass.

They each had a drink to consummate the toast, playfulness twinkling in their eyes.

"So I'm just Girlfriend, then?" she asked.

"You seemed to like it a little while ago," he replied.

"Yeah, Girlfriend is good, but it doesn't have the same oomph as Honeybunny."

"True," Remy agreed. "Maybe we should give you a more tantalizing moniker."

"Moniker?" she repeated, starting to laugh. "Who the hell uses the word moniker? What are you, like a hundred and fifty years old?"

*If you only knew,* he thought, feeling another twinge, not over falling in love, but because he was unable to share the truth of himself with her.

It just wasn't the proper time. Things were still young, fresh, and the burden of his reality would surely kill what they were currently sharing.

Some other time, perhaps.

"Give me a break," he said with a chuckle. "I have a word-of-the-day calendar on my desk."

That made her laugh again and he absorbed the sound, relishing how good it made him feel.

"Maybe I should just call you Jerk-Woman," he said, feigning indignation.

"Oh really? Jerk-Woman?" she asked, pretending that she was offended, but not able to hide her smile.

"I'm just going to sit here and finish my dinner and think of all the other fabulous words from my calendar that I still haven't had the opportunity to use," he said as he made a show of dismissing her.

Linda reached across the table, taking his hand in hers and giving it a powerful squeeze.

"Your girlfriend is perfectly fine by me," she said as he looked up into her smiling face, feeling his heartbeat grow faster as the blood rushed through his veins.

"Yeah, I wasn't too thrilled with Jerk-Woman," he said, watching as she brought her wineglass up to her mouth.

"Oh good," she said, just before taking a drink. "Wouldn't care for that moniker," she teased, wrinkling her nose with distaste.

"I was thinking about one of the classics, like the Old Ball and Chain."

The words had barely left his mouth when she started to laugh while in midsip.

Remy knew right then how impossibly special she was, still sexy as hell even with wine coming out of her nose.


*Jericho*
*26 AD*


Simeon soon learned that no matter how hard he tried, the bliss of death was now denied him. Driven nearly insane by the Nazarene's actions, the resurrected man wandered, searching for a way to return to the bosom of God.

His body still bore the effects of the time he had spent rotting in the grave, his seeping flesh a home for insects, muscles pulled away from bone. He was a monstrosity, feared and reviled wherever his travels took him, and his hate of life grew, even as his body healed, for he remembered what had been taken from him.

And a hate of God, and all that He was, blossomed, as well.

It was in the place called the Skull, a place named Golgotha, that Simeon finally came to understand his purpose for being in this world. The Nazarene, now an adult, had been arrested and tried for his crimes. He had been sentenced to die, crucified between two common thieves. From the crowd Simeon watched the King of the Jews suffer, reveling in the fact that the one who had snatched him from death was suffering as he himself had.

"My God, my God, why have you forsaken me?" the Nazarene cried out as he hung upon the cross, and Simeon took great pleasure in seeing that the Almighty seemed to ignore this man, as well, this man who called Him father.

Simeon wanted to go to him, to stand beneath the slowly dying man and ask him to take back his gift of life, that perhaps the Lord of Lords would look kindly upon this act, and allow him release, as well.

And just as he was about to force himself through the lingering crowd, the skies grew gray, then black, and the ground beneath his feet began to move as if alive.

"It is finished," the one called Jesus cried out from the cross.

Sensing that his opportunity was fleeting, Simeon pushed against the mass of people, some weeping for their assumed savior, others waiting eagerly for his death.

"Nazarene!" Simeon cried out, finally breaking through the throng.

A Roman soldier stepped forward and struck him across the temple with the butt of his sword, sending Simeon to the ground, fighting to remain conscious.

And it was then that he heard the last words of the one who had taken away perhaps his only chance at regaining the rapture he had briefly known.

"Father, into your hands I commit my spirit."

And it was done. Jesus of Nazareth, the King of the Jews, was dead.

Simeon looked upon the face of his tormentor through the blood that dripped from the wound on his head, and saw the peace of death.

And he knew then and there that if he was to be denied that bliss, he would do everything in his power to see that it was denied to all.

He would take away their Heaven.

The evening had been next to perfect, and Remy did everything he could to hold on to the satisfying feeling of contentment he was experiencing. As they drove back to Boston, Linda Somerset snuggled close to him in the front seat of his Toyota, her head resting upon his shoulder as the new Brandi Carlile CD played on the stereo.

But when he drove, his thoughts tended to wander, and that very seldom lent itself to anything good. He found himself thinking of the dream he'd experienced, the one where he talked with the Almighty in the form of an old man, who Remy had once imagined was the personification of a perfect, human existence. Everything that he had wanted and would ever want for himself.

*"I need your help, Remy,"* God had said in the dream, his bare feet awash in the coming tide. *"The Kingdom of Heaven needs your help."*

Remy reached for the radio, turning up the volume in the hope that Brandi's gorgeous voice would drown out the memory of the words and what God had asked of him.

*"There is a war coming, Remy Chandler,"* the old man had told him. *"And I need you to stop it."*

No pressure.

"It was a nice night," Linda said groggily, as Brandi sang.

"Yeah, it was," Remy answered, grateful for the distraction.

He put his arm around her and pulled her closer.

"You know it doesn't really bother me," she said.

"What doesn't?" he asked, keeping his eyes on the road.

"When you're gone . . . for work and stuff," she explained. "It doesn't bother me 'cause I know that's your job . . . and I know you'll be back."

Remy pulled her even tighter to him. "That's good to know."

"And if you don't come back I get to keep your dog."

He laughed, happy that she and Marlowe had become so close. Remy wouldn't have had a clue as to what to do if the black Labrador hadn't liked Linda, but that was something he would never have to concern himself with. The dog had been pretty much smitten the first time he'd laid eyes on her.

"Don't let him find out about that," Remy said. "He'll try to figure out a way to keep me out of Boston indefinitely."

She laughed, rubbing her cheek against his chest. "Aw, Marlowe loves you more than he's letting on."

"Oh yeah? How can you tell?"

"He told me," she said.

"Really," Remy said bemusedly. "He talks to you now?"

"I can understand him," Linda said. "We chat all the time about stuff."

Remy found the conversation particularly amusing since he actually did have the gift of language. He was able to speak the languages and understand the tongues of all life upon the planet, including Labrador retrievers.

"You talk about stuff," Remy repeated.

"We do," Linda answered. "All kinds of stuff."

"I'm sure it's very interesting," he said.

"You'd be surprised," she answered.

The search for the ever-elusive parking space on Beacon Hill went as poorly as it usually did, forcing him to put his car on Cambridge Street, which meant that they had to endure the hike up Anderson Street to his home on Pinckney.

By the time they reached Revere Street, Linda was hanging all over him, jokingly telling him that she wasn't able to go any farther and that he was going to have to carry her. He joked about leaving her there and going for help, which got them both laughing and holding each other close. And that just led to kissing.

At this rate they'd never get to the house, and the neighbors would be calling the cops for the indecent public display of affection.

"We should probably take this inside," Remy said, looking deep into her eyes.

"Yeah, you're probably right," she answered, reaching up to touch his face, her fingernails on the roughness of his five-o'clock shadow sending currents of electricity down his neck and into his spine.

She suddenly didn't have any problem climbing the remainder of the hill, urging him to follow with a seductive wag of her finger.

Remy pushed himself the rest of the way, catching up to her at the top of the street, and grabbing her around the waist. He was about to kiss her again, when he saw that they weren't alone.

Steven Mulvehill sat on the front steps of Remy's brownstone, legs splayed out onto the sidewalk.

"Hey," the Boston homicide cop said as he casually looked up from his phone. Steven was one of the few people who Remy truly called friend, even though that relationship had been going through some difficulties of late.

"Hey back," Remy said.

Steven had gotten a little too close to the secret world that Remy navigated, and had almost paid a deadly price. The friends hadn't really spoken since.

"I was hoping I'd catch you," Steven said. "Didn't realize that you'd have company." He reached down and picked up the paper bag at his feet. "We can do this another time. I'm Steven by the way," he said to Linda, sticking out his hand as he stood. "You must be Linda."

"Yeah." She gave him a spectacular smile and took his hand. "Yeah, I am. It's really nice to finally meet you."

Steven's own smile slowly waned as he returned his attention to Remy. "Give me a call. I know I've been out of touch, but I'm back now. We need to talk."

Remy was about to reply, when Linda beat him to the punch.

"Hey, you know, I've got to get up early tomorrow," she said, her eyes darting to Steven and then to Remy. "I was planning on going right to bed. Why don't you stick around, Steven?"

Linda looked at Remy. He saw what she was doing, and loved her all the more for it.

"Why not," Remy agreed.

She smiled briefly at him, and then turned it to Steven. "Promise you won't keep him up all night." Her eyes dropped to the paper bag in his hand. "Or that you won't get him too drunk."

"Promise," Steven said, holding up his hand in a Boy Scout salute. "I know what a sloppy drunk he can be and I wouldn't want to subject a sweet thing like yourself to his shenanigans."

Linda laughed out loud.

"Shenanigans?" she repeated. "Who uses these words? Let me guess, you have a word-of-the-day desk calendar, too."

"He gave it to me for Christmas," Steven said with a completely straight face, pointing at Remy. "Why?"

The silence on the roof of Remy's brownstone was practically palpable.

He and Steven had grabbed some glasses and filled a bucket full of ice in the kitchen before heading up to the rooftop deck. Marlowe had been ecstatic to see his friend Steven and had insisted on joining them. He now lay beside Steven's chair, looking up at him lovingly, tail wagging.

"How ya been?" Steven finally asked, breaking the silence, reaching down with his free hand to pet the black dog's blocky head.

"Are you asking me or the dog?"

"Both," Steven said. He brought his tumbler of Glenlivet 18 to his mouth and carefully sipped at the scotch.

"I'm doing all right," Remy said, having some scotch of his own. "How are you doing, Marlowe? Steven wants to know."

"*I love Steven,*" Marlowe said, tail thumping excitedly upon the rooftop. "*Miss him.*"

"Well?" Steven asked.

"He says he's good," Remy said, not bothering to share the extent of the dog's emotions. "He said he missed you."

"I missed you, too, buddy," Steven said, leaning over in the chair to scratch Marlowe behind the ear and accept a wet, sloppy kiss.

Remy swirled the ice around in his glass, deciding to tackle the six-hundred-pound gorilla in the room. "Here's the real question," he said. "How are you?"

Steven moved uneasily in his chair, looking out at the twinkling lights of the city.

"I'm good now," he said. "I'm getting there . . . getting better. I'm all healed up physically."

"You know I'm sorry for what happened," Remy told him. "If I had known what I was asking you to do would put you in any danger I would never . . ."

"It's cool," Steven said. "If it wasn't, I wouldn't be here."

"When you wouldn't answer my calls . . ."

"If we talked then it wouldn't have been all right," Steven said, downing the remaining contents of his glass. He set the empty tumbler down on the patio table and fished a pack of cigarettes from his coat pocket, tapped one out, and lit it. "I just needed some time to think about stuff," he said, blowing a stream of smoke into the cool night air. "I needed to think about what I'd seen . . . and how it was connected to you."

Remy listened, sensing that his friend had more to say.

"I know you'd told me stuff in the past," Steven said with a nervous chuckle. "But I never imagined . . ."

Steven's voice trailed off, cigarette smoldering in his hand as he stared off into space. Remy was certain that he was experiencing it all again—his nearly fatal brush with the supernatural.

"I never meant for you to be exposed to that part of my life," Remy said. "You asked me to keep it as far from you as possible, and I thought I'd done a pretty good job until . . ."

Steven looked at him with fear in his gaze. "It's terrifying," he said. His hand was shaking as he brought the cigarette up to his eager lips. "The things I saw . . ." Steven finished the smoke, stamping out the remains in an ashtray on the table.

"I know," Remy said. "I'm sorry."

"How do you sleep?" Steven asked, pulling the stopper from the bottle and pouring another few fingers of scotch into his glass. He added some ice as an afterthought.

"I'm not sure you remember, but I'm not human," Remy said. He quickly looked to the doorway that led onto the roof, just to be sure that Linda wasn't there to overhear, before looking back to his friend. "This kind of thing—I'm sort of built for it."

"And I'm not," Steven Mulvehill said, bringing his glass to his mouth for a sip of his drink. "But now I know what's out there . . . not just what you've hinted at . . . what's *really* out there, and I'm terrified . . . terrified to have anything to do with you because it might force me to come in contact with something that, this time, would finish me off in the most horrifying way imaginable."

"I figured as much," Remy said, sipping what remained of his drink.

The two were silent, the sound of Marlowe's deep snoring the soundtrack to the moment.

"So how about now?" Remy finally asked him. "Are you still scared of what's out there? Of me?"

Steven laughed, looking at his friend.

"Fucking terrified."

That made Remy laugh, too, and shake his head.

"I wish there was something I could say or do to take away your fear, but . . ." Remy stopped, considering his words. "But it doesn't change the fact that those threats are out there, and now with what happened in Back Bay . . ."

"You were involved with that," Steven stated. "How did I fucking know you were involved with that?"

"You are a police detective," Remy said. He leaned forward in his chair and reached for the bottle.

"I was out there," Steven suddenly stated.

"Where?" Remy asked as he poured more scotch over the dwindling ice in his glass.

"The streets around where that business was happening."

Remy sat back. "Did you see . . ."

"More shit that I wish I could unsee," he said.

"Why would you go anywhere near something like that if you knew . . ."

"I saw it on TV and just about shit myself," Steven explained. "I knew it—as soon as that special news report started, I knew that it must've had something to do with the crazy shit that you'd gotten me involved with."

"Still doesn't explain why you would go out into it," Remy said. "Especially after what you'd gone through before. I don't get it."

"I was afraid," Steven said.

"Yeah, I get that, but it doesn't tell me why—"

"The fear was eating me alive," he interrupted. "It was all I knew. . . . I woke up with it. I had lunch with it. . . . It was with me constantly, and it liked to remind me that it was the fucking boss."

Steven took a big long drink, almost draining his glass.

"And when I saw that business on the television I wanted to pull the curtains and hide myself away. . . . That was what the fear was telling me to do."

Remy continued to listen, urging him on with a glance.

"But I didn't want to listen anymore," Steven continued. "I didn't want to hide anymore."

"So you went out there, out onto the streets to confront your fears? Is that what you did?"

Steven chuckled, taking another cigarette from his pack.

"Sounds pretty fucking stupid doesn't it?" he said, starting to laugh harder.

Remy laughed, too. "It really does."

"But that's what I did. I put my gun in my pocket, drove as far as I could, and walked as close as I was able."

"And did you face your fears?" Remy asked.

"I don't know what I fucking faced," Steven said. "It was pretty horrible . . . but I faced it, and I lived to tell about it."

Remy raised what was left in his glass to him in a toast.

Steven lifted his empty glass in response.

Remy finished off his drink, thinking of how he was going to word his next question.

"So what now?" he asked. He decided to have something more to drink. "Are you planning on walking the mean streets looking for evil to vanquish?"

Steven smiled. "Nothing so dramatic," he said. "I'm back at work, doing my thing, but I see things differently now."

"How so?"

"I know what's really out there now, waiting in the shadows, as do a lot of people, I think, since what happened at the Hermes Building."

"They were blind, but now they see," Remy said grimly.

"Yeah, but I at least understand what I'm seeing," the homicide detective said.

"So, you're good?" Remy asked. "You're dealing with this okay?"

"As good as can be expected," Steven said in all truthfulness. "Am I still afraid of what could be waiting for me around the next corner? You bet your ass I am, but I'll be damned if I let the fear win."

They again raised their glasses in a toast, both of them drinking at the same time.

"Marlowe wasn't the only one who missed you," Remy said casually.

"You just missed the free booze," Steven said with a knowing nod.

"Am I that transparent?" Remy asked.

"I was blind but now I see," he said, throwing Remy's quote back at him. Steven was smiling and finishing his latest cigarette when . . .

"Ah!" he said, turning in his chair toward his friend.

" 'Ah'?" Remy asked. " 'Ah' what?"

"Malatesta," Steven said, snapping his fingers. "The guy from the Vatican . . . What was that all about?"

"Guy from the Vatican?" Remy asked. "What guy from the Vatican?"

A sick feeling swirled with the alcohol that had pooled in his belly.

"His name was Malatesta," Steven explained. "He was waiting for me outside my apartment right after the business in Back Bay."

"What did he want?" Remy asked cautiously.

Steven shrugged. "He wanted to know what I could tell him about you."

"And you told him . . ."

"Everything," Steven said, his face suddenly very serious.

Remy wasn't quite sure how to react when his friend caved.

"I'm just fucking with you," the detective said. "I told him that I knew you were a Boston PI, and that we'd crossed paths a few times in our chosen professions, but that was about it."

"Did he ask you anything else?"

Steven shook his head. "He verified your office address, thanked me, and left. I figured he was on his way over to talk to you."

"No, never saw him," Remy said, suddenly slightly concerned, and very curious.

"I wonder what it's all about," Steven pondered.

"I haven't a clue," Remy answered.

"The Pope doesn't know that you're . . ." Steven made flapping movements with his hands.

It was a tricky question, and one that Remy wasn't sure he wanted to answer in detail at the moment, so he decided to keep it simple. "No. No, he doesn't."

But there had been other popes in his lifetime upon this planet, and one in particular a very long time ago.

### On the Outskirts of London Town
### 1349, During the Time of the Great Pestilence

The angel Remiel, wearing the guise of a man, sat upon the edge of the child's cot, holding her hand.

The plague was about to claim her life, as it had her father, mother, older brother, and sister.

And he did not wish her to pass from life alone.

The child was burning with fever; the fingernails on the tiny hand that he held were black with gangrene. She thrashed on the straw-filled mattress, and he leaned in close to whisper words of comfort and ease her into the arms of death.

"Fight it no longer, sweet one," Remiel whispered into the tiny ear inflamed with fever. "Let the sickness that has already taken your family take you, and you will no longer be alone."

She was looking up at him now, eyes red and bleary with the intensity of the warmth radiating from her small body, mouth moving as she struggled to speak.

The angel listened intently, trying to understand. Squeezing her hand in his, he brought it to his mouth and kissed it gently, lending her some of his own strength.

"What is it, child?" Remiel asked her. "What are you trying to say?"

She was fighting to breathe, lungs clogged with congestion, the glands beneath the skin of her throat black and swollen; but despite her condition she continued to fight to get the words out.

"Where . . . ?" she wheezed.

He was about to answer her, to tell her where her force of life would soon be, joining with her family and the many others who had been taken by the plague this day, but she had not yet finished her question.

"Where's . . . Dolly?"

Remiel did not understand what it was she asked.

"Dolly?" he repeated. "You want to know the whereabouts of Dolly?"

"Where . . . Dolly . . . ?" the small child gasped, now moving about more wildly upon her bed as if searching for somebody . . . or something.

He was holding her down, to keep her from rolling onto the cold, dirt floor, when he saw it lying crumpled in the corner, beside the hearth. A doll of straw, wearing a dress of burlap.

*A dolly.*

He left the child momentarily to retrieve the toy and bring it to her upon the bed.

"Is this what you were asking for?" Remiel asked, showing it to her before placing the doll in her waiting arms.

Her bloodshot eyes became wider as she took the toy, hugging it to her body, and she seemed to relax, beginning the process of giving in to the sickness that consumed her.

"That's it," Remiel whispered, tenderly wiping a lock of sweat-dampened hair from the child's forehead. "You can go now that Dolly is here with you."

She seemed to grow smaller, her body, once tense with the pain of disease and impending death, now relaxing under his watchful gaze. The child's face grew slack, and there was a brief crackle of bluish white energy that only he could see.

Israfil, the Angel of Death, then appeared to collect the last of the child's life energies, but the powerful angel did not acknowledge Remiel's presence there.

The Angel of Death departed as quickly as he had come, and Remiel stood up, looking down at the shell of cooling flesh that had once housed the stuff of life. He looked about at the remains of the child's family, their bodies in more advanced stages of decay, having passed from the world earlier. It was a house void of all life now, except for the disease and vermin that thrived upon the corpses that rested there.

Remiel let his arms drop to his sides and called forth the fire of God, allowing it to flow into his hands. The fire was hungry, eager to consume anything it was set upon. The angel walked about the tiny home gently caressing the sparse furniture and the bodies that lay putrefying in death, leaving behind the fire of Heaven to quench its insatiable hunger.

Stepping through the door, roiling fire at his back, the angel Remiel wondered how many more he would need to comfort on their way to death before the virulent plague ran its course.

The whinnying of horses distracted him from his thoughts, and the angel, clad in the clothes of a simple man, looked to see that he was now being watched.

The knights sat upon their horses, watching him with suspicious eyes. He could have easily willed himself invisible and gone on his way unhampered, but these armored soldiers, there was something about them.

Something that made him curious.

The shack behind him had become like a ball of fire, and he continued to watch the knights, their horses made nervous by the intensity of the divine flames.

"There was great sickness here," Remiel spoke above the roar of the flames. "But I have put an end to it."

The knights continued their silence, watching him with scrutinizing eyes.

"Is there something I can do for you, brave knights?" Remiel asked, his curiosity getting the better of him.

"Our master wishes an audience," said one of the soldiers.

"With me?" Remiel asked. "Why would someone of obvious power wish to speak with one such as me?"

"He knows what you are, soldier of God," said the knight, bowing his head.

The other knights followed suit in reverence to the angel.

"Will you accompany us to nearby Bohner Castle to speak with the Holy Father?" the knight asked.

"Holy Father?" Remiel repeated, curious about the title they had given their master.

"Yes, warrior of Heaven," the knight said. "The Holy Father, Pope Tyranus of the Holy See."

They had brought along a riderless horse, and presented it to him.

"Will you ride with us?" the knight asked him, as the other knights watched. "Or would you prefer other means in which to reach our destination?"

Remiel had grown temporarily disenchanted with the wearisome task of ministering to the dying, and believed that this might be just the kind of distraction that he required at that moment.

"Take me to your master," he said, climbing up onto his mount. The flaming home behind him collapsed with an animal-like roar, tongues of angelic fire lapping eagerly at the damp, night air.

"Take me to Pope Tyranus."

# CHAPTER TWO

Steven's visit had left Remy's mind buzzing.

After his friend had decided to pack it in for the evening, he'd stayed on the roof for a while pondering the questions of an uncertain future.

His dreams warning of an impending war, and now the Vatican looking for him, made him very anxious indeed.

But what to do about it?

Remy downed the last of his scotch, not allowing himself to feel the effects of the alcohol. Marlowe was looking up from the floor where he lay.

"We should think about heading down," Remy said, his mind still annoyingly abuzz.

*"Yes,"* Marlowe agreed, in the voice of his species.

Remy stood, grabbed the nearly empty bottle of scotch and the two tumblers, and started for the doorway. Marlowe cut him off, zipping down the stairs in front of him to get inside first, his toenails clicking on the wood steps as he made his way down.

"Don't make too much noise," Remy warned the beast. "You don't want to wake up Linda. You know what she's like when you wake her up."

Remy laughed as he heard Marlowe's bark of a response. *"Monster!"*

"Exactly," Remy replied as they reached the first floor.

Most of the lights were off, but Remy had no problem moving around in the darkness. With just a thought, he could adjust the structure of his eyes, and see in the black as though the sun was coming in through the windows.

Marlowe drank sloppily from his bowl of water in the kitchen corner as Remy set the bottle on the counter and put the dirty glasses in the sink.

No matter how hard he tried to slow it down, his brain simply refused to cut him that slack. Something was brewing, and he knew that it likely had to do with the return of Lucifer to the prison dimension of Tartarus to remake it in his own image.

To turn it into Hell.

Remy had always feared something like this happening—the forces of God once again pitted against the Morningstar.

He needed to know what was happening; needed to know how close the impending disaster was, and how much danger the world of man would be in.

It was time to make a call.

He moved away from the sink and caught sight of Marlowe watching him from the corner, his shiny black coat blending with the shadows. The dog's tail immediately started to wag.

"What?" Remy asked.

*"What?"* the dog repeated in a throaty growl.

Remy was just about to ask him if he wanted to go for a ride, when suddenly they were no longer alone.

Linda sleepily rubbed at her eyes as she leaned against the kitchen doorframe. "What are you guys doing?" she asked, stifling a yawn.

Remy couldn't help but stare at her. She was wearing the gray, extralarge *Walking Dead* T-shirt they had bought at Newbury Comics the week before and nothing else, her long, shapely legs looking even longer and shapelier than they usually did. Her hair was tousled, suggesting that she had been asleep for a bit. She ran her fingers through the long, dark locks, pushing them back from her face.

Though half-asleep, Linda smiled at him, and he felt that sudden flush of humanity that he had learned to appreciate so much.

"Want to fool around?" she asked, biting at her lower lip, her hair falling back over one half of her face.

She couldn't have been sexier if she'd tried.

"What kind of a man do you take me for?" he asked, crossing his arms in mock indignation.

She padded toward him. "The kind that stands around in a dark kitchen with his dog, stinking of booze," she said. She kissed him hard upon the lips, then pulled away.

"And tasting of booze, too," she added, making a face.

She turned, heading back for the doorway, walking in such a way that he had no choice but to watch her. "If you have any interest at all in my offer, you know where I'll be," she called over her shoulder as she passed through the door into the room beyond.

"Huh." Remy looked at Marlowe.

*"Bed?"* Marlowe asked, his blocky head cocked to one side.

"Eventually," Remy said. "A little playtime first."

*"Playtime?"* Marlowe repeated eagerly. He looked about the darkened kitchen for one of his toys.

"Sorry, pal. Not that kind of play." He patted the dog's head as he passed him. "People play."

He heard Marlowe sigh pathetically behind him, and turned to see his friend sitting dejectedly, head low, in the darkened kitchen.

"I'll tell you what. Once Linda and I are finished playing, I'll take you out for a walk." Remy told him.

The Labrador's thick tail thumped furiously on the kitchen floor.

*"Walk!"* Marlowe barked, his sadness suddenly forgotten.

Remy placed a finger to his lips, warning the dog to be quiet. "After playtime," he assured the dog, starting toward the flight of stairs that would take him up to his bedroom. Once again, Marlowe rushed past to get there first.

"Stay off the bed!" Remy warned as the dog bounded up the stairs. The sound of Linda's surprised scream, followed by hysterical laughter and a dog's playful growl proved that the one obedience class they'd attended had certainly done the trick.

*England*
*1301*

Since being touched by the Nazarene, Simeon could not die.

It was not as if he hadn't tried; it was just that death would not have him.

Even the passage of time could not harm him, the man looking just as flush with life as he had before he'd died so very long ago.

Plagued by the curse of immortality, he chose to wander, to experience everything that this world—now his prison—had to offer.

The good as well as the bad.

Simeon found himself drawn to the darker corners. Where the sane and rational mind might flee the terrors that hid in the shadows, the eternal man found himself moving toward them eagerly.

He was desperate to know what secrets they might share, how they might help him someday to see Heaven fall from the sky. Simeon had gathered much in the way of knowledge over the centuries he had lived and wandered, but it was the ways of sorcery and black magick that had proven the most useful.

The forever man had an aptitude for the black arts, and his hunger for this particular type of knowledge had become insatiable.

During his travels, as he sought out those in special circles who could teach him, there was one name often spoken in both reverence and great fear.

Some said he was only a legend, an amalgam of all the world's greatest sorcerers and wizards, while others believed that he truly did exist, a living repository for all the magickal knowledge that had ever existed.

The name of the legend was Ignatius Hallow, and Simeon had traveled long and far to finally find him.

Standing on English soil, in the pouring rain, the forever man looked upon the ruins of the castle he had been directed to, and felt the beginnings of despair.

"How can this be?" he asked the foul elements, as he stumbled through the mud toward the ruins.

In a tavern in the town of York he had met an old man whose neck had been broken but he still managed to be alive. Those in the tavern whispered that this one was so insane that neither God nor the Devil wanted him, and they had sent him back to the world. They also said that the man with the twisted neck knew things—dark secrets that he would share for a price.

That had been good to know, for Simeon had need of such information.

By its appearance, the castle had been taken a long time ago, in some long-forgotten conflict that had caused its battlements to fall. There was not a sign of life to be found.

Simeon snarled as the realization that he'd been had began to sink in. He and the insane old man had made a deal: the first digit of his little finger from his right hand in exchange for the whereabouts of the legendary magick user. A bizarre price to pay, but it was what the man with the broken neck had demanded for his services. The madman had said that he could see the remnants of many years in Simeon's eyes, which made him—as well as pieces of him—so very special.

The eternal man could still hear the old-timer's cackle as he wondered aloud whether perhaps Simeon had been discarded by Heaven and Hell as he himself had been.

Simeon stared down at the bloody bandage wrapped around his hand. He could feel it throbbing with the angry beat of his heart as what had been cut away slowly, painfully, grew back.

Looking out over the ruins as he was assaulted by wind and rain, Simeon debated his next course of action. There was a part of him that wished to continue on his way, wandering to the next location, hoping for a piece of forbidden knowledge to add to his growing arsenal.

Or he could return to the tavern in York, for a piece of the twisted old man.

The wind pushed him even closer to what remained of the forgotten castle's walls, as if the elements were urging him to be certain that the madman had indeed been wrong. He was about to step back, to prepare himself for the long trek to York, when the ground in front of him began to churn.

At first he believed it to be a trick of his eyes, the way the heavy rain pelted the muddy patches of exposed earth, but he quickly came to realize that wasn't the case at all.

The vines, their bodies as fat as the thickest rope, and covered in large thorns that looked as though they could strip the flesh from his body, erupted from the saturated ground in a writhing tangle. Simeon managed to throw himself back, away from the thorn-covered tendrils, only to have another patch of the virulent growth explode from the ground behind him. Everywhere he looked the ground churned, and more of the serpentine vines grew, reaching for him, ensnaring him in their constricting embrace.

Simeon screamed as the thorns dug into his skin, tearing it through his garments. The tentacle-like growths held him tight, and began to squeeze the life from his body.

The more he struggled, the tighter the vines became, until his bones began to snap like pieces of dry wood.

Simeon's screams filled the night, diminishing to little more than a pathetic whine as his blood flowed, watering the hellish vegetation. He was waiting for the inevitable death that would not hold, when through a darkened stone doorway in the ruins of the castle something appeared and began to move toward him.

The man was tall and of indiscriminate age, clad in robes that seemed to be cut from the fabric of night. He leaned on a staff as he slowly approached—a walking stick that appeared to have been carved from bone.

The figure stopped mere inches from him, and stared deeply into his eyes.

"You should be dead," the magick user, Ignatius Hallow, said in a voice ripe with curiosity.

"That I should," Simeon managed, though his throat was clogged with bile and blood.

"Why have you come?" the sorcerer asked.

Though it took all the strength that he had remaining, Simeon managed to answer.

"To . . . learn."

And then he died, his body no longer able to sustain his life as a result of the abuse his fragile human form had endured.

But as before, death would not have him.

## Now

"Do you like it?"

Simeon's eyes were focused on the bare skin of a waitress's arm, or more specifically, on the tattoo that curled its way around her pale flesh.

*Thorny vines.*

That was all it took to stir the memories of long ago.

He pulled his eyes from the tattoo to gaze up into the woman's face. She was attractive in that used sort of way, the deep lines around her eyes and smiling mouth hinting at a hard life.

"Quite lovely," Simeon told her, forcing a friendly smile. He didn't want to be rude and draw attention to himself.

"I had it done when I was just a kid," she said, taking his empty wineglass and placing it on her tray. "Wished I hadn't as I got older, but now I think it's kinda nice."

She smiled again, as he agreed.

"You're new in here, aren't you?" she then asked, becoming more personal.

This was what he'd hoped against. Simeon had needed to get away by himself, away from the demonic trio that served him, even for just a single drink.

Methuselah's was the best place he could think of. He'd always wanted to patronize the strange bar that catered to the most unusual clientele. And looking around, he was glad that he had.

A golem of stone wiped the surface of the bar with a damp rag, as a minotaur checked identification at the heavy wooden door. In one corner of the darkened establishment sat creatures more reptile than human, served by a waitress whose skin was nearly translucent, her internal workings on view for all to see. Four succubi that had followed a group of humanoid travelers down a hallway leading to the restrooms emerged from the darkened passage, dabbing at their mouths with lacy handkerchiefs.

Methuselah's was a most fascinating place, and Simeon was glad he'd come, but he caught sight of what was coming through the door and knew it was time to leave.

He smiled again at the waitress, ignoring her question as he took some bills from his pocket and placed them on her tray. "Keep the change."

"Next time you're in," the waitress said, eyeing the cash before slipping it into a pocket on her apron, "you be sure to ask for Katie."

He stood up, staring at the three demons that had just entered the bar. Their eyes were shifting about the room. They were looking for him.

"I'll be sure to do that, Katie," Simeon told Katie, reaching out to take hold of her arm in a firm grip. "But I'm afraid that in a little bit you won't even remember I've been here."

She seemed a little startled, a bit perplexed at first, but then he watched his magick seep deep into her flesh, and spread throughout her body, and as he released his grip, she was already moving toward her next table.

His presence forgotten.

The demons had come closer, waiting for him to notice their presence.

He turned to them. "You've found me."

"When we noticed you were gone . . . ," one of them began.

"You were worried?" Simeon asked. His coat was hanging over the back of another chair and he retrieved it, pushing past the demons on his way to the door.

"Was it wise for you to come here?" another asked in a voice low and soft, so as not to be heard.

Simeon stopped as he hung his coat over his arm.

"Your concern is really touching," he said, trying the smile again but certain to make it appear as obviously insincere as he could manage. "But it's nothing you need to worry yourself about."

"Hold this," he ordered, handing his coat to one of the demons smart enough to keep her mouth shut.

Simeon walked away from his pale-skinned escorts and placed his hands together, allowing the two rings, one on the ring finger of each hand to briefly touch, before raising his hands in the air.

"Excuse me," he called out, feeling the ancient power imbued in the two pieces of jewelry flow through his hands and out into the tavern's patrons. "Just to be on the safe side," he said as they listened. "I was never here."

He watched the memory of him leave each and every one of those present, all of them going back to whatever it was they were in the middle of doing before the pale-skinned man with the curly black hair called on their attention.

"Happy?" Simeon asked the demon that had questioned him, stealing back his jacket from the other, and throwing it over his arm.

He headed toward the door, ahead of his entourage.

"Have a good night," he told the minotaur as it opened the door for him and the demons that followed.

Remy stopped to let Marlowe sniff the base of the parking meter, before the dog lifted his leg to spray it with urine.

"Where do you keep it all?" Remy asked him.

*"What?"* the dog asked, already moving Remy along the nearly deserted early-morning street.

"The pee," he said. "I can't imagine one dog having so much of it inside him. You must have some sort of storage tank or something. Is that what it is? Do you have a storage tank?"

Marlowe had no real idea what Remy was talking about and answered in the expected manner.

*"No."*

Remy chuckled, walking down Boylston Street with Marlowe sniffing at the ground and pulling slightly on his leash.

He and Marlowe had been careful not to make too much noise as they got ready to leave the house on their walk. Buttoning his shirt while Marlowe patiently waited just outside the door, Remy had watched Linda sleep. His body still tingled with the memory of their lovemaking, and he considered crawling back beneath the covers for another go, but a faint, pathetic whine from the hallway was enough to reignite his other purpose.

He had a call to make that couldn't be made from his cell, and besides, he'd promised Marlowe a walk.

Remy loved the hum of the city by day and night, but this time of the early morning, when things were so remarkably still and quiet, was high up there on his list of favorite times. It was almost as if the day to come was waiting, tensed, at the starting line, eager for the pistol shot that would signal what was to come.

He loved this city and the humanity it coddled, which made the reason he'd left his lover, and his bed, to head out into the early morning, all the more pertinent.

If war was on the horizon, he needed to know exactly how close it was, and what could be done, if anything, to prevent it from overflowing onto the world of man.

Remy pulled back on Marlowe's leash, standing on the corner of Boylston and Dartmouth, preventing the overeager beast from heading out into the street. Traffic was light, but all it would take was one taxi driver or delivery truck not paying attention.

"You really need to be more careful," Remy told the dog.

Marlowe looked up at him, his dark eyes dark filled with adoration. *"You careful for me."*

The coast clear, the two crossed, passing by an entrance to the Copley Square T station, Remy tugging Marlowe past several early commuters, their eyes bleary as they headed for work. They stopped near an unobtrusive door in a darkened corner of the Old South Church, one of the last places of worship that Remy had been in.

He was about to take Marlowe into his arms and wrap his wings about them to take them inside, when something moving in a patch of shadow caught his eye. Remy shifted the configuration of his eyes to see that it was one of the many homeless people who slept on Boston's streets. An old woman's head popped up from a filthy sleeping bag to stare at them.

"No need to be scared, fella," she said, addressing Marlowe.

It took everything that Remy had to keep the dog, tail wagging, from pulling himself over to her.

"Marlowe, no," Remy ordered.

"It's all right," she said, her hands coming out from within the sleeping bag to eagerly clap. "C'mon over and see old Dottie."

Remy let up on the leash, letting him go to the old woman. It wasn't long before he was licking her weather-worn face, and she was scratching him behind his velvet soft ears, cooing affectionately to him.

"You're a sweet one, aren't ya?" she said as Marlowe administered some of his patented affection, licking every inch of her face, neck, and ears.

"Marlowe, go easy on the poor woman," Remy said.

"Marlowe?" the woman asked. "Is that your name? Marlowe?"

If the dog could have crawled into the sleeping bag with her, he would have.

" 'Why should you love him whom the world hates so?' " old Dottie quoted, glancing at Remy to see if he was listening. " 'Because he love me more than all the world.' "

Remy realized that she was reciting from Elizabethan dramatist and poet Christopher Marlowe.

He smiled at her and nodded. "Nice," he said. "But not that Marlowe, I'm afraid. He's more Philip Marlowe."

The woman laughed as the dog continued to lick her face.

"Ah!" she exclaimed. "Raymond Chandler."

"That's it," Remy agreed.

" 'Down these mean streets a man must go who is not himself mean, who is neither tarnished nor afraid,' " Dottie said, quoting Remy's favorite author. " 'He is the hero, he is everything. He must be a complete man and a common man and yet an unusual man.' "

The woman stopped, smiling a toothless grin.

"Pretty good, right?"

He gave her the thumbs-up. "Awesome."

"I read a lot," she told him, scratching roughly behind Marlowe's ears, but the dog didn't seem to mind. Not one little bit. "And stuff just seems to get stuck up there." She stopped scratching Marlowe to point to her head, upon which sat a floppy, knitted hat. "Can't forget the stuff even if I tried—especially if I like it."

"Not so bad of a curse as far as curses go," Remy told her.

"I guess."

Marlowe had plopped down beside the woman, shimmying as close to her as he was able. He was a good judge of character; if Marlowe liked her, this woman was probably special.

They were silent for a bit, as old Dottie continued to stroke Marlowe's ebony fur.

"He likes that," she said, looking deeply into the dog's dark eyes.

"That he does," Remy said.

Dottie let her eyes leave Marlowe's and fixed her gaze on Remy. He could see that she was staring really hard, squinting her watery eyes as if she was having some difficulty focusing her sight.

"What is it, Dottie?" Remy asked. "Something wrong with your eyes?"

"No," she said, with a shake of her head. "No problem . . . just that I see things a little differently from most."

Remy continued to listen to her, sure that she was about to say more.

"I see things about folks that they can't see themselves," she said.

"That another curse?" Remy asked her. He had moved closer to them, squatting down so that he, too, could pat his dog.

"All depends on how you look at it," she said. "Makes it kinda tough to have a normal life . . . to keep a job and stuff."

She was staring at him again, old eyes squinting.

"Do you see something with me?" he asked.

"Yeah, I do," she said. "You're not like everybody else, are you?"

Remy smiled. It wasn't entirely unusual, but it was rare. There were a select few people out there in the world with the ability to see things— those who could peer into the shadows and see what was actually lurking there behind the veil.

Those who could see things as they truly were.

"No, I'm not," Remy said, looking away from the intensity of her gaze.

"So, what's your story?" she asked him, her face now very serious. "Haven't come to take me, have you?"

Remy laughed as he patted Marlowe's head. The dog was in heaven with all this attention.

"Not my job," he told her with a shake of his head. "So no worries there."

"Good," Dottie said, happy that he wasn't the Angel of Death. "Been seeing a lot of your types walking around recently, and have gotten a little nervous."

Dottie's words hit him hard, her observations worrying.

"You've seen a lot like me around?" he asked her to be sure.

The old woman nodded. "Oh yeah, just strolling around." She waved a hand around in the air. "Like they were checking the place out or something."

*Or something,* Remy thought, certain that the angels she had seen were doing reconnaissance . . . but for which side? Perhaps both? It was truly bothersome, but it made what he had come to the Old South Church for all the more pertinent.

"Was that what they were doing?" Dottie asked him, interrupting his train of thought.

"Yeah, it probably was."

"Something up?"

"That's something I need to find out," Remy answered, rising to his feet and looking at the church before him.

He needed to get himself inside to do what he had to do. He had been planning on taking Marlowe in with him, but now maybe he wouldn't.

"Hey Dottie, want to do me a favor?" he asked the old woman.

"Sure, if I can," she said, stroking Marlowe's side.

"Want to keep an eye on Marlowe while I take care of some business?" he asked her.

She smiled warmly, looking to the dog.

"What do you think, pal?" she asked him. "Can you stand to hang around here with Dottie for a little while longer?"

Marlowe panted heavily, his tail wagging happily in response.

"Will you be okay, buddy?" Remy asked the Labrador.

*"Okay with Dottie,"* Marlowe grumbled, extending his thick neck to give her another big wet kiss on the side of her face.

"That's great. I should only be a little while," he told the dog.

"Take your time," Dottie called out as he started to walk around to the back of the building.

To make his direct call to Heaven.

# CHAPTER THREE

Remy pictured in his mind's eye the Old South Church as it was the last time he had entered, and willed himself inside with a rush of air and the flutter of wings.

He had attended a fund-raiser for the Congregationalist parish to help finance repairs of damage done by the ravages of age and nearby construction. Tonight, it was just as beautiful as he remembered, even in darkness.

Remy pulled his wings back into his body and strolled down the center aisle, admiring the elaborate woodwork and stained glass. His eyes fixed upon the enormous organ pipes to the left of the altar, and he remembered the glorious sounds they had made when played at the fund-raiser.

If he listened very carefully, straining his preternatural senses to their maximum capacity, he could still hear the lingering residue of the countless prayers that had been spoken here.

Now he was about to add his own to the fray.

Remy stood no more than a few feet from the altar and turned his gaze to the ceiling. Shedding his human visage, he appeared as the angel, Remiel, Seraphim and soldier of Heaven. Wings spread wide and armor-covered arms outstretched, the angel began to pray. Up through this place of worship, Remiel projected his petition, spoken in the language of the Messengers, hopefully to the ears of God.

Or whoever might be listening on His behalf.

Remiel needed answers. He had to know if the world that he cared so deeply for, the people that he loved, would be safe. He needed to know if there was anything that could avert the coming hardship.

It had been a very long time since Remiel had asked Heaven for anything, but now it was time to put aside old hostilities for the sake of something so much bigger.

Exhausted, Remiel fell to his knees, listening with all his might for an answer, but except for the sounds of the city coming to life outside, the place of worship remained silent. Slowly, the angel climbed to his feet, abandoning the guise of a Heavenly warrior and slipping comfortably back into the guise of humanity he had worn for so many years.

Remy looked around the church, senses on the alert, but still there was nothing.

Still there was no response.

*Is this how it's to be now?* he wondered. *Is no one listening to me anymore? Or is there some other reason that my prayers go unanswered?*

Perhaps the drums of war beat much louder than even he suspected.

He was ready to leave, ready to reveal his wings again and take himself back outside to reunite with Marlowe and Dottie, when he felt a sudden change in the atmosphere of the church.

As if something had been added.

Remy turned, eyes scanning his surroundings, and he found it—someone sitting tall in one of the pews, staring straight ahead toward the altar.

"Hello?" Remy called out.

At first the figure did not react. But then he spoke, his voice soft yet powerful. "Hello, Remiel.

"I would have come sooner," the figure continued as he turned eyes as dark as space to Remy, "but, as you can probably guess, things are terribly hectic."

"There's a war brewing, don't you know."

\*       \*       \*

His name was Montagin, and Remy had not seen him since the first war against the Morningstar. How apropos that he would be the one to come to Remy now.

"How long has it been?" Montagin asked, turning to face the angel as Remy slid into the pew.

"Let's just say that it's been a long time," Remy replied, trying to keep it friendly.

"It was right after the war, wasn't it?" the angel asked. His eyes twinkled mischievously.

This was one of the many reasons that Remy had left Heaven: Angels were basically assholes.

"It was," Remy agreed tightly.

"Right before your little tantrum that ended up with you settling . . ." Montagin's dark eyes darted about, seeing not only the church, but the world outside it. "Here."

Remy didn't respond to the angel's malicious grin.

"So how have you been?" Montagin then asked, unbuttoning his suit coat so that he was able to cross his long legs without wrinkling the linen. The off-white suit appeared very expensive, and he was wearing what looked to be Italian loafers, without socks.

Very stylish for a creature of Heaven; Remy had to wonder how long he'd been in this world.

"Fine," Remy said, casually nodding. "I'm surprised to see you."

Montagin smiled. "Just happened to be listening and I wasn't too far away. Actually it should have been Aszrus who answered, but he had some business to take care of tonight."

The mention of Aszrus caused an icy chill of concern to pass through Remy's body. "Aszrus is here?" he asked.

Montagin nodded. "Has been here for quite some time. We've always anticipated that what's happening would occur."

"And what exactly is that?" Remy asked.

Montagin chuckled coldly. "You're not that far removed from what you are, Remiel," he said. "You'd have to be deaf, dumb, and blind not to know—not to see—what's been unfolding all across this planet."

"You mentioned a war," Remy prompted.

"And that will likely be the end result," Montagin acknowledged, slowly rotating his foot. Remy was reminded of a cat's tail languidly swishing back and forth just before it pounced.

"I'm sure you know that the Morningstar has returned to Tartarus and is in the process of reshaping it into who knows what?" Montagin leaned forward toward Remy.

"Yeah, I'd heard something about that."

"Good," the angel said. "Then you're not as far gone as I feared."

"So this is all about the Morningstar," Remy said, ignoring the barb.

Montagin was staring intensely now.

"Are you just playing dumb, or are you really that stupid?" he finally asked.

"I just don't see an imminent threat," Remy told him.

"Lucifer has returned to power," Montagin said a little slower and a little louder. "Lucifer has returned to power, and has gone back to Tartarus . . . back to Hell."

"So he's gone back to where the Almighty put him to begin with."

"Is this what living here among the monkeys does to one of us?" Montagin asked with a sneer.

"What does it do, Montagin?" Remy retorted. "Does it make me ask questions, and not fly off the handle at the slightest things? If that's the case, then yeah, I guess living here has done that to me."

The angel's face wore an expression of absolute disgust.

"Even after everything you saw during the war, you can still be blind to what Lucifer is capable of."

"I know what he's capable of, but the question is, what is he doing now?"

Montagin rose to his feet, buttoning his suit jacket as he stood.

"If you can't see his influence in everything that has been happening here on the world of man, then I'm afraid there's really nothing more I can say to you."

"Are you serious?" Remy questioned. "You think that what's been happening here is all Lucifer's fault?"

"Whether it is or isn't doesn't matter to the overall picture," Montagin said. "The fact is that Lucifer Morningstar is free, and as long as he is, he poses a danger to God and the Kingdom of Heaven."

"And Earth?" Remy asked the million dollar question.

"Yes, to Earth as well," Montagin said, almost begrudgingly. "To think of the Morningstar in control of this world . . . We will not stand for it."

"So that's why Aszrus is here," Remy stated.

"As well as others in various aspects of reconnaissance," Montagin said. "I just so happen to have been assigned to assist the general." He stepped into the far aisle. "And I believe I've answered your pleas."

Remy could feel his disbelief turning to anger. "After everything we've already been through," he began incredulously, "after everything we lost, we're willing to do this all again?" He stood and moved back into the center aisle. "Didn't we learn anything?"

Montagin considered the question as brown wings reached from his back, readying to embrace his form.

"Maybe we learned that the Lord God Almighty was far too merciful to those who challenged His holy word."

Remy couldn't believe his ears. What had happened to these supposed divine creatures to make them so bitter?

"That if He'd tempered His mercy then, we wouldn't be having this conversation now," Montagin continued, as his wings folded about him.

And he was gone, as silently as he'd appeared.


Dottie and Marlowe were right where Remy had left them, only the old woman had rolled up her sleeping bag, and the two were sitting side by side, Marlowe draped partially across her lap. They were sharing a bag of Cheez-Its.

Marlowe was first to notice the angel's return. *"Hello,"* he woofed, spewing orange crumbs.

Dottie turned toward him and smiled, popping a Cheez-It into her mouth. "There he is," she said to the dog. "I told ya he wouldn't be long."

Marlowe's tail wagged as she gave him another one of the treats.

"He wasn't any trouble was he?" Remy asked.

"No trouble at all," Dottie said, reaching out to pat Marlowe's head. "He even watched my stuff while I ran in the store to get us something to eat."

"A regular watchdog," Remy said, bending over to scratch his friend's ear.

*"Watchdog!"* Marlowe barked, and then began sniffing for stray Cheez-It crumbs.

"Well thank you for watching him, Dottie," Remy said, taking the end of the leash from the woman.

"No problem at all, it was a pleasure," she said. "So how did it go?"

Remy cocked his head, unsure of the question. "Go?"

"Inside." She motioned toward the church with her head. "Did you get to talk to who you wanted to."

"Not really," Remy acknowledged, giving the leash a slight tug so that Marlowe would stand.

"Huh," Dottie said. "That doesn't sound good."

"I'm afraid it isn't." Remy found himself thinking of his dream and the foreboding words of the old man, and what Dottie had said earlier about seeing angels on the streets.

The old, homeless woman was carefully watching him as he wrapped the leash around his hand and started to lead Marlowe away.

"Thanks again," he said, turning to head back up Boylston toward home.

"So what're you gonna do?" Dottie's voice called after him.

Remy turned to face her.

"What are you gonna do?" she asked again. "You know, to fix the problem . . . what're you going to do?"

It was a very good question, and one that Remy didn't have an answer for. Instead, he shook his head, then turned back up the street, her question hanging in the air like a bad smell.

# CHAPTER FOUR

The weeks that followed were without catastrophic event, but the potential for disaster was never far from Remy's mind, and he found himself watching for angels in the strangest of places.

*What are you gonna do?*

The answer to old Dottie's question still evaded him.

*I honestly don't know, Dottie. I really don't.*

He was doing the last bit of paperwork on a workman's comp job he had done for an insurance company out of Lexington—an incapacitating neck injury that wasn't so incapacitating that it kept the claimant from participating in a bodybuilding competition—when there was a knock at his office door.

"Come in!" Remy called out, stapling the pages of his report together and placing them inside a file that also contained some photos taken at the Mr. Power Competition in Tampa.

The door into the office swung open and a man stepped in. He was wearing a dark suit on his average-sized frame, his blond hair cut short. He looked around the office, taking it all in as he carefully closed the door behind him.

Something wafted off of him like the smell of aftershave.

Something with the potential for danger.

"Can I help you?" Remy asked as he stood, all of his senses on alert.

"Remy Chandler?" the man asked, a hint of an accent in his voice. *Italian, most definitely Italian.*

"That's right," Remy said, feeling the power exude from the man in waves.

"My name is Malatesta," he said, stepping forward and extending his hand. "Constantin Malatesta."

Remy had been wondering when the Vatican representative who had paid Steven Mulvehill a visit would finally get around to meeting him face-to-face. He shook his hand, a strange electrical tingle coursing up through the angel's arm reaffirming what he had felt in the air when the man entered.

"What can I do for you, Mr. Malatesta?" Remy asked, feigning ignorance of the man's identity as he released his hand and gestured for him to take a seat in front of the desk.

"Thank you." Malatesta unbuttoned his suit coat as he took the offered chair. "First, let me say how good it is to finally meet you."

The man smiled.

"Have you been wanting to meet me, Mr. Malatesta?" Remy asked, curious, as he cocked his head.

"For quite some time," the man acknowledged. "But it's only been recently that there has been a reason to make the journey to Boston."

"You have me at a disadvantage," Remy said. "You obviously know who I am, but I can't say the same of you."

"Where are my manners?" Malatesta said, reaching into his suit coat pocket to extract a small, leather identification case. He opened it, and leaned forward to place it on the desk in front of Remy.

Remy examined it and smiled. "Yep, you're from the Vatican, all right," he said, and handed it back to his guest.

"Ah, so you are aware of me?" Malatesta asked.

"Detective Mulvehill informed me that somebody from Rome was asking questions about me, yes."

"Then you lied a moment ago," the man said, putting his identification away. "You do know something about me."

"Only what Detective Mulvehill could tell me, which wasn't much.

But what I'd really like to know is what could the Vatican possibly want with a private investigator from Boston?"

Malatesta crossed his legs and smiled, saying nothing.

"Well?" Remy prompted. "Care to explain?"

"Our records on your whereabouts were relatively accurate until the mid-thirties," the man said, picking a piece of lint from his pant leg and letting it drop to the office floor. "But then things got a little sketchy."

Remy remained silent, glowering at the man sitting across from him.

"There were a few sightings here and there, but it wasn't until a few years ago that we received some solid information on your location."

Remy leaned back in his office chair, hands clasped behind his head. "You keep mentioning *we*."

"Of course, the people that I work for."

"At the Vatican."

"Yes, at the Vatican."

"May I ask who these people are?"

Malatesta chuckled softly. "I doubt that you've ever met any of them, but they are very familiar with you, Mr. Chandler. They are the people charged with tracking things of . . . an unusual nature. Many of these things—these items in our possession—are ancient writings and artifacts of power, while others are of a more transient nature."

"And do these people have a name?"

"They're known simply as Keepers," Malatesta said.

"And, are you a Keeper, Mr. Malatesta?"

The blond-haired man seemed amused by the question. "Oh, no, Mr. Chandler. I simply do their bidding," he explained, slowly shaking his head. "I am but one of their humble agents out in the world."

Remy knew where this was going and resigned himself to the fact.

"Would you like some coffee?" he asked, rising from his desk chair and going to the coffee cart he had set up in the corner beside an old file cabinet.

"Yes," Malatesta answered. "That would be lovely."

Remy went about the steps to prepare a pot. He'd had multiple cups at home before leaving for the office and hadn't even thought about making coffee when he'd gotten in that morning. That alone should have told him that something was off about this day.

As the machine burped, hissed, and gurgled, Remy spurred the conversation on. "So your employers, the Keepers of the Vatican's secrets, have sent you out into the world looking for me."

"They sent me to Boston, yes," Malatesta said. "There have been quite a few incidents in this region of the world that have caught their attention of late."

Remy should have seen this coming, and deep at the back of his mind, maybe he had. With what was going on out there in the world, and the potential for so much worse, he just couldn't bring himself to care all that much about what the masters of the Catholic Church would be up to.

But whether he wanted to know or not, now he did, and it appeared that they had been looking for him.

"There has been quite a lot going on around here lately," Remy acknowledged with a knowing nod.

Malatesta reciprocated with his own slow nod. "Quite a bit, yes."

The coffee was just about done, and Remy looked to see if the mugs he had were clean. One was. The other wasn't, its bottom covered with a gross brown stain. Remy took the cup and went to the small washroom at the far end of the office space. He ran the hot water into the cup and washed away the old coffee residue.

"So, I'm curious," he said, leaving the bathroom. "How did you narrow it down? How did you find me?"

Malatesta folded his hands in his lap, shifting his weight, as if he was considering what exactly he should share, and what he shouldn't.

"There are others out there in the employ of the Keepers, even though most are totally unaware that the data they provide is being collected, compared, and contrasted. The name Remy Chandler has popped up a number of times in connection to some of the more unusual data that was being reviewed."

Remy poured his company a cup of coffee.

"And the more bizarreness that occurred in this region . . ." He brought the mug over to his guest. "Do you use sugar? I don't have any milk, but I might have some powdered creamer if . . ."

"Black is fine," Malatesta said, taking the offered mug. "Thank you."

He brought the edge of the mug to his mouth and sipped.

"More bizarreness in a particular corner of the world would cause us to focus our attentions, and narrow said focus on certain locations . . ."

"Or people," Remy finished, bringing his own cup of coffee back to his desk, careful not to spill it as he sat down.

"Or people," Malatesta agreed, having some more of his steaming drink. "Your name quickly moved to the top of our list."

"Lucky me," Remy said.

The Vatican representative chuckled. "We were very discreet in our interview process," he said.

"Who else did you talk to beside Detective Mulvehill?"

Malatesta was bringing the mug up to his lips. "Some former clients who all spoke very highly of you . . . if they spoke at all."

Remy cocked his head, confused by the statement.

"Some of those we talked to would give us only the basic information, as if they were somehow protecting you . . . protecting your secret."

"Most don't even know that I have one," Remy said, taking a sip of his coffee. "It's something that I work on."

"I can imagine it would be complex," Malatesta acknowledged. "You said *most*. . . . There are some who . . ."

"Very few."

"Detective Mulvehill?"

"Let me guess. He got all squirrelly when you started asking about me."

"Squirrelly," Malatesta repeated and laughed. "Yes." He drained his coffee and leaned forward to set the mug on the edge of the desk.

"Want another cup?" Remy asked. "I've got a whole pot."

"No, thank you," Malatesta said. "I'm trying to limit my caffeine, and I'm afraid to say that cup has put me over my allotted amount."

"No worries," Remy answered, as he stood and headed for the pot. "More for me."

"So, now that I know how you found me, Mr. Malatesta," he said, filling his mug, "why don't you tell me what I can do for you?"

"Not for me per se, Mr. Chandler," Malatesta answered. "It is what you can do for a changing world."

Remy chose to stand, steaming cup of coffee in hand.

"And what, I'm afraid to ask, is that?"

"The Keepers of the Vatican wish you to work for them, Remy Chandler."

Remy thought about this for a moment before bringing his mug up to his mouth. "I worked for the Vatican once, a long time ago," he said, taking a sip of the hot liquid, reveling in the scalding sensation as it burned his lips and tongue. "Let's just say it didn't turn out so well."

### England
### 1349

"Do you eat?"

Pope Tyranus did not rise from the head of the vast banquet table as Remiel was led into the dining hall by the soldiers of the Vatican.

The table was covered with all forms of repast: roasted chickens, quail, a wild boar the size of a small child, and bowls of peas, carrots, and potatoes. There was enough to feed a small village laid out before the holy man.

"Would you prefer that I speak in Latin?" the Pope asked in the tongue of the Church, seemingly impatient with the lack of immediate response. "Or perhaps Italian?"

Remiel fixed the old man in an icy stare. "Occasionally I indulge," he replied to the first question. "But it is not necessary for my survival."

"Then, will you do me the honor of indulging me?"

The old man gestured for him to take a seat at the corner, by his side. Remiel noticed the jewelry that clattered upon his wrist, and the rings that adorned his long, slender fingers.

There was something in the tone of the holy man's voice, something that told him to acquiesce to the Pope's request of him.

Pope Tyranus smiled as Remiel approached the table.

A servant appeared from a shadowed corner of the hall, pulling out the heavy wooden chair so that the angel could sit, before scampering out of view again.

"She's actually one of the few left alive here," Pope Tyranus said, drawing Remiel's attention back to himself. "The lord of this manor, his family, and most who served them have succumbed to the pestilence."

He reached for a silver decanter and poured a libation into a tarnished goblet. "Wine?" the Pope offered.

Remiel found himself taking a goblet in hand and holding it out so that the holy man could fill it.

They both noticed the servant girl now standing nearby, watching the holy man, a look of horror upon her face.

"Please, your holiness, please allow me to pour . . . ," she began.

"Off with you, girl," the Pope said, setting down the decanter. "My guest and I wish for privacy."

He turned his cold, gray eyes to Remiel.

"And we're both human enough to serve ourselves," he added with a smile.

Remiel turned his gaze to her, reassuring the girl with a kind nod. She turned away, darting into a passage behind a scarlet curtain.

Pope Tyranus leaned forward in his chair, sinking his long fingers into the eye socket of the roast boar, rooting around, and removing the gelatinous remains of the wild pig's eye.

"Excuse my lack of manners," the Pope said as he brought the dripping organ of sight toward his eager mouth, "but I'm simply famished. You should be honored that I waited for you."

He slurped the eye from his fingers and chewed happily.

"You said that the lord of this manor and most of his servants are dead," Remiel began. He picked up his goblet of wine.

The Pope waited for him to continue, using his silken robes to wipe away the ocular fluid that dribbled down his chin.

"So why are you here?" Remiel asked as he sipped from his silver cup, his eyes never leaving those of the Pope. "Why would one such as yourself risk exposing himself, and his servants"—Remiel turned slightly in his chair to glance at the soldiers who remained at attention in the entry to the dining hall—"to the potential of plague?"

"Exactly," Tyranus reiterated. "What could be of such importance that I would leave the safety of Rome and expose myself to all of this . . ." He waved his bejeweled hand around in the air beside his head. "Death," he finished dramatically.

The Pope sipped more wine, as if he needed the soothing effects of the libation to continue.

"These are dark and dangerous times we live in, soldier of God," Tyranus told him. "There are forces of darkness afoot that wish to squelch the goodness of the true faith."

Remiel was amused by the statement—as if one faith of humanity were somehow better than all the rest. As if one specific religion would somehow place its followers closer to God than all the others.

Pope Tyranus must have caught the look on Remiel's face. "Do you not see it as you make your way in the world, angel?" he asked, his annoyance clear in his tone. "Things lurking in the shadows that lust to see your most holy radiance snuffed out like a candle's flame."

Remiel slowly rotated his goblet upon the wooden table, carefully considering his words.

"This world has always been plagued by darkness, but there has also been light. There is a balance here, I believe."

"Balance?" Tyranus sneered. "I'm afraid I see a world teetering on the edge of the abyss. Balance was lost a very long time ago."

He picked at some pheasant meat that he had torn from the body of the bird and placed upon his plate.

"I plan to keep this world from plunging headlong into damnation."

"And this has brought you here? To England?"

Tyranus slowly chewed the piece of pheasant meat he'd put in his mouth. "Exactly, angel."

"And how do you plan to prevent the world from being swallowed up by this darkness you see?" Remiel asked, curious.

"I sense that we don't necessarily agree on the level of the threat that the good people of the world face," Tyranus stated.

Remiel shrugged. "It is a matter of perception," he explained. "When one has seen true darkness . . ."

The angel remembered the war against the Morningstar, and the lives of his brothers that he was forced to take. The taste of angel blood was suddenly in his mouth, and he quickly picked up his goblet to wash it away with wine.

"Perhaps, but from the look I see upon your face now . . . you've experienced something akin to what I see out there." The Pope pointed beyond the dining hall, out beyond the castle, out into the countryside racked by plague and things of a far more sinister nature.

"Though my brothers and sisters of the blessed faith disagree with my methods, I believe I have found the answer to stifling the flow of evil into the world."

Remiel waited for the revelation, still hearing the ghostly sounds of Heaven's war echoing in his ear.

"By fighting fire, with fire," Pope Tyranus confided. "Darkness used in the service of light, against darkness."

The angel considered this, and found the concept interesting, but still could not quite fathom why he had been summoned here. What was his part to play in all of this?

"And my role in this battle against the encroaching shadows?" he asked.

Pope Tyranus smiled, his icy eyes twinkling.

"The lord in whose house we now reside summoned me with knowledge of an item of incredible power." The old man spoke in a whisper that only they could hear. "A ring once given to the great King Solomon by the Archangel Michael."

Remiel immediately perked up, remembering the ring, and how it would give whomever possessed it control over the demonic.

"I can see that you know of this item," Pope Tyranus spoke.

"The sigil ring," Remiel said. "As far as I know, it was lost after the death of the wise king."

"And for a time it was," the Pope acknowledged, slowly nodding. "But it was eventually found, though not by any who shared the great king's connection to the divine."

Tyranus paused, playing with a silver ring upon his finger, slowly turning it around, and around.

"The ring found its way from one eager finger to the next, as all who possessed the powerful, magickal artifact fell victim to an evil successor."

"And the lord who succumbed?" Remiel asked. "He had knowledge of who now possesses the sigil ring?"

"Oh yes," the Pope said, his voice a chilling hiss. "He had succumbed to the plague before my arrival, but that did not prevent me from . . . extracting the information by supernatural means."

Remiel looked at the holy man, offended by what he was suggesting.

"Fire with fire, soldier of God," he clarified. "Though it pained me to do so, I recalled his spirit to the earthly realm, and for the good of the world forced it to give up the ring's current owner and location."

"Who now possesses this artifact?"

"It has come into the possession of a powerful necromancer," the Pope said. "One who has learned to harness the power of the dead and dying."

"Where?" Remiel asked, already suspecting he knew the answer.

"Somewhere right outside this door, angel," Pope Tyranus said. "Can you think of a better place for one who harnesses the power of death, than a region besieged by plague?"

"His magick will be strong," Remiel said.

"But not as strong as a soldier of Heaven," Pope Tyranus said, leaning back in his chair, again fiddling with the ring upon his finger.

"You're going to help me, angel," the Pope told him. "You're going to obtain Solomon's sigil ring, and do your part in keeping the world from sliding into darkness."

Remiel was stunned, shocked that one such as Tyranus felt that he could give orders to an angel of the holy host Seraphim as if he were a mere lackey.

But for reasons then unknown to him, the angel Remiel held his tongue, knowing that he would do everything in his power to perform this chore, and to obtain the ring of Solomon for the one who asked it of him.

For Pope Tyranus of the Holy Roman Empire.

\*    \*    \*

"I'm sorry," Remy told the Vatican representative. "I have no interest in working for you, or the Keepers, or anybody else associated with the Vatican."

Malatesta just stared.

"I know it's probably hard for you to believe, but—"

"No," the man interrupted. "After reviewing what I could find on your original involvement with us . . ."

"I'm surprised there was anything left for you to review," Remy said. "Since Tyranus' name was removed from the lineage of popes."

"Even though his reign was erased, there are still some records to be found about the Black Pope, and his actions during the Middle Ages."

Remy chuckled. "Kinda like that stain on the rug you can never get completely out."

Malatesta tilted his head ever so slightly to one side. "A stain on the rug?" he asked, obviously not getting what Remy was talking about.

"It's nothing," Remy said. "Just trying to draw a comparison."

Malatesta nodded, sliding to the edge of the chair to drive home his point. "The Keepers have given me full authority to apologize profusely for any past transgressions, and to offer you substantial payment, within reason, for your time and services while working with us."

Remy shook his head.

"I'm really sorry, but I'm just going to have to say no."

It felt good saying no to the Vatican representative, not at all like when he was dealing with Pope Tyranus.

"There's nothing that I can say or do to change your mind?" Malatesta asked.

Remy shook his head again. "I'm afraid not."

Malatesta looked as though he was going to continue, but then appeared to think better of that. "I guess there's nothing more to say," he said, standing up.

Remy stood also.

"Thank you for your time, Mr. Chandler," Malatesta said, and extended his hand.

Remy reached out, taking his offered hand, and as their flesh touched . . .

There was a flash, and a hum, like unrestrained power coursing through a live wire lying in wait upon a street after a storm. If there had been any doubt that this man, this Constantin Malesta, had some sort of a knack for the arcane art of magick, there wasn't any now.

His power coursed through Remy, amplifying the sensations that he had been experiencing for quite some time, reminding the angel of what was out there in the world, and the dangers that it would soon be facing.

"Perhaps another time," Malatesta said with a final squeeze, before releasing his grip.

And before Remy could even respond, the Keeper agent was gone. But what he had stirred up in Remy with just a touch remained, and it lingered disturbingly for the remainder of the day.

# CHAPTER FIVE

The next few weeks passed without incident.

The world rolled on, the trivial and the not so trivial, the kinds of events Remy had grown accustomed to in his time with human civilization, as days passed into weeks.

But that did not mean he wasn't waiting for the so-called other shoe to fall. He found himself staring out the windows of his office and down onto the city streets far more attentively, watching the evening news broadcasts, and trolling the Internet with more frequency as he looked for signs.

He found nothing serious enough to alert him to impending doom, and started to eventually let his level of caution drop; still, he kept one eye open and his superhuman senses on alert for any notable change in the ether.

But life marched on; it had the habit of doing that, and Remy found himself more fully engaged in his ordinary human life than he had been for quite some time.

Business was good—not great, but good—enough to keep money coming in to handle the rent on the office space, and pay for the inordinate amount of coffee he drank.

On a personal level things couldn't have been better. The more time he spent with Linda, the more the trepidation that he'd felt at becoming involved again—falling in love again—slowly crumbled away. He needed a partner to be whole, to be the person he wanted, and needed, to be. Linda was that partner—of that he no longer had any doubt.

The August night had been dreadfully humid, but a quick-moving thundershower while they had been out on a walk with Marlowe had brought with it a welcome drop in temperature. Refreshing cool breezes made the curtains in the house flap and wave like something out of an eighties music video.

While he dried Marlowe off with a towel, which was more of a tug-of-war match than anything of real use, Linda kicked off her sneakers and peeled her soaking-wet T-shirt and running pants from her body. She left the wet clothing where it had fallen, in a trail that led to the stairs that would take her up to the bedroom.

"Coming?" she asked as she started to climb, wearing only a sports bra and panties.

"Oh, do I have to?" Remy mockingly whined.

Linda laughed, padding up the wooden steps.

Telling Marlowe that Linda and he had some business to attend to met with some minor protests—Linda had been staying with Remy and Marlowe far more often lately, and the Labrador was feeling just the tiniest bit neglected—but the offer of a smoked pig's ear was just the balm the retriever needed to feel as though he was still loved.

Remy picked up Linda's discarded wet things as he followed their path to the stairs, finding the bra and panties waiting for him at the top.

"You're never going to find yourself a good man with these cleanliness issues," Remy said as he added her underthings to the wet pile, and dumped them in a hamper in the corner of the bedroom.

"Guess you'll be stuck with me," she said, propped up on her elbows in bed, a sheet barely covering her naked body.

"Great," Remy said with a heavy sigh that made the woman laugh. He started to remove his own clothes, also damp from the summer rain, as she watched him from the bed.

"Is it so hard?" he asked her, as he tossed his shirt into the open hamper. "Dirty clothes go in there."

He shed his sweatpants and underwear, putting them where they now belonged.

"Is that where they go?" Linda asked, wearing an exaggerated, dumbfounded look. "I thought that was the trash barrel."

Remy shook his head in mock disgust.

"And they said I would be sorry for bringing a mail-order bride over from Blugrovia."

She started to giggle, the sheet sliding down to reveal her nearly perfect breasts.

"I may not be the most tidy, but I can shine in other ways," Linda said, holding out a hand and beckoning him to join her in bed, beneath the sheets.

"Shine away," Remy said, crawling into bed with the woman he loved.

Their lovemaking was passionate, yet gentle. There was a hunger present, each of them attempting to appease the other until the air of the bedroom became filled with the sounds of labored breathing, gentle sighs, and pleasure-filled moans, before falling eventually to contented silence.

Exhausted by the act, Linda swiftly drifted into a deep sleep, Remy's arm around her body as she snuggled up tightly against him. He lay there in the soothing quiet, listening to the sounds of the city outside.

There came a creaking of the wooden steps, and he lifted his head from the pillow to see Marlowe's head peak up over the rise.

Remy put a finger to his mouth.

"C'mon," he told the dog. "But be extra quiet."

The Labrador contemplated his jump up onto the bed before doing it, seeming to defy gravity for an animal his size as he leapt into the air, before coming down upon the mattress with hardly a ripple.

"Good boy," Remy whispered, reaching his hand down to pat the dog's rump as he lay down with a heavy sigh at the foot of the bed.

*"Good boy,"* Marlowe repeated, licking his chops noisily as he settled in for the night. It wasn't any more than five minutes before Remy heard the dog's breathing change as he drifted off into sleep.

Remy lay there for what seemed like hours but was more likely much less than that, staring up at the ceiling, listening to Linda and Marlowe, an odd symphony of heavy breathing, moans, and grunts.

As a creature of Heaven he did not require sleep, and had often used this time of night, when loved ones were embraced in the arms of Morpheus, to escape to a kind of fugue state where he thought about his life, and the events and people that had helped to shape him into the man he was, for better or worse.

And some nights he would just watch TV.

Remy was about to carefully extract himself from bed to go downstairs and see what he might find on-demand that he hadn't yet seen, when he felt a sudden change in the atmosphere. He knew in that instant that he was no longer the only one awake in the room.

Montagin appeared in the far corner, in front of the hamper, his wings unfolding in the darkness to reveal the angel that had been within their feathered embrace.

Remy leapt up from his bed, feeling his own angelness rising to the surface. He had no idea why Montagin had come, and assumed the worst.

Assumed that he was there to harm him and those that he loved.

Remy's first thoughts were to the safety of Linda and Marlowe, but he noticed that the two were still deeply asleep, their breathing regular and heavy.

He reached over to brush some hair away from Linda's peaceful face, as Marlowe snored loudly, certain now that the angel had done something to keep his loved ones in slumber.

"You better have a really good reason for being here," Remy warned, looking away from his woman to lock Montagin in his fiery gaze.

"I didn't know what to do," the angel said, his eyes wide and darting about the room. "It's terrible."

"What is it, Montagin?" Remy demanded.

The angel's eyes seemed to focus upon him, as if remembering where he was and why he had come.

"It's murder, Remiel," Montagin spoke, his voice a whisper filled with disbelief.

"General Aszrus has been murdered."

## Heaven
### At the Close of the Great War

Remiel stood on the battlefield, the Kingdom of Heaven looming ever so large at his back, the corpses of his fallen brothers strewn upon the ground before him.

The air was heavy with the stink of death, and the taste of blood was bitter in his mouth.

"Stand down, Seraphim," a voice ordered from behind him.

Remiel spun, his bloodstained sword at the ready in his gold, gauntleted hand.

General Aszrus emerged from a shifting haze that seemed to rise up from the bodies of the dead that littered the ground.

"I ordered you to stand down," he repeated.

Realizing that they'd fought on the same side, Remiel lowered his blade, turning back to the carnage for which he had been partially responsible. The sword was suddenly heavy in his hand, and seemed to grow heavier with each passing second.

"It is a sight," the general said as he moved to stand beside Remiel.

"It is," Remiel agreed, feeling a bottomless sadness open up at his core.

"But we are victorious," Aszrus added.

The words were as sharp as a dagger, and Remiel flinched as if struck.

"Victorious?"

"Aye," the angel general said, with the hint of a crooked smile upon his chiseled features. Remiel studied the figure then, noticing the dried blood that flecked his pale, perfect flesh. "Many of our brothers perished in this great conflict, but so did our enemies."

"Enemies who were our brothers not so long ago," Remiel reminded the general.

Aszrus' gaze intensified.

"Brothers who turned against the Lord God to follow the edicts of the Morningstar," he said firmly. "Making them brothers no longer."

Remiel sensed the presence of others and turned to see the last of the general's men, their haggard faces a reflection of the battle that had been fought. Here were faces of beings once touched by the glory of God, now forever changed by what they had seen, and been forced to do.

"But that is behind us now, soldier," Aszrus proclaimed, reaching out to lay a heavy hand upon Remiel's armored shoulder. "Those still faithful to the Morningstar have been routed, and the adversary himself has been captured, and awaits the Almighty's edict for his treasonous acts."

Aszrus paused, allowing his supposedly inspirational words to sink in.

"It's over, brother," the general added.

Remiel could not take his eyes from the carnage, and the more he looked, the more he saw.

The more he came to understand.

"You're right," the Seraphim said. "It is over."

*And it was.*

There is nothing sadder than a dead angel.

Angels were a durable breed, but even they could not function when their hearts were cut out. General Aszrus was indeed dead.

Sensing the wrongness of the situation, Remy had risen from bed, thrown some clothes on, and told Montagin to take him to Aszrus.

The angel had just stood there, staring off into space and talking about how horrible it all was. Remy had been forced to reach out and take hold of Montagin's arm and to squeeze as hard as he could.

The angel's face quickly registered pain, and then anger, but before he could lash out at the one causing it . . .

"Take me to Aszrus. Now."

Remy had watched as the anger churned there, behind the angel assistant's dark eyes, but the rage gradually receded, as what Remy was asking of him gradually sunk in.

Montagin pulled his arm away, reaching up to rub at where Remy had grabbed him.

"That better not leave a bruise," the angel warned as he brought his wings around to embrace them both, and transport them away from Remy's bedroom to . . .

Here.

They appeared in the corner of a room—a study—that Remy would have given one of his kidneys to have.

It was enormous, filled with floor-to-ceiling bookshelves and heavy pieces of leather furniture. Lying in the center of what was obviously a priceless Persian rug was the sprawled body of angel General Aszrus.

Remy glanced to his left, through the opening in the slats of a shuttered window, and saw a spectacular view of the sea washing up on a rocky beach outside.

"Where are we?" Remy asked, walking away from Montagin toward the body.

"Newport," the angel responded. "I believe it's in a state called Rhode Island."

"What brings an angel soldier and his assistant to Newport?" Remy knelt beside the corpse.

"You would have to ask him," Montagin replied. "Perhaps he saw a picture in one of the human magazines he enjoyed reading."

Remy looked down at the general, remembering how he'd last seen the powerful being. Once again, his face was flecked with small spatters of blood, but this time it was his own.

"Tell me everything about finding him," Remy ordered.

He was already starting to notice things that were . . . *curious*.

Montagin had crossed the room, over to what looked to be a portable bar in the shape of an old globe. The angel lifted the cover, revealing the inside of the planet to be filled with bottles of alcohol.

"I came in for one of these, actually," Montagin said, removing a decanter of scotch from the hollow inside of the globe, along with a glass, and filling it halfway.

Remy looked away from the corpse, to the angel.

"He was the one to introduce me to the joys of alcohol," Montagin said. "Especially scotch. Got to be one of the only things I admired about this monkey cage of a world."

"So, you came in for a scotch—go on."

Montagin came cautiously closer, drink in hand.

"I didn't expect to find him in here, especially in this . . . condition."

The angel took a large gulp of his drink and swallowed it down without any hesitation, his eyes briefly closing as he savored its taste. It was obvious to Remy that the angel wasn't lying when he said that he'd learned to love alcohol.

It wasn't often that one could observe an angel in the throes of pleasure.

"Aszrus wasn't supposed to be here. He'd gone out earlier in the evening and wasn't expected back until much later—if at all."

"Where did he go?" Remy asked.

The angel shrugged. "Out," he answered. "The general did not share his every bit of business with me, only items that pertained to maintaining God's will and the glory of Heaven."

"Right," Remy muttered in response. "The glory of Heaven. So you don't have the slightest idea where he went last night?"

"Not the slightest," Montagin said as he drank some more.

Remy scowled, not liking that pieces of the puzzle were missing. "Go on. You came in . . ."

"So when I came in and found him like this . . ."

"And this is exactly how it was when you entered?" Remy asked. "You didn't touch anything?"

The angel shook his head. "Not a thing." He considered the question again, before adding to his answer. "I had a drink, but that was all."

"And then what did you do?"

"Drank my drink, and thought about who could have done such a thing, and what it would mean to the grand scheme of things."

"And then?"

"And then I thought of you, and how if there was anybody on this forsaken world that could keep this situation from blowing up it would be you."

"I'm guessing that you already suspect who's responsible," Remy said, rising to his feet, eyes still rooted to the corpse of the angel general.

"Isn't it obvious?" Montagin scoffed.

"No, not really," Remy said, looking away from the corpse to the angel.

Just as he was about to take another swig from his glass, he stopped. "You're not sure?" Montagin asked. "Who else but the Morningstar would be responsible for such a blatant disregard for protocol? Somebody entered the dwelling of a general serving in the army of Heaven and cut out his heart. Who else but Lucifer would dare—"

"He wasn't murdered here," Remy interrupted, looking back to the corpse.

"What?" Montagin asked, thrown by the statement. "What do you mean he wasn't murdered here?"

"There isn't enough blood." Remy pointed down to the Persian rug beneath the corpse. "If Aszrus' heart was cut out here, the rug would be stained with his blood. There isn't more than a drop here and there beneath him."

Montagin downed what remained of his drink, placed the empty glass on one of the bookshelves, and stalked closer for a look.

"You're right, but if he wasn't murdered here, then . . ."

"He was murdered someplace else," Remy finished. "And I think that wherever that is will likely tell us who is responsible."

"But who else would dare?" Montagin began.

The stink of scotch wafted from the angel's breath, causing Remy to wrinkle his nose.

"I could be wrong, but I'm just not feeling the work of the Morningstar here," Remy said.

"Then who?" Montagin demanded.

"Don't know." Remy was looking at the body again, searching for something—anything—that he might have missed the first few times. "But something tells me that if the Morningstar was involved, he wouldn't have gone through all the trouble of killing the general, and then bringing the body back here. I'm guessing it would have been left where it fell."

"How can you know that?" Montagin asked.

Remy shrugged. "I can't," he said. "It's just something that I'm feeling in my gut right now. This doesn't feel like an act of war. It feels more . . . personal."

"But that's exactly what this is," Montagin stressed.

Remy understood the ramifications of this act, and did everything possible not to break out in a cold sweat.

"Right, but we've got to do everything in our power to prevent folks from finding out about it right now until . . ."

"Until?" Montagin wanted to know.

"Until I figure out who's responsible."

# CHAPTER SIX

The clock was ticking, and since Montagin didn't have any information as to where the general had been the previous night, Remy figured that it wouldn't hurt to ask some of the house staff if they knew anything.

Montagin had pissed on the idea, but Remy knew better, insisting that the angel would be surprised at how much was known by people who supposedly didn't know a thing.

They locked up the study and proceeded through the labyrinthine corridors of the estate to a huge kitchen, where a squat old woman sat at a table peeling potatoes, the filthy skins dropping from her knife onto a spread-out newspaper.

The smell of freshly brewed coffee permeated the air.

"This is Mr. Chandler," Montagin announced as they entered the kitchen, and Remy watched as the old woman jumped at the sound of his voice. "He has some questions to ask you, and I would appreciate if you answered them."

Montagin then looked to him. "I will be in the study if you should need me," the angel announced before turning to go back the way they'd come.

"Would you like some coffee, Mr. Chandler?" the woman asked, pushing back her chair as she started to stand.

Remy watched her, and knew at once that she was blind. It was no surprise to him; Angels who functioned on Earth had a tendency to surround themselves with the sightless. There was something about the affliction that lent itself to the service of Heavenly beings.

Some said it had something to do with the sightless being able to see—*sense*—angels as they truly were and not as their human alter egos.

"That would be very nice, Ms. . . . ?"

"Bridget will suffice," she said with a pleasant smile, fingers gently laid upon the tabletop as she moved around the furniture to get to the stove, where a pot of coffee sat.

She poured him a steaming cup of the dark liquid and carefully set it down in front of him without spilling a drop.

"Cream and sugar?" she asked. "Or would you prefer milk?"

"This is fine," Remy said, picking up the cup and taking a careful sip. It was some of the best coffee he'd had in ages. Madeline would have called it rocket fuel it was so strong, but that was just the way he liked it.

Bridget continued to stand there, fingertips resting atop the table.

"Excellent coffee, Bridget," he told her, expecting her to find her way back to her chair; but she continued to stand before him, sightless eyes gazing off into the kitchen.

"Glad you like it," Bridget said, again with a tender smile. "It's one of my special talents."

Remy wholeheartedly agreed and took another drink of the scalding brew, the older woman still standing in front of him. He was about to ask her if there was something wrong, or something that he could do for her, when she began her question.

"Would it be forward of me to ask to touch your hand?" Bridget asked.

For a moment he didn't understand, but he quickly came to realize that she wanted to *see* him as he truly was.

"Normally I have far better manners than this, but in you I'm sensing . . ."

Remy did not wait for her to finish. Instead, he reached out, gently taking her hand in his.

"How's this?" he asked, watching the expression upon her face change.

"Oh my," Bridget whispered, her cheeks beginning to flush pink. "You're lovely."

"Why, thank you," Remy said with a laugh.

The old woman then lovingly patted his hand and returned to her seat.

"And why haven't I seen somebody like you around here before?" she asked as she lowered herself down into her seat, and felt out a potato to begin peeling again.

"Let's just say your master and I don't run in the same circles," Remy said.

She seemed to accept that, nodding in understanding.

"Mr. Montagin said that you have some questions for me," she said, her knife expertly separating the skin from the body of the potato.

"I do," Remy said. "When was the last time you had contact with Aszrus?" he asked.

She stopped her work, thinking about the question.

"Last night, before supper," she said. "I was going to make a roast chicken, but he told me not to bother—that he was going out for the evening."

"And that was it?" Remy asked. "You didn't speak with him again?"

"Only briefly, when he asked if I would make him shepherd's pie for tonight." Her smile was beaming. "He loved my shepherd's pie."

"I'm sure it's something amazing," Remy responded, finding all of this absolutely fascinating. Here were angels of Heaven, creatures not known for their love of humanity's ways, embracing many of the habits for which he himself had been ostracized by his kind.

"Perhaps if you and the master could put aside your differences—at least long enough to have a good meal—you might be able to see just how amazing."

"That certainly is something to consider," Remy said, finishing up the most excellent cup of coffee, and rising from his chair. He reached across the table to touch her hand again. "Thank you so much for your time, and the coffee."

She told him that he was most welcome, but as Remy pulled his hand away, she grabbed hold of his fingers in a passionate grip.

"Why exactly are you here, Mr. Chandler?" Bridget asked. "Is everything all right?"

Remy could sense her rising concern, and did everything in his power not to let on. It was still too early for the fate of her master to be revealed.

"I'm helping Mr. Montagin with an investigation," he told the concerned old woman. "As soon as we've gathered all the facts, I'm sure we'll be speaking again."

Remy felt bad that he couldn't tell her more, but was afraid that if he did, things would soon spiral out of control.

She released his hand without another word, and he left her there, staring off into space, alone with her curiosity and concern.


Remy found Montagin in the foyer of the home, finishing up his talk with the remaining staff.

"And if you should remember anything out of the ordinary, please do not hesitate to inform me."

The random assortment of men and women, young and old, all sightless, responded that they most assuredly would, and proceeded to slowly go about their duties.

As Remy watched them he could see that there was some hesitation there, that some of them were attempting to get up enough courage to ask what this was all about. He used the opportunity to inject himself into the scene, canceling out their opportunity.

"Mr. Montagin," Remy said aloud, announcing his presence.

He watched those who had not yet left rethink their next action, then disappear into the house along with their curiosity.

"Anything?" Remy asked.

"If they did hear something, they've chosen not to talk about it," Montagin answered. "Was Ms. Worthington any help?"

"Bridget?" Remy asked. "No. She had a brief exchange with the general last night before he went out." He kept his voice low in case there were any ears close by.

Remy took hold of Montagin's elbow, steering him back toward the study and the scene of the crime.

"What now?" Montagin asked. "If we report this to the proper authorities, you know what the outcome will be."

Remy knew exactly what would happen; it was as sure as dropping a lit match into a bucket of gasoline.

*War.*

The forces of Heaven were looking for an excuse, any excuse at all, to begin another war with the legions of the Morningstar.

"We need to keep what's happened a secret as long as we can," Remy said as they stood in front of the heavy wooden doors leading into the study.

"I'm not sure how long that might be," the angel assistant said. "Aszrus had certain responsibilities."

"They'll need to be canceled," Remy stated.

"Canceled?" Montagin protested. "Aszrus was a leading general of the Heavenly legions here to assess the situation brought on by the reemergence of the threat of Lucifer Morningstar. His responsibilities cannot just be canceled."

Remy's eyes darted around the hallway, making sure that no one was around before he spoke. "Well, guess what? They're going to have to be, unless our friend in there is going to show up at one of his meetings sporting a lovely hole where his heart used to be."

They glared at each other, the immensity of the situation weighing on them both.

"Perhaps it wouldn't unfold like we think," Montagin suggested. "Maybe if we stress your belief that the Morningstar wouldn't—"

"You know as well as I do that's exactly how it would unfold," Remy interrupted. "War would be declared as soon as they saw the body—

and since when would any of the Heavenly host have anything to do with what I have to say? They can't fucking stand me."

"True," Montagin agreed. "But I don't know how I'm going to keep this secret for very long."

Remy looked at the doors. "First, we have to seal this up," he said.

"Seal it up?"

"Nothing gets in there," Remy explained. "We're better off if no one knows he's dead."

"A locked door will not keep a being of Heaven from getting inside," Montagin informed him.

"True, if we're going the traditional route," Remy said.

Montagin stared, unsure of where this was going. "Go on."

"Magick," Remy said. "We'll find a magick user strong enough to weave a spell around the study, to keep anybody from getting in. Hopefully that will buy me enough time to come up with something to keep the dogs of war on their leashes."

"And how do you suggest we locate this magick user?" Montagin questioned. "Should I look him up in the phone book, or use one of those computing devices and find him on the interweb?"

"I'll take care of that," Remy said. "I think I know enough to find somebody that should be able to handle the job. The payment might be steep, but considering the alternative . . ."

Montagin laughed—one of those freezing-cold displays of emotion popular with these creatures of the divine.

"Did I say something funny?" Remy asked him.

"All this effort, and we're not even sure if it's true or not," the angel said, shaking his head.

"If what is true?"

"That Lucifer isn't somehow responsible for this," Montagin said. "Responsible for what's gone on in there." He pointed briefly to the closed doors, the horrible secret on the other side just pushing to get out and explode upon the world.

"That's something I'm just going to have to find out," Remy said.

"That, and a magick user to put the granddaddy of all padlocks on that door."

## Castle Hallow
## 1301

Simeon vaguely recalled the sound of the heavy metal bolt in the door being slid back, and the creak of rusty hinges, before being taken by unconsciousness again.

It was the intense pain of claws scratching across his lower body that drew him up from the pool of oblivion.

Simeon screamed.

He opened bleary eyes to gaze upon a foul sight: a demonic creature of pale gray flesh with a humped back and a circular, tooth-ringed mouth like that of a leech. It had dug its long, filthy claws into his belly and was digging bloody rivulets into his fragile flesh.

His screams echoed mournfully throughout the dungeon.

"How do you do this?" asked a voice from somewhere within the room of torture.

Simeon could see that it was not the beast who spoke, its ringed mouth not likely made for speaking. With great effort he lifted his head from where he hung naked, chained by the wrists and ankles, and squinted bloodshot eyes to see what addressed him.

Something tugged excruciatingly from below, and his eyes dropped to see that the demon had torn a hole in his belly. It had withdrawn a rope of his innards and was now feeding it into its circular maw.

Simeon felt himself on the verge of tumbling back down into the black of the abyss when the voice spoke again.

"Every bone broken—mended in a matter of days," the voice said. "Stabbed, flayed, and now disemboweled and eaten while still alive."

The darkness crept closer around his eyes, threatening to claim him once more, when the figure that was speaking stepped into the faint light thrown by a smoldering brazier. Earlier it had heated instruments of torture that had been used upon his flesh.

Ignatius Hallow stood before him, clad in heavy robes, a skullcap of glistening copper atop his head.

"I ask you again, what manner of thing are you?"

Simeon answered before he could again be pulled down into temporary death. "I . . . I am . . . I am a man."

He vomited a stream of blood on the demon squatting below him. The hellish beast didn't seem to mind, its gray skin now speckled with color.

Hallow laughed.

"Oh yes. Of course you are."

As the demon excitedly tugged more length from the coiled intestines inside his belly, Simeon briefly died.

Briefly.

When he came round once more, he was no longer chained to a wall, but had been strapped to a wooden table, the tall figure of Ignatius Hallow hovering over him.

"Ah, you're with us again," the necromancer stated.

"Yes," Simeon croaked, doubting he would be for very long.

And he was right.

Hallow lifted a blade and brought it down with all his might into Simeon's chest, causing his heart to explode as the metal blade perforated it.

Simeon died again in a white-hot flash of agony, before the coolness of the dark dragged him below.

"The Nazarene," said a voice that pulled him up from the depths of nothing.

Simeon opened his eyes, and found himself gazing at his own reflection in a blood-flecked mirror. As his eyes slowly began to focus, he could see the form of Hallow looming behind him, hard at work, delicate metal instruments probing the bloody insides of his head. The top of his skull had been cut away, his neck and head strapped tightly to the back of a chair.

"How do you know of him?" Simeon asked weakly.

"The brain is a most magnificent organ," the necromancer stated, putting down one of his surgical tools only to have another placed within his bloody hand by a demonic assistant. "If one were to look closely enough, I feel that one could find the secrets of all existence. . . ."

Hallow jabbed the point of his metal tool into a specific spot of the soft, gray matter of Simeon's organ of thought.

"Or at least yours," Hallow finished as stars erupted before Simeon's eyes; he could not help but laugh hysterically, though he did not know the reason.

He laughed and laughed until he could no longer breathe, and another bout of death came round to see if this time would be the last.

It wasn't.

When next he lived, Simeon opened his eyes to the sight of Hallow sitting upon an enormous throne of intricately carved wood, directly across from him, goblet of wine in hand, staring intensely.

"Fascinating," the necromancer stated before bringing his drink to his mouth.

Simeon then realized that he was seated in a chair, and not bound in any way; that his plentiful wounds had been allowed to heal, and that his previously tortured flesh was adorned in robes of heavy wool.

"Bring him some wine," Hallow ordered, and another creature of demonic origin scampered over with goblet and pitcher. "I imagine continuously dying might work up quite the thirst."

The monstrous thing poured the wine sloppily into the cup, and then placed it in Simeon's trembling hands. He was about to thank the foul thing but thought better of it.

"Touched by the hands of God's supposed son," Hallow said from his throne of oak. "And now you cannot die."

Simeon attempted to sip from his cup, but his thirst was too great to hold back, and he greedily gulped at the liquid.

"Is this a blessing?" Hallow asked, swishing the contents of his goblet around as he pondered his own question. "Or is it a curse?"

Simeon lowered his cup. "Some more?" he asked, unsure of what the question might bring. He thought he might find himself strapped to a table, being forced to drink until his stomach bloated so badly that it eventually exploded.

"Give him more," the necromancer commanded his monstrosity.

The beast responded with a throaty growl, loping back to refill the cup.

"Are you . . ." Simeon began, before partaking of any more wine. "Are you going to kill me again?"

Hallow laughed, a booming sound that echoed throughout the vast chamber of his castle home.

"It is a possibility," the necromancer said with a slow nod. "But for now I believe I have seen enough."

He drank deeply from his goblet, his steel gray eyes never leaving Simeon, seated across from him.

"When you first arrived here . . . when my vines took hold of you, I asked why you had come," Hallow said. "You said that you'd come to learn."

Simeon had finished the wine that had been poured in his cup, and was starting to feel its effects. His head had grown light, and the pain from his healing body didn't seem quite so bad.

"I did," Simeon answered. He looked toward the demonic creature squatting beside its master's throne and held out his cup, giving it an impatient shake.

The demon hissed, showing off rows of razor-sharp teeth, as it looked from Simeon to his master, and then back to Simeon.

"Give him more," Hallow stated, and the demon begrudgingly obeyed.

"To learn," the necromancer then said as the demon poured more wine into Simeon's cup. "That is an awfully broad statement. What have you come to learn?"

Simeon stared at the older man over the metal rim of his cup.

"Everything that you know."

Hallow laughed—a loud, braying sound. "Everything, you say. Do you realize how long I've lived to know what I do?"

Simeon stared intensely, wanting the necromancer to know how serious he was.

"How long it would take for you to learn even a fraction of what I've already forgotten?" Hallow asked.

Simeon could not help but smile at the older man. "Doesn't matter," he stated flatly. "I've got all the time in the world."

The necromancer at first seemed startled by the sudden levity of Simeon's words, but then the true meaning permeated through his copper skullcap, and down into his brain, and Ignatius Hallow began to laugh.

Sharing the joke of the forever man. Sharing the joke of the man who could not die.

# CHAPTER SEVEN

A certain energy once again radiated from the brownstone on New-bury Street, but up until recently, that energy had been missing.

Remy hoped to kill two birds with one stone on this visit. Climbing the concrete steps to the front door, he let himself into the entryway as he fished for the key that would get him into the building.

The fact that people actually lived in the building again seemed to give the old brick structure a life of its own, and Remy could feel it in the air as he stepped into the lobby.

Francis was back, reclaiming the building that had been left to Remy when the fallen Guardian angel was thought dead, killed during the upheaval in Tartarus caused by the return of Lucifer Morningstar.

But he had returned, unscathed, and with a new employer. Though the identity of his fallen friend's new boss had yet to be discussed, Remy had his suspicions.

One does not walk away from an upheaval in Hell and not have scars to show for it.

Remy figured Francis would have the inside scoop as to what might have happened to Aszrus and on whether the Morningstar was inter-ested in escalating a conflict with Heaven. He headed for the door leading to the fallen angel's basement apartment, and immediately sensed that his friend was not at home. He pulled open the door anyway, but the silence confirmed his suspicion.

No matter. He'd hook up with Francis later. Instead, he turned his attention to the second bird. He was in need of a magick user, and Francis just so happened to have one living in his building.

Angus Heath wasn't the most pleasant of individuals. A former member of a band of sorcerers interested in the acquisition of supernatural knowledge and power in order to influence the world, he and Remy had recently been forced to work together in order to stop a renegade member of his former cabal.

Heath had since claimed an empty apartment on the third floor, and Remy quickly took the stairs two at a time to reach his destination. It was surprisingly cool outside, and the steam heat in the long hallway hissed like a snake, as if in warning.

Remy rapped on the door with his knuckle, listening to see if he could hear anything inside. Thinking that he might have heard movement, he knocked again.

"Angus," he called. "It's Remy Chandler. I need a favor."

There was movement behind the door, and Remy stepped back on instinct as it came open to reveal not at all who he was expecting to find.

"Hey, Remy," the creature named Squire said. His arms were filled with items as if he'd just come from grocery shopping, but they'd run out of bags. Squire was attempting to hold on to a loaf of bread, a jar of mayo, multiple packages of cold cuts, and a king-sized bag of potato chips.

"Did I knock on the wrong door?" Remy asked, checking the number.

Squire now lived in the building, too, after helping out with the same case that had introduced Remy to the sorcerer, Heath. Squire was a hobgoblin from an alternate version of Earth where something really horrible—something that he wasn't too keen on sharing—had transpired. He had the ability to use shadows as a means of transport. He was also pretty good in a fight.

"No, you're good," the hobgoblin said, closing the door behind him, but dropping the loaf of bread in the process. "As you can guess Angus isn't home."

"Which is why you're helping yourself to his food," Remy said.

"Exactly," the squat, homely creature said. "Could you grab that bread for me?"

Remy bent and picked it up, watching as Squire headed down the hall to an apartment on the other side.

"It's unlocked," he said, motioning with his chin for Remy to open his door.

Remy turned the knob and pushed it open, Squire heading in first.

"Make yourself at home," the hobgoblin said as he walked into the kitchen area, putting his plunder down atop the counter. Remy tossed him the loaf of bread as he looked around.

The apartment was practically empty, except for a leather couch and a beat-up old recliner. There was a large, flat-screen television hanging on the wall.

"Can I make you a sandwich?" Squire asked. He had torn into the packages of cold cuts and the bread and was making a monstrosity of a meal. "I got roast beef, provolone, and ham."

"No, I'm good," Remy said. He watched the goblin construct his lunch in awe, multiple pieces of meat and cheese creating a sandwich at least five inches thick. And since he didn't appear to have any silverware, he just dipped his chubby fingers into the jar of mayonnaise and smeared it on the meat and bread. He then placed some whole pickles and a handful of potato chips onto the heap of cheese and meat.

"There, that oughta hold me for a bit," he said, proudly placing the other piece of bread on top and pushing it down with a muffled crunch.

Squire grabbed the huge sandwich off the counter and started toward the living room.

"I'd offer you a drink, but I forgot to see what Angus had in the liquor cabinet," he said, hopping up into his recliner. A cloud of dust shot up into the air as he hit the seat.

"Love what you're doing with the place," Remy said sarcastically.

"Can you believe that somebody was throwing this chair out?" Squire asked. With the hand that wasn't clutching his snack, he found the remote control and pointed it at the television.

The sounds of moans and shrieks of pleasure filled the apartment, and Remy glanced toward the screen to see a naked man and woman in the midst of a pornographic act that was probably illegal in at least fifteen states.

"Really?" Remy asked, looking back to the grinning creature.

"Not a fan of the arts?" Squire asked with a cackle. He pointed the remote again and turned the porn off. It was replaced with *The Price Is Right*.

"So, what do you need Angus for?" the hobgoblin asked, taking a huge bite of his sandwich as some of the contents between the two bread slices spilled out from the bottom onto his shirt.

Squire really didn't seem to care.

"I need a magick user for a case I'm working on," Remy answered. "Any idea where he went?"

"Pretty sure he headed over to Methuselah's," Squire answered with his mouth full. "Said something about planning the dinner specials for the week."

Remy nodded, reminded that the sorcerer was the cook at the tavern located at the edge of multiple realities.

"Let me finish my snack and I can open a shadow path and take you over," Squire suggested.

"Wouldn't want to take you away from your art," Remy said with a smirk.

And the hobgoblin began to cackle, the last of the sandwich unappetizingly visible from his open maw.

The corridor of shadow opened up just outside the large, wooden door with the neon sign flashing METHUSELAH'S hanging above it.

"I always thought you needed a key to find this place," Remy said. He had a key. It had been Francis', but he'd left it back on Beacon Hill.

"Yeah," Squire replied. "But I've got a knack for finding shit that ain't supposed to be found."

"Good to know," Remy said.

The hobgoblin and Remy stood in the stone alleyway, total darkness at their backs.

"Are you coming in?" Remy asked. "I'll buy you a drink."

"Naw," Squire said. "I gotta get back to the apartment. I'm getting cable installed and they're supposed to be there between ten and five."

"No worries," Remy said. "I owe you one, then."

"And don't think I won't take you up on it," Squire said, turning back to duck inside the shadow portal.

Remy was walking toward the ancient, wooden door, when Squire called out from behind him.

"Hey, Remy."

He turned to see the hobgoblin peering out from inside the passage as it grew smaller around him.

"Don't tell Angus you found me in his place," Squire said. "You wouldn't believe how sensitive he is about that shit."

"Your secret's safe with me," Remy said, giving him a wave before turning back to the entrance to Methuselah's.

The door opened before he could even knock.

A minotaur loomed over him in the doorway, its nostrils flared and dripping.

"What do you want?" the brown-furred beast demanded, its eyes dark and reflective in the strange glow of the alleyway.

"Is that any way to talk to a customer?" Remy asked, advancing to push past the beast.

The minotaur moved to block his entrance. "If I owned the place I wouldn't let you holier-than-thou types through the door," he growled.

"Good to know," Remy told him, looking deep into his eyes. "When Methuselah hangs it up, I'll be sure to lose the address."

The monstrous bouncer was giving it his best, trying to outstare him, but Remy didn't have the time for this kind of nonsense. He was about to get a bit more physical with the door beast, when the bar's owner called out from inside.

"Let him in, Phil," the gravelly voice of Methuselah ordered.

The beast turned its massive, horned head to look inside the bar.

"You heard him, Phil," Remy said, shoving the large-bodied mythological doorman aside to step into the dingy bar.

Remy could sense the minotaur coming up quickly behind him, and spun around just as Methuselah called out from behind the bar.

"Phil, you heard me!"

The minotaur had raised his huge fists, like twin cinder blocks, and was preparing to bring them down on Remy.

"Do it and pay the consequences," Remy warned, the power of the Seraphim now coursing through his body, causing his voice to echo. "Don't and we both go about our business. It's really pretty simple."

Phil loomed above him, nostrils wet and pulsating as he clenched his huge fists.

"What's it going to be . . . Phil?" Remy asked, the fire of Heaven blazing in his eyes.

"It's a good thing Francis is your friend," the minotaur said, lowering his muscular arms and returning to his post in front of the door. "Wouldn't want to offend him by stomping your holy ass."

Remy let it go, sidling up to the bar.

Methuselah, in his stone golem body, placed an empty glass on top of the bar and began to fill it from a dust-covered bottle of whiskey.

"Sorry about that, Chandler," Methuselah said, filling the glass by half with golden liquid. "Phil has just never warmed to you angel types."

He slid the glass across to Remy.

"On the house."

Remy didn't want to seem rude by refusing the offer. He picked up the glass, tossing back its contents in one gulp. He was certain that if he'd allowed himself to feel the alcoholic effects of the beverage, his head would have been spinning.

"Hit you again?" Methuselah asked, ready to pour some more.

"I'm good," Remy said, placing his hand over the mouth of the glass.

"So what brings you in?" Methuselah returned the dusty bottle to the display behind the bar. "Sorry to say that it's usually nothing good."

The bar was pretty empty, only sporadic tables here and there occupied by customers.

"No wonder Phil doesn't like me," Remy said. "Is Angus around?"

"Heath?" Methuselah asked. "Yeah, he's out back in the kitchen."

Remy slid from his stool, heading toward the double doors that would take him out back. "Do you mind?"

"Go ahead," Methuselah said, waving one of his squared, stone hands. "Try not to wreck the place."

Remy passed through the swinging doors into the kitchen, eyes scanning the good-sized room for a sign of Heath. He was surprised at how clean it actually was.

Three creatures of some insectlike species watched him with their bulging, compound eyes. One had grabbed a rather large knife.

"Angus Heath," Remy said, speaking the language of the insect creature. "Is he around?"

The insect kitchen worker, startled by Remy's question and how it was asked, pointed with the knife blade to an area in the back, near the walk-in freezer.

"Thanks," Remy said, walking where the insect had pointed.

He found Heath leaning upon a scratched and gouged butcher block table, a legal pad laid out before him. It looked as though Squire had been right about what the sorcerer was doing here. He was planning the dinner specials.

"I bet you make a mean shepherd's pie," Remy said as he approached.

The heavyset sorcerer looked up. "Fancy seeing you here. To what do I owe the occasion?"

"I need a favor," Remy said.

"Let me guess," the rotund sorcerer stated. "Something, something, something . . . the end of the world."

Remy smirked but with little humor.

"Yeah, a little something like that."

It didn't take Heath long to agree to help once Remy explained what was at stake.

The promise of substantial payment for his services didn't hurt, either.

"I'm going to need some things from my apartment," Heath announced to him as they came through the double doors into the bar.

"Where are you going?" Methuselah asked, pouring a guy wrapped from head to toe in heavy robes a drink of something red and churning.

"There's something I need to take care of," Heath said. "But I'll be back before the dinner crowd shows."

Methuselah glared at him.

"Would it help if I told you that it's something really important?" Remy asked, following Heath to the door.

"Isn't that how it always is with you, Chandler?" Methuselah asked. "Make sure you get him back here in one piece. He's the best cook this place has had in over seven hundred years."

"Take it easy, Phil," Remy said to the minotaur as he passed, and the tavern's door was loudly slammed closed behind them.

"I take it that you and the minotaur don't get along," Heath commented as they walked along the stone corridor to the doorway waiting for them at the end.

Heath pulled a fancy-looking gold key from inside his pants pocket, and slid it inside the lock, opening the door.

"Had an entrance installed inside my apartment," the sorcerer said, putting a finger up to his mouth as if uttering a secret he didn't want repeated. "Takes the problem of being late for work when I oversleep off the table," he said, swinging open the door into a pool of shadow.

Remy followed Heath inside and was closing the door behind him when something was suddenly in the Methuselah's alley—something desperate to join them.

It moved more quickly than even Remy could see, forcing its way through the doorway and into the cool space beyond.

"What the fucking hell!" Remy heard Angus bellow, as the door slammed closed on them, and they were all engulfed in total darkness.

There was a struggle in the pocket of black, and a strange sound like blasts of air being shot down a hollow tube. Remy reacted, jutting out his arm and filling his hand with the fire of the divine, which illuminated a closed door in the shadowy oblivion before them.

Then there followed a rush of flame, and the door disintegrated in a flash of smoke and fire. They emerged from the closet into the apartment.

"What is going on?" Heath asked in a near hysterical shriek, and Remy noticed that the sorcerer's chest was bleeding.

"You've been hit," Remy said, holding on to the large man as he began to fall to his knees.

That strange blowing sound filled the air again, and Remy reacted in an instant, throwing himself atop Heath's body.

The apartment was filled with smoke from the exploding door and the smoke alarm wailed. Remy brought forth his wings, flapping them wildly to clear the air and find their attacker.

The shooter took aim from the kitchen and Remy recognized him to be the cloaked customer at the bar for whom he'd seen Methuselah pouring a drink as he and Heath had left.

The shooter raised a long, sleeved arm and fired again.

Remy leapt above the intense blasts, and angled his descent down toward his assailant, connecting with him before he could fire his weapon again.

Landing atop the would-be assassin, Remy drove him savagely to the floor. There was a clattering sound as they hit, and Remy watched as the weapon flew from the attacker's hand and slid across the black-and-white linoleum tile.

The weapon was unlike anything he'd ever seen before. It appeared to be made out of yellowed bone, and looked almost like the intact skeleton of something that had once been alive, petrified into the shape of a gun.

The figure lashed out at the angel straddling him, the strength of the blow knocking Remy to the floor.

Scrabbling across the kitchen, the assassin went for his weapon. Remy dove as well, grabbing handfuls of the attacker's robes, and willing them to burn.

The cloth went up as if doused in gasoline.

The assassin screeched, throwing off the burning garment to reveal his true form.

There was no doubt that the attacker was a member of a demon species, one of the mysterious races of creature that angels believed existed in the darkness before God brought forth the light of creation, but even that was purely speculation.

His pale, naked flesh scorched by divine fire, the demon snarled, showing off yellow, razor-sharp teeth as he snatched up his bony weapon from the floor and began to shoot.

Remy beat his wings powerfully, propelling himself back and through the kitchen as the demon fired. In a dish strainer beside the sink Remy found a cast-iron frying pan, using the cooking tool as a means to defend himself.

As well as a weapon.

He infused the metal handle with the fire of God, the metal beginning to glow white-hot almost instantly in his grasp. The demon shot, and Remy lashed out, swatting the projectiles aside, listening as they clattered noisily to the floor. Remy glanced down to where one of the bullets had landed, and was shocked to see something that resembled a tooth lying there.

The assassin dashed from the kitchen, his movements so fast that it was almost as if he had disappeared. Burning frying pan in hand, Remy pushed off with his wings, the cramped conditions of the apartment preventing him from being able to take flight.

Remy saw the demon pulling the door open to make his escape, and hurled the burning pan in his direction. The demon ducked as the pan struck the doorframe beside his pale head. He snarled once more, raising his gun of bone and firing multiple shots again before racing out the door.

Remy barely managed to get out of the way as the organic-looking bullets chewed into the wall not far from his face.

He was already in pursuit when he heard the most ungodly of screams emanate from the hallway outside the apartment, and he quickened his pace to get there.

Careful, just in case he might be fired upon again, Remy darted from the apartment in a low crouch, prepared for just about anything that might follow.

Except for what did.

What was left of the demon lay upon its back in the middle of the corridor, the pale flesh now burned to a blackened crisp. Jagged bolts of supernatural energy wove through the body's ashen remains, as if searching out any part of the demon's form that was still flesh.

The energy then shot from the remains, like serpents of electricity, causing the blackened assassin's body to crumble away, leaving nothing more than a large pile of ashes in a humanoid shape.

The energy then returned to the man standing no more than five feet away, coalescing in the palm of his outstretched hand.

"Thought you might need a hand," Constantin Malatesta said as the magickal energy he'd wielded was absorbed back into his flesh.

"I certainly hope you don't mind."

Remy withdrew his wings as he walked toward the assassin's remains.

"Have you been following me, Mr. Malatesta?" Remy asked, kneeling down to sift through the ashes, retrieving the strange weapon of bone.

"I didn't care for how our first meeting ended," the Vatican representative said. "So I made a conscious effort to reconnect with you. Lo and behold, you were summoned to Rhode Island, as was I."

Remy stood, eyeing the man.

"You weren't at the mansion."

"Not inside, but I was there," Malatesta explained. "I received a message from one of my Keeper informants that something was going on, and that you had been called in. Let's just say, my curiosity was piqued."

"Doesn't explain how you ended up here," Remy said.

There was a click and the creak of a door opening as Squire stepped out into the hall, his stocky, leathery-skinned body wrapped in a bath towel.

"I called him," he said.

Remy glared.

"What?" the hobgoblin protested. "Vatican boy said he'd give me fifty bucks every time I saw you. A guy's gotta make some scratch on the side somehow."

He then turned his stare back to Malatesta.

"I needed to know where you were, what you were up to," Malatesta explained. "The Keepers believe . . ."

There was a moan of pain from the doorway behind them.

"Holy crap, Angus," Squire said. "You look like shit."

The sorcerer slid down the doorframe to the floor, as Remy was on the move.

"I think he's been shot," Remy told them.

Squire and Malatesta helped get the injured sorcerer back into the apartment, dragging him over to an overstuffed sofa in the living room.

Adjusting his towel as it began to slide off, the hobgoblin then tore open Heath's shirt to get a look at the wound. It was nasty looking, seeping blood as well as some other yellow, viscous fluid.

"That doesn't look right," Squire said. "What was he shot with?"

Remy remembered that he was still holding the weapon, and held it out for Squire to see.

"Oh, isn't that cute?" the hobgoblin said. "Does it fire regular bullets?"

"No," Remy stated. "It looked like it fired teeth."

"Swell," Squire muttered, just as Heath began to convulse, a spurt of blood and puss erupting from the wound.

Squire tore the towel from around his waist, bringing it down on the strange bullet wound.

"Get out of the way," Malatesta said, pushing Remy aside, and kneeling down beside Heath convulsing upon the couch.

"Remove the towel," the Vatican representative said.

The hobgoblin started to protest, but shut his mouth when he saw that the man's hand had started to glow an eerie blue, and pulled the towel away.

The sudden blast of stink was almost palpable, and Remy stepped back.

"What's wrong with him?" Remy asked.

"The projectile has released its poison," Malatesta said. "If I don't act quickly . . ."

The Vatican representative plunged his fingers down into the wound, the blue energy radiating from the tips of his fingers causing the blood, puss, and flesh to froth and sizzle.

Heath moaned in his unconsciousness, head thrashing from side to side, the agony great as it wreaked havoc on his body.

Most of the fingers of Malatesta's right hand were buried deep inside the wound as blood and discharge bubbled and smoked.

"I have done all I can," he said finally, withdrawing his gore-covered fingers. He held them up, showing the broken pieces of what used to be a tooth. "Hopefully I got them all."

Malatesta then took the towel from Squire and wiped his hand.

"I would suggest covering the injury with a bandage," he said. "Wouldn't want it to get any more infected than it already is."

"Is he gonna be all right?" Squire asked. He had left the living room, and had gone into the kitchen, returning with a roll of paper towels and a bottle of whiskey.

"I believe I got all of the projectile, and hopefully burned away most of the poison," he explained. "If his constitution holds out, he'll probably recover over time."

Remy watched as Squire tended to his friend, cleaning the wound with paper towels soaked in the whiskey.

"So I'm guessing he's out of the picture for a while," Remy said.

"I doubt he'll regain consciousness anytime soon," Malatesta answered. "Would I be forward to ask what it was that you needed him for?"

Remy considered the situation, and suddenly found himself with an answer.

"I'm in the middle of a job and require somebody with a certain skill set," Remy said, looking away from the unconscious Heath to the Vatican agent, who was still wiping the blood from his hands. "But I think I might've found an alternative."

Malatesta cocked his head inquisitively.

"From what you did to the assassin out in the hall, and what you did to save our friend, it looks as though you have some special talents."

"Yes?" Malatesta inquired.

"Exactly how good of a sorcerer are you?"

# CHAPTER EIGHT

*The Northern Ukraine*
*Within the Zone of Alienation*

Simeon stood in the window of the office building, looking out through the cracked and broken panes of glass onto the abandoned Chernobyl nuclear power plant.

The forever man remembered how dangerous it had once been, the levels of radiation so high as to cause skin to blister, and wreak irreparable damage at a cellular level.

It had been a true place of death, which is why he had first been drawn to it. No matter how many times he had failed in his pursuit of the final sleep, Simeon never gave up hope that perhaps, someday, he would at last be given that which he desired most of all.

That at last he would be granted the bliss of death.

But the Almighty was unnaturally cruel, allowing everything within a thirty-kilometer radius of the damaged facility to wither and die.

Everything except for him.

In the first days following the evacuation of the city of Prypiat and some of the villages closer to Chernobyl, Simeon had walked the lonely streets, feeling the effects of the deadly radiation, but never succumbing.

Though it did not give him what he most wanted, he grew to admire this place, reveling in its eerie quiet.

It was as if a tiny corner of the world had simply stopped.

A place of death, and it gave him something to aspire to.

But all good things . . .

From the window, Simeon watched a rabbit emerge. It scampered out from beneath some overgrowth, near a section of rusted chain-link fence that had been taken down by a fallen tree.

Twenty years later, life was slowly returning to the region. He'd even heard rumors that people were again being allowed to walk the evacuated streets, a once-forbidden curiosity to be explored.

He so despised letting go of things he'd grown to love. If he had to be around forever, so should at least a few of the things that gave him some bit of happiness. Simeon snarled, and wondered what his chances were of finding some discarded nuclear material to spread around in order to raise the radiation levels and preserve the solitude of this place.

And then he realized he was no longer alone.

The demon Beleeze stood silently in the doorway to the office.

"Yes," Simeon sighed, knowing that what was to follow would not be good, for he had left specific instructions that he not be disturbed.

The demon flowed farther into the room.

It always impressed him how silent this species was, as if sound itself was scared away by the primordial creatures.

Beleeze still did not speak.

"Tell me," Simeon commanded, twisting the ring upon his left hand.

"There's a problem," the demon said.

"Where?" Simeon asked, catching sight of a tuft of brown fur as it blew across the cursed earth. He had taken his eyes from the rabbit for only a moment, but it was gone now, tufts of bloody white and brown fur all that remained. Whatever had happened had only taken an instant.

It reminded him of how quickly things could go awry.

"The island," Beleeze grunted, as if the words themselves were adorned with razor-sharp edges that savagely cut as they left his mouth.

## England
## 1349

They had retired to a great den in the nearly empty castle, the stone walls covered in fine tapestries, a roaring fire burning in the huge stone fireplace.

The Pope sat upon a formidable wooden seat—a throne, really—its upholstery the color of fresh blood. Remiel sat in his own chair, a simple chair in comparison to Tyranus', but it suited the angel just fine. Both had been set before the fire, a small table for their wine goblets positioned between them.

"Would you like this castle, angel?" Tyranus asked. He held out his goblet, waiting for the servant girl to attend to his needs. She scurried over, filling his cup, careful not to spill a drop.

Remiel pulled his eyes from the mesmerizing flames and looked at the Pope.

"This castle," Tyranus stated again. "Would you like it? I could make it yours."

"I have no need for a castle."

The servant girl was now hovering beside Remy, eager to refill his goblet.

"I am fine, girl," he told her, and she bowed her head and scurried off.

"Certainly a place to call your own would not be a bad thing," the Pope continued, as he drank his wine. "A place to settle down . . . a place to call home."

"This could never be home," Remiel said grimly. He gently sipped what little drink he had remaining in his cup.

"Do you actually have a place in this world, soldier of God?" Tyranus asked. "What would drive one such as you from the Golden City of Heaven to this place of such turmoil?"

Remiel felt an odd compulsion to tell the holy man of the Great War, but he managed to suppress the urge, rising from the chair to stand before the fire. "Tell me of this necromancer," he said instead, changing the topic. "The more I know, the swifter will be his defeat."

The angel leaned upon the stone mantel, staring into the roaring flames, waiting for the Pope's answer. When he did not respond, Remiel turned to see him reclined on his throne, his goblet of wine resting in his lap. He was watching a young boy, dressed in Vatican finery, setting an ornate wooden box down upon the table between the two chairs.

"What is this?" Remiel asked.

"You wish to learn of the necromancer," Pope Tyranus replied. "This will tell you all that you need to know."

Remiel approached, observing the boy as he began to unsnap metal latches that held the box closed. He then pulled the two sides of the box apart to reveal what was inside.

The head was ancient, the skin like parchment stretched taut over the bald pate and the angular bones of the face. The eyes were squeezed tightly shut and sunken in, the orbs of sight behind the withered flesh a long time ago food for the worms and beetles.

"Let me guess," Remiel said. "One of the ways you fight fire with fire."

Tyranus smiled dreamily, multiple goblets of wine at last having their effect. "If you are suggesting that the oracle is an object of supernatural power, then you are correct," the Pope admitted. "Through it I first learned of the necromancer's existence, and that he possessed Solomon's sigil."

Remiel continued to stare at the disembodied head. "What does it do?" he finally asked.

With those words, the boy reached beneath his fine garments and produced a small knife. He stared at his master.

"Pay the oracle," Tyranus proclaimed as he drank once more from his cup.

Remiel watched as the boy raised the knife to his index finger, slicing the pad with a pained hiss. As the scarlet fluid bubbled out from the slash, the child brought his finger to the head's pursed lips, smearing the blood there.

The child's blood beaded upon the dry, leathery flesh, before slowly being absorbed. At first Remiel believed it be a trick of the flickering light thrown by the fire in the stone hearth behind him, but came to realize that the lips of the corpse were swelling, and then a tongue, dried and withered like a piece of tree bark, snaked out from between the engorged lips to partake of the boy's offering.

The boy squeezed his wound to bleeding again, and brought it down to the writhing mouth.

The head opened its awful mouth eagerly, and the boy stuck the bleeding digit into the gaping mouth, where it was at once suckled upon.

The child gasped as the head continued to suck greedily.

"That's enough, boy," Pope Tyranus ordered from his throne. "Make the oracle work for its sustenance."

With a growing revulsion, Remiel watched as the child withdrew his finger from the corpse-head's eager mouth. It began to emit a horrible, high-pitched keening.

"Silence, oracle," the Pope commanded.

The head ceased its noise, its nose twitching as if attempting to locate the scent of the one who commanded it.

"You have been fed, and now you will tell us of what we ask," Pope Tyranus proclaimed.

"The payment has been made," the head spoke in a weak, high-pitched voice. "You will be told what the oracle knows."

The boy had removed a lace handkerchief from somewhere within his robes, swathing his bleeding finger in the finest material.

"Tell us of the necromancer," Pope Tyranus stated. "You will tell us of the necromancer called Hallow."

The oracle considered what was asked of it, the lids covering the empty sockets of its eyes moving as if there were something beneath them, something squirming around to eventually be free.

"One of twins born of human, and protohuman," the oracle wheezed. "They were to be the guardians of magick, one representing the light, and the other, the dark. They were to maintain the balance, to keep one power from overwhelming the other."

The oracle stopped talking, its mouth moving hungrily.

"Go on, oracle," Remiel commanded.

"So dry," the head hissed weakly. "So very, very thirsty."

"Finish your tale and we shall see about quenching that thirst," Tyranus stated cruelly.

The oracle noisily smacked its parched lips together, building up enough moisture that it could go on.

"One power believed itself stronger than the other, throwing the balance into turmoil. The light would take from the dark, both powers amassed in one . . . but the darkness would not stand for this and a great battle was fought—the light versus the darkness . . . brother against brother. . . ." The oracle's voice trailed off.

"And this battle," Remiel said. "The light versus the dark—it continues?"

"Yes," the oracle replied. "The opposing forces collect their objects of magickal power in the hopes that one will eventually triumph over the other, and claim the might of the opposition."

"The necromancer . . . Hallow. He has Solomon's sigil?" Remiel asked.

"Yes," the oracle hissed. "A prize coveted by many who know the ways of the weird, and especially by one who serves the light. This will be the prize most viciously sought, for it will upset the balance once and for all, and the power of magick both black and white will rest in the hands of . . ."

"We are done," Pope Tyranus proclaimed, empty chalice clattering to the floor as he stood up from his throne.

Remiel stared at the Pope, curious of the interruption.

"The oracle is a tricky creature," the Pope said. "It will continue to prattle just to hear itself if it believes it will be fed."

Tyranus gestured to the boy. "Put it away."

The child snapped to it immediately, going to the case, his bloody finger still wrapped in the dainty handkerchief. He started to close up the sides, eliciting a reaction from the oracle.

"Wait!" it squeaked. "You promised me more. . . . You promised to quench this unbearable thirst!"

The boy considered the head's request, turning to gaze at his master for confirmation.

"Close it up, boy," Pope Tyranus ordered.

"Please," the oracle begged as the two sides of the case were slowly brought together. "The thirst . . . It hurts so badly. . . ."

The oracle's pleas fell upon deaf ears as the case was closed, and the latches were refastened.

The sound of muffled cries of sorrow trailed off as the boy carried the box from the room.

Having already been to the Newport mansion, Remy was able to locate it again.

He opened his wings, allowing Malatesta to emerge, as he wished the feathered appendages away. They had appeared just beyond the elaborate home, on a cliff overlooking a tumultuous sea.

"An impressive way to travel," Malatesta said, stumbling a bit to one side. Remy grabbed hold of his arm to steady him.

"As long as you know where you're going it beats public transportation," he said. "It's a little disconcerting at first, but you get used to it."

The Keeper representative shrugged off Remy's assisting hand, and turned to face the mansion. "Is this it?" he asked.

"That's it," Remy answered, and both began walking toward the quiet road that ran in front of the impressive front gate.

"Is the reason a Bone Master wants you and your sorcerer companion dead why I am needed here?" Malatesta asked as they crossed the road, the crash of the turbulent sea upon the cliffs filling the air behind them.

"I believe it is," Remy said as they reached the heavy wrought iron gate. "So you're familiar with our attacker . . . this Bone Master? What can you tell me about them?"

Malatesta grabbed hold of the black iron and gave the gate a shake to see if it opened. It didn't.

"Keeper agents have encountered them from time to time, assassins of a demonic nature. From what we've been able to piece together over the centuries, the Masters have somehow genetically engineered an animal that once dead becomes their weapon of choice. They bond with these mysterious animals on a psychic and physical level from child-hood, and when coming of age, ceremonially slay the animal, and peel away the flesh to reveal the weapon specifically bred for them."

Remy called forth his wings once again, grabbing Malatesta and hauling him up and over the gate.

"Thank you," the Vatican agent said, appearing a little startled by this, smoothing down his shirt, and pulling at the sleeves of his suit jacket.

"The special weapon," Remy said, walking up the driveway. "It fired what looked to be teeth."

"Yes," Malatesta answered, jogging to catch up. "The Keepers found that to be particularly interesting. As I mentioned, the weapon and the master are bound together both spiritually and physically, and the special gun is capable only of using its master's teeth as ammunition."

"So I'm guessing these Bone Masters—they have a lot of teeth?"

Malatesta nodded. "Very much like sharks' teeth; one is removed and another grows in to take its place. We at the Keepers believe that once a Bone Master finally runs out of ammunition—teeth—they, and their weapon, die."

They were climbing the steps to the double front doors.

"Do you realize how crazy all that sounds?" Remy asked, rapping his knuckles on the door. "And that's coming from somebody like me."

The door started to open, one of the blind servants visible on the other side.

"Get away from that door!" a voice boomed from somewhere inside.

The servant jumped back away from the door, and had started to close it again as it was yanked from his grasp. Montagin appeared in the entryway, his eyes burning with an unnatural light.

"Oh, it's you. What took you so long?" he demanded to know.

"Had to find what I was looking for," Remy said, pushing his way inside with Malatesta in tow. "And then there was the matter of some-body trying to kill me and the person who I found to take care of our problem."

Inside the elaborate foyer, Remy saw that the servant still lingered there, waiting.

"Be off with you," Montagin commanded, and the servant hurried off, hand upon the wall as he felt his way farther into the home.

"Is this that person?" Montagin asked, looking Malatesta up and down.

"No, he's my substitute," Remy explained. "Montagin, this is Constantin Malatesta."

The angel was already on the move toward the study, as Malatesta stood there, hand extended, his offer ignored.

"Hurry this way," Montagin said.

Remy and the Keeper representative followed.

"So, seeing as an attempt was made on my life," Remy called after the angel. "Any chance that we might have a leak here?"

Montagin stopped before the study doors.

"No one but you and I has been inside this room since the discovery," the angel said. "And from what I know about you, Remiel, the idea of somebody trying to kill you doesn't seem all that uncommon."

Malatesta looked to Remy.

"He thinks he knows me, but he doesn't," Remy said to him.

Montagin unlocked the door, the smell of death wafting out to greet them like an eager puppy.

"I'm guessing that I'm here because someone has died," Malatesta said, hand going up to his nose.

"Not just someone," Montagin said as he closed the door tightly behind them.

Remy pointed out the corpse lying on the floor.

"He's there."

The Vatican representative slowly approached the large figure lying there, his chest cut open.

"Oh my," Malatesta said. "Who was he?"

"General Aszrus," Remy said, staring at the corpse and noticing for the first time that the angel's wings were visible, crumpled and bent beneath him. "A very important figure in the looming war between the forces of Heaven, and those of the Morningstar."

Malatesta looked at Remy, his eyes filled with shock and awe.

"Yeah," he said with a nod. "Hadn't heard about that had you?"

Malatesta knelt carefully on the rug beside the corpse. "I can't imagine what would be strong enough to do something like this to something like him."

"It's what I intend to find out before the news of his murder starts a war, with humanity stuck smack in the middle."

"What do you need me to do?" Malatesta asked, his eyes traveling across the angel's body.

"We need something to keep people out," Remy stated. "The longer we can keep this secret, the better off we'll be."

Montagin was pacing back and forth, long arms folded.

"I don't know how I let you talk me into this," the angel grumbled. "It will likely be all for naught."

"Don't worry, this will work," Remy assured him.

"It would probably be easier for me to go to the war council and let them know what's occurred," Montagin replied. "We'll likely end up with the same result anyway, only a little bit sooner."

"You'll do no such thing," Remy instructed, moving to stand before the general's assistant. "There's far too much at stake. You know as well as I do that the war council is just looking for an excuse to start swinging their swords."

"What does it matter, Remiel, whether they start swinging now or later?" Montagin asked, on the verge of hysterics.

The sound of someone noisily clearing their throat got them to stop. Remy and Montagin both looked to the man kneeling beside the corpse of the angel general.

"If you two would like me to try to erect some sort of shield to seal this room, I'm going to need some quiet in order to concentrate."

Montagin sneered. "You'll have all the quiet you need and then some once the war horns blare, and all life upon this planet is burned to a cinder."

Malatesta cleared his throat again, his eyes never leaving the angel's. "Let's see what I can do to prevent that, shall we?"

It looked as though Montagin might have something more to say, but Remy took him by the arm, dragging him toward the exit.

"Let's leave him alone to work his magick," Remy said as he opened the door, and led the ruffled angel out into the hall.

"I don't even know that person," Montagin huffed, attempting to go back inside the study.

"You don't have to," Remy said. "He's a Vatican magick user. . . . I think he can handle this."

"He's from the Vatican?" Montagin asked as Remy nodded.

"This just keeps getting better and better," the angel said, bringing a trembling hand to his head.

Remy's phone began to ring. It was Linda.

"Look, let me get this," Remy said. "Why don't you go to the kitchen and see if Bridget will give you something to eat? She was making shepherd's pie this morning."

"I love shepherd's pie," Montagin said, heading toward the kitchen.

"Hey," Remy said into the phone.

"How are things?" Linda asked.

"Good," he answered. He couldn't bear to think of what might be waiting around the corner, if the news of Aszrus' death got out. He had seen what a war fought between angels was like, and couldn't even imagine this world experiencing something so devastating. "Got some things that I'm working on."

"I was calling to see if you want me to take Marlowe with me, or if you'll be home?"

"Would you take him, if it isn't a bother? I'm not sure when I'll be able to wrap things up, and I don't want the boy hanging around with his legs crossed."

"Oh, can't have that," she answered with a short laugh.

"Nope."

"All right, I'll let you go, then," Linda said.

"Okay," he answered, wanting to continue to talk with her, but knowing that the longer he was away from figuring out who, or what, had killed Aszrus . . .

"Give me a call later?" she asked.

"Sure," he answered. "Tell the boy that I'll see him later."

"I will," she said.

He was about to hang up, when he realized that there was something that he had to say. "Linda?" he called out.

"Yeah?"

"I love you," he said, and knew that it was completely true.

There was a long pause, and he could just about make out the sound of her breathing.

"Hello?" he asked. "Are you there?"

"I love you, too."

"Good," he said.

"Good," she repeated, and then broke the connection.

# CHAPTER NINE

Remy slipped the phone back into his pocket, and was considering heading back inside the study to see how Malatesta was doing, when he noticed one of the female staff members staring blankly ahead from the end of the corridor.

It was as if she was watching him, but he knew that wasn't the case. Maybe sensing him was more like it.

"Hello," he called out to her. "Is there something I can do for you?"

She advanced slowly, carefully, her fingertips running along the wall to guide her way.

"He's gone," she declared.

Remy was taken aback, but tried not to show it. "Excuse me?"

"The master . . . He's gone."

"That's something you're going to have to take up with Mr. Montagin," Remy said, turning toward the door to the study.

"I knew it was only a matter of time," she said. "Only a matter of time before the sin of the world had its way with him."

Remy froze for a moment, then slowly approached the woman.

She was younger than she looked initially, straggly blond hair falling down across her face. She smiled, chasing away the years.

"He called himself a creature of God," she began, her fingernails scratching at irregularities in the wall. "If that's the case, I wasn't aware that God was so awful and cruel."

It wasn't the first time Remy had heard that servants to the angels were treated less than humanely. Many of the divine creatures considered humanity little more than God's pets.

*Sea Monkeys in an aquarium.*

Remy was standing directly in front of the woman now. The fingers that had just been picking at the wall wagged before him.

"Do you fancy yourself a creature of God?" she asked, and he caught a hint of disdain in her tone.

"Aren't we all?" Remy asked.

The woman laughed, a high-pitched sound that very easily could have been tinged with madness. Serving angels certainly took its toll.

"What's your name?" Remy asked her.

She considered the question for a moment before answering.

"Marley," she said, almost in a whisper. "And you're Mr. Chandler."

"Remy," he told her. "Call me Remy."

Marley smiled again. "All right."

"Why do you think that something bad has happened to your master, Marley?"

"It was inevitable," she answered matter-of-factly. "Even the divine will fall when surrounded by so much . . . sin."

"I don't understand," Remy admitted. "What was Aszrus surrounded with?"

Marley remained silent, picking at the wall again.

"Marley, what was your master doing that was so bad?"

Her face twisted up in disgust. "He was no better than the vermin that walk the streets," she snarled. "He let himself be tempted. And it changed him."

"Tempted by what?"

"Things, Remy," she replied. "Are you tempted by things?"

"I don't really understand what—"

"I'll show you," Marley interrupted, reaching out for his hand. She led him down the corridor, abruptly stopping just before the kitchen.

She turned toward the wall and pushed on a wooden panel. "Secrets," she muttered, as part of the wall slid inward with a click.

She led Remy through the tiny opening, closing it behind them and plunging the small hallway into total darkness. Remy altered the configuration of his eyes so that he could see where they were.

A stairway stood directly in front of them. Marley, still holding tightly to his hand, led him up the steps.

"Where are we going, Marley?" Remy asked.

She giggled. "Where the sins are, where he hid them."

There was another door at the top of the stairs, and Marley paused briefly. She let go of his hand long enough to reach into the pocket of her maid's uniform to extract a key. Feeling for the lock, she inserted the key and turned it, opening the creaking door.

"I was the only one he allowed inside," Marley said. "The only one that he would let tidy up."

She reached for Remy's hand again, and drew him inside.

"This is where he would come," she told him. "Where he would spend hours upon hours surrounded by his vices."

Though he could see perfectly fine, Remy reached out to a table lamp to bring some light into the gloom. The light came on, and to say he was taken aback by what he saw there in the room was an understatement.

"You've got to be kidding me," he said, taking it all in.

Marley stifled a laugh and crossed her arms defiantly in front of her chest.

"These were his prizes," she said with disdain. "His most cherished possessions."

The room looked as though it might have belonged to a teenage boy, or maybe a first-year college student. Video game systems sat on the shelves of an elaborate entertainment center; empty plastic cases littered the floor. Aszrus appeared to have been a fan of first-person-shooter games. There were stacks of magazines just about everywhere: magazines about cars, about food, and porn—more porn than anything else, which complemented the plethora of pornographic DVDs stacked haphazardly beside a high-backed leather easy chair in front of a sixty-inch television monitor.

Remy slowly turned in the center of the den, taking it all in. There was a wheeled bar cart not far off, loaded with liquor—all top shelf. A tiny refrigerator hummed beside it.

On the table that held the lamp beside the easy chair, there was an ornate box, and he could only imagine what he would find inside. Remy reached out, carefully removing the carved lid. The inside of the case was compartmentalized: loose pot on one side, with rolling papers in another section beside it. In another section was what looked to be cocaine, and beside that what he guessed to be heroin. There was a hypodermic in its own thin section beside it.

From what he could see, every human vice was represented in some degree here. Remy had heard of angels becoming obsessed with the ways of the Earth; hell, even he had been accused of it, but he would never imagine an angel of Aszrus' stature falling so hard.

"He loved this . . . stuff more than those who would give their lives for him," Marley said. Lurching suddenly to one side, toward the small table beside the chair, she shoved the box of illicit drugs and the lamp to the floor. The room was again plunged into darkness. "And then not even this would do; he had to go even farther from us, outside the home to find whatever it was he was searching for."

"Where outside the house?" Remy asked, taking advantage of a potential opportunity.

She was breathing heavily now, the fear of repercussions for her actions weighing upon her. It looked as though she was thinking that perhaps she'd gone too far.

"What was he doing outside the house?" Remy pressed.

Marley carefully squatted down, attempting to clean up after herself, her fingers carefully picking up the pieces of the shattered lamp.

"It got to be that he barely acknowledged our existence," she said, quietly. "It was like we weren't even there anymore, our presence invisible as the car pulled up in front of the house, and he left for the evening, not returning until the early morning hours."

"He used a car?"

Marley slowly stood, broken lamp pieces carefully held in her hand. "It was another of his vices. . . . He loved cars and has an entire underground garage filled with them."

"But you said a car came for him."

"Yes, it would beep its horn once to let him know it had arrived."

"So he had a driver," Remy prodded.

"Yes," Marley agreed.

"Does this driver live here with the other staff members?"

Marley shook her head, a broken piece of the lamp in her hand falling to the floor from the movement.

"No," she said. "Normally he would drive his own cars."

"But in some instances he chose not to drive himself to wherever it was he was going."

Marley was quiet, her blind eyes staring into the darkness around them.

"Elite Limousine," she said.

"That was the name of the service he used?"

"Yes," she answered him. "I heard him through his office door once . . . and he asked for Neal to drive him."

Now they were getting someplace.

"You've been very helpful, Marley," Remy said gently. "Thank you."

He went for the door, turning toward the young woman.

"Are you coming?" Remy asked her.

She shook her head. "I'd like to clean up."

So he left here there, standing perfectly still in the darkness of the room, a darkness she had grown accustomed to.


Beleeze quickly left his master's presence so as not to incur his wrath.

His master had the most unpredictable of natures, and sometimes, when things did not go as planned, he would display a vicious temper.

Images that had branded themselves in the demon's mind flashed before his eyes, images of those that had brought their master news that he deemed . . . disappointing.

Beleeze still found disconcerting the memory of one of his kind being turned inside out, and yet still living. None who still served Master Simeon cared to put their own endurance to the test.

They had survived too much to suffer such an ignoble fate.

Beleeze and the other demons were of the species Demonicus, extracted from the darkness of oblivion by the necromancer, Ignatius Hallow, and enslaved by the power of Solomon's ring. They had served the death wizard for nearly a century before their servitude was transferred to the one named Simeon.

But with that transference, came the birth of purpose.

The demon descended the refuse-strewn steps into the main lobby of the deserted office building to find the others waiting.

"Well, at least you're still alive," Dorian commented.

*Is that actually concern in her dark eyes?* Beleeze wondered.

"How did he take it?" Robert asked.

Beleeze had yet to get used to the demon's change of names. Robert had been Tjernobog until a few centuries ago, when he'd changed it to fit in better with the world in which they existed.

Even though they were all working toward seeing it brought to ruin.

"Surprisingly well," Beleeze replied.

"What did he say?" Dorian asked. She was standing closer to him now, the long, spidery fingers of her hand briefly touching the sleeve of his jacket.

*Is it possible that after all this time, she finally realizes the feelings I have for her?*

Beleeze slowly shook his head. "He didn't say anything."

Robert hissed. "That's not good," he said, and started to pace. "Not good at all. That's the same thing that happened with Teloch."

"Teloch?" Beleeze questioned. There had been so many more of them—so many that had met their fates at Simeon's angry hand.

"Teloch!" Robert boomed, barely stopping his pacing. "Short, circular mouth ringed with teeth? Loved intestines and bone marrow?"

Beleeze remembered his demon brother, and his fate.

"He didn't say anything to Teloch, either, and then . . ."

Images flashed through Beleeze's memory—images of Teloch's

body suddenly swelling as if filling with fluid, and then exploding like a human child's toy balloon.

Beleeze did not recall the news Teloch had brought their master that had garnered such a horrendous response, but as he dwelled upon it, he realized that it could have been nearly anything: an ingredient for a particularly complex spell not being readily available, the premature return of the Morningstar to his hellish domain, the weather in whatever corner of the world they were currently residing being too hot, too cold, or too rainy, or the ancient god Dagon meeting with an untimely demise.

It could have been something, or really nothing at all. It didn't matter.

They were all quiet then, in the lobby of the dead building, thinking of Teloch and so many others that had met an ugly fate after delivering messages that did not please their master.

Would they be next?

*It is possible,* Beleeze thought worriedly. But what choice did they have? Master Simeon had the ring, and as long as he did, there was nothing else but for them to obey.

But despite the looming potential for death, the demons and their eternal master shared a common goal. They both hated God, the Almighty, the Lord of Lords, or whatever else the Being that brought forth the light to a universe that was once only darkness, was called.

Those who served and worshipped this heartless Deity believed that there was nothing until He made His illuminating declaration, but that couldn't be further from the truth.

There were things living in the sea of black that existed before He even became aware of His own existence; worlds and peoples thriving in the cold, endless void.

And so many met their end with the birth of this creation, their lives burned away with the utterance of four little words:

*Let there be light.*

Beleeze recalled the blinding flash and the screams of millions as they died, but somehow he, and others of his kind, had managed to survive, finding pools of shadow deep enough to hide themselves.

For where there is light, there must also be shadow.

Beleeze left his thoughts at the sound of footsteps.

"This is it," Robert muttered with a gulp.

But Beleeze did not believe it. Though their master might sometimes be unpredictable in his wrath, Beleeze felt somewhere deep down in the pocket of shadow that churned at the center of his being that their mutual hate would spare him.

The others he did not know about, but as for himself, he somehow knew that his and Master Simeon's fates were intertwined. They would witness the fall of Heaven together, and watch the world and the universe around it, gradually return to darkness.

Simeon stepped into the lobby, his dark eyes fixed upon the demons. The others averted their gazes, but Beleeze was not afraid.

"Take me to the island," their master commanded, pulling at the white cuffs of his shirt just below the sleeves of his dark sports jacket. "Let's see what I can do to keep this from turning into one huge clusterfuck."

Overjoyed that they were not murdered, Beleeze watched as Dorian and Robert conjured a circle of transport upon the lobby floor that would take them all to their destination.

And toward what Beleeze believed would eventually be his destiny.

Remy found his way back down to the first floor of the mansion alone, exiting from the secret door into Montagin's path.

"Where have you been?" the angel demanded, eyeing him, and the door, as Remy closed it behind him with a click.

"Finding stuff out," he said.

"Stuff?" Montagin asked. "What kind of stuff?"

The angel moved around Remy to examine the door. "Where does this go?" he asked. "I've never seen it before."

"Doesn't surprise me," Remy said. "Seems as though your boss might have been keeping some things pretty close to the vest."

"Things?" Montagin questioned with a sneer.

"Looks like Aszrus was a little more infatuated with this world than he led you to believe."

He could see that the assistant's demeanor was changing, his ire on the rise. There was nothing somebody like Montagin hated more than to not be aware of the total picture.

"Explain, Seraphim," Montagin demanded.

Remy looked him straight in the eyes with a stare that suggested he back off.

The angel's demeanor softened.

"Did you find something that could explain who . . ."

"Maybe," Remy said, starting back toward the study with Montagin eagerly walking beside him. "It seems that your boss liked to hit the town some nights, and he used a limousine service to get there."

"Why would he do that?"

"That's what I'm hoping to find out," Remy said as they approached the study doors. Montagin used his key to open the door, and they were greeted by the sight of Malatesta kneeling beside the dead angel's body, one of his hands buried deep within the open wound that had allowed the angel's killer access to his heart.

The sorcerer looked up from his work.

"I'm not quite finished here, but—"

"I have to leave," Remy interrupted. "Finish what you started and lend a hand if necessary." He turned to Montagin again, and saw that spark of panic ready to ignite once more. "You just keep it together until I get back with some answers."

"I'll try," Montagin replied, his eyes drifting over to the globe-shaped liquor cabinet in the corner of the room.

Remy was just about to leave when he remembered something he would need. He stopped, turning back toward Montagin.

"Do you think I can borrow a car?" he asked. "I hear there's an entire underground garage of the things."

# CHAPTER TEN

*England*
*1349*

**P**ope Tyranus' carriage followed the line of soldiers sworn to defend the holy man and his mission at any cost.

Remiel sat across from the Pope, the wings that he had yet to summon itching beneath the guise of humanity he wore, eager to perform the task that had been requested of him.

He could have flown to their destination on his own, but Tyranus required his company on the ride. The angel had no choice but to obey.

"Tell me," the Pope began, pulling aside a red velvet curtain to gaze out upon the bleak, English countryside. The weather was foul, as it had been for days, as if in anticipation of the conflict against the forces of darkness to come. "Tell me why you walk the earth."

Remiel did not wish to speak of it, but the words came nonetheless.

"There is a simplicity here that speaks to me," he said.

Tyranus chuckled. "Where you see simplicity, I see the complexities of this world . . . complexities that I must master."

Remiel remained silent, hoping no more questions would come, but knowing better.

"How could you leave your God?" the old man asked. "For is He not your everything? Your sole reason for existing to answer His every whim?"

"It was."

The images came again, the war and the killing of his brethren.

The death of so much more.

"There came a time when I could be there no more," Remiel offered. "When the difficulties of Heaven weighed far too heavily upon my winged shoulders."

Pope Tyranus studied the angel, his head resting against the back of the red velvet seat.

"Where is the difficulty in serving your master?" the Pope finally asked. "If there is trust in Him, there should be no question."

Remiel saw the deaths of those he had once loved, those corrupted by the message of the Morningstar. He had hoped there would be another answer, that the Lord God Almighty would find a solution other than war.

But Remiel had been forced to take a side, and the solution was death to those who fought against His holy word.

"There was trust . . . ," Remiel said softly. "For a time."

This response seemed to rankle the holy man. "Are you saying that the Almighty is not to be trusted?"

"I'm saying that my trust in Him was tested," Remiel explained. "And it was a test that I failed."

The coach came to a sudden, lurching stop, leaning precariously to one side. Outside, Remiel could hear the chatter of the soldiers and the cries of horses in distress.

"What is happening?" the Pope asked, a slight tinge of fear evident in his voice.

Remiel cautiously opened the coach door, to be certain that they were not under attack. They were not, but somehow the soldiers had marched themselves deep into the center of a marsh, thick fog closing in on them from every direction. Several soldiers were attempting to lead their horses to solid footing, but to no avail, the panicked beasts' cries echoing strangely across the misty moor.

"What is it? What's happening?" Pope Tyranus demanded to know.

"Stay here," Remiel ordered, leaping down to the muddy ground, slamming the carriage door closed behind him.

"Captain of the guard!" Remiel cried, feeling the earth suck at his boots, trying to lock him in place.

The sounds of the panicked horses, mingled with the screams of soldiers who had wandered into the bogs were eerily disturbing.

Remiel caught sight of the captain standing, holding tightly to his horse's reins, staring out into the shifting mists.

"Captain," he yelled, grabbing the man by the shoulder and spinning him around.

The man looked at him, eyes bulging with fear.

"How could you have led us into . . . ," Remiel began to ask.

"We weren't anywhere near a marsh," the captain cried, shaking his head from side to side as his voice quaked with emotion. "A mist blew out onto the road, a mist so thick that . . ."

He stopped speaking and slowly turned back to the nightmarish scene as the wetlands claimed even more of the soldiers.

"And then we were here," the captain finished. "May the Lord God Almighty preserve us, we were here."

The captain let go of his horse's reins, and the animal galloped madly off into the marsh. For a moment, Remiel lost sight of the animal in a writhing gray cloud, but then the cloud shifted; even the angel wasn't sure of what he was seeing.

The captain's horse was struggling mightily in the mire, which appeared to be hungry. When it seemed that the muscular beast would manage to free itself, something Remiel could not quite discern in the haze reached up from the water and mud to drag it back from whence it had escaped.

The Seraphim glanced toward the captain and realized he was no longer beside him. Remiel saw him wandering off in another direction, as if answering some siren call.

It was then that the angel sensed it. It had been hidden at first, mingling with the damp, heady smell of the marshlands, but the angel found it as the screams of animal and man intensified, and the shapes of things that might have once been human pulled themselves up from the clutches of the moors to shamble through the fog.

It was the scent of dark magick.

Remiel reached beneath his robes for the sword that hung there, the blade immediately igniting as it became engorged with the fire of the divine.

The light of the blade cut through the unnatural shadows and shifting mist, illuminating the horrors that were making their way directly toward him.

"What is the meaning of this?" Pope Tyranus cried out, clambering out of the carriage onto the moist ground. "I do not care to be kept waiting!"

It took a moment, but the Pope finally saw what was illuminated in the light of the angel's sword.

"What in the name of all that is holy?" he stated, staring numbly ahead at the sight of the men, women, and children that had been sacrificed to the bogs so many years ago, their strangely preserved bodies . . .

Now returned to ghastly life.

It didn't take Remy long to find Neal's address, seeing as there was only one employee with that first name working at the Elite Limousine Company out of Warwick, Rhode Island. Doubting that they'd be willing to hand out personal information over the phone, Remy had paid a visit to the office.

It was quiet at Elite that morning, and willing himself unseen, Remy had whispered in the office manager, Ginny's, ear that things were incredibly slow, and maybe she should go grab herself a coffee over at the Dunkin Donuts down the street to keep herself awake.

Ginny had heeded his suggestion, leaving him with access to the company's files, where, after a little searching, he found the address of one Neal Moreland of Providence.

Seeing as the Mercedes that he'd borrowed from Aszrus' garage had a GPS, it didn't take long at all to find the driver's residence in downtown Providence. Remy parked the car as close to the old apartment building on Pequot Street as he could, and walked around to the back of the building. There was a back door, and Remy quietly climbed the six steps up to it, peering in through the curtained window to see an entryway, and a back flight of stairs leading to the apartments above. He took a brief look around to see whether anybody was watching before unfurling his wings. He quickly wrapped himself in their embrace, and thinking about the hallway on the other side of the door, suddenly appeared there. According to Elite's schedule book, Neal had had a late-night international pick-up at Logan last night and was supposed to be driving somebody back to the Boston airport later that afternoon, so this would probably be an awesome time to catch him. Remy slowly climbed the steps up to the second floor, and was making his way to the third when he felt it.

It was like walking into a curtain of spiderwebs, a strange tickling sensation across his bare skin alerting him that something of an unearthly nature had recently manifested itself in the area. He immediately went on guard, focusing his preternatural senses on his surroundings.

The wood creaked as he stepped onto the third-floor landing. A short hallway was before him, Neal's apartment at the end.

Remy listened carefully to the sounds of the old building, hearing only the creaks of centuries-old wood, the distinct hum of multiple refrigerators, and in one apartment, the contented purr of a cat. Attuning his hearing to the apartment he wanted, Remy didn't hear any signs of life, and was fearful that Neal had already left for the day.

Standing in front of the driver's door, Remy was about to knock, just to be sure, when . . .

"He ain't home," said a voice from behind him, nearly causing him to explode out of his skin.

It took a second or two to realize that he knew that voice.

Remy turned to see Francis leaning against the wall behind him.

"Where the hell were you hiding?" Remy asked, annoyed, but also glad to see his friend. A second set of hands was always helpful.

"I've been right here all along," the balding assassin said. "Guess those ninja correspondence courses were da bomb."

"What are you doing here?"

"Working," Francis said, pushing off the wall to approach the door. "But the person I was sent to check on isn't home."

"Huh," Remy said, interested in the fact that they seemed to be here to see the same person. "And you've been sent here to see this person by your current employer?"

"I was."

"This has the potential to be very bad," Remy said to his friend.

He assumed that his friend's mysterious new employer was Lucifer Morningstar, although Francis had never actually confirmed that.

"Care to share?" Francis asked, his eyes a cold and piercing gray behind his dark-framed glasses.

Remy wasn't sure how much to say, for if Montagin's suspicions about the legions of the Morningstar being responsible for Aszrus' murder were correct, then this could very well blow up in his face, and spread exponentially from there.

"Let's just say that I'm working on a potentially explosive case, and wanted to talk to the individual who lives in this apartment."

Francis stroked his chin with a long-fingered hand. "A potentially explosive case," he repeated. "And it just so happens to be somebody that I'm checking up on as well. What are the odds of that?"

"Those are some pretty crazy odds," Remy agreed with a slow nod.

"Aren't they?" Francis replied.

His friend had already turned to the door, and was reaching inside his pocket for the knife that had once belonged to one of Heaven's most powerful angels. Francis had learned that he had been manipulated by this angel, part of his memory cut away by the very blade he now had in his possession.

Francis had killed that angel for the indignity, and for his troubles, had kept the knife.

He inserted the ultrathin blade into the lock on the door, and slowly turned it. The door swung open.

"Would you look at that?" Francis exclaimed. "It's unlocked."

"Imagine that," Remy said, following the former Guardian angel inside.

The door opened into a small kitchen. They both looked around.

"See anything?" Francis asked.

The apartment was relatively tidy, all things considered, and Remy didn't see anything that set off any alarm bells. Silently, he walked toward the living area, focusing on a tiny desk against the wall and the laptop that was resting there.

"Well, since you're not being all that forthcoming, let me start," Francis said. He was in front of the refrigerator, examining some notes held in place by magnets.

"Neal Moreland is doing some work for my employer."

Remy quickly turned his gaze to his friend.

"A limousine driver from Providence, Rhode Island, is working for Lucifer Morningstar?"

Francis glanced at Remy, then back to the fridge.

"I never said who my employer was." There was a hint of coldness in his tone.

"Cut the shit, Francis. I know," Remy said. He was poking around the desk, careful to not mess anything up.

"How?"

"People usually don't come back in one piece when the Hell dimension they're trapped in is completely reconfigured by the most powerful fallen angel to exist. In fact, they usually don't come back at all."

"I'm lucky like that," Francis said. He was now looking through the fridge, and was about to drink from a carton of orange juice.

"And you have the pistol," Remy told him, remembering the case he'd taken not long after Madeline's death that involved the Pitiless weapons. One of the Pitiless had been a Colt Peacemaker, a weapon that never missed its target.

A weapon that had been forged from the power of the Morningstar. A weapon that Francis now held in his possession.

Francis wiped his chin of orange juice, and carefully placed the carton back on the shelf in the fridge. "I know how you are about this shit which is why I kept it to myself," he said as he joined Remy in the living room.

Remy didn't care for secrets, no matter how badly they were kept, especially when they had something to do with an opposing force of Heaven.

"So, does this make us mortal enemies or something?" Francis asked.

"All depends on whether what you're doing here has anything to do with starting a war."

Francis stepped back, and made a face. "You've lost me."

Remy stared at him, attempting to read his friend.

"Seriously." Francis put up his hands in mock surrender. "I haven't a fucking clue what you're talking about. This face wouldn't lie," he added.

No matter what else happened between them, Remy trusted Francis not to lie to him, and if he said he didn't know anything about a plan to start the war machine rolling, he believed him.

"Why don't you start by telling me what Neal was doing for your boss? Then I'll see if I can fill in the blanks from there."

"I'm only agreeing to this because you're my friend, and I hated to keep that shit about my employer secret," Francis said.

Remy couldn't help but think of the secret he had yet to share with Francis: his involvement with the woman with whom Francis had at one time been obsessed.

But there was a time and a place for everything, and this was neither for that.

"Neal is a driver with a local car service," Francis began. "And one of his clients—"

"Is General Aszrus," Remy stated flatly.

"Bingo," Francis said, pointing at him. "So, Neal drives for the general, they chat a bit on the way to wherever it is they're going, and when Neal drops off his customer, he makes a little call."

"Neal was an informant?" Remy asked.

Francis nodded. "Yeah, kept the big boss in the loop as to how one of Heaven's generals was spending his downtime."

"I don't suppose the big boss knows anything about the latest piece of hot information?" Remy said.

"And what might that be?"

"Aszrus is dead. Somebody cut his heart out."

Remy was good at reading reactions, and Francis' was most definitely genuine.

"Get the fuck outta here," he exclaimed. "Who . . . ?"

"What I'm trying to find out," Remy answered.

"If Aszrus is dead, how come the sky isn't filled with angels with swords and hard-ons for fighting for the glory of whoever's fucking side they're on?"

"Because nobody knows."

"You're shitting me," Francis said. "Damn, got any other secrets you're sitting on?"

Remy kept himself from flinching at the question. There was a time and place.

"I've managed to keep the information locked up for now, but I don't know how much longer we have. Montagin is babysitting the corpse with the help of a Vatican magick user by the name of Malatesta."

"Montagin," Francis said with a sneer. "I'm surprised he hasn't sent out a mass e-mail yet."

"You might be surprised," Remy said. "He seems just as concerned as I am about the potential for some really nasty shit to go down if this information gets out before we can figure out who's responsible."

"So you think driver Neal might have something?"

"It's all I've got right now," Remy said. "If he could at least tell us where he took Aszrus last, we might be able to move backward from there."

"Sounds like a plan," Francis agreed. "Why don't we go grab a coffee and wait to see if . . ."

A heavyset man, his arms full of groceries, was standing just inside the door, staring at the two men in the living room.

"Does Neal know you're in here?" he asked, shifting the plastic shopping bags.

Remy took a step forward, but Francis took point.

"Yeah, he left the door open for us," Francis said with an enormous smile. "We're supposed to be meeting for lunch. I'm surprised he's not here yet."

"Are you sure it's today?" the man asked.

"Yeah, I just talked to him this morning," Remy said, taking out his phone.

"Well he must've forgot," the big guy said, already losing interest in them. " 'Cause I just saw him getting into his car. If you bust a hump, maybe you can catch him."

Remy looked at Francis, and he at him.

"Son of a . . . ," Remy began, darting across the kitchen to the window. He looked through the filthy glass onto a rusty fire escape and the alley below, where he saw a navy blue Town Car start to pull away.

"It's him," Remy said, pulling open the window and climbing out onto the fire escape.

He wasn't about to let this guy get away.

Remy was starting down the metal stairs, not wanting to risk releasing his wings and being seen, when something fell past the fire escape at great speed. It landed in front of the Town Car only to be struck by the vehicle. He heard the sounds of twisting metal and breaking glass.

Remy leapt down the final stretch of stairs to the alley just in time to see Francis peeling himself from the front of the smashed Town Car bumper, a geyser of steam from the ruptured radiator hissing like the king of all serpents.

"No need to thank me," Francis said, checking his suit jacket for rips. "I do this shit all the time."

The driver's side door opened with a screech.

"What the fuck!" Neal Moreland bellowed as he crawled out from behind the inflated airbag. "Look what you fucking did to my car!"

Remy was suddenly beside the guy, taking his arm in a steely grip.

"You were in quite the hurry, Neal," he said. "Late for a pick-up?"

Francis stepped around the car, brushing pieces of glass from the fabric of his jacket.

"Who the hell are you two supposed to be?" the man asked defiantly, trying to pull away from Remy's hold with little success.

Neal was older than he first looked. His thick head of hair was dyed an inky black and too many trips to the tanning salon had left his skin lined and leathery.

"Management sent me," Francis stated flatly, his gaze boring into the driver's. "Do you understand?"

Neal quit struggling, knowing exactly what Francis meant.

"Yeah, sure," he said quickly. "Why the fuck did you have to wreck my car?"

"Because we wouldn't have been able to talk with you if we hadn't," Remy explained.

Neal looked at him. "I got a call saying that I pissed somebody off with my job last night," he said. "Said I might want to lay low for a while."

"Your job last night is exactly what I'd like to discuss," Remy told him, pulling him back toward the fire escape.

"Hey, I can't help if he never came out," Neal protested as Remy began to push him toward the first step. "I waited until they told me not to."

"Who told you?" Francis asked.

"A guy came out and said Mr. Aszrus would be finding another way home."

"Where did you take him?" Remy asked.

"Where he told me to go," Neal said.

He looked as though he was going to say more, but stopped, staring at something in the opposite direction.

"Now what the fuck is that?" he asked.

Remy barely had a chance to look when the driver was snatched away. Francis and Remy reacted as one, jumping aside as the tendril of smoke dragged a flailing Neal Moreland up into a roiling black cloud that was drifting in from the opposite end of the alley.

Remy and Francis knew that it wasn't really a cloud at all.

Neal screamed horribly as he was taken inside the billowing substance, and a rainfall of blood began pattering down atop the roof of the limousine and the alley floor.

"Black Choir," Remy announced, already flexing the muscles of his shoulders to make his wings emerge.

"No shit," Francis said, drawing the golden Colt from inside his suit jacket, already on the move toward the threat.

The Black Choir was the most horrible example of the fallout from the war in Heaven: angels who chose not to take a stand during the Great War, cursed to be accepted by neither God nor Lucifer, and warped to monstrous proportions by their inability to take a side.

They were true abominations, their misery provoking their foul deeds.

Remy searched the alley for something to use as a weapon, finding a length of an old wooden pallet lying up against the side of the apartment building beside the Dumpster. It would have to do.

He reached for the piece of wood in midstride, his wings lifting him from the ground as he took flight.

The Choir's writhing, cloudlike environment descended toward Francis, who opened fire with the Pitiless pistol. Shrieks of the eternally damned echoed from within the shifting black and gray miasma. The cloud expanded, flowing out from the ground. Francis spun, attempting to outrun the roiling storm, but he wasn't fast enough, turning to fire into the black cloud even as it engulfed him.

Remy descended from above, the piece of wood in his clutches now burning with the fires of Heaven. He could see glimpses of shapes within the shifting fog, the accursed angels now neither damned, nor divine. They were a horrible sight to behold, their thin, pale bodies warped by the hatred they felt for God and His opposite.

He dropped within the cloud, lashing out with the burning board, the fires of Heaven illuminating the numbing atmosphere within. He swung the flaming club, striking at the Choir and driving them away from his friend.

Francis fired the pistol with deadly accuracy.

It was like a world unto itself within the cloud—a horrible world of misery and torment—and Remy and Francis fought together to be free of it.

"Get me the fuck out of here, Chandler," Francis cried out.

"I'm working on it," Remy shouted, swinging his makeshift weapon at his foes, while also attempting to illuminate a path to escape. Briefly he caught a glimpse of the smashed-in Town Car, and flapped his wings, flying toward it. "Follow me," he ordered, swinging his burning weapon at the withered angels who tried to prevent their leave.

Francis' gun boomed, and angels fell, as they fought their way toward freedom.

"Get out," Remy told Francis, pushing him out of the shifting cloud and back into the alley.

"What about you?" Francis asked as he fired his weapon three more times in succession, the screams of the damned nearly deafening in response.

"I'm right behind you," Remy said, infusing the piece of pallet with even more divine fire than it could contain, and tossing it toward the Black Choir angels who were slithering closer to them through their misty environment.

The wood exploded as it fell among them, the Choir screaming out in rage and pain, driven deeper into the cloud by the blinding light of Heaven.

Remy emerged to find Francis standing at the ready, gun in hand.

The living darkness of the Black Choir writhed and shifted before them. Something darker than the area surrounding it moved within, and the Seraphim was at the ready, wings spread to propel him into action.

The body of Neal Moreland was ejected from the cloud, spit out like an old piece of gum to land broken and bloody beside his wrecked limousine. Seemingly having accomplished what it had come to do, the Black Choir drifted back and away, disappearing as quickly as it had appeared.

"Son of a bitch," Remy hissed, pulling the aspects of his true nature back within himself and squatting beside Neal's corpse.

The driver's body was withered and pale, as if drained of life energies as well as fluids. It was a horrible way to go.

"So much for answers," Remy said.

"We might be able to get some more," Francis said, putting the Pitiless back inside his jacket.

"What do you mean?" Remy asked.

Francis knelt down beside the corpse, and from another inside pocket extracted the special knife. "This thing is better than a Swiss Army knife," the former Guardian angel said as he plunged the glowing blade into the back of Neal's head. "Let's see what I can find."

Francis seemed to drift off for a moment, staring blankly into space.

A smile suddenly appeared on his face.

"What is it?" Remy asked.

"Yahtzee."

# CHAPTER ELEVEN

**M**ontagin watched the magick user weave his spell.

"How much longer?" the angel asked before taking a long drink of his second scotch.

Malatesta continued to mutter, pausing only when he appeared to run out of breath.

"This is a more difficult task than normal," the Vatican sorcerer finally said. "We must repel not only the household staff, but also those of an angelic nature. For such a spell to work on an angel, it must be layered, spell upon spell, magick atop of magick."

"And that will keep any and all away?" Montagin asked, not sure if he truly believed that was possible.

"I certainly hope so," Malatesta said. "Now, if you'll excuse me."

The sorcerer went back to work, laying down another layer of magick to keep the contents of the study a secret—how long it would last was a question that gnawed at him.

Montagin finished his drink, and poured another. He was allowing the alcohol to calm him. It was the only thing keeping him from panic. What he was helping to hide here could very well lead to a war that would rival the one already fought in Heaven so very long ago. The angel brought the glass to his mouth, gulping the liquor, eager to dull the anxiety that nibbled at the periphery of his thoughts. All he had to do was stay focused until Remiel returned. Hopefully, he would have the answers they needed.

But what if Remiel's investigation verified what Montagin had first suspected: that the legion of the Morningstar was indeed responsible, and this was but the first attack?

"Are you sure you're a proper sorcerer?" Montagin suddenly blurted out.

Malatesta glared at him, his hands suddenly aglow with preternatural power. "I began my training with the Keepers of the Vatican before my tenth birthday. Before puberty, I had risen to the top of my class in almost all forms of spell casting."

Montagin stared, uninterested, finishing up his latest attempt at calming his fragile nerves.

"If you wish me to finish this spell, you will leave me alone," the sorcerer demanded. "No more questions . . . no more interruptions. Do I make myself clear?"

The angel seriously contemplated lashing out against such disrespect. Instead, he strode across the room, placing his empty glass upon a bookshelf as he headed for the door. He was just about to open it when he felt the disturbance. At first he thought it was a manifestation of his nerves, but quickly realized that wasn't the case.

"Angels," Malatesta said.

"Damn it," Montagin hissed.

He turned to the sorcerer, doorknobs in hand. "Finish what you have started, or we'll all be dead," he proclaimed before stepping out into the hall and closing the double doors tightly behind him.

Montagin stopped just outside the study doors and took a deep breath, centering himself, before he marched down the corridor toward where he sensed the emanations were strongest. Turning the corner at the end of the hallway, he found the servant, Marley, bowing her head in reverence to a gathering of three angels who stood in the entryway.

The three wore human appearances and attire, exuding discomfort as they looked in his general direction.

"Ah, Dardariel," Montagin said, attempting to hide his own unease. "To what do we owe this visit?"

"The general," the angel responded curtly. "Take me to him at once."

Montagin suddenly felt as though his verbal skills had completely left him. He stared at the three soldiers of the divine.

"He isn't here," he managed, feeling as though millennia had passed before he was able to answer.

Dardariel glared, his dark predatory eyes glistening in the light of the hallway.

And then the laughing began—not from the angels, but from the girl.

"Silence, woman!" Montagin roared, his body momentarily taking on the guise of his true form, a being of fiery light.

The blind woman sensed his displeasure, and carefully backed away from the angels. "I meant no disrespect," she said, although Montagin could see that she was still stifling a smirk.

"Leave us," Montagin commanded, and Marley quickly turned, hand upon the wall as she nearly ran from them.

"Why do you tolerate such lack of respect?" Gromeyl asked, a look of disgust on his smooth, perfect features.

Montagin once again assumed his human form. "That one, I'm afraid, is a bit touched in the head," he explained. "But a favorite of the general."

"I cannot even begin to understand how you bear to have them among you," Sengael said. "They are such filthy, untrustworthy beasts."

"And yet the Lord God Almighty loves them so," Montagin added.

The three angels turned their gazes to him, and Montagin resisted the nearly overwhelming urge to step back.

"Until He doesn't," Dardariel said, his voice as cold as the vacuum of space.

"Perhaps," Montagin begrudgingly agreed.

"Take us to the general," Dardariel repeated. "He told us to meet him here, on this day, at this time. A commander of Heaven's armies would not be so vulgar as to not be here."

"And I'm telling you that—"

"I know not what games you're playing, Montagin," Sengael snarled.

Dardariel sniffed the air. "He is here," the angel soldier stated. "And you will not keep me from him."

He brusquely shoved Montagin aside, the two other soldiers following close behind, glaring menacingly as they moved past him down the corridor.

"And don't think the general will not be told of this," Gromeyl threatened.

Montagin didn't know what to do. He seriously considered an attack on the three, but realizing the folly in that, entertained the idea of coming clean.

Letting them know exactly what was going on—what had happened.

"Please, my brothers," Montagin stated, following the angel soldiers. "The general's essence covers this dwelling; there isn't an inch that doesn't hold his powerful scent."

He'd managed to come around them just as they reached the study, blocking the doors with his body.

"Why would I wish to keep you from your meeting?" Montagin asked, desperately hoping that they could not read his panic.

Dardariel reached out, laying a hand menacingly upon Montagin's shoulder.

"Get out of the way," he ordered, and Montagin began to feel the heat of Heaven's divine fire start to flow from the soldier's hand.

The doors to the study opened abruptly and Montagin released a pathetic scream as he turned to look into the face of General Aszrus.

"General," Montagin stated in disbelief.

"What is the meaning of this?" the general demanded, stepping out farther into the hall, closing the doors behind him.

"General Aszrus," Dardariel said, stepping back along with his two companions, all three bowing their heads. "You're attendant was attempting to keep us from . . ."

"My attendant was doing exactly as he was told," the angel general said, looking to his aide.

Montagin shrugged off the shock. "I tried, General," he said. "But they did not wish to listen."

Aszrus fixed them all in a withering stare.

"Then perhaps they'll listen to me," he stated. "Leave my home. I have no time for conference today."

"But General," Dardariel began. "The war council is meeting in two days and . . ."

"Have you lost the gift of tongues, soldier?" Aszrus asked. "Am I speaking some language that you are incapable of understanding?"

"No, sir," the angel soldier answered quickly, averting his eyes.

"Then leave," Aszrus commanded. "Do not return until you are summoned again."

The three angels raised their eyes to their superior. Montagin waited for some sort of challenge, but it did not come.

"As you wish, my general," Dardariel responded, obviously chagrined.

Dardariel's gaze then fell upon Montagin, and the angel did all he could to suppress a smile of petulant satisfaction, and supreme relief.

Without another word, the three soldiers opened their wings, and with a rush of air, were gone from the mansion.

It was a moment before Montagin could react.

"What madness is this?" he shrieked as he turned to face the general.

The general's appearance began to melt away, revealing the form of the smiling Vatican sorcerer.

"Besides being top in my class for offensive and defensive spells," Malatesta offered, "I also excelled in the art of glamour."

## Castle Hallow
## 1349

Simeon could not find his master.

He'd searched high and low, but the whereabouts of Ignatius Hallow were unknown even to his demonic servants.

The old necromancer had mentioned that Simeon's lessons would start earlier than usual, and would be more challenging than ever before.

Simeon's thoughts raced through the years he had spent in service to the necromancer called Hallow. None of them had ever been easy, and many of the things he had learned had resulted in his own death. But that was not such a high price to pay when cursed with eternal life.

Hallow had called him the perfect student, hoping if he'd had time to sire a son, he would have been as obedient—and enduring—as Simeon.

But today Simeon was to be challenged.

He had searched everywhere for his master—every place but one, which was forbidden to him.

Hallow called it his sanctum, a place only for him. Simeon always believed that was where the most powerful of the necromancer's knowledge was kept, and he wondered if this day would be the day that the special room was revealed to him.

The sanctum was located in a hidden chamber, deep beneath what was believed to be the final room in the castle. It was part dungeon, part torture chamber, and part wine cellar. The only reason Simeon even knew of its existence was that he'd followed his ancient master one night, and unseen, watched as the old man opened the secret door and descended even further into the bowels of the earth.

Simeon moved aside some old wooden barrels and began to search for a way to make the entrance appear. Eyes squinted and hand glowing with a supernatural light he ignited with a simple spell of illumination, he looked, but could not find any trace of a door.

He was about to call forth a spell of unraveling, when the door suddenly appeared. It began as a spot of shadow, growing steadily until a dark passage was revealed.

Smiling with the belief that this was the day he yearned for, Simeon entered the cool darkness, carefully making his way down steps that appeared constructed from bricks of solid shadow. His breathing quickened, and his heart beat at a frantic, excited pace. Simeon could only imagine the magick that was stored here, and how it could eventually help him toward his purpose.

The descending passage seemed to go on forever, but then he saw the hint of a flickering light below him. Careful not to stumble—he might have been immortal, but he still would rather not go through the rather unpleasant experience of breaking his bones—Simeon continued down the steps.

Unsure if he had reached the bottom, he reached out with a foot to test the darkness, probing for something solid with the tip of his boot. The darkness beneath it was firm, and did not yield, and he knew that he had arrived.

The dancing light was not too far ahead, and he plunged into the sea of pitch black, moving toward it like an insect to flame. It was not long before he realized that he had been traveling a long, stone corridor that emptied out into an enormous, domed chamber.

"There you are, Simeon," said an ancient voice from within the underground room. "I suspected you would find me."

Simeon stepped into the vast, circular room, and found his suspicions confirmed. The room was indeed a vast storeroom of ancient texts, scrolls, and rare arcana.

But what he then witnessed almost brought a scream to his lips.

Ignatius Hallow had taken his books and scrolls and had placed them all in an enormous pile upon the stone floor. Squatting, huge and loathsome, not far away was a monstrous entity of some twisted kind. It resembled a gigantic toad filtered through the mind of a madman, the bulbous black eyes protruding up from its lumpy head riveted to the necromancer before it.

Hallow, wielding a shovel, was taking large scoops of the ancient works and tossing them into the cavernous, gaping maw of the demon toad, which was filled with unnatural flame.

"Stop!" Simeon cried, running across the room toward his master. "You can't do this!"

"I can, and I will," Hallow said, grunting as he shoveled a particularly large shovelful of texts and scrolls into the waiting mouth of the beast. The fire hissed and billowed as the writings were consumed, the great demon toad chewing and swallowing noisily before opening its mouth once more.

Hallow was digging for more when Simeon grabbed hold of the shovel.

"You can't," he bellowed, taking Hallow by surprise.

The demon toad let out a horrific sound of warning, steam escaping from its nostrils with a hiss.

"I know what this must look like to you, boy, but I do what needs to be done," the necromancer told him. He pulled the shovel away from Simeon with a display of great strength. "There isn't much time. . . . They're almost here."

Hallow bent and dug into the dwindling stack.

"I have no idea what you're talking about," Simeon said, watching as scrolls and forbidden, flesh-bound volumes made their way into the inferno inside the great, reptilian beast's mouth. "This knowledge is irreplaceable, why would you see it destroyed?"

"This knowledge is power," the necromancer spoke. He paused to wipe away the sweat pouring out from beneath his copper skull-cap. "And I cannot afford for him to have any more than he already has."

"Who?" Simeon demanded, unable to take his eyes from the potential knowledge and power being eaten by the flames within the monster's mouth.

"I always knew this day would come," Hallow said, resuming his task. "That he would someday gather a force, and have enough power to come at me . . . to take what I have collected."

"Who?" Simeon asked again, his voice a plaintive cry. He stepped into the path before more could be tossed within the demon toad's furnace of a mouth.

Hallow stopped midtoss, the books upon the shovel falling to the stone floor.

"The leader of the Church," Ignatius Hallow said. "Pope Tyranus . . ."

Hallow paused, his glassy eyes reflecting the fire from inside the demon toad's mouth.

"My brother."

It was as if Simeon has been physically struck. "Your . . . brother?"

"The one born in light," the necromancer explained. "Who seeks my birthright of darkness."

Hallow leaned on the shovel, showing a weariness that Simeon had never seen in him before.

"That is why this all must be destroyed," he explained. "He can never have it."

"We will fight him," Simeon proclaimed. "We will be the ones to take away his birthright instead."

The old man smiled sadly. "I'm afraid my brother has grown quite powerful since last we dueled, and the spirits of the dead tell me that he has acquired an even more powerful ally." Hallow paused, as if not wanting to say aloud what it was they would be facing. "A soldier of Heaven serves his cause."

Simeon could not believe what he was hearing; from what he understood, the winged messengers served only one master.

"How?" he asked incredulously. "How is it that an angel of God serves a being of mere flesh? Is it his position of authority with the Church?"

Hallow raised his right hand, showing Simeon the ring that adorned his middle finger. "I wear this ring forged for King Solomon to control the demonic; my brother wears its opposite."

"But Solomon had only one ring," Simeon said, feeling foolish in correcting his master.

The necromancer slowly shook his head. "There were two sigil rings: one to control the demonic . . ."

Simeon was stunned.

"And the other to control the angelic."

"Now do you see?" Hallow asked. "Now do you see why these texts and scrolls must be destroyed?"

"But—," Simeon began to protest.

"But nothing," Hallow roared. "My brother is ravenous for the power contained within these walls. . . ." He held up his hand again.

"And what rests upon my finger."

\*   \*   \*

Francis cut a tear in the fabric of reality with his fancy knife, and he and Remy stepped from an alley in Providence to . . .

"Where are we now?" Remy asked, standing beside his friend, taking a look around.

The cut quickly healed behind them, the makeup of the universe not tolerant of holes in the material of existence.

"This is where I saw Neal take Aszrus," Francis said. "Although in daylight it doesn't look like much of a happening place."

They were standing outside a tall, chain-link fence that surrounded a vast property, which looked as if it was being prepared either for demolition or renovation.

"Are you sure this is it?" Remy asked, his fingers gripping the fence as he peered through the links.

"As sure as if I'd done it myself," Francis said.

Remy studied the brick building. There was a cornerstone with 1913 chiseled into it just after the broken concrete steps that led up to the front entrance. Over the rounded stone entryway, it read LEMUEL.

"I think I know what this is," he said, turning to his friend.

Francis was already on the other side, walking toward the entrance. "Connecticut," he said over his shoulder.

Remy unfurled his wings and flew over the fence.

"We're in Connecticut," Francis said again. "There's a sign for the demolition company hanging on the fence."

"Then I definitely know what this is," Remy said as they entered the cool shade thrown by the ominous brick building looming above them.

"Gonna share?" Francis asked.

"This is the Lemuel Institute," Remy explained. "A prominent psychiatric facility that ended up with quite the reputation when some of its more experimental methods of rehab were exposed in the sixties."

"Let me guess," Francis said. "They were less than humane."

Remy started up the steps toward the doors. "Sounded like it was a regular house of horrors—the mentally retarded mingling with the criminally insane, and the medical staff working practically unsupervised. The reports of unauthorized medical procedures were staggering. The place was finally shut down in the early seventies." He stood at the door, peering through the filthy glass at the corridor beyond.

"Are we going in?" Francis asked.

"Yeah," Remy sighed. "Not that I want to, but we need to figure out why Aszrus would come here."

Remy stepped closer to Francis, sweeping him up into his winged embrace, and the two disappeared from the front steps to reappear in the hallway beyond the front door.

The institution was no more pleasant on the inside. It was in the midst of decay, the floors covered with plaster from broken walls and collapsed ceilings. It was obvious that trespassers had frequented the building, leaving behind their own, spray-painted scars upon various surfaces.

"Okay," Francis said, looking around. "I'm not seeing why a general in the army of Heaven would have any business here."

To the right of the entrance was what looked to be a large sunroom. Filthy blankets and fast-food trash were strewn about the floor.

Something flashed briefly, and Remy gradually changed the shape of his eyes to better focus. Shades of people—some standing before the windows staring out, other sitting in chairs in front of an old nineteen-inch television, others pacing back and forth as if in a trance—appeared to him.

Residual impressions left upon the building.

Ghosts by any other definition.

They did not see him, and wouldn't, even if he attempted to communicate with them. This was perfectly common for buildings such as this, with powerful emotional energies charging the very environment like a battery.

"We've got ghosts," Remy announced, hooking a finger toward the sunroom as he started to follow Francis, who was standing at the far end of the corridor in front of a pair of swinging doors.

"No shit," Francis responded, pointing through the broken glass of one of the doors.

Remy came up alongside him to see what he was pointing at.

There was a nurse in the hallway, wearing a proper white dress and cap with a blue stripe around the top. She was pushing a cart filled with trays of small, paper soufflé cups, disappearing into rooms to dispense her meds before coming out again. They could actually hear her white, rubber-soled shoes squeaking on the tiled floors as she went about her business.

"Probably a residual haunt," Remy said. "Just like the ones in the sunroom."

The nurse suddenly lifted her gaze to them.

"Are you going to stand there and gawk, or are you going to help me?" she asked.

"I don't think she's residual," Francis said.

She placed her ghostly hands upon her hips and stared at them in annoyance. "Don't tell me that agency has sent me another couple'a newbies," the nurse said in disgust. "I've got five nurses out with the trots, and I don't have time to hold hands with new nurses. You two either help me with this med pass, or you can head on out of here."

She left the cart, passing through a closed door into the room beyond it.

"She thinks we're nurses," Francis said.

"And new ones at that," Remy answered.

"What should we do? Ignore her?"

"That would be sort of rude, wouldn't it?"

Francis shrugged. "It's not like we could really help her."

"Yeah," Remy agreed. "I wonder if she could help us though."

"What, like maybe she saw something?"

Remy nodded and pushed through the swinging door, cutting a swath through the plaster and other detritus left on the corridor floor.

The nurse walked through the wall and stopped to stare at him.

"Well?" she asked petulantly.

"Sorry," Remy said. "But we can't help you."

"Then what did they send you for?" she asked huffily.

Remy shed his human guise, allowing his true form to manifest itself: a winged being of radiance, transcending humanity.

"They didn't," he said, stepping closer to the nurse. The name tag pinned to the front of her white dress identified her as LeeAnne.

LeeAnne's expression turned to one of panic.

"No," she cried, stepping back. "I'm not ready to go. There are still so many who need their medicine . . . who need to be taken care of. . . . Please . . ."

"Great," Francis said from where he stood just outside the door. "You're scaring the shit out of her."

"I don't see you doing anything to help," Remy quipped.

"Hey, I got us here."

Remy returned to his human shape, hoping it would calm the spirit.

"It's all right, LeeAnne," he said, soothing her fears. "No one is going to take you anywhere you don't want to go."

She was still in a tizzy. "There're so many here . . . so many that need looking after."

And she was right.

Remy looked down the corridor to see the ghostly shapes drifting out from behind the walls and closed doors, slowly floating down the hallway toward their caregiver.

"This could be bad," Francis warned.

"We're not here to hurt you," Remy tried to explain. "We're not here to hurt anybody."

The ghosts stood just behind LeeAnne, and Remy could see evidence of some of the twisted medical experiments. Even in their nearly translucent form, jagged lobotomy scars showed upon their shaved skulls.

"Then why are you here," LeeAnne asked.

"We're looking for some answers," Remy said. "Someone like me was here not too long ago, and we'd like to know why."

"Like you?" LeeAnne questioned.

"Angel," Remy said. "A powerful angel."

The nurse shook her translucent head.

"There hasn't been any like you here that I can remember," she said. She nibbled at a ghostly fingernail as she thought. "But it's been so busy . . ." She seemed to drift off then, staring at something Remy could not see.

"LeeAnne?" Remy prompted.

But it was as if she could not hear him. She turned and went back to her medication cart, resuming her duties.

"Well, I guess that's that," Francis said, still at the swinging door.

The patient-apparitions drifted off as well, many fading away as they headed farther into the building.

Remy shrugged and was heading back toward his friend when Francis suddenly pointed down the corridor past him.

"Look."

Remy turned around to see a single ghost dressed in pajamas and a bathrobe standing there, watching them.

"Hello?" Remy called to him.

"Let me try," Francis said, passing Remy on his way down the hall toward the ghost.

"Did you see something, old-timer?" Francis asked.

The ghost began to shuffle off.

"Hey," Francis called after him.

The ghost stopped, turned ever so slightly, and motioned for them to follow him.

Remy joined Francis, and they did as the ghost had ordered.

Nurse LeeAnne was back at her cart again, fussing over ghostly meds as they passed her.

"Are you going to help me?" she asked them.

"We're supposed to be working another floor," Remy told her.

She seemed to accept that with a shrug, and resumed medicating the patients on the first floor.

Remy and Francis continued to follow the old ghost. Every once in a while he would stop, as if resting, and then he would continue.

The place was labyrinthine in its design.

"Do you think he knows where he's going?" Francis asked when the ghost had stopped yet again at another set of double doors.

The sign above the doors indicated SURGERY.

Remy felt a change in the atmosphere almost immediately, a sense of weight, as if the air had gained some sort of substance. "Feel that?" he asked.

"Yeah," Francis answered. "And it doesn't feel right. . . . In fact, it feels awful."

"I'm guessing some really bad shit went down in this part of the building."

The ghost disappeared through the doors and Remy pushed through them after him. The ghost was gone, leaving Francis and him in the darkness of the corridor.

"Where'd he go?" Francis asked.

They may have lost their guide, but the corridor was filled with others.

These ghosts were agitated. Snippets of their moans and shrieks could be heard upon the periphery of sound, and given the way this section of the facility felt, Remy could understand why.

"We're close to ground zero," he said.

He felt that they had arrived before seeing it. In a deep patch of bottomless shadow there was a doorway darker than the darkness surrounding it.

"Here," Remy said.

The specters were watching him, some trying to warn him of something, but he continued forward, passing through the chilling dark of the doorway into the room.

*The room.*

He knew where he was the minute he stepped inside.

Francis cautiously joined him. "Feels awful in here."

"Awful is what was done here," Remy replied. He could see staccato images of this room's past: surgery after surgery, skulls cut open and brains played with as if nothing more than modeling clay.

"Shit," Francis said.

Remy looked toward his friend. The old ghost who had led them to the surgery was standing beside a rusted operating table upon which was his own body. A bloodstained surgical team surrounded him.

"He wanted us to see this," Remy said.

"There's something else, though." Francis' eyes were riveted to the nightmarish scenes unfolding around them.

Remy looked away from the ghosts. "What?"

"I didn't think of it until now," Francis said. "Charnel houses."

"Charnel houses?" Remy repeated. "Isn't that another name for a slaughterhouse?"

"Yeah, among other things; but it's also the name used for special places of ill repute."

"A whorehouse?"

Francis nodded. "For special customers with special tastes."

"What do they have to do with . . ."

"They're not located in this reality," Francis started to explain. "You can find them on other planes of existence—really bad places that have been sealed off."

A ghostly surgeon with a saw was cutting into the head of a man who struggled against his restraints, sending geysers of phantom blood into the air.

"So how would one get to these charnel houses?" Remy asked.

"There are weak spots," Francis explained. "Wounds in the flesh of reality that allow these bad places where the charnel houses exist to temporarily bleed through."

"And where can these weak spots be found?" Remy asked, the pieces starting to fall into place.

"From what I understand they move around, appearing at random times in places where the most horrible acts of cruelty have occurred."

"So you think that a passage to a charnel house opened up here?" Remy asked.

They watched as the doctors worked, feeling the psychic scars that the surgeons were leaving behind in this reality.

"This place would be a prime candidate," Francis said.

Remy walked farther into the operating room, passing through the lingering specters. "So, what, you just show up in a place where something really bad happened, and hope that the entrance to one of these charnel houses opens up?" he asked, turning back to his friend.

"It's not as random as that," Francis said. "These houses are pretty exclusive."

"So you'd have to be a member or something?"

Francis nodded. "Yeah, something like that."

"An invitation?" Remy suggested.

Francis shrugged. "Wouldn't know where to show up without one."

"We should head back to the mansion," Remy said, passing Francis as he walked from the operating room out into the hall.

The old ghost that had led them there bidding them good-bye with a wave.

# CHAPTER TWELVE

Gareth had been crying nonstop for at least a day.

Left alone to think about what he had done, the young man could only huddle in the corner of the concrete bedroom and pour out his emotions to the shadows.

When his keepers had learned of his transgression, there was hell to pay, and he had been banished to his room.

He pulled his legs up closer to his chest; a whiff of body odor mixed with that of drying blood wafted up to tease his senses, and to remind him of the act he'd committed.

The hate had always been a constant companion; it was with him when he awoke every morning and when he closed his eyes at night. It was the only thing he could truly count on in his troubled life, and he was certain that his brothers and sisters felt the same. Hate gave them the strength—the power—to survive in a world that wished to see them dead.

Gareth's mind wandered back to the moment that had filled him with such distress. He hadn't been told who the large man with the booming voice was, but when he saw him, Gareth knew.

The hate told him.

And the hate that Gareth never dreamed could grow any stronger did just that, and it took everything he had not to lose control of it.

He wanted to tell somebody about the man, and had considered bringing it up to one of his brothers or sisters, but he wasn't supposed to have been at the house. He was supposed to stay on the island with the others like him—with his siblings—but since he'd learned his special trick, he hadn't been limited to the island anymore.

Gareth was the eldest, and he briefly wondered if the others would soon be able to come and go as they pleased as well.

*But don't let Prosper know.*

Prosper ran the house, and also took care of him and his siblings on the island. Prosper was also a mean son of a bitch.

He said they all owed him their lives, and that was probably true—but it wasn't like their lives were worth anything anyway. From the youngest of ages they had been told how worthless they were, how they had been cast away like so much garbage, and that only Prosper gave two shits about them.

But that was about all he gave. Two shits.

Gareth had finally managed to calm the hate down to a dull roar, and had never said anything about the man to anyone.

But then the man who made Gareth's hate sing had come to them. Had come to the island.

It was Prosper who had brought him, and Gareth could see that Prosper was nervous in the man's presence. As if he was afraid; but that wasn't possible, was it? There was only one other person that Prosper was afraid of, and he didn't come around all that often.

Just every now and again to make sure that Prosper wasn't screwing up.

Prosper had taken the man who stirred Gareth's hate to the building that he used as his dwelling when he visited the island.

Gareth distinctly remembered how he had felt when he'd seen the man again: how he had wanted to follow Prosper, how he had felt as though he might rip out of his skin, revealing somebody completely different than he currently was—somebody forged from the fires of pure hate. But he had held back, knowing that it wouldn't have been wise for any of them to interfere with Prosper's business.

Soon after, Gareth and his brothers and sisters were summoned to

Prosper's dwelling. The others were excited; attention from Prosper, whether good or bad, was something to look forward to.

They didn't know who this man was—what this man was. But Gareth did. And since he'd seen this man, his temper had grown, and he'd spent more time torturing the island rats before eventually killing them.

He had changed with the sight of this man, and he wondered if his brothers and sisters would be affected as well.

Wedged deep into the corner of his room, awash in the stink of himself, Gareth relived the experience.

Those who kept watch over them, the walking dead men, had herded them all into a line, marching them single file into the broken-down concrete building that served as Prosper's home. The others giggled and shared nervous glances. They thought that something big was going to happen, something important, and in hindsight, maybe they were right.

Gareth was the oldest, and the others looked to him as they marched toward their destination, their furtive gazes desperate for answers. But he revealed nothing, for they had to see for themselves.

Their own hate had to show them—tell them.

They entered Prosper's dwelling. It was so much nicer than the squalor in which they lived. As they lined up in the front room, Gareth could hear Prosper and his guest talking in the next room, the man demanding to know why he had been brought to such a forsaken place.

Gareth remembered what Prosper had said.

*"Just you wait and see."*

The wind outside Gareth's room howled, and he could hear the incessant patter of rain against the building. It was like the hate inside him, raging against the confines that kept it locked away.

Gareth didn't want to remember anymore, but the memory was crystal clear in his mind, and would be, he was certain, for what remained of his life.

A door at the far end of Prosper's front room opened with a sharp click, followed by the whine of hinges rusted by the heavy, moisture-filled air of the island. Prosper led the guest into the room with a guiding hand, although he seemed careful not to touch him.

Gareth could not look away from the man, as if his stare would tell the man who he was. . . .

*Who they all were.*

Then an odd sensation filled the stale, damp air of Prosper's quarters. Gareth managed to tear his gaze from the powerful figure that stood before them, and looked toward his brothers and sisters.

Their hate . . . their hate was coming alive as his had.

They knew this man as well—this powerfully built, finely clothed figure that looked at them with dripping contempt.

Their hate knew him, as Gareth's did.

And the air around them began to crackle with a power both awful, and awesome.

What soon followed was why Gareth was here, alone in his room. Even in the darkness he could see the blood on his clothing. He lifted his trembling hands and stared at the dried gore of his brutal act. His hands remembered what they had done, and shared with him the memory.

For the briefest of times, the hate had been replaced by something else. Hope? *Was it hope?* Gareth wasn't sure, but the hate was quickly back again as he learned what the man wanted of them.

What he wanted to make them.

Gareth would not stand for it.

The ripping and tearing, the screams of pain and anger, and hate so much greater than it had ever been before. The hate had changed him. . . .

The hate and the blood had transformed him, and given him the special talent to change the others.

And he would do just that, if he was to survive what was to come.

If he was to survive his punishment.

Gareth was suddenly distracted by the sound of someone approaching his room. He figured it was time. Perhaps he would finally leave this life, but he was all right with that.

For he would leave satisfied, covered in the blood of the one who had abandoned him, one of those who had cast him and his siblings aside as if they were filth.

Covered in the blood of his father.

The door opened with a creak and a figure silently entered the room. Gareth had seen this man before. This was the man that Prosper feared, the one who came from time to time to check up on Prosper.

The man casually looked at him before turning around, finding the chair, and sitting down across from him.

He said nothing, staring at Gareth, who gazed back, not sure what he should be doing.

Finally Gareth could stand it no longer.

"Who—," he began, his voice sounding dry and old, perhaps changed by his act.

"Simeon," the man said. "My name is Simeon."

He crossed his legs, and looked at Gareth even more intently, tilting his head to one side. He played with a ring on his finger.

"And your name is Gareth."

Gareth nodded slowly.

"You have created quite a problem for me, Gareth," Simeon said, turning the ring round and round.

"So, how are we going to make things right?"

Remy and Francis appeared in the foyer of Aszrus' Newport home. They were in the midst of conversation.

"If there are any clues to the whereabouts of this charnel house, they'll probably be in here somewhere," Remy said as he folded his wings, already on the move toward the study.

"Are you sure about me being here?" Francis asked, attempting to keep up.

Remy was just about to tell his friend that he was certain everything would be fine when a blast of divine fire flashed by his face, striking Francis and sending him hurtling backward, engulfed in the flames of Heaven.

Spinning toward the source, Remy released his wings again, hurling himself at this latest seemingly endless array of adversaries. He was shocked to see that it was Montagin.

The angel had shed his fussy, human form and appeared as Remy remembered him during the Great War, adorned in shining armor and mail of silver, his wings a black-flecked white, a burning sword in his hand.

"Montagin!" Remy raged, pulling back to flutter before the angel. "What do you think . . . ?"

"How dare you bring him here!" Montagin screamed. "Do you not know who he serves, Seraphim?" He flapped his powerful wings, swaying from side to side. "Have you brought him here to kill *us* as well?"

*Is that slurring?* Remy wondered, instantly convinced that it was. The angel, Montagin, was drunk.

*Great.*

"That's about enough of that," Remy warned, advancing toward the inebriated creature of Heaven.

Montagin flew backward, slamming into the wall and a table that held an expensive-looking pitcher and chamber pot. The table crashed to the floor, the pot and pitcher shattering upon impact.

"Perhaps you've allied yourself with him," Montagin considered. He started to raise his sword. "Perhaps you've weighed your options and believe that siding with the Morningstar would be more beneficial to your pathetic human existence upon this forsaken mud ball that you—"

Remy lunged at the angel and grabbed hold of his wrist.

"You dare!" Montagin raged, attempting to pull his hand free.

"You've got some fucking nerve," Remy said, bending the angel's wrist in such a way that he could easily have snapped the bone.

Montagin continued to struggle, but it was useless, and Remy drove his fist into the angel's drunken face. Montagin's head snapped back, arms and wings flailing as he dropped to the hallway floor.

"How dare you!" the angel roared again, scrabbling for the sword that he had dropped.

"Stay down," Remy commanded, his stare intense and piercing.

Montagin must have sobered up just a tad with the warning, for he stayed where he was.

Remy turned his back on the angel, and rushed down the corridor to where his friend lay. He was glad to see that the divine fires had been extinguished, but Francis' entire body was now covered in what looked to be a thick membrane of solidified darkness.

The package of shadow writhed upon the floor, and a razor-thin knife blade suddenly pierced the fabric of night from the inside out, slicing downward. Francis, looking none the worse for wear, crawled out from the incision.

"Okay," Remy said cautiously, not sure of what he was seeing.

"I know," Francis replied. "Pretty fucking cool, isn't it?"

His eyes traveled down the hall to Montagin who leaned against the wall, armored legs splayed out in front of him.

"What's up with him?" Francis asked.

"He's drunk," Remy responded with supreme annoyance. "So drunk that he's forgotten that he can shrug off the effects of the alcohol with just a thought."

"That *is* drunk," Francis agreed with a slow nod.

Remy started down the hall again. "Montagin," he called.

The angel's head was leaned back against the plaster wall, eyes closed. The effects of Remy's blow were still evident around the angel's mouth.

"Are you going to hit me again?" Montagin asked. "Or maybe you'll slay me just like you did all those others during the war."

Remy had heard enough. He reached down and grabbed hold of the angel's armored chest-plate, pulling him to his feet. "What is wrong with you?" he demanded. "Do you seriously think getting soused is what we need right now?"

"What's the use," the angel groused, his voice still slurring. "They've already been here . . . and it's only a matter of time before they come back and then—"

"Who?" Remy demanded, giving the angel a violent shake.

"Aszrus' subordinates. They were looking for him but . . ."

Malatesta came around the corner at the end of the hall then, his hands glowing with magickal power.

Francis, Pitiless pistol in hand, reacted with the speed of thought, and aimed.

"Not necessary, Francis," Remy said. "He's on our side."

"Who is he?" Francis asked, hesitating a moment, before lowering the gun's barrel.

"Works for the Vatican."

Francis let out a loud laugh. "You're fucking kidding me?"

"Is everything all right?" Malatesta asked. The power in his hands receded as he took the magick back into himself.

"Everything's just fucking ducky," Remy said, annoyed to no end with the entire situation.

"He saved us . . . for now," Montagin said, looking toward the magick user.

"Do I dare ask?" Remy questioned Malatesta.

"The angels showed up and were demanding to see Aszrus," he explained. "So I showed them Aszrus."

"Glamour spell?"

Malatesta nodded. "Yes, and it worked."

"Nice," Remy replied. "That'll buy us some time—not a helluva lot, but enough to put some things together."

Montagin began to laugh.

"Did I miss something?" Remy released his hold on the angel.

"It's all quite comical," Montagin said. "Here we are scrambling to hold on to a secret, and you've brought someone who could very well be responsible for the murder right into our midst." He looked to Francis with a snarl. "I know what you are, Guardian," Montagin spat. "And I know what your master has done."

Francis reached into his pocket, and Remy prepared to respond, but his friend simply removed a pack of cigarettes, tapped one out, and placed it in his mouth.

"Why don't you fill me in?" Francis suggested, lighting the smoke with a lighter.

"There's no smoking in here," Montagin snapped.

Francis ignored him, taking a huge draft, and blowing a cloud of smoke in the angel's direction.

Montagin pushed off from the wall threateningly, and Remy pushed him back.

"There will be no more of that," he told him. "I trust Francis with my life."

Montagin looked at him incredulously.

"If he says that he or the Morningstar aren't involved, I believe him."

"The prince of lies, and you believe him?" Montagin asked with a disgruntled shake of his head. "Why did I ever bother coming to you for help?"

"Maybe it was my low-interest payment plan," Remy suggested sarcastically.

"Good one," Francis chuckled, still sucking on the end of his smoke.

"I don't need any more help from you," Remy told him, and the fallen angel shrugged.

"And what will we do when the angels return?" Montagin asked. "Another glamour perhaps?"

"You could have a drink," Francis offered.

Remy gave him the hairiest of eyeballs.

"Go ahead and joke," Montagin said. "We'll see how funny it is when full-scale war is declared between Heaven and your master."

Remy knew that Montagin was right. The angels would definitely return for their general, and Malatesta's magick would only work for so long.

"We have to move him," Remy said, thinking out loud.

"Who are we moving?" Francis asked.

"Aszrus. We need to move his body so there's nothing for them to find when they return."

"Move the body?" Montagin repeated.

"Do you have a better idea?" Remy asked.

The angel remained quiet.

"Do you have any suggestions as to where we put him?" Malatesta asked. "Perhaps the Vatican could assist."

"No, that's all right," Remy said, the gears turning inside his head. He cast his glance at Francis.

"What?" Francis asked. "Why . . . ?"

And then the expression on the former Guardian's face told Remy that Francis understood what he was thinking.

"I see," he said thoughtfully.

"What?" Montagin asked. "What do you see?"

Francis finished the last of his cigarette, squeezing the flame from its tip before slipping the remains into the pocket of his suit coat.

"I've got a place."

Remy looked at Montagin and Malatesta.

"He does," he said with what he hoped was a reassuring nod.

They'd been tearing the room apart for hours, but hadn't found a thing.

"I've always wanted to see this," Francis said, holding up a DVD case for the film *Forest Hump*.

"You're not helping," Remy said.

"And you have no appreciation for fine cinema," Francis added, tossing the case aside and continuing to rummage through the stacks of magazines littering the floor.

Remy leaned back against the chair and again surveyed the room around him.

"We don't have time for this," he said, feeling his frustration rise. "We don't even know what we're looking for."

"Nope," Francis agreed, as he flipped through some magazines. "But I'm thinking we'll know it once we see it—at least I hope that's the case."

Remy's eyes drifted over areas that he'd already inspected numerous times, searching for something he might have missed. Then he noticed that Aszrus' drug box had been returned to the table beside the recliner; Remy dropped his gaze to where Marley had swept it to the floor.

And that was where he saw it: a small corner of white sticking out from beneath the chair.

Remy bent down, pulling the item from where it had slid. It was a photograph—a Polaroid—and it showed a baby, probably a few months old. There was the impression of a thumbprint on the corner of the picture, where it had started to burn from being held.

"What do you have there?" Francis asked. He had found a beer in the dormitory refrigerator and had helped himself.

"I have no idea," Remy answered, staring at the picture of the baby.

Francis took the picture as he drank from the bottle of beer.

"Cute kid," the former Guardian angel said. "What's it got to do with Aszrus?"

"I have no idea," Remy said again, taking the picture back.

"You say that a lot."

"Seems to be the go-to response for this case."

"Think the one who brought you up here originally might know something?" Francis asked, having some more of his beer.

"Marley?"

"Yeah."

"It couldn't hurt to ask."

Marley had retired to her room on the far side of the mansion. Remy and Francis found their way to it, knocked on the door, and waited.

"Come in, Mr. Chandler," Marley called out.

Remy opened the door to find her sitting in a chair by the open window, the room rich with the scent of the sea. He could see by the way she craned her neck and positioned her head that she was reading his angelic aura.

"Oh, and you've brought a friend."

"Yes," Remy said as Francis entered behind him. "His name is Francis."

"Hello, Francis," Marley said. She had been reading the Bible and closed it as they entered. "You're an interesting one," she added, her blind eyes fixed upon where Francis was standing. "You're dangerous, aren't you, Francis?"

"And these are dangerous times, Marley," Francis replied.

"Yes, I suppose they are," she said. "What can I do for you?"

"I was wondering if there's anything else about Aszrus that you haven't told me," Remy suggested.

Marley smiled. "Like what, Mr. Chandler?"

"Secret things, Marley," he said. "Things like his room that he might have kept from the others but may have shared with you."

The servant gazed directly ahead, blankly.

"I'm afraid I have nothing more," she said.

"I found a photograph," Remy told her. He took it from his pocket, staring at it once again.

Marley smiled. "The master had many photographs," she said. "Often of things he most desired."

"The picture was of a baby," Remy told her.

"Perhaps he was thinking of acquiring one in the near future," the woman said.

"Like a pet?" Francis asked.

Marley moved her head from one side to the other. "Some treat their pets as if they were children," Marley observed.

"So you don't know of anything else that might be useful to us," Remy said.

"I'm afraid I don't, Mr. Chandler," Marley confirmed.

Remy noticed that her hand went to her throat, where the flesh had become blotchy, as if she was suddenly nervous.

"Are you sure, Marley?" Remy stressed.

He stepped closer, and watched her become all the more anxious.

Francis seemed to sense it as well. "You're holding something back, Marley," he said, his voice suddenly cold. He reached down, brushing the top of her hand with his fingertips.

She gasped, and pulled her hand away.

"Where there is warmth in the others, you are incredibly cold," she stated. "There's something missing in you."

"You're right," Francis agreed. "I've fallen, so the grace of God has been missing in me for quite some time." He moved closer to the woman, allowing her a better sense of his presence. "And you know what?"

He leaned in close, his mouth mere inches from her ear.

"I don't miss it one little bit."

Marley began to tremble.

"Francis," Remy started, not fully comfortable with his friend's tactics.

But the former Guardian held up a finger.

"What are you hiding from us, Marley?" Francis continued.

"I told you," she said. Her teeth were chattering as if the room had become incredibly cold. "I don't . . ."

Francis leaned in closer. Her body was trembling even more violently as her hand continued to fumble about her throat.

"It's nothing. He . . . he gave it to me before he stopped loving us," she said, her voice shaking, not with cold but with emotion.

"What did he give you, Marley?" Remy asked, motioning for Francis to step back, which he did.

"I was only to wear it in his presence, but . . ." Marley reached into her blouse and withdrew a gold chain; a black key dangled at the end of it.

"A key," Remy stated. "He gave you a key?"

She nodded vigorously. "He said that when I wore it, I would be his special one," she said, tears leaking from her blind eyes.

Francis fingered the key about the woman's neck.

"This isn't just a normal key," he said. "I can feel the magick in it."

"What's the key to, Marley?" Remy asked.

She shook her head. "I . . . I don't know," she said, as if finding it difficult to catch her breath.

"Marley, please," Remy insisted. "This could be extremely important."

"I'm telling you the truth, Mr. Chandler," she said, flustered. "I was only to wear it when I was with him, but I so yearned to be his special one all the time."

Francis gave the chain a quick yank, breaking it. Marley let out a pathetic scream and leaned forward, attempting to retrieve her prized possession with flailing hands.

"Catch," Francis said, tossing it to him.

Remy caught the key one-handed and felt it almost immediately—an electric shock as the special magick contained within the black metal reacted to contact with him.

And Marley reacted as well, going completely rigid in her seat.

"Do you see this?" Francis asked, observing the stiffened woman.

"Yeah," Remy said, noticing something else. He moved closer to the woman. A blackened hole had appeared in the base of her throat.

"That's new," Francis said. He reached down, ready to put his finger inside the hole.

"Do you mind?" Remy asked.

"What?" Francis replied.

"Don't you think it's a bit odd that my contact with the key caused a hole to appear in this woman's throat?"

"Coincidence?" Francis questioned with his typical wise-ass smirk.

Remy stepped closer to the woman. "Here goes nothing," he said, carefully inserting the key into the fleshy hole.

He felt it immediately as something took hold of the key inside the woman's throat. He felt compelled to turn it. To unlock something.

The woman shuddered, and looked as though she was about to gag.

"Now you've done it," Francis said, stepping back just in case she was going to hurl.

Marley didn't hurl. An expression came over her face as though the woman who they had just been talking with had left, replaced by another being entirely.

"Greetings," she said in a masculine voice, a grin stretching her face from ear to ear. "How nice to hear from you so soon. Would you care to learn where Rapture will be manifesting itself next?"

"Yes," Remy stated.

"Excellent," replied the voice. "You are in luck. Rapture will be in your area tonight."

"I can't believe this," Francis said. "This is some sort of prerecorded message about where the charnel house is going to appear."

"Shhh," Remy said, listening as the voice gave the location and address where the charnel house, called Rapture, would next appear.

"We look forward to again meeting your every, special need," said the voice, before going silent.

Marley's face went slack.

Remy reached for the key, pulling it quickly from the hole as the strange orifice began to gradually heal, appearing as little more than a red blotch in a matter of seconds.

Marley swooned, and he thought she might tumble from her chair.

"Give it back!" she screeched, completely recovered but appearing to have no idea what had just occurred.

Remy pulled back so that she could not take it. "Marley, I . . . ," he began, but she wasn't interested in anything more that he might have to say.

"I'm going to need to take this with me and . . ."

"I think you should both leave," she said, slowly rocking in her chair, her clenched fist held close to her heart.

"Certainly," Remy said, gesturing for Francis to head toward the door. "I'll return the key to you just as soon as . . ."

"I want nothing from you," she snarled. "Go."

And having finally found what they had been searching for, Remy and Francis did just that.

Respecting the woman's wishes.

# CHAPTER THIRTEEN

*England*
*1349*

The Seraphim soldier was ecstatic to be free.

Remiel flapped his powerful wings, hovering over the marshland, in the midst of battle with the animated corpses that had once rested beneath the muddy mire.

They came at him in force, gliding atop the spongy surface as if insubstantial, but they were far from that. Remiel dropped down, snatching one up from the gaggle, and carrying it above the fray.

The mummified corpse struggled in his grasp, and Remiel stared deeply into sockets that had once held windows to the soul, but now only contained cold, oozing mud. He needed to be sure there was nothing there, that there wasn't some fragment of God's spark still residing within the animated corpse, before he unleashed his power.

Before he unleashed the full fury of the Seraphim.

There was nothing inside these things but dark magick, and Remiel felt a wave of satisfaction wash over him as he allowed the divine fire of Heaven to flow through his body and into his hands, to set the sodden flesh and rags of the struggling corpse aflame.

Remiel waited until the flailing body was fully engulfed, before casting it down to the other monsters below. The burning corpse ex-

ploded on contact with the others of its kind, God's fire leaping hungrily from one bog mummy to the next.

Remiel dropped among them with a predator's cry, ripping into the
moving corpses with the zeal of a warrior long devoid of purpose.

There were far more of them than he had imagined; for every single
one that the Seraphim destroyed, three more rose up from the wetland
to come at him.

But Remiel did not mind, for it had been too long since his pen-
chant for battle had been satisfied. He destroyed them with abandon,
one after the other, animated flesh turned to so much ash by Heaven's
fire.

The marsh was alight with burning bodies, and Remiel gave an
eagle-eyed search through the fog and smoke for the location from
which the next assault upon him would come. He saw some of the
Pope's men struggling to pull themselves from the clutches of the mire,
but they were not his concern. He turned his nose to the fetid wind; it
stank of dark magick, making the hair at the back of his neck stand
erect.

"Is it done?" asked the Holy Father from somewhere in the shifting fog.

"Stay where you are!" Remiel commanded, catching sight of Tyranus as he left the safety of the carriage.

He spread his wings to their fullest, readying to return to the Pope's
side, but the muddy ground began to seethe as something larger than
a mummified human body surged up from beneath. His instincts at
full attention, Remiel pushed off from the soft surface. But he wasn't
fast enough.

A massive vine unfurled from the bubbling mud, lashing out to
entwine the angel's ankle, preventing his escape. Remiel cried out as
thorns like teeth punctured his divine flesh. Wings pounding the air
frantically, he struggled in its grasp, but the thorns bit deep, holding
fast to his skin. Remiel hacked at the unholy growths with his sword of
fire, but another vine, and then another, shot up from the swamp to
wrap around his wrist and arm, preventing him from swinging his
burning blade.

The Seraphim strained against the multiple tendrils of biting vine. He let the fire come, oozing from his skin to burn away the intrusive vegetation, but the dark magick was strong, and even more of the vines whipped out from beneath the muddy ground.

Though he struggled mightily, the angel was gradually pulled to the ground. Filth-encrusted corpses lifted their heads from the bubbling mud, waiting to aid the accursed vegetation in taking him down.

His wings restrained, Remiel had little choice but to fall, the frothing surface beneath him now opening like a hungry mouth to pull him inside. The viscous fluids hissed and bubbled with the intensity of the heat thrown from his body, but the bog knew no pain, steadfastly continuing its purpose of disposing of the angelic threat he comprised.

The muddy water was freezing against his white-hot flesh, and Remiel continued his struggle to keep his face above the swamp's clutches, but his labors appeared to be for naught.

He was going down.

The sound that preceded the blast was like something emitted from Gabriel's horn. The clamor moved the very air, and caused the mud that was attempting to draw him down to tremble. There was magick in that tremulous sound, and it moved across the swampland with purpose.

Remiel felt himself wrenched from the hold of the vines and mud, picked up like a child's toy and tossed away. It took him a moment to recover, but when he did, he found himself lying upon solid ground.

Solid ground, dry and smoldering.

Through the dissipating haze, Remiel saw it before him, looming and ancient looking: a castle, once hidden by powerful magicks but now revealed.

The angel climbed to his feet, fluttering his wings to remove the dust and remains of the muck and vines. He turned to see those that remained of the Pope's men also standing upon the solid surface. Pope Tyranus was there as well, stooped, and holding on to the side of his carriage as if tired.

"Go," the Pope said, eyes fixed upon Remiel. "Go and bring me back what is rightfully mine."

And the angel Remiel had no choice but to do so.

*　　*　　*

Malatesta's question lingered in the air like an offensive smell.

"Did you hear me, Remy Chandler?" the Vatican magick user asked, his voice raised over the roar of the sports car's engine. "I said, perhaps after this situation is remedied, you might reconsider the Keepers' invitation to . . ."

"I heard you just fine," Remy said as he shifted the fire-engine red Ferrari into a higher gear, the engine's powerful whine growing louder as the car surged forward.

"And?" Malatesta persisted.

Remy did not answer, hoping that his silence would speak for him. But from the corner of his eye he saw the sorcerer smile slightly, nodding his head.

Besides, there were far more important things that required his attention. And who knew, within days there might not even be a Vatican—*or a world, for that matter*—to work for.

Finding the charnel house that Aszrus had visited the night before his death was a piece of the puzzle that they desperately needed.

"This place we are going to," Malatesta began. "This . . . charnel house, did you call it?"

"Yeah," Remy said, keeping his eyes on the road, as well as the speedometer. The Ferrari Enzo was probably the fastest thing he'd ever driven, the ride so smooth that it was easy to go over the speed limit without even realizing it. Since he had never been to the address that Marley had given them in her trancelike state, he'd had to borrow one of Aszrus' many cars, the Enzo being the fastest choice.

"Charnel houses," Remy explained. "They're like houses of ill repute—whorehouses. This particular one is named Rapture."

"Why would a place of pleasure be called a charnel house?" the sorcerer questioned.

"I'm no expert, but from what Francis tells me, these houses exist on multiple planes. The magick that keeps them hidden attunes to a specific kind of negative energy in order for them to manifest themselves in a specific place, and that energy happens to be the kind left behind in locations where pain, sadness, and misery were the norm."

Remy glanced over at the sorcerer.

"Places of hopelessness and death," he said. "Metaphorically speaking, charnel houses."

Malatesta stared straight ahead.

"And why would a creature of Heaven feel the need to frequent one of these sad places?"

Remy wasn't sure if he wanted to open that can of worms—especially to someone in the service of one of the largest religious organizations on the planet.

"Let's just say your perception of divine beings, and what they are like, might be a tad off," he said, hoping to leave it at that.

"What is there to mistake about beings who serve the every whim of the Lord God Almighty?"

*Here we go,* Remy thought. He was going to have to maneuver this one carefully.

"That they might be a bit more self-serving than you realize," he explained carefully. "That the Lord God might not always fit into their plans. They might say that He does, but that's just a good excuse to do something they want to do."

"Are you saying that God might not be aware of what His divine creations are doing?" The sorcerer chuckled with disbelief.

"I'm saying that He has a tendency to be a bit lax when it comes to holding on to His dogs' leashes."

Malatesta looked horrified.

"What can I say?" Remy said. "From what I've observed over the millennia I've been here, He really doesn't appear to be paying attention a lot of the time."

The sorcerer fell silent then, likely pondering Remy's words and their meaning for the faith that he served, wondering whether the angel could be believed.

And wasn't that what it always came down to? What to believe, and what not to.

Remy watched the speedometer climb past ninety, and took his foot from the gas. He was tempted to turn on the radio, but was afraid he might hear that the war between Heaven and Hell had begun.

Instead, he focused on the things that were currently in motion, things that would prevent what he feared most from transpiring.

"Why did you need me to come with you?" Malatesta asked, breaking the silence. "I would think that your fallen friend, Francis, would have been a far superior choice to enter a charnel house than I."

There was no one on Earth, or any place else, that Remy would rather have watching his back than Francis, but the former Guardian had special skills that were best used elsewhere.

"Aszrus' body needs to be watched over by somebody who can handle a potentially explosive situation," Remy explained. "Francis is the right choice for that job."

"And I am the right choice for this one?"

"Don't sell yourself short," Remy said. "You've handled yourself quite well. And that glamour you pulled to send those angels looking for Aszrus packing is exactly what I'll need once we reach Rapture."

"Thank you," he said with a bow of his head. "Hopefully I won't disappoint."

"I hope so, too," Remy said, steering toward their exit.

It was going to be interesting, especially when the imposter Aszrus tried to bring a guest to the party.


The Bone Master sat quietly in the tree across from the brownstone on Pinckney Street, watching the front entrance for signs of his prey.

He was cloaked in patches of black, having used the existing shadows from the trees to weave a quilt of darkness to hide in. The Master had been up there for quite some time, witnessing only the comings and goings of his prey's female and his four-legged pet.

The angel had not yet returned.

The Bone Master rested his weapon across his legs, gently running the tips of his fingers along the curves of its ribs. A psychic response of pleasure vibrated in his mind, telling the assassin that his weapon was content, but would not know its own full potential until its current task was fulfilled.

Until death was delivered to their quarry.

He'd heard that one of the other Masters had met their fate—that the angel was proving to be a far more competent adversary than originally believed.

The Bone Master recalled his meeting with the client who wished the angel Remy Chandler killed. There was much rage in that one, and when asked why the angel needed to die, the client simply explained that the angel had insulted him, causing him to lose face.

Remy Chandler's death would be an attempt to reclaim this honor. And the amount of honor lost must have been great indeed, for this Master knew that others of his assassins' clan had been hired by this same client. But it was no matter, for he knew that he would be the one to take the angel down.

The Bone Master had accepted this venture, not really caring why he was killing the angel, only that he and his weapon would be allowed to do what they had been born to do.

Memories of his youth, when his weapon was still a living and breathing thing, flashed through his mind. Even then he knew that their bond was something special, that there would be nothing to stop them from achieving a special place in the history of the Bone Masters.

He wanted to be the greatest of them all, as did his weapon. They would be legendary in the annals of their demon sect. Their number of kills would be in the multitudes, and they would remember each and every one, each death a step in achieving the greatness for which they had been born.

But the Bone Master was getting ahead of himself; there were still many kills in his future, and his journey would continue with this latest.

There was movement from the dwelling, and the Master quickly changed his position, weapon at the ready.

The female stepped out from behind the door, the four-legged pet on a leash, tail wagging excitedly as they headed out on another walk.

The Bone Master's eyes were following the pair, when the animal suddenly stopped, turning his snout to the air and beginning to sniff. It growled and barked, trying to pull the female across the street toward the tree where the assassin waited, concealed.

The Bone Master tensed, his weapon vibrating with the potential to deliver death. He reached up to his mouth, gripped one of his pointed teeth, and with a vicious twist and pull, removed the ammunition. He did this, again and again, loading the weapon. Finally he slid the last tooth into the weapon, and feeling its acceptance, waited to see whether its use would be necessary.

The woman spoke harshly to the animal, yanking him back to the other side of the street and reining him in. They then continued down the street, the dog trying to turn back, until they rounded the corner and were gone.

The weapon's disappointment buzzed in his mind, and he reassured it that the chance to inflict death would be awarded soon enough.

It was just a matter of time, and patience.

And to achieve the greatness that was to be their destiny, they would have to have plenty of both.

Remy moved farther away from the car so he could have some privacy.

"I don't have a clue. Maybe he saw something in the tree?" Remy suggested into the phone. He was speaking to Linda, who was complaining about Marlowe's bad behavior on their walk.

"Well, tell him that you're going to bring him to the pound if he gives you any more trouble," Remy told her jokingly. "And tell him that I told you to do it."

Remy chuckled as he heard her do just that, and then heard the sound of Marlowe barking wildly in protest.

His eyes wandered around his surroundings, and he felt his momentary lightheartedness quickly dispelled by the grim pall that seemed to hang over the dilapidated factory structure.

Linda then told him that Marlowe was mad, laughing as she did this. And then came the inevitable question of when he was coming home. Remy wanted to be there with her and Marlowe right then, would have loved to say fuck it to the whole current situation, but he knew that he could do no such thing.

A timer was ticking away, and it was attached to something akin to an atomic bomb, only worse. At least an atomic bomb would be quick.

"I'm really not sure," he told her, glancing over to the car, and at Malatesta, who was leaning against it, watching the building with an unwavering eye, waiting for something to happen.

"I'll be back as soon as I can, I promise."

Suddenly they weren't alone. More cars approached, headlights blazing as they carefully made their way down the severely damaged stretch of road that would bring them to the factory.

Malatesta had turned, and was looking toward him. It must have been time.

"Listen, I have to go," Remy told Linda.

She told him to be safe, and not to worry about them, that they were doing just fine.

He then joked about what might have been hiding in that tree. They had a good laugh, and she told him that his dog was likely insane.

"All right, I gotta go," he said, not wanting to, but knowing that he must. His only consolation was that the quicker he figured out who was responsible for killing the general, the faster that he could get back to her.

They both ended the call with "I love you," and Remy tucked those feelings away for when he could appreciate them. For love would be seriously out of place where he and Malatesta were going.

"Everything all right?" Malatesta asked, standing beside the car.

Remy opened the passenger door of the Ferrari and placed his phone in the glove compartment. He doubted that he would need it where they were going, and didn't want to lose yet another phone.

They had parked in a deep patch of shadow, away from the fence that had been erected around the abandoned factory grounds.

A quick Google search back in Rhode Island had shown that Prometheus Arms in Bridgeport, Connecticut, had been one of the biggest producers of guns on the East Coast for at least twenty-five years before eventually shutting down in the early eighties.

The place had a history of safety violations that spanned most of its existence. The old place had seen a lot of death and pain in its day.

It was no wonder that it was the chosen location for the charnel house to appear.

"It seems that we are not the only ones to use this particular entrance," Malatesta said.

They watched from the shadows as figures left their vehicles, walking toward the fence that surrounded the abandoned building.

"We might want to get ready," Remy said, watching as the first of the individuals reached the padlocked, chained gate. Within moments, the rusted chain had fallen with a loose jingle to the ground, and the gate had swung wide to allow all of them access.

Malatesta had closed his eyes, and was mumbling something entirely alien sounding beneath his breath. Remy took notice of the fact that the flesh of his face had begun to tremble violently, so violently that the movement created a kind of blurry aura that began to spread from his neck, to his shoulders, and downward.

Within minutes the Vatican sorcerer had transformed himself into the angel, Aszrus.

"Impressive," Remy said, walking around the sorcerer to see the entire package. "It would fool me."

"Let's just hope that it's good enough to get us inside," Malatesta answered, straightening his suit coat, and adjusting his tie.

"We'll never know until we try," Remy said, gesturing for the magick user to proceed.

The two of them walked toward the doors of Prometheus Arms, and into the arms of the unknown.

# CHAPTER FOURTEEN

Prosper could barely recall what he had once been, and was the happier for it.

He vaguely recalled Heaven in faded fragments, visions that would come to him in tattered images when he had imbibed to excess.

But what followed Heaven were the memories that proved more distinct—the tortures of Tartarus, the prison where angels who had sided with the Morningstar were incarcerated, forced to relive their sins against God until deemed worthy of release. But once freed, Heaven was still denied those angels; instead they were forced to continue their penance on the world of God's favorite pets, humanity.

*Penance,* Prosper thought with a grin as he walked into the howling winds and rain that tried to push him back. He doubted there was a single thing he'd done since arriving on Earth that could be considered penance.

He had found the world of man to be cruel and decadent, but he'd managed to build a life for himself far away from the fragmented memories of Heaven. Prosper had built his own paradise in the hundreds of years he'd been exiled, and gladly let the recollections of God's kingdom slip away.

It was the vices that he learned to exploit, the twisted pleasures enjoyed not only by man, but the other supernatural beings that had found themselves upon the Earth. His places of forbidden pleasures—his dens of inequity—were the bane of his rivals. None could offer what he did, and the human, as well as the unearthly, sought out his establishments with vigor.

Fighting the wind-swept rain, he paused long enough to realize that he was being watched. He shielded his eyes against the stinging downpour and looked at the gray, concrete buildings around him. Prosper wanted to know which of them had chosen to skulk in the shadows, watching him, reveling in the idea that he had been summoned here now.

Eager to see him punished as he often punished them.

If he had his way they would all be dead, and the current situation that was causing him so much grief would never have transpired.

Prosper scowled as he gazed at the seemingly empty windows, hoping that they saw the displeasure upon his face.

He reached the building that housed his office, and found one of Simeon's demon lackeys waiting for him in the entryway.

"Prosper," Beleeze said with a courteous nod.

"He's already here?" Prosper asked, moving toward his office door.

"Oh yes," the demon replied. "He's been waiting for quite some time."

*Damn it all,* Prosper thought, managing to appear cool on the outside. He had been hoping to reach his office before Simeon arrived.

He knew the forever man would have one question after another and had wanted time to prepare.

*Damn it all to Hell.*

"Simeon," Prosper said with a smile as he threw open the door. "I hope you haven't been waiting long. I was in the middle of—"

"I've been waiting longer than I care to," Simeon interrupted. He was sitting on a leather couch in the darkest part of the office.

"I'm sorry about that," Prosper said. "There were some loose ends that needed cutting."

He made his way to his desk, pulling out the high-backed leather chair. "Can I get you anything to drink?" he asked before sitting down. "Maybe a snack?"

"I should be snacking on your still-beating heart," Simeon snapped, standing bolt upright, seemingly without bending his legs.

"Now, Simeon," Prosper said, attempting to soothe the man. "There's no need for that."

"No need?" Simeon asked, slowly walking toward the desk. "One of your charges slips away and commits murder, shitting on plans that I've had in motion for years, and you don't think I have reason to be upset?"

"Honestly?" Prosper asked. "No, I do not."

Prosper didn't even see him move. Suddenly he felt himself lifted from his seat and thrown viciously over the desk to the floor beyond. He lay on his back, stunned, with the grinning visage of Simeon looming above him.

"Do I look like someone who enjoys being fucked with?" the forever man asked, his eyes bulging so wide that they looked as though they might pop from his head.

"I meant no disrespect," Prosper began, offering no attempt at retaliation. He was smarter than that.

"Too late," Simeon said, stepping back and allowing him to stand.

"I didn't want you to worry needlessly," Prosper explained. "Yes, this is a bit of a glitch, but I'm dealing with it."

Simeon's back was to him now as the forever man stood in front of a window boarded up tight to keep the frequent wind and rain from coming inside. "You're dealing with it," Simeon repeated with a laugh. "If this is the best you can do I shudder to think of how bad things would be if you weren't paying attention."

Prosper bit his tongue, the desire to flaunt his achievements nearly overwhelming. Simeon stood quietly, perfectly rigid, the potential for violence exuding from him in waves.

"Has news of the murder gotten out?" Simeon finally asked.

"No," Prosper said, climbing swiftly to his feet. "From what I understand it's still pretty much contained."

He made his way around to his desk and pulled open a side drawer. There was a good bottle of Irish whiskey and two glasses there.

"First things first, there was the matter of the driver," Prosper said. He held up the bottle and glasses. "Drink?"

"And?" Simeon asked.

"And, I dealt with it," Prosper said, pouring himself a few fingers of the whiskey.

"And how did you deal with it?"

"I hired somebody . . . a group of somebodies, really," Prosper said, sipping the golden liquid.

Simeon's stare said that he wanted more.

"The Black Choir," Prosper said. "I hired the Black Choir to remove him."

Simeon's gaze grew laser-beam focused, and Prosper felt the tingle of sweat beginning to form at the back of his neck.

"A little dramatic just to deal with a driver, don't you think?"

"The driver and someone else," Prosper explained, certain that he would not like where the conversation was going. "An outsider."

"An outsider?" Simeon came closer to his desk.

"Yes," Prosper said. "One of their own, but not part of the establishment. An investigator of some kind."

"An investigator," Simeon said. "You do realize that this isn't good."

"Of course I do," Prosper snapped, and then quickly smiled benignly. "Which is why I took care of it. Which is why I brought in the Choir."

Simeon's stare bored into his skull.

"And they've been successful, this Black Choir?"

Prosper poured himself another finger. "Partially," he said, watching the fire again ignite in the forever man's eyes. "But like I told you, there's no need for concern," he continued quickly. "The Choir missed their first crack, but they are still after him. Shouldn't be long now."

Prosper brought his drink to his mouth and smiled.

"Seems like the Black Choir has a real hard-on for this guy." He took a drink and then chuckled.

"I wouldn't want to be that poor bastard."

Simeon had started to pace back and forth.

"So you believe once this . . . investigator is removed from the board, things will return to normal?"

Prosper considered the question.

"Maybe not normal, but definitely better," he said, wincing. "At least we should have enough time to clean things up here, and as far as the angels go, one side will blame the other, and bang. Isn't that where you wanted all this to end up anyway?"

It looked like a smile had started to crease Simeon's face, but Prosper couldn't be sure. For all he knew it could have been a grimace of pain.

"Where I wanted this to end up?" Simeon repeated. "Like you have any idea where it is that I want to be."

With those words Simeon spun on his heel, heading for the door. But just as he placed his hand upon the knob, he stopped and turned back to face Prosper.

Prosper waited, nervously holding his breath.

"This investigator for the angels who we won't be worrying about soon," Simeon said. "He has a name?"

Prosper gasped, air filling his lungs as he nodded.

Simeon raised a hand, gesturing for him to continue.

He racked his brain, trying to recall the name. He'd heard it only once.

And suddenly it was there.

"Remy," Prosper blurted out with a proud smile. "Remy Chandler."

Simeon's expression turned to stone. "Are you certain?"

Prosper nodded. "I remember because of the Choir's reaction when I told them who their target was. I guess they have a bit of history."

Simeon stared.

"History," he repeated, and there was that smile that might not have been a smile again, before he turned away, leaving the office.

Prosper felt his legs go suddenly weak, a trembling passing through them that made it feel as though they had turned to jelly. He dropped into his seat with a heavy sigh.

*That could have gone worse,* he told himself, reaching for the whiskey with a trembling hand.

Eyes fixed to the door, hoping—*praying*—that Simeon did not come back.

\* \* \*

Dardariel returned alone to his general's dwelling.

Something had not felt right.

The soldier of Heaven parted his wings in the hallway of the elaborate human mansion, sniffing the air for a hint of his superior.

There was something in the air of this place that tickled his nostrils but eluded his divine senses as soon as it was perceived.

The others that had accompanied him were afraid to follow, afraid to further incur the wrath of the great general. But Dardariel's concern overruled his fear, leading him back here to this place Aszrus called home.

Dardariel stood in the hallway, awaiting the attentions of the human staff, but none came. *Odd,* he thought, assuming his human guise and walking the silent halls. He followed his senses, tracking the elusive scent, searching for signs of life, but the grand home was eerily silent.

It wasn't until he got closer to the spot where he and his fellow soldiers had last encountered the angry general that he finally heard something: the sound of activity, and someone softly crying.

Dardariel strode with purpose down the corridor and turned the corner to General Azrus' study. The angel paused, listening to the sounds of sorrow, and what could only be the bristles of a brush moving across fabric from behind the closed doors.

One of the doors to the study was opened a crack, and the angel was drawn to it, as if some invisible force had hooked him and was effortlessly reeling him in. He passed through the doorway and immediately felt his flesh begin to tingle, as if assailed by something that had once been there—something to deter his presence. The powerful aroma of cleaning products assaulted his complex sense of smell.

But it was what lay beneath the noxious, soapy smell that birthed his ire.

A female member of the house staff—Dardariel wasn't sure if this was the one they had encountered earlier, for all the hairless monkeys looked the same to him—was on her hands and knees, a bucket of foaming liquid by her side. She was scrubbing at a dark stain in the middle of the carpet.

A dark stain that gave off a smell that caused Dardariel's every sense to cry out in protest.

It was the smell of blood. The smell of blood rich with the stink of violence.

"What is this?" the angel demanded, no longer holding on to his human visage. Dardariel was suddenly armored, his brown and black spotted wings fanning outward as he set upon the sobbing woman.

She froze, turning her blind eyes toward the booming sound of the angel's voice.

"Please . . ." was all she could manage before his hands closed about her throat, and he hurled her across the study.

The angel soldier stared at the haze of bubbles, and at the fading spot on the rug beneath them. Dropping heavily to his knees, Dardariel bent closer to the carpet, his nose mere inches from the bloody blemish.

It was Azrus' blood; of that there was no doubt.

Dardariel heard the pathetic whimpering of the human woman and turned, eyes aflame with rage and indignation, toward where she had fallen. She lay upon the floor, up against the book-lined wall, her limbs bent and twisted unnaturally.

"Where is he?" Dardariel demanded.

"I—I don't—," she stammered between grunts of pain. She flopped around upon the floor of the study like a wounded bird.

Dardariel rose to his feet and stomped across the room. "What has happened to the general?" he demanded, grabbing the woman's broken arm and hauling her to her feet.

Her scream was piercing, but it was music to his ears if it would supply him with the information he sought.

"The general," he repeated, shaking the woman's arm, feeling the broken bones grind beneath their fragile flesh covering.

Her eyes fluttered, and she moaned. He was afraid that she would lose consciousness, so he drew her close, blowing the breath of the divine upon her face, and watching her instantly revitalize.

"You're . . . you're so beautiful," the blind woman said, her empty eyes tearing up as her senses were overwhelmed.

"Who are you?" Dardariel asked, trying to keep his voice calm.

"Marley," she said. "My name is Marley."

"Tell me, Marley," Dardariel said, still holding on to the woman's arm, his face mere inches from hers. "What has occurred here? What has happened to your master?"

He could still smell the blood, and it made him want to scream, and rage, and tear this dwelling down to the ground.

"Something . . . something bad," she said, and started to sob again.

The fire of Heaven surged within Dardariel, and it took all that he had to keep himself from burning like the sun.

"What?" he asked. "What . . . bad, has happened here?"

"I don't . . . I don't know," she told him. "He kept us away. . . . I tried to see, but . . ."

"Who kept you away?" Dardariel asked.

"Montagin," she said in a pain-filled whisper. "Montagin did not want us to know that something . . ." She started to writhe in his clutches. "But I knew. . . . I could feel it. . . . My love of him was too strong. . . . I knew that something had happened to him."

She was crying again, sobbing for the love of her master, and perhaps for the pain she was currently enduring.

His eyes were drawn back to the mark on the carpet, almost as if it were calling to him, mocking him. What did it all mean, he needed to know. Here they were on the precipice of war, and now this.

"Where is he?" Dardariel demanded.

"I don't know," she said. "They took him away from here. . . . I wanted to see him. . . . I needed to. . . ."

He was suddenly sick of her babble and cast her aside without further thought. Again there was screaming, but he didn't care. Dardariel was back at the stain. Reaching down with a finger, he scraped his elongated nail along the fibers, attempting to raise the scent.

The smell grew stronger. He brought his finger to his nose and, moving past the chemical stink, took in the scent of blood. Then his tongue darted out, licking his fingertip, and his senses came alive.

Dardariel found himself screaming, his head tilted back as he proclaimed his fury to the world. There was fire on his body now, radiating from his armor, his hands, his wings, and the top of his head.

There was no more keeping it in. He had what he needed; there was nothing more to be learned in this place. And as for what had happened here, like the stain the human had been attempting to remove, it would be cleansed from the earth.

The fire leapt from his body, engulfing a nearby chair and sofa, leaping onto the first of the bookcases, and the books upon the shelves.

Marley had rolled onto her stomach, and was lifting her head to capture his eyes. Dardardiel rewarded her tenacity by looking at her.

"I loved him," she said, her voice a screeching mess as the flames blossomed, and rushed to claim her.

The angel could not help but laugh as his wings fanned the burgeoning fire.

"What does something like you know of love?"

Dardariel listened, wondering whether she would try to answer him as she was consumed, but as he expected, he heard only screaming.

With the scent of Aszrus' life-stuff in his nostrils, the angel leapt into the air, crashing up through the ceilings and floors until he was hovering above the burning estate. He tilted his head back and cried out for his brothers, calling them to him, as he began to follow the trail.

Following the scent of spilled angel blood that would lead them to their wayward general.


The general's body was starting to stink.

Francis and Montagin had moved Aszrus from his Newport abode to the basement apartment of the Newbury Street brownstone, and the corpse now lay on the floor of Francis' living room, a trash bag shoved beneath him just in case he leaked.

"A stinking body is bad," Francis said, gazing down at the corpse, his hands on his hips. "A stinking angel body is really bad." He paused, remembering the position of authority Aszrus held in the angelic hierarchy. "The stinking body of an angel general is so bad that I'm getting a headache even talking about it."

"We should have left him where he lay," Montagin fretted. "With the sorcerer's magicks at work, there was a chance we could have lasted until Chandler got back."

"A chance," Francis said. "But a slim one. If the general's playmates stopped by once, they'll definitely stop by again. We couldn't take the risk."

"But the smell," Montagin said. He pulled a monogrammed hand-kerchief from the inside pocket of his suit jacket and held it to his nose.

"Yeah, it's getting pretty bad," Francis agreed, staring at the bloated corpse on the floor. He'd met Aszrus a few times in Heaven, before the beginning of the war, and had never really liked him. The guy was pretty full of himself.

*Now look at him,* he thought. *Full of nothing but gas.*

"We gotta move him," Francis said aloud.

Montagin looked at him incredulously. "Again?" he whined. "We just moved him here."

"Yeah, I know," Francis said. He was already heading toward the door. "But we can't just leave him here, stinking to high heaven. A smell like this could lead the general's buddies right to my door."

"Where would you suggest we put him, then?" Montagin asked. "There's not a place on earth that—"

"Exactly," Francis interrupted. "I'll be back in a minute."

He climbed the stairs from the basement to the lobby, and on up to the third floor. The smell of violence lingered in the hallway, and Francis remembered that someone had tried to punch Angus Heath's ticket there the other day. He noticed a dark, ashen stain on the rug in the corridor, and made an educated guess as to what had left it.

Francis approached the door and gave it a solid kick. "Hey," he said, leaning in close. "Quit spanking it to porn and open the door."

The door opened suddenly and Francis was staring down into the ugly, hobgoblin face of Squire.

"What, do you have a fucking hidden camera in here?" he asked with a snarl.

"Nope," Francis said, pushing his way into the apartment. "Just figured that's what you'd be doing."

"To what do I owe this visit?" Squire asked, slamming the door behind him.

Francis saw the large shape of Angus Heath lying on the couch. He was covered with several blankets, but he was still shivering. "He all right?" he asked the hobgoblin.

"He got himself poisoned by a Bone Master," Squire said.

"Bone Master?" Francis repeated. "Sounds like what you might've been watching when I knocked."

"You're a fucking riot," the hobgoblin said as he walked past the angel and approached the shivering sorcerer, laying a stubby hand upon his brow. "He's still pretty feverish, but he does feel cooler than he did a while ago."

Francis glanced over to the television and was surprised to see what seemed to be a show about cupcakes. "Cupcakes?" he asked.

"What can I say," the hobgoblin answered with a shrug. "Fucking shoot me, I like cupcakes."

Heath mumbled something unintelligible, and began to thrash, knocking his blankets to the floor.

"Did you pop by to borrow a cup of sugar?" Squire asked, picking up the blankets and draping them over his friend. "Or is there something else?"

"Something else," Francis said.

"Go on," Squire urged.

"Got a favor to ask."

"Yeah?"

"Got the body of an angel general rotting in my basement apartment," Francis said matter-of-factly. "I was wondering if for storage you could stick it in one of those shadow places you so often frequent."

"Oh, is that all?" Squire replied, rolling his eyes.

# CHAPTER FIFTEEN

**R**emy and the glamour-wearing Malatesta approached the entrance to Rapture.

A doorman, a huge specimen of inhumanity squeezed into a black tuxedo, was greeting people at the door and checking their keys.

"Do you have the key?" Remy asked from the side of his mouth.

"Got it," Malatesta said, holding it up for Remy to see.

In front of them, an elderly woman and a much younger male were greeted and allowed to step inside with just a casual glance, and Remy hoped that it would be just as easy for them.

Malatesta presented the black key for the doorman to see, looking straight ahead as he was about to pass through the entrance. Remy hugged closely behind the sorcerer, thinking that maybe something would go right for them.

The doorman's large hand planted itself in the center of Remy's chest, stopping him.

"Excuse me, General," the doorman said. His voice was rough, as if it were a strain to speak.

The hand resting upon Remy's chest was like ice, and closer examination of the man showed that he probably hadn't been alive for quite some time. Zombies were all the rage in supernatural circles, he was hearing. They never got tired, and he guessed that they seldom complained about the long hours, and the low pay. They were probably just happy not to be rotting in a grave someplace.

This particular walking dead man must have been a professional wrestler or some sort of bodybuilder before he shuffled off this mortal coil to Zombieville.

Malatesta turned, wearing a look of annoyance perfect for the face of the angel general.

"Is there a problem?"

The zombie shifted on cinder-block-sized feet. "Actually, sir, there is."

Malatesta glared like a true champion. *He's good at this,* Remy thought. *Damn good.*

"And what might this problem be?" Malatesta demanded in his best authoritative tone.

"We know who you are," the zombie said. "But who is he?"

The walking dead man pointed a finger at him that looked like a big, gray Italian sausage.

Remy decided to keep his mouth shut, and trust Malatesta's skills. If he had been working for the Vatican all these years, he must have learned something about throwing weight around.

"He is my guest," Malatesta declared.

"Yes, of course," the zombie stammered. "But the rules of the house state—"

"The rules of the house don't apply to someone like me," Malatesta growled. "Do you have any idea what my presence in your establishment does for your reputation?"

"I'm sure that—"

"I don't think you do," the disguised sorcerer said, stepping in close to the animated dead man.

"Sir, we must have the proper verification of all guests before—"

"He is Remiel, of the host Seraphim," Malatesta spoke in his most booming voice. "One of Heaven's finest warriors, who fought by my side during the Great War with the Morningstar."

The zombie looked away from the general to fix Remy in a milky stare.

"I don't like to brag," Remy said with a smile and a shrug of modesty.

"I believe that is all you really need to know," Malatesta said.

The zombie looked as though he might continue the argument, but thought better of it.

"That's more than sufficient," the zombie said, with a nod to the general. "Enjoy your evening, General."

He turned his dead gaze to Remy.

"And you as well, sir."

The doorman then looked away from both of them, before something else could arise, and began to speak with those who were lined up behind them.

"Are we going in?" Malatesta asked of him.

"I guess we are," Remy said, following the form of the angel general through the doorway and into the building.

Remy could feel it immediately, his location shifting from the Prometheus Arms building to someplace else completely.

"Did you feel that?" Malatesta asked quietly.

"I certainly did," Remy replied.

They were suddenly standing in front of two enormous double doors, intricately carved with depictions of various sexual acts, vases of flowers, and fruit.

"Tasteful," Remy said.

Malatesta's eyes seemed transfixed as they moved over the surface of the dark wood.

Remy reached for the door handles and immediately felt the pulsing beat of blaring music from the other side tickling the flesh of his hands.

"This should be good," he said, moving the handles down, and pushing the doors open to allow them inside.

It was like a sensory attack, the music loud, with voices raised in conversation and laughter heard over throbbing dance tunes. The air was thick with the smell of cigar and cigarette smoke, as well as anything else that could be rolled and puffed upon. And there was also the smell of hundreds of sweating bodies, eager to do—or continue to do—what they came to this sinful place for.

The lights were turned down low, casting just about everything in thick, liquid shadow as Remy and Malatesta moved from the doorway and into the writhing crowd.

The room was cavernous with small alcoves in the walls, where people, and things not of the earth, were enjoying themselves in as many ways as one could, or could not conceive.

A woman holding a silver tray of drinks approached who she believed to be General Aszrus and with a sly smile handed him a golden goblet of something. Malatesta accepted the offering, and Remy watched as the woman stood upon her toes to kiss the angel's cheek. A faint glimpse of her tongue showed as she quickly licked the side of his face, before continuing on with her tray of drinks.

Malatesta casually looked in Remy's direction, goblet in hand, and raised it.

There was a brief pause in the music, before a new tune that sounded pretty much like what had already been playing began. Remy made his way through the lingering crowds, many of whom were locked in what appeared to be heated conversations. Every form of life that he had ever encountered in his long existence was represented here: angels and devils, beast-men, and vampires. There were things that he'd previously only glimpsed from the corners of his eyes, and had wondered whether they were even real.

And they were here, and partying hardy at the Rapture.

Remy became aware of a presence staring at him close by, and turned to look into the face of a very attractive woman. She, too, was holding a serving tray.

"Drink?" she asked him.

"What do you have?"

"What do you like?"

"How about a scotch on the rocks," Remy said, leaning in close so that she would hear him over the racket disguised as music.

She lowered the tray and moved her hand over a glass filled with ice. There was a crackle of white energy and the glass was filled with what he had asked for.

Remy was impressed, but didn't want to let on.

She handed him his drink with a lingering look and a grin, and angled her way back into the crowd, on to her next customer.

The scotch was good, really good, he noticed as he stopped for a sip while searching the sea of faces and bodies for a sign of Malatesta.

Remy saw that he was standing within one of the sunken alcoves locked in what appeared to be a rather intimate conversation with a woman clad in a black leather jumpsuit, its zipper pulled down past her navel.

Navigating the crowd, Remy made his way toward them, catching Malatesta's eye as he approached.

"Ah, here he is now," Remy heard the sorcerer say.

The woman looked in his direction and smiled predatorily.

"Hello there," she said. He was surprised that she wasn't licking her lips as she gave him the once-over.

"Hi," Remy said.

"This is Morgan," Malatesta said. "She and I enjoy each other's company."

*Could he have said that any more awkwardly?* Remy wondered. A couple more lines like that and red flags would be going up all over Rapture.

"Oh you do?" Remy said. "Is she one of the ones you were telling me about?" He sipped his drink, gazing over the rim of his glass at the woman, who covered her mouth demurely as she laughed.

"It's not polite to talk to your friends about our personal business," Morgan said to Malatesta, wagging a scarlet-nailed finger.

He chuckled, sipping from his goblet. Remy wondered what the golden cup contained, and whether it was healthy for the sorcerer to be drinking.

"He didn't tell me much," Remy interjected, causing the woman to turn her attention to him. "Only the juicy parts."

He imagined Linda hearing him speak like that, and the beating that would have followed.

Morgan laughed, gliding closer to him.

"And how did he describe my juicy parts?" the woman asked without even cracking a smile. He was amazed that she had the ability to say something like that and not start laughing.

"Spectacularly?" Remy suggested, taking a long sip from his drink.

"Sounds about right," Morgan said, and entwined her arm with his, leading him from the alcove. "Why don't we go someplace where you can judge for yourself?"

Remy turned to see that Malatesta had been approached by yet another employee of Rapture. It appeared that the general was quite familiar with, and popular among, the staff of the charnel house.

"Don't worry about him," Morgan said, squeezing his arm. "She's almost as good as I am."

And as they walked, the crowds moved aside, like Charlton Heston as Moses, parting the Red Sea, leading his people to salvation.

Remy doubted that there would be anything even slightly reminiscent of salvation to be found at the end of this journey.

"I swear he's gotten heavier," Montagin said with exertion, holding on to Aszrus' shoulders as they maneuvered the angel general's corpse through the opening Francis had slit in reality from his basement apartment to where Squire was waiting.

"Maybe it's the stink," Francis said, gripping the corpse's legs as he stepped through the fluttering passage. "Stink has to weigh something, right?"

Montagin came through and they prepared to lay the body down.

"Got any tarps or trash bags handy?" Francis asked, remembering how the body had leaked.

"Got a few *Boston Herald*s lying around," Squire responded.

"Yeah, that'll do," Francis said.

The hobgoblin shot into the kitchen, returned with a small stack of newspapers, and began to lay them on the floor.

"Got it," he said as he finished.

Francis had begun to position himself to lower the bottom half of the dead Aszrus down, when Montagin released his end, the angel general's skull sounding like a dropped bowling ball as it bounced off the hardwood floor beneath the newspaper.

Francis just glared at the angel.

"What?" Montagin protested. "It isn't like he's going to feel it."

He was about to wipe his hands on his pants when he thought better of it.

"I need to wash my hands," the fussy angel proclaimed.

"Go right ahead," Squire told him. "But I'm fresh out of lavender bath soaps."

Montagin fixed the hobgoblin in a withering stare.

Squire looked right back at him, refusing to back down.

Francis knew that he liked the little guy for a reason.

Montagin left the scene disgusted as he went in search of a sink to wash his hands.

"Don't forget to lift the seat, Mary," Squire grumbled beneath his breath as the angel passed.

The passage Francis had cut from his apartment to here healed shut noisily with a sucking sound, leaving nothing behind to show that the tear had ever been there.

"Now what?" Francis asked.

"Now we get him someplace where it won't matter if he stinks to high fucking hell."

"Sounds like a plan," Francis agreed.

Squire rubbed his stubby hands together. "First off, we need a nice piece of shadow."

The hobgoblin was in the process of moving his sparse furniture around, so that the sun coming in from the unshaded window provided them with the largest area of shadow that they could have, when the explosion caused the apartment to shake.

"What the fuck?" Squire cried out.

Francis was already on the move, pistol in his hand as he left the living room, in pursuit of the commotion going on down the hallway in the first bedroom.

He wasn't sure what he expected to see, and was relieved that it was only Montagin, his chest burning from where he had been struck. He rose to his feet, wings spread.

"You dare use your filthy magick upon me!" the angel bellowed, facing off against an unknown assailant in the bedroom.

A blast of crackling energy whipped out, striking where the angel had just been standing. He leapt above the latest assault, propelling himself into the bedroom with a thrust of his wings.

Francis aimed his pistol from the doorway, the racket of battle rising up from the skirmish unfolding before him.

"For the love of Christ," he cried, slipping away his gun. "Break it up you two!"

He entered the room, careful to avoid magickal spells that were missing their intended target and striking nearby walls. If this kept up he could see some pretty hefty repair work in his building's future.

"Knock it off!" the former Guardian angel screamed again as he watched Montagin and the sorcerer, Angus Heath, thrashing about on the floor of the bedroom.

There was a flash of divine fire, and Francis knew that things were about to get even more serious as he dove forward to grab Montagin by the shoulder, hauling him backward with a show of inhuman strength.

"Get your filthy hands off of me," the angel said with a snarl, turning a flaming hand toward Francis.

The gun was shoved up underneath Montagin's nose.

"I will turn the top of your head into a fucking Frisbee," Francis snarled.

A blast of magickal energy struck Montagin from behind, causing him to cry out. He fell to the ground, his body crackling in a magickal corona.

"Oh, don't make me threaten you, too," Francis said, aiming his gun at Heath.

"He attacked me," Heath proclaimed, swaying unsteadily on stumpy bare feet.

"I used the bathroom to wash my hands," Montagin said, rising to his knees, his wings slowly fanning away the excess magickal power that had engulfed him.

"I didn't know who you were," Heath explained.

"Montagin, Angus Heath," Francis said. "Angus Heath, Montagin. We all BFFs now?"

Squire appeared in the doorway. "Is it safe?" the hobgoblin asked.

"Yeah, everything's just hunky-dory," Francis said, putting his gun away. "Think we might be able to—"

The building shook.

"It wasn't me," Heath immediately responded, covering his ass.

Montagin was staring at Francis. Clearly the angel felt it, too—that certain feeling in the air when *they* were around.

"What the fuck now?" Squire grumbled.

"Angels," Francis said, already on his way from the room. "We've just been fucking invaded."

Constantin Malatesta wore two masks.

The woman who had brought him to the small apartment, off a winding hall away from the main lobby, stood above him as he sat, her eyes fixed upon him hungrily.

"Can I get you anything?" she asked. She'd told him that her name was Natalia, and that she had heard things about him.

Things that she wanted to experience for herself.

He didn't know what to do; any slight deviation in his concentration could cause the spell that allowed him to masquerade as the angel general to slip, and where would he—and Remy Chandler for that matter—be then?

"A drink? Drugs? Something stronger?" Natalia asked. She had already taken his goblet and was holding it in her hands, suggestively running them along the shaft of the golden cup.

Malatesta didn't even want to look at her, for it made his thoughts go places that he would rather they not—for the sake of the glamour spell that he wore, as well as the mask of sanity that had been his for these many years, since being indoctrinated into the ways of the Keepers.

Two masks that could potentially fall away if . . .

Natalia tossed the goblet aside and dropped to her knees in front of him.

"Or we could just begin with this," she suggested, leaning into him, resting her arms on his legs as he sat. One of her hands began to wander in the direction of his crotch.

Panic—sheer, electric panic—shot through him.

Malatesta suddenly stood, nearly knocking the woman over.

Natalia appeared shocked, but then began to laugh.

"I know Morgan is your usual, but there's no need to be shy," she told him with a throaty chuckle.

Not knowing what to do, he fixed his gaze upon the golden goblet lying there, and snatched it up from the floor.

"I think I will have something to drink," he said, just to have something to say, doing everything in his power to maintain his masquerade.

"You go right ahead," she told him. "We'll have many hours to get used to one another . . . many hours to play."

He felt his heart begin to hammer in his chest as he approached the bar cabinet in the corner of the room. Letting his eyes wander over the multitude of bottles, he settled on what he thought was whiskey, and poured himself a full cup.

It wasn't supposed to be this difficult; he'd been trained for years by the Keepers to keep these dangerous feelings in check.

To keep the Larva locked away.

Malatesta had been sixteen when first approached by the Keepers. At that time he was imprisoned in a boy's reformatory for crimes of sexual deviancy against the women of his village. Constantin had been told by the village priest that he had a devil living inside of him, for he had been born out of wedlock, and on the Sabbath. Malatesta would struggle with that evil spirit infestation for as long as he was alive, the priest had said. In moments of lucidity, he would pray that he would be kept locked away for his own good, and for the good of the world. Nobody, especially those of the female persuasion, would be safe if he was allowed to roam free.

But his condition did not cause the Keepers concern; in fact, they had sought him out because of it.

Malatesta stiffened, spilling the contents of his goblet as the woman came up behind him, wrapping her arms around his chest.

"I didn't figure you for shy," Natalia said into his back, her eager hands caressing his chest and stomach.

He began to find himself aroused, and with that, so was the Larva—the evil spirit locked away inside him.

The Keepers believed he was perfect for their cause, a lost soul already infected by the blight of the supernatural—these were the types that they were looking for: those already inclined to the ways of the weird. And they had been right. Once they secured his release from the reformatory, they brought him to a secret monastery where his training began in earnest.

But first they showed him how to keep the monster inside him in check, and for many years, other than the occasional backslide when he was younger, foolish, and overconfident, he had done just that, and had continued to do so while serving his Vatican masters.

Until now.

The Larva was fully awake, clawing at his insides, demanding to be paid attention to. Malatesta fought to remember all that he had been taught, every last bit of the minutiae he had been shown to control the filthy spirit that resided within him.

Natalia's hands were all over him, traveling down to the forbidden place that grew hard as she teased him. It was like ringing a dinner bell for the damnable fiend inside him.

Using all the strength he could muster, Malatesta held on to the beast, but in doing so felt the glamour spell begin to slip.

And he could not allow that.

Malatesta abandoned his drink, spinning himself around to face the woman who gazed at him longingly. The spirit was there, taking full advantage of this weakness. It grabbed Natalia by the shoulders in a grip surely meant to hurt.

The woman gasped as he squeezed, the monster inside him wanting to turn the flesh and bone in his grasp to a red pulp that would ooze from between his fingers.

Constantin was expecting her to cry out; the look in her eyes was one of shock and awe. The Larva liked that. It would feed off of her fear, but slowly. It had been a very long time since it had fed, and it wanted to take full advantage of the meal that was being presented.

Her mouth opened, and he prepared himself for the inevitable screams, but surprisingly, they did not come.

"That's it," Natalia said, her face flushed from the pain he was inflicting. "Show me what you can do. . . . Show me what you like."

Malatesta was shocked by the words, but the spirit—the spirit had just been given the main course. He was nauseated by its excitement, its unbridled enthusiasm, as it tore free of any restraint that he had managed to maintain.

Though he wanted to look away, he couldn't. His eyes—now the demon's eyes—were locked upon their prey. Malatesta wanted to say that he was sorry, and that he would pray for her soul when the atrocity was complete, but the Larva refused to let him as it picked the woman up from the floor and savagely threw her across the room, where she struck a high part of the wall, leaving behind a bloody impression before dropping to the bed, and rolling onto the floor.

Malatesta wanted to cry out his sorrow, but the Larva had taken that away as well, replacing it with a hysterical laugh.

Temporarily sated, he was able to restrain the beast, to use the mental constraints taught to him by the Keepers to wrestle the beast into submission.

Malatesta leaned upon the bar, breathing heavily from the exertion of keeping the monster from emerging again while also maintaining the glamour. He thought about leaving the room and finding Remy Chandler before his act was discovered, and they were all put in jeopardy.

He walked toward the door, but was compelled to stop—to stare at the body of Natalia. The bloody smear on the wall above the bed told him that she was injured, quite possibly even dead, but he needed to know.

The Larva chattered excitedly inside his head, eager to deface the woman's body in some foul way; but Malatesta remained strong, holding the leash tight.

Natalia lay crumpled upon the floor, her limbs bent in ways that suggested to him bones broken in more than one place. And the way her head hung limply to one side . . .

He believed that she might be dead.

The Vatican sorcerer had begun to utter a special prayer for the dead when he saw the body twitch. For a brief moment he was overjoyed by the idea that he hadn't killed her, but was still nauseated by what he—the Larva—had been allowed to do.

Compelled to move closer, Malatesta found himself kneeling before the woman, reaching out to lay a comforting hand upon a leg bent disturbingly in the wrong direction.

Natalia's eyes came open, staring.

He could not contain the gasp that escaped his lips as she began to thrash, hauling herself upright against the bed.

Wanting to tell her to stop before she could injure herself further, Malatesta remained strangely silent, watching entranced as she adjusted herself accordingly, setting limbs and bones straight, the way they should have been.

Natalia saw that he was watching, and laughed.

"I knew the bad angel that Morgan told me about was in there somewhere." She adjusted her arm, bone grinding against broken bone. "Just give me a minute to heal, baby," she told him, her lips stained with blood.

"Then we can really have ourselves a party."

# CHAPTER SIXTEEN

It was as if the building on Newbury Street and Francis were connected on some level. He had lived in the brownstone since its construction back in 1882, and they'd been through quite a bit together, seen a lot of things.

This angelic incursion was just the latest.

Standing silently in the lobby, Francis closed his eyes and reached out, feeling as the building felt, hearing the sounds, smelling the smells both old and new.

The angels had come in from the roof. The magickal wards that Francis had set up so many years ago were signaling the invasion. He doubted that the invaders had even noticed them, and if they had, they hadn't given them a second thought.

These were angels of Heaven's war legion, and Francis seriously doubted they gave one lick that they were trespassing.

Which was why he was going to teach them a little lesson on respecting others' space.

Still standing in the entryway, senses fanning out through the building like a spider's web, he was able to trace their movements. There were six of them, spread out, investigating every apartment, probably trying to pick up the scent of the general's stinking body.

Francis opened his eyes, and pulled his knife from inside his suit coat pocket. Squinting from behind his dark-framed glasses, he found a weak point in reality, and swiftly cut a passage that would take him to the first of the home invaders.

The first of his prey.

The angel Montagin looked as though he might burst into tears at any moment.

"We're dead," he whined, as he nibbled on a fingernail. "Might as well just accept our fate."

"I'm not accepting anything," Squire said. "What I am gonna do is what Francis asked me to."

The angel watched him.

"You're going to hide the body?" he asked. "What's the use?"

Squire turned at the door. "You have a better plan, Mary? Gonna stand here and wait to be slaughtered? I don't fucking think so." Squire stopped, eyeing Heath and Montagin. "Are you coming or not?"

It didn't take Heath long to make up his mind. "Your plan is better than no plan," he said, walking as if drunk, still experiencing the effects of the Bone Master's poisonous bullet.

Squire continued to stare at the angel. "I'm not gonna ask you twice."

"So what, then?" Montagin asked as he strode over to join them. "We hide Aszrus' body, and then what of us? Are you going to hide us, too?"

Squire led them down the hall to the living room where the angel general's corpse was still waiting.

"One thing at a time, Tinkerbell." Squire stopped in front of the dead angel's body. "Now help me move this furniture around. I'm gonna need the biggest shadow we can make."

Taking down an angel of the Lord was all about surprise, and capitalizing on their sheer arrogance. As far as angels were concerned, nobody was as badass as they were.

Francis begged to differ.

He stepped from the rip he'd cut in the stuff of time and space, and quietly darted for a patch of shadow in the upper corridor, just as one of the angel soldiers rounded the corner. The angel was armored, what light there was on the abandoned floor glinting off Heavenly forged metal. In one hand he held a sword, and it glowed as if just pulled from the heart of the sun.

This guy had *meanmotherfucker* written all over him, but Francis wasn't fazed in the least. He'd watched a lot of mean motherfuckers cry for their mothers when faced with something meaner than them.

Francis put away his knife and drew his pistol, waiting for the angel to come closer. He stepped from the shadows, striking at the soldier of Heaven. The angel did not even have the opportunity to raise his fiery sword before Francis drove the butt of his weapon into the angel's forehead.

Wings of chocolate brown flecked with white erupted from behind the warrior of Heaven like a parachute. Perhaps it was to startle his attacker, or maybe to provide a means of escape, but either way, it didn't work. For Francis stuck to him like glue, hitting him again and again, until the angel crashed to the floor and remained still.

The blood was flowing freely from the fissure that Francis had put in the angel's forehead, but at least he was still alive. How easy it would have been to slip the knife from inside his pocket and end this being's life permanently, or fire a single shot from his gun into the unconscious soldier's heart, or skull.

But that wasn't what this was all about. Instead, he stifled his urge to kill, and used the knife to cut another passage to his next encounter.

Besides, he didn't want to have to listen to Remy complain about his use of excessive force.

Montagin watched as the hobgoblin and the sorcerer moved the furniture, using what little sun was coming through the window to create a particularly large patch of shadow.

"Thanks for the help, Precious," Squire said as he finished moving the recliner.

"You're welcome," Montagin responded, before realizing that the little creature was being entirely sarcastic.

He had never encountered one of these hobgoblin creatures before, and now figured it was probably because they had all been slain for their infuriating, antagonistic ways.

At least that was why he would kill one.

"Now, what should we do with this patch of shadow?" the angel asked.

"*We* do nothing," Squire retorted. "But *I* will use my special gift to open a passage to a place that exists on the other side of all shadows, and remove this particularly fragrant bag of angelic rot from this plane of existence."

The hobgoblin's words were like a blow to the heart, but Montagin managed to suppress his anger at the creature's lack of respect.

"You're going to put him in the dark," Montagin said, going to Aszrus' corpse, and kneeling down beside it.

"Yeah, it's pretty dark there on the shadow paths."

Montagin wasn't a particularly emotional being—most angels were not—but during his time upon Earth, he'd found that certain human characteristics had begun to rub off on him. He'd developed quite the affection for the general over the course of his service to him.

For a being that had once burned with the light of divinity, to now be stored away in darkness . . . it just seemed so incredibly sad.

"Do you want to say a few words?" Squire asked. "Y'know, before the angel apocalypse rains down on our fucking heads."

Montagin turned his gaze from his former master.

"Just do it, you foul thing," he said with a snarl.

"Only because you asked nice," Squire said with a crooked grin as he cracked his knuckles.

The hobgoblin squatted at the edge of the shadow, reaching out and allowing just the tips of his fingers to brush against the floor where the darkness lay.

"That should do it," he said, tilting his head to the side like an artist admiring his canvas. Then he turned to the angel. "Help me drag him over."

"No," Montagin said. "I'll do it myself."

The angel placed his arms beneath the body of General Aszrus, and lifted the corpse with ease. At the edge of the shadow, he stopped and peered down into the darkness. It reminded him of a pool of oil.

"What should I do now?"

"Lower him down," Squire explained. "This particular passage looks as though . . ."

The shadow exploded upward in a geyser of liquid black. Montagin recoiled. Stumbling back, he lost his balance and fell to the floor with the stinking body of the angel general atop him.

"What is this?" he managed, rolling the body aside to see a giant tentacle, its underside covered in what looked to be hungry mouths, waving in the apartment air before them like a cobra waiting to strike.

"I hate when that happens," Squire said, watching the monstrosity.

The tentacle lashed out, its movement a blur as the muscular appendage wrapped around one of Aszrus' legs, dragging the corpse toward it.

It was bad enough that the general was going to be put into the darkness, Montagin thought as he allowed the divine power that churned within him to ignite his body, but he would be damned if he was going to allow his angel master to end up in the belly of some shadow-born abomination.


The fiery sword cut a crackling swath through the air not far from Francis' face.

"Fuck," the former Guardian growled as he leapt back from the blade's path. He hadn't hit this particular soldier of Heaven hard enough.

The angel soldier roared, his ivory wings carrying him through the air toward Francis. Francis dove out of the way, but he was too slow and the angel's booted foot caught him on the temple, sending him sprawling to the hallway floor.

Through blurred vision Francis watched as the angel touched

down, and strode eagerly toward him, burning sword ready for another strike.

Was that a smile he saw on the angel's chiseled features?

Francis managed to push himself up into a sitting position, reaching into his suit coat as the angel prepared to deliver what was certain to be a killing strike.

"Hold that pose," he said as he withdrew the Pitiless pistol and fired a bullet into the angel's armored knee.

The scream was horrible. The soldier of Heaven pitched to one side, his fiery blade burying itself in the hardwood floor, angrily sputtering and crackling. He looked as though he were about to say something, but Francis didn't wait to hear it.

"Say good night, Gracie," the former Guardian said as he struck his foe on the side of the head with the butt of the gun.

The angel went down with a grunt, but fought to remain conscious, another weapon of fire beginning to materialize in his grasp.

Francis hit him again, and then one more time for good measure. He waited a moment to be sure that the angel was down, using the time for a much needed breather. He was surprised that he felt so winded after having dealt with only five of the home invaders. *Too much living the good life is probably the answer,* he thought.

There was still one more angel to go, and he was pretty sure that it was the leader, and would likely be tougher than the others.

He took a deep breath, put the gun away, and pulled out the knife again. He was just about to slice into the fabric of time and space when he caught movement from the corner of his eye—the angel he had thought was out for the count launched himself at Francis with a predator's shriek.

The enraged soldier of God tackled Francis, sending the blade of the knife he was about to use into the substance between here and there, slicing a crooked line sideways as the two flew backward to the floor.

The angel screamed like some bird of prey, flapping his wings crazily while raining blows down upon Francis, finally knocking the special knife from his grasp.

"Son of a bitch," Francis hissed as one of the angel's fists connected with his face, knocking off his glasses and filling his mouth with the taste of blood. He tried going for his gun, but the fists just fell all the faster.

*Fuck*—a few more hits like that and Francis was sure that he wouldn't even remember his name.

He knew what he had to do to survive.

It was the same sort of decision he'd made while standing before the Lord God, when he'd thrown himself on the mercy of his Creator. He'd known he'd fucked up in taking the side of Lucifer Morningstar and hadn't been afraid to admit it.

And he'd fucked up again now, letting this piece-of-shit angel get the jump on him.

He called upon the special reserve of strength he always set aside for times like this, arched his back, and launched himself up toward his attacker, the flat of his forehead connecting with the angel's face. Francis took a certain amount of pleasure in the snapping sound the angel's nose made as it broke.

The angel was stunned as blood poured from his nostrils. Francis grabbed the angel by his breastplate and threw him to the floor. The angel yelled, his wings beating wildly. Francis had had enough. Reaching into the mass of feathers and taking hold of the angel's wings, he savagely bent and twisted until he heard the sweet, sweet sound of snapping, followed by a wail of agony.

But Francis did not stop there. He straddled the angel, driving his own fists down upon the warrior to stun him further, and then taking hold of his head slammed it down repeatedly against the floor. Before long, the angel soldier wasn't moving anymore, and Francis made sure that he wasn't playing possum by giving the back of his head a few more hits before letting it limply fall upon the floor.

His own face felt broken and sore, and he could have used a few hours of rest, but he knew he still had one more soldier of Heaven to deal with. He was about to continue on his way, when he felt himself being grabbed from behind.

"You have got to be shitting me," he managed as he was yanked backward, into the jagged rip that had been accidentally cut through time and space.

Simeon had Tjernobog, also known as Robert, construct a shelter from an old tarp, and the forever man was now sitting in what would have been the mining city's square when the coal town had welcomed its first inhabitants back in 1887.

He was curious, and felt that this might be the perfect way to satisfy that curiosity without raising concerns. The rain was coming down in sheets, but the makeshift lean-to was doing an adequate job of keeping him dry. A small fire burned in front of him under the shelter of the tarp.

He had ordered his servants not to disturb him, but he knew they kept a watchful eye on him from the cover of some nearby buildings. Simeon really did admire their loyalty, but sometimes it proved to be a little too much. Who would have thought that the promise of Heaven destroyed could elicit such devotion?

As he stared into the fire, he was again reminded of the orphan, Gareth, and the problem his change from child to adolescent had begot. And what of the others?

Would Gareth's change somehow affect them?

That was what he intended to find out, sitting there in the rain, waiting for them—the orphans—to notice.

It didn't take long. He felt their eyes before he actually saw them. They peered out from hiding places in the various abandoned buildings that surrounded the square. Simeon pretended not to notice, focusing on the fire and the rain.

He heard the sound of someone approaching, and looked up to see a young girl standing before him. She was wearing a heavy, leather jacket, two sizes too big for her thin frame. Her T-shirt, which was also too big, announced in fading letters that she was a Sexy Bitch, and her jeans were faded and torn at the knees.

Simeon was fairly certain that this was Mavis. She and Gareth had been two of the first to be saved from death. He smiled, hoping that he was doing it properly. It had been a very long time since he'd had a reason to smile, and he didn't want to scare her.

"Why are you sitting here?" Mavis asked.

He didn't answer her right away, instead focusing on the churning fire.

"Hey!" she said impatiently.

"I heard you," Simeon replied, tossing another piece of wood onto the fire. He looked at her from the corner of his eye. "I was hoping one of you would come and talk to me."

"You're that guy," Mavis announced. "The guy that comes to speak with Prosper."

Simeon attempted another smile, nodding. "I am that guy."

"You scare him, you know?" Mavis said. "We can tell when you're coming because he acts all different . . . nervous."

"I have that effect on some people," Simeon answered. "As you might someday."

He threw that last bit out there; a baited hook, fishing for a response.

"What do you mean?" Mavis asked. "Why would anybody be afraid of me?"

She stepped closer to him—as if curiosity compelled her.

A piece of wood popped and snapped, tumbling from the pyre he had built. He moved it closer to the burning mass with the side of his shoe.

"I spoke with your friend not too long ago," Simeon said.

"What friend?" she asked with caution.

"Gareth."

Simeon looked up in time to see a certain amount of excitement showing in her dark green eyes, which she quickly attempted to suppress.

"He did something very bad . . . didn't he?" she asked.

This young woman didn't know the half of it. Simeon had had plans in motion for a very long time, plans that had been affected by this young man's actions. "Yes, he did."

"Has he been punished?" Mavis asked.

"Not yet," Simeon said, slowly shaking his head.

"Will he be?"

"Perhaps."

Simeon picked up a piece of wood from the stack next to him. A beetle, its shell glistening in the firelight, emerged from a knot in the wood, as if suspecting it was wise to leave. And it might have been, if only it had made the decision to act a little faster. He dropped the wood on the fire, watching the death throes of the insect.

"When I spoke with Gareth, I learned that he had developed special . . . talents."

Simeon tore his gaze from the fire to look at the girl. She had moved even closer to him now, and the look in her eyes told him that she knew exactly what he was talking about.

"An incredible talent that allowed him to leave the island without anyone knowing," he continued. "You wouldn't happen to know anything about that . . . would you?"

Mavis shook her head quickly.

"No?" Simeon asked. "I was afraid of that." He rubbed at his chin, pretending to be deep in thought. "Hmm, then I guess poor Gareth is a freak," he said. "An aberration."

"Aberration?" Mavis repeated, uncertainty in her tone.

"Something unlike all the others," Simeon explained.

"Is . . . is that bad?" she asked. "To be an aberration?"

"In this case, my child, it is. You see, Gareth did something very bad, and to be sure that something like that doesn't happen again we must—"

"What if there are more?" Mavis interrupted.

"What do you mean?"

"What if there are more . . . more aberrations? Would that keep Gareth safe?"

"More aberrations?"

From the ruins of the mining town stepped the other orphans. They were of all ages, some having been on this world no longer than a few years, while others were older—like Mavis and Gareth. Simeon suspected that they were the ones who should generate the most concern.

They walked through the rain toward Mavis. Then he saw their eyes grow cautious, and turned to find that his own demon servants had emerged from their hiding places.

"Who are they?" Mavis demanded, ready to flee if necessary.

He motioned for his servants to stay where they were. "Only those who help me with my day-to-day," Simeon said.

Mavis turned, telling the others that it was all right with just a glance. He wondered if that might be her special gift, to be able to communicate with others of her ilk without making a sound.

She turned back to Simeon. "Gareth isn't the only one," she admitted, looking down at the ground.

"Then there are others like him?" Simeon asked. "With special gifts?"

She nodded quickly. "It's the older kids," she explained. "Though some of the younger ones can feel something coming."

"What is your gift, Mavis?" Simeon asked.

The girl looked embarrassed, rocking from side to side as her fists clenched and unclenched within the long sleeves of her leather jacket.

"Don't be shy," he encouraged. "It's all out in the open now."

"It hurts," she said. "It hurts when I use it."

He continued to stare at her, his gaze demanding that she show him despite the discomfort.

Mavis closed her eyes. Almost immediately, the air around her began to shimmer. Then flames grew from her body, forming a pair of fiery wings that fanned the air, throwing intense amounts of heat. The rain hissed as it attempted to land upon her, creating roiling clouds of steam that billowed across the ground toward him.

And as if that wasn't enough, Mavis tossed her head back, raised her arms and unleashed gouts of white-hot fire from her hands, fire that burned so intensely that it caused concrete to burn.

Yes, the situation was exactly as bad as he'd originally thought.

She settled down, her breath coming in labored gasps. Simeon noticed that the flesh of her hands had been charred black, but was already beginning to heal.

"Am I an aberration?" she asked, her chest heaving from the exertion.

He noticed that some of the older children in the background were now showing off as well; one floated above the ground on invisible wings, while another levitated stones, some far bigger than even Simeon.

He had seen enough. He stood up from the bucket upon which he sat, and stepped forward, exposing himself to the elements.

Mavis stared at him intensely, waiting for her answer.

"Hey, you didn't answer," she said. "Am I?"

He stood there in the rain, his demon followers coming to stand with him.

"Yes," Simeon told her. "Yes, you are."

The girl seemed to accept that, as she'd likely accepted every other indignity that had been heaped upon her since she'd been born into this cruel world.

"Will this help him?" she asked. "Will it help, now that Gareth's not the only one?"

"Yes," Simeon said, and she smiled briefly.

"For now," he added, as he turned and walked away, leaving Mavis and the others to decide whether something good had occurred.

Or bad.

# CHAPTER SEVENTEEN

**R**emy glanced nervously toward the door and wondered how Malatesta was holding up.

He had a bad feeling. With the two of them separated, the potential for disaster was pretty damn high.

The woman, Morgan, emerged from the bathroom where she'd gone to freshen up. She had relieved herself of her black leather jumpsuit, and was dressed only in a lacey bra and panties.

"Hope you don't mind that I changed," she said with a sexy smirk. "That jumpsuit can be a bit warm."

Remy took a sip from the glass of scotch she had poured for him, as she padded barefoot across the room.

"So," she continued, sitting beside him on the leather couch, curling her bare legs beneath her. "I know pretty much all I need to about your friend, but what do you like, Remiel?"

Remy shifted to face the beautiful woman. He was reading something from her, but couldn't quite put his finger on what it was. There was something different about her.

"Tell me about my friend," he said, waggling his eyebrows as he took another drink of his scotch.

"Oh, you're like that," she purred. "Well, let's just say that the general likes his playtime rough," Morgan told him.

"Really," Remy said. "How rough?" He was goading her on, trying to make her think that this sort of thing was a turn-on for him.

"Very," she said, her voice nearly a whisper. "Very, very rough."

"Did he hurt you?"

She nodded vigorously as she unfurled herself and crawled atop Remy. "Would you like to hurt me?"

Remy didn't want this, but to reject her advances might destroy his opportunity for information.

She straddled his lap, facing him. "I asked you a question, Remiel," she urged, as she removed her lacy bra.

He could see the deep scarring in the flesh around her nipples as she leaned forward, pressing her breasts against his chest.

"Did he do that to you?" Remy asked her.

"Uh-huh," she whispered softly in his ear. "But that's all right, I heal quickly. Would you like to leave your own scars?"

She leaned back, and dug one of her long, scarlet fingernails into the flesh above her left breast, causing the blood to flow.

"You can if you like," she told him.

She began to grind her hips against Remy's lap, as she dipped her fingertip in her blood and brought it to his lips. He tried to move his head, but she was insistent, smearing her blood on him. As soon as it touched his lips, as soon as the coppery scent of it filled his nostrils, Remy saw what she actually was.

The blood triggered an explosion of images in his mind; Morgan's life-stuff telling the story of a mother's interaction with divinity, the conception and abandonment of a half-breed child, and the life that she—the child—had been forced to lead in the wake of her rejection.

Remy tried to shake his head clear and reached up, gripping the writhing woman by the shoulders, looking her straight in the eyes.

"You're Nephilim." He watched surprise register on her face, then her expression quickly changed to one of pleasure.

"Of course I am," she said. "How else could I survive the kind of shit you guys like?"

In the eyes of the various angelic hosts that served the whims of God, the Nephilim were considered a blight. The offspring of angel and human were the trickiest of things. Most of the time they appeared perfectly normal, until puberty, and then the end result was usually anything but. An actual human form imbued with the power of Heaven was a recipe for disaster.

Now here was one of those children, forced into this kind of life, a sexual plaything for the unearthly.

"What, you have something against Nephilim?" Morgan asked. "If that's the case, you're in the wrong fucking place. All the playthings here are Nephilim."

Morgan's blood still engulfed Remy's senses; the smell and taste, and the images continued to bombard him as he twitched upon the couch beneath her. He saw Aszrus in this very room, wrapped in the throes of passion with multiple Nephilim. Suddenly, the women were cast aside; Aszrus cried out as a knife plunged into his chest. And then Remy could see the attacker, a young man with shaggy blond hair. His attack on the angel general was vicious—relentless—as he drove the blade into the angel's chest again and again.

And then he began to cut, slashing and digging with his fingers, trying to reach the still-beating prize inside.

"Are you all right?" Morgan asked. She climbed off of him, and stood in front of him, staring. He could see that her breast had already healed. "Are you having a bad trip or something?"

It took a moment for Remy to pull his wits together, and then he asked her, "Did something happen to Aszrus here?"

"I'm not supposed to talk about other—"

Remy flew from the couch and grabbed the girl by the arm.

"This is very important, Morgan," he said with the intensity of the Seraphim.

"Yeah," she said quickly. "A few nights ago . . . some crazy got in and came at the general."

"A crazy?"

"Yeah, Prosper didn't know who it was."

"Prosper?"

"Rapture's owner."

"So Aszrus was attacked?"

"Yeah, guy came out of nowhere with a knife, started screaming and trying to stab the general."

"What happened then?"

She shrugged. "I didn't hang around to find out—security came. I can't tell you how relieved I was to see Aszrus tonight and know—"

The door to the room suddenly slammed open then, and the zombie that had been checking IDs at the door stormed in with a group of five other walking dead.

"What the fuck, Charlie?" Morgan shrieked, just as he backhanded her across the face.

The six zombies then turned toward Remy, who allowed his true nature to emerge. He sprang from the couch and plowed into the first of the walking dead, driving him back into the others and causing them to tumble like bowling pins. Then he grabbed an ashtray from a nearby side table and infused it with the fire of Heaven, until it glowed like a tiny star, tossing it at the first zombie to rise to its feet.

The burning ashtray bounced off the zombie's chest and landed on the floor, hissing like a giant snake.

It took a second for Remy to grasp what had happened, which was just long enough for the zombies to reach him. As he struggled with the mass of living dead men, he caught sight of the jewelry around their necks, confirming his suspicion that they were magickally protected against beings such as him.

*Of course they are,* he thought, as they pummeled him with fists like cinder blocks, driving him to the floor. Remy dropped to his knees, struggling against multiple blows. His gaze fell on the doorway, where he saw more zombie security guards entering the room; Malatesta was in the hallway, no longer wearing the guise of the angel general, his face swollen and bloody, his hands bound behind his back.

There were far too many now, and Remy's wild swings landed harmlessly on flesh that had been dead for some time. As he fell to the floor beneath a sea of fists and kicking feet, he caught sight of Morgan, now in a silk robe, watching the beating with a certain amount of interest.

It was all he could do to stay conscious, and he was just about to give in to the sweet arms of oblivion when he saw Morgan reach for something on the floor. It took him a moment to realize it was the picture he had found in Aszrus' secret room—the picture of the baby with the thumbprint burned into it.

She looked at it, and then to him.

Her look told him that it meant something to her.

And then everything faded to black.


Montagin couldn't believe his eyes.

Not only had some foul abomination from the depths emerged from the conjured passage of shadow, but it had now claimed the corpse of his master as its own.

"No!" Montagin roared, shucking his human shape to assume the form of the angelic warrior that had fought alongside the brave general during the Great War against the legions of the Morningstar.

"Let it go!" Squire was screaming. "It's more trouble than it's fucking worth."

"I will do no such thing!" Montagin extended his arm, imagining his weapon, and suddenly it was there, traversing the planes of reality to find its way into his waiting hand.

It had been a long time since he'd felt the grip of a Heaven-forged weapon in his hand.

Aszrus' feet had reached the edge of the shadow patch, and he was about to be drawn over the edge, when Montagin attacked. Wings spread to their fullest, he leapt into the air, sword of crackling fire raised to strike.

The blade came down upon the mouth-covered flesh, severing a thick limb just above the point where it entwined the general's ankles. From the darkness of the patch, a wail from a thousand mouths resounded throughout the room, and the warrior angel reveled in the cries of his enemy.

The sword disappeared as Montagin knelt to pull the general's body away from the edge with both hands, but the attack suddenly intensified. Multiple tentacles of different sizes, shapes, and widths squeezed their way up through the opening, splintering the floor, and bending back pieces of the floorboards as they eagerly sought their prize, and more.

"I fucking told you to let it go!" Squire screamed from behind the couch.

One of the limbs lashed out, slapping Montagin and sending him sprawling across the apartment.

"Keep away from the TV!" he heard Squire yell, and seriously considered killing the hobgoblin before dealing with the tentacles that hungered for his master.

Three of the damnable limbs had wrapped themselves around Aszrus' waist, and were already dragging his body back toward the passage, while another larger, thicker limb—this one adorned with a shiny, black claw—was slithering across the floor toward Montagin.

The angel scrambled to his feet as the tentacle reared up, the claw already beginning its descent. He was fairly certain that the foul appendage could slice through his battle armor from stem to stern, and disembowel him. He spun around, saw the television, and tore it from the wall, using it as a shield. The tentacle descended and the claw slashed through the monitor, cutting it nearly in two.

He could hear Squire screaming, and took a certain amount of pleasure from his pain, as he launched himself atop the writhing appendage, staying clear of the slashing claw. Holding on to the bucking limb, Montagin again called forth a weapon from the armory of Heaven. A burning dagger appeared in his grip, already beginning its descent down into the muscular, orifice-covered surface.

The angel stabbed the limb again and again, the divine fire leaking from the blade finding its way beneath the accursed flesh. The tentacle flailed all the wilder now as it burned.

Montagin leapt from the dying arm, looking toward the body of his general, saw that Squire and Heath were doing their part to keep it from being taken into the darkness. Each had hold of one of the general's arms, Aszrus the prize in a bizarre game of tug-of-war.

"Can you close the passage?" Montagin asked, rushing toward them as even more tentacles began to force their way up from the holes in the floor.

Squire looked suddenly confused.

"Make up your goddamned mind!" he screeched. "Do you want the passage open or closed?"

The angel took hold of his master's arm, pushing the hobgoblin out of the way. "Close it. Now!" he roared.

"Fucking angels," Squire muttered, crawling on all fours toward the edge of the shadow passage, trying desperately to avoid the thrashing tentacles.

The hobgoblin reached out a finger toward the edge and the tendrils reacted, attempting to wrap themselves around it. Squire recoiled with a yelp.

"Son of a bitch."

"Do it!" Montagin shouted again, not sure how much longer he and the sorcerer could hold on to the general's body.

Again Squire made a move, his chubby hand reaching, but the tentacles were there, and he had to fight to keep from being dragged into the opening himself.

The tugging on Aszrus also grew more vicious.

"I'm losing it," Heath cried out, trying to maintain his footing, as he slid to the floor.

It was as if the tendrils entwined around the great angel general's body could sense that they were winning, and intensified their hold. Montagin heard the sounds of breaking bones as the tentacles constricted even more tightly about Aszrus' waist.

"You will not have him!" the angel bellowed, summoning all the strength that he still had remaining, and pulled.

There was a terrible ripping sound, and suddenly Montagin and the sorcerer were tumbling backward. Montagin was horrified to see that they still held the general's torso, internal workings trailing away as the tentacles claimed what they could, dragging his legs toward the shadow.

Squire saw his opportunity, and leapt beneath the writhing tendrils, plunging a finger into the shadow pool. He used his innate control over shadows to will the passage closed, returning it to a normal patch of darkness.

One moment it was a doorway, the next it wasn't, and the many-mouthed tentacles that had not withdrawn into the dark dimension were quickly severed, writhing on the floor as they began to decompose in an environment of light.

Montagin stared in horror at his master's body. Was it not bad enough that he'd been murdered, his heart taken? But now this.

Squire rose from where he'd been lying, kicking aside some of the tendrils that still thrashed upon the floor. "Happy?" he asked sarcastically.

Still upon his knees, Montagin pulled the upper half of Aszrus closer, cradling the remains in his arms.

"Goblin, I don't know the meaning of the word."

Francis allowed himself to be yanked through the haphazard cut that had been made in reality on the second floor of his brownstone.

He had no idea what he would find on the other side, but he did have the idea that it would probably be the last of the invaders.

"I seem to have caught a rat," said the angel, as he hauled Francis through the crackling rip.

Francis was ready, spinning around to face his attacker, drawing back a fist to deliver a decisive blow that would render the angel numb, and easy to dispatch.

At least that was the plan.

Their eyes locked and Francis knew at once that he was in trouble. He knew this angel; even after all the time that had passed, the gaze of the one who had felled him during the Great War was not something easily forgotten.

"You," Dardariel said, the angel's grip upon him firm.

Francis' first instinct was to kill the fucker, before . . .

Dardariel reacted, hoisting Francis up and slamming him to the floor with all the force he could muster. The floorboards shattered on impact, sending clouds of dust billowing upward.

"I should have known you would be involved in this, Fraciel," Dardariel growled.

Francis lay stunned on the floor, remembering the last time he had seen this angel.

The war was reaching its inevitable end.

How many had he killed? How many of his own brothers had he violently brought down, believing in the message of the Morningstar? Francis—*Fraciel*—did not want to think of such things, still holding on to the hope that the one he served would be victorious, and that the Lord God would be forced to see the error of His ways.

But the more he fought, the more death that he dispersed, and Fraciel was beginning to see—*to think*—that maybe the Morningstar was wrong. And that was when he encountered the angel, Dardariel.

The look on Dardariel's face now was so bloody familiar.

The angel ignited the fires of Heaven in his hand, and he leaned toward Francis' face. Francis dug his fingers into the flooring, pulling away a jagged piece of pine with a snap, and stabbing it through Dardariel's fiery hand of doom.

Dardariel pulled back in pain, allowing Francis to scramble away.

The former Guardian withdrew his gun from his coat and took aim at his opponent, but Dardariel didn't miss a beat—still the deadly son of a bitch he'd been during the siege of the Golden City. The angel lashed out with an extended wing, swatting the pistol from Francis' hand. It felt as though some of his fingers might have been broken in the process, but Francis kept moving.

"Where are you off to, Fraciel?" Dardariel asked. "You have about as much chance of escaping me now, as you did during the war."

Francis wanted to put some distance between them, to lead him away from Squire's apartment, and Azrus' body. He dove for the stairs, almost believing that he'd made it, when he felt himself yanked violently back by the collar of his shirt.

Francis squirmed in his grasp, but Dardariel held him aloft as his powerful wings fanned the air, and a dagger of fire formed in his free hand.

The sudden sounds of struggle coming from Squire's place momentarily distracted the angel, providing Francis with a much-needed opportunity. Francis lunged, throwing his weight toward the burning knife clutched in Dardariel's hand. Dardariel tried to pull the blade back, but Francis gave it his all, twisting the angel's wrist toward his foe's midsection, and using every bit of strength he had remaining to drive the blade into Dardariel's side.

The angelic soldier screamed his rage, casting Francis aside like a rag doll.

Francis bounced off a nearby wall, landing on all fours.

His plan was to make a break for his apartment, where he had plenty of weapons hidden, and to finally put an end to . . .

Dardariel was on him like a horsefly on fresh shit, dropping out of the air before Francis even had a chance to move.

"I should have killed you when I had the chance," the angel taunted, grabbing him by the throat and squeezing.

Francis imagined his eyes exploding from his head like something out of a Warner Brothers' cartoon as the grip intensified. There was only one thing left he could do and he knew he would regret it. He fumbled inside his suit coat again, found the dagger, and used it.

The blade was thin and sharp, and it sank into the flesh of Dardariel's throat with very little resistance.

The look on the angel's face was priceless, and Francis felt the grip upon his neck begin to loosen . . .

Before it grew viselike again.

Dardariel threw him away, his body rocketing down the corridor and smashing through the door to Squire's apartment.

He wouldn't have any luck at all if it weren't for bad luck.

Francis struck the arm of the filthy couch, sliding across the floor, and ending up against the wall. "I'm okay," he lied as he realized all eyes were upon him.

He struggled to stand, and then saw Aszrus, or what was left of him, cradled in Montagin's arms.

*This is gonna be so much worse than I figured.*

Dardariel made his entrance then, flying through the doorway, blazing sword in hand. He touched down in a crouch, eyes scanning the room like a hawk.

Francis winced as the angel's eyes touched upon the remains of his beloved general. He opened his mouth to warn the others, just as Dardariel seemed to explode, a searing flash of divine radiance accompanied by a mournful cry that turned into a shriek of berserker fury.

Jumping to his feet, Francis tried to get across the room, but the angel Dardariel was already on the move.

Heath was the first to fall, a magickal spell roiling in the palm of his hand as the angel delivered a blow that sent him sprawling, the magick in his hand gone harmlessly awry.

Montagin didn't even try to escape, bowing his head in submission as Dardariel lashed out, slapping Aszrus' assistant to the floor.

"This way!" Francis heard Squire cry out, and turned to see the hobgoblin holding open a cabinet door beneath the sink.

Francis was about to head in that very direction, when the room was filled with the deafening roar of flapping wings. He knew what had to be done.

"Get the fuck out of here," he ordered Squire, then turned to face the horde of Heavenly anger that now descended upon him.

"Hey, fellas," Francis said with a devilish smirk as he held up his hands in surrender.

"Long time, no see."

# CHAPTER EIGHTEEN

*Castle Hallow*
*1349*

The castle trembled violently.

Simeon squinted through the dust and bits of rock that rained down from the ceiling, looking to Hallow for guidance.

"It appears that our first lines of defense have been breached," the necromancer said, suddenly looking much older.

"What should I do?" Simeon asked, ready to fight.

Hallow listened to the sounds from outside, head cocked ever so slightly. "If you stay here with me you will most certainly die," the necromancer said. He turned his wizened gaze to the forever man. "I could order you to leave, but something tells me that command would fall upon deaf ears."

Simeon stumbled to one side as the castle again quaked.

"The spell that prevents their access will not stand up to much more of this assault," Hallow said. He was making his way toward the stairs, beginning his climb.

"Where are you going?" Simeon demanded.

"I'm going to meet our guests," the magick user told him.

"No." Simeon rushed up behind the old man, grabbing at the back of his robes.

Hallow lost his balance and fell backward into Simeon's arms.

"I won't let you kill yourself," Simeon told him.

"Is it that obvious?" Hallow asked. "Not even about to give me a fighting chance." He chuckled sadly.

"You're still a great necromancer," Simeon said, helping to steady the old man. "Show it."

Normally for such impertinence he would have been beaten, or worse—killed, and maybe killed again—but this time was different.

"I'm tired, Simeon," Hallow said. "My brother and I have been fighting this war for far too long." He paused, catching his breath.

"It's time for it to end."

Simeon reached out, gripping the necromancer's arm. He was shocked at how bony it felt through the heavy cloth of Hallow's robes.

"Everything that I have has been put into the castle's defense," he said, "but still he advances."

"You must continue to fight," Simeon told him.

The old man nodded. "And fight I will," he said. "Until I cannot fight anymore."

"You yourself said that Tyranus cannot be allowed to win."

"No truer words were ever spoken," the necromancer said. He started to climb the stone steps again. "Of that, I have no intention."

Hallow reached the doorway.

"In days past it was all about the battles, who would win, and who would lose," he said. "But now, in my waning years I've come to understand that the answer I sought—that my brother and I both sought—masked a lie."

The structure trembled again, the iron chandeliers that hung above the grand room swaying in the rubble that crumbled down from above.

"I . . . I don't understand," Simeon said. He had his hands atop his head to protect himself. "What lie?"

"Victory," the old magick user said. "There can be no victory in this game."

The building shook again, and Simeon fell to one knee, as his master clutched the doorframe with a withered hand.

"I don't . . ."

"We exist to maintain a balance," Hallow spoke, over the sounds of his home under siege. "If one defeats the other, what is maintained with that? Nothing. The balance is lost no matter who lives, or dies."

There came a commotion from outside that told him that the magickal barriers had fallen, and he looked toward the huge, wooden doors. The demon staff was scrambling to place heavy pieces of furniture in front of the opening, hoping to buy more time.

"But someone will reign victorious," Simeon said.

Ignatius Hallow shook his head. "None must be victorious. For balance to be restored, the Keepers must be removed from the equation."

"But . . ." Simeon began, not quite sure he understood.

"With both of us gone, nature will take its course—a natural balance will eventually occur."

"So much power going out into the world."

"Better it go out into the world than be in the hands of one," Hallow said.

The doors into the castle blew inward with a deafening roar, the pieces of furniture laid before it doing little to prevent what wished to gain entrance from coming inside.

Simeon had been blown down from the explosion, rising to his feet to see that his master now stood in defiance of what had entered.

It was a visage of power, a soldier of Heaven clad in armor that appeared to be forged from the surface of the sun; in its hand was a sword seemingly broken from the point of the nearest star.

Simeon could do nothing but stare, and loathe it with all his heart and what little remained of his soul.

He dreamed of a time when he was not in control.

Images exploded from the darkness. Remy, the Seraphim, had been riled to war, finally battering down the magickally fortified doors to the castle, allowing him and the Pope's soldiers inside.

There was such anger then, with nary a thought as to why he would feel so much rage for someone that he didn't even know. But if Tyranus wished Hallow vanquished, that was more than enough for him.

And Remiel didn't even think to question that.

The images came fast and furiously, accompanied by a droning sound track of Latin prayer.

He didn't think that this had been the case back then, the screams of those dying in battle being the only score that he could recall accompanying the siege.

His entire focus then was to find the necromancer and destroy him utterly, for that was what Pope Tyranus had commanded. It was all so very simple; he needed to do what the Pope told him to do.

And he did so, with nary a question.

The Latin prayer was louder now, and he realized that he could not understand it. How was that even possible? Remiel could understand all prayers, all languages. . . .

*What's going on?*

It felt as if he was falling . . . so very fast, but his wings would not come.

And he struck the earth, shattering his every bone and causing his skin to split and all that was inside him to spill out into the world.

And then all was darkness.


Remy awoke with a start. He quickly looked around, trying to get his bearings, and to remember what had happened.

He was in a storage room, cartons of alcohol and crates of wine stacked against cinder block walls.

The sound of Latin prayer still echoed in his mind. Turning his head toward the other side of the room, Remy realized that he wasn't alone. Constantin Malatesta was slumped in a wooden office chair beside him, hands bound behind his back.

And Remy realized then that he, too, was bound.

"Hey," Remy said, tugging on the restraints, but finding that they held him fast. They hadn't used rope on him; his restraints were made from chains, and as he moved he could feel the tingle of enchantment coursing up the lengths of his arms.

He remembered the zombie security guards, and how they'd been protected from his angelic talents.

*Rapture. The charnel house. This place was all set to deal with folks like him if things got out of hand.*

"Constantin . . . hey," Remy called out again. "Listen to me."

The praying at last stopped, and the Vatican agent slowly turned his gaze to him.

Remy didn't like what he saw at all.

"What have they done to you?" he asked.

Malatesta looked as though he'd aged twenty years, his face battered, bruised, and covered with drying blood.

"It's this place," the man said, his voice trembling. "It makes you weak . . . unable to fight. . . ."

Malatesta began to squirm then, crying out as if suddenly in torment.

And from the look of what was happening to his body, he was. It was then that Remy knew that the Vatican magick user had a deadly secret.

His flesh began to writhe and twist, as if there was something on the inside of him that was trying to get out. His eyes had gone completely yellow, and he looked to Remy with a pointy-toothed snarl.

"Been awhile since I've been this close to the surface," the monstrous entity growled. "Feels good."

And the creature laughed, before crying out in protest and pain as Malatesta tried to take control of his form once more.

"Can't let the Larva free," the magick user told him. "But it's so strong . . . so damn strong."

Remy could see that the effort was practically killing him, and wished that he could have done something to help the man, but at the moment, there were some larger issues that needed to be dealt with.

He knew that trying to break his bonds was probably futile, but he couldn't help but give it the ole Seraphim try. The backlash of the magick was something incredible, almost sending him back to the dark place he'd been before waking up.

A place where he hadn't been in control, and wasn't even aware.

Shaking off the pain, he looked around for something, anything that might trigger a useful thought.

He couldn't help but look to Malatesta, who had started praying again, even as the evil spirit inside the man struggled to emerge once more.

The door to the basement storage swung open with a creak, distracting Remy from another futile attempt at trying to break the chains around his wrists.

A man sauntered in as if he owned the place, which he probably did. Remy guessed that this was the guy Prosper that Morgan had talked about. He was followed by two exceptionally large zombies.

*Where the hell does he find these guys?* Remy wondered. It wasn't as if behemoths of this size were dying every day, but then again, maybe they were and he just wasn't being told. Wouldn't have been the first time he was kept out of the loop.

"I'd get up and shake your hand," Remy started. "But I'm a little tied up."

Prosper didn't even crack a smile, staring at the two bound figures before him like somebody might study a particularly troubling stain upon a carpet.

"I can't believe you ended up here," Prosper said, barely containing his annoyance.

Remy stared at the man, realizing that he was an angel, but one of the fallen kind—a Denizen.

Denizens had served time in the Hell prison of Tartarus, before being released to Earth to serve out the remainder of their penance.

Remy wasn't really sure how many Denizens actually ever finished their sentence. This might be something to ask the Big Guy upstairs, if they ever got a chance to chat again.

But right now Remy had more pressing concerns.

"It's great that you found yourself a good living," Remy said. "But do you think that whorehouses are on the accepted list of businesses for parolees?"

Prosper just stared blankly.

"I can see why the Black Choir hates your fucking guts," he finally said.

Malatesta's praying started to get louder, creating a distraction.

"Shut up," Prosper ordered, to no avail.

Remy could see a spark of something not quite right go off in Prosper's eyes, telling him that the fallen angel probably hadn't learned the error of his ways while imprisoned after the war.

"I said to shut your fucking mouth." Prosper leaned in closer to Malatesta, speaking louder, as if the Vatican sorcerer was hard of hearing.

Malatesta kept right on praying, and Remy could see that this wasn't going any place good. He made an attempt to defuse the situation by trying to get Prosper's attention.

"So tell me about the Choir," Remy said. "Did they talk about me a lot? Did they mention what I did that bugged them . . ."

Prosper barely nodded, and one of the zombies stepped in, delivering a smashing blow that snapped Malatesta's head viciously to one side. Remy was spattered with the magick user's blood.

"Hey, there's no need for that," Remy hollered.

The distraction worked this time, and Prosper turned his cold, dead gaze to the angel. Again, there came the barely perceptible nod, and the zombie with the sledgehammer right hook was beside him, giving Remy a taste of hurt.

The blow practically tore his head from his shoulders, but at least he had gotten the focus away from Malatesta.

"So, as I was saying," Remy said, spitting a mouthful of blood onto the floor. "The Choir really has no love for me. Did they charge you, or did they agree to do me in for nothing?"

Prosper pretended to smile, but Remy could see that there was no real happiness behind the facial contortion. He'd seen this in quite a few Denizens after they'd been freed from Tartarus. It was as if they had no idea what happiness was anymore, and any chance of knowing it again had been taken away.

"Do you want me to kill you? Is that what you're trying to make me do?" Prosper asked.

The zombie stepped in again, and Remy tried to brace himself, but it really didn't do much good.

"Now why would I want you to do something like that?" Remy asked, feeling blood dribble from the corner of his mouth, and down to his shirt.

"Maybe because you know what's coming," Prosper suggested, and again there was that smile, only this time there might have been something akin to pleasure behind it.

"And what might that be?"

"I hate to waste things," Prosper said. "If I can turn waste into profit, I'm ahead of the game."

"So you're gonna turn me—us—into profit?" Remy asked. "Is that what you're saying?"

Prosper folded his hands in front of himself and stared. "In my business I have all sort of clients, and some of those clients have certain needs that are very specific, and quite difficult to fulfill."

"I've heard that," Remy said. "Like General Aszrus, he liked to play a little rough."

This time Prosper didn't wait for his living-dead bodyguard to do the dirty work. The fallen angel delivered a succession of blows that showed Remy he had struck a nerve.

*Go him.*

"You had to go poking around." Prosper shook his hand out and Remy could see that his knuckles were torn and bloody.

*That'll show him.*

"Just doing my job," Remy managed from a mouth feeling swollen and out of shape. "Like you . . . making my client happy."

He thought he might get hit again, but Prosper managed some level of restraint.

"Glad you understand," he said instead. "I have clients who would give me anything I want for some time with the likes of a Seraphim."

Prosper smiled. There was definitely some pleasure there, but it was the dirty kind that made the hair at the back of the neck stand up, and the skin prickle.

"Now would this be a dinner date, or just lunch?" Remy asked, knowing the question would probably be bad for him, but it felt good to ask.

Prosper surprised him by laughing out loud. It wasn't too pleasant a sound. "Yeah, you could call it that. A dinner date, yeah." He was laughing again. "You'll be the fucking dinner and they'll be eating you alive, among other things."

That idea made him laugh all the harder. Remy could just imagine the perversity inside the fallen angel's head, and was glad that he couldn't share in it.

A knock at the door interrupted their fun.

One of the zombies opened it a crack, and Remy caught sight of a pretty, older woman standing outside.

"What?" Prosper said, without even looking, annoyance in his tone.

"Got a problem upstairs," the woman said.

He looked in her direction then. "What kind of problem?"

"The kind that can cause a shitload of damage if it's not taken care of," she stated. "A Summerian battle god whacked out of his gourd on joy juice is threatening to rip the roof off the place if somebody doesn't bring him a ten-year-old virgin."

"Son of a bitch," Prosper spat, moving toward the door. "We don't have any?" he asked as he and his zombie thugs pushed past her, closing the door behind them.

Remy was left alone to deal with his own problem. He looked at Malatesta who was coming to, moaning as if being prodded with a hot poker.

The doorknob rattled again, and he was half expecting to see Prosper back for more fun and games, but instead the woman entered, closing the door quietly behind her.

"Forget something?" Remy asked.

The woman glared as she stalked toward him.

"Where did you get it?" she asked, tension like that of a coiled spring ready to snap in her voice.

"I don't understand," Remy said, looking into her distressed eyes.

"Where did you find it?" she repeated, as if English was his second language. She reached into her pocket and removed the picture that Morgan had picked up from the floor in her room. "This," the woman held it out to Remy, "where did you get it?"

She was frantic, her eyes darting between Remy and the door, obviously expecting Prosper and his buddies to return.

"What does it mean?" Remy asked her.

She looked at the picture, a look of genuine longing spreading across her face.

"I was told they had died at birth," she said. "But this . . ."

"Why would Aszrus have that picture?" Remy asked, watching the woman's reaction.

"Aszrus," she repeated. "You got this from Aszrus?"

She was looking at the picture again, tears welling in her eyes.

"Who is it?" Remy asked.

She seemed to be struggling with his questions. "They weren't supposed to be able to have babies," she finally said, sobbing. "But here they were, pregnant."

"Who?" Remy prodded, desperate for answers. "Who was pregnant?"

"My girls," she said. "It wasn't natural, but it happened."

"The Nephilim?" Remy asked. "The Nephilim were getting pregnant?"

He'd never heard of such a thing, and as far as he knew, it wasn't even possible. Nephilim were supposed to be sterile.

There was a muffled sound from outside the room, and the woman turned, bolting for the door.

"Who got the girls pregnant?" Remy asked as she turned the knob, ready to flee. "Was it the angels? Was it Aszrus?"

The look on her face told him all he needed to know as she quickly slunk out of the room, carefully closing the door behind her.

Remy had more than he did before, but the puzzle's picture was still not yet defined. He had to get out of here.

He looked over to Malatesta, who was again muttering in Latin.

"Listen," Remy said. "We're in some pretty big trouble here," he told the sorcerer.

Remy didn't know whether he was listening, but went on, assuming that he was.

"We need to get out of here as quickly as we can before we end up as part of the entertainment." He was straining against his chains again, feeling the magick charging up to prevent him from getting much farther.

"As much as it kills me to admit it, I'm useless right now—these chains prevent me from doing anything that could be even remotely useful, and I'm guessing that whatever is keeping you in that chair has probably done a job on your magickal mojo as well."

Malatesta's head turned ever so slightly, looking at him from the corner of a swollen eye.

"I'm going to ask you to do something pretty horrible," Remy said, letting his words permeate a bit before he continued. "And it involves that thing inside you."

"No," Malatesta objected outright. "You . . . you don't understand what you're asking."

"I know exactly what I'm asking, and I'm sorry, but it's the only way. The spirit, or whatever it is inside you, is our get-out-of-jail-free card—they don't know about it, so they didn't do anything to prevent it from getting free."

Malatesta was crying and furiously shaking his head.

"I can't. . . . I can't. . . . You don't understand what that would mean."

Remy knew exactly what the sorcerer was talking about, having spent the last hundred years, give or take a century, attempting to keep the warlike aspect of his angelic nature in check.

"You'd be surprised at what I know," he said. "But if we're going to get out of here, you have to trust me—this is the only way."

"No," Malatesta said again, now starting to thrash around in his chair. "I won't let the Larva out, I've worked too hard to—"

There was the muffled sound of voices from outside, and Remy knew that time was just about up.

"Do you hear?" Remy stressed. "This is it—they're coming for us."

Malatesta had tucked his chin deep into his chest, straining to keep the monstrous force inside him imprisoned.

"It's almost too late," Remy roared.

Malatesta continued to struggle, his body racked with sobs of terror and strain.

"As a soldier of the Lord God . . . as an angel of Heaven I command you to set it free."

The voices were louder now, almost to the door.

Malatesta was looking at him, his gaze begging Remy not to ask this of him.

"I command you," Remy said again.

"Please . . . ," Malatesta whined.

"Do it."

Malatesta's eyes slowly closed, and his head sank down, his chin touching the top of his chest. "I hate you," he whispered. "I hate you with all my heart and soul."

"I'm sorry," Remy replied, hearing the sound of the door opening. "If there was any other way . . ."

Two zombie security guards entered.

"Hey, guys," Remy said. "Miss us?"

The zombie that liked to hit came at him, hands like catchers' mitts, reaching. He guessed that they were being taken elsewhere, maybe to a certain someone who'd paid a lot of money to do something really horrible to a soldier of Heaven.

The other guard had gone to Malatesta, and was trying to haul him up from the chair. Remy glanced over to see that the zombie was having a bit of trouble, Malatesta's hands holding on to the back of the furniture.

"I'll break those hands," the zombie murmured menacingly.

But that just made Malatesta start to laugh and laugh, and that was when Remy realized it wasn't the sorcerer who was laughing.

The laughing abruptly stopped, and then Remy heard what could only have been the muffled sounds of bones popping from their joints. He watched in awe as Malatesta was suddenly free from his restraints, his arms bending in directions that should have been impossible.

Malatesta was laughing again, as he sprang onto the seat of his chair, then up and over the towering zombie, grabbing hold of the walking corpse's chin and yanking back as he went. There was a loud crack as the zombie's neck was broken, and he tumbled backward to the floor.

The zombie that had been beside Remy was already on the move toward Malatesta. The possessed sorcerer continued to laugh and giggle, evading the zombie with ease, even springing up onto, and sticking to the side of the wall like Spiderman.

The zombie lunged, crashing into wooden crates of wine and boxes of booze as he attempted to rip the insectlike sorcerer from his perch. The zombie with the broken neck was now struggling to stand, his heavy head lolling about horribly as he tried to assist his partner.

"Larva!" Remy called out, still restrained.

Malatesta was padding across the ceiling and looking down on those who were attempting to reach up for him. The demon turned his eyes from his foes to Remy.

"What are you wasting time for with mere animated corpses, when you could be tangling with a soldier of Heaven?" Remy asked it, enticing the accursed thing.

The evil spirit laughed at him, reaching down from the ceiling to rip at one of the zombie's faces, snatching away one of its eyes and popping it into his mouth like a cherry tomato.

The zombie flailed about, now partially blind.

"Come on," Remy taunted. "When was the last time you tasted angelic flesh?"

He wasn't sure if the spirit ever had, but figured if it hadn't, it certainly would want to. It continued to taunt the zombies.

"Now I know why Malatesta was able to keep you locked up for so long," Remy stated over the commotion. "You're weak . . . a minor entity. Nothing more than an annoyance."

He was counting on the thing's arrogance and stupidity, and he wasn't disappointed.

Forgetting its zombie opponents, the Larva came scrabbling across the ceiling, and dropped down atop Remy, sending the chair flipping violently backward to the floor. Remy heard the sound of the chair moaning beneath their weight, as the evil entity hissed and slashed. He rocked from side to side, straining the chair's integrity while attempting to evade the creature's razor-sharp claws.

He needed something more to get free of the chair, and his prayers were answered in the form of two linebacker-sized zombies, one with a funky neck, barreling across the room to get their escaped prisoner back under wraps.

They hit the Larva like two runaway freight trains, landing atop them in a heap of powerfully muscled dead flesh that ended up doing exactly what Remy had hoped for. The chair's back snapped beneath their thrashing bodies, allowing Remy to slip free of the magickally enhanced chains.

He'd had just about enough of animated corpses wrestling atop him and brought forth the fires of Heaven. The light of divinity caused his body to glow, sending the spirit screaming away, and attaching itself again to the ceiling like a spider.

The zombies were driven back from the light, still wearing the protections that kept him from dealing with their likes before. Not wanting them to have a chance, Remy acted, grabbing for the leg of the broken chair that had held him and smashing it into the side of one of the zombie's heads, and then the other's.

One of them crashed into a stack of boxes, causing the bottles of liquor inside to smash to the floor in an expanding puddle.

Seeing as they were already dead, Remy didn't hesitate, flicking his fingers as if flipping droplets of water; but instead of water he was flipping fire.

The zombie went up in a rush of flame, the sprinkler system in the ceiling raining water down upon the room in an attempt to extinguish the fire. The other zombie, his head flopping about loosely, made a dash for the door, but the Larva sticking to the ceiling above had other ideas.

The possessed man dropped down upon its prey, finger claws slashing, ripping away the zombie's clothes, and finally the dead flesh beneath.

Remy turned his focus to the burning dead man. The zombie was attempting to roll around on the ground, trying to put out the flames. Approaching the flailing figure, Remy took the chair leg, and drove it down into the zombie's face, and into the brain, shutting the burning corpse down for the count.

He then returned his attention to the Larva.

The possessed Malatesta was crouched atop the zombie, his head buried in a gaping hole that he had torn in the dead man's gut.

Remy was disgusted.

But there hadn't been any choice.

"That's enough of that," he said, using a tone of authority.

The Larva turned its bloody face to him and smiled, a flap of zombie flesh dangling wetly from the corner of his face as he continued to chew.

"Give me Constantin back," Remy said, moving closer.

The evil spirit chuckled, licking his bloody fingers one by one.

"Constantin is gone now," the Larva told him in its horrible voice. "Now only I am here."

Remy surged forward, catching the creature by the throat as it was about to leap up onto the ceiling. The Larva screeched and struggled in his grasp.

"You will give me Constantin Malatesta or I will destroy you, and this host body," Remy ordered.

The Larva continued to struggle. "You lie, Creature of God."

Remy willed fire into his grip, starting to burn the flesh of the host body's throat. From the sound that came from the spirit entity, it was quite painful.

"I never lie," Remy told the monster, looking into its horrible, dark eyes. "Give me what I want, and you return to the darkness inside the sorcerer and continue to exist. Deny me . . ."

The Larva snarled, spitting a wad of bloody spit into Remy's face. The blood sizzled on Remy's cheek as he let his internal fire begin to intensify.

"It will never be as deep again," the Larva said. "It will always be so very close. . . . We'll be just like brothers," the damnable spirit went on, cackling crazily, before suddenly stopping.

Malatesta went suddenly limp in his hands, and Remy let him slump to the floor. He watched the Vatican magick user, waiting for a sign that he was again in control.

Malatesta moaned.

"Are you all right?" Remy asked.

"Fuck off," Malatesta growled, pushing himself into a sitting position.

By the sounds of it, the human side of the man had regained control.

\* \* \*

The youngest of the Bone Masters waited in the shadow of a cellar alcove in the building where the human lived. He had been there for days, the shadows draped over him like a cloak, watching the comings and goings of his human target, and waiting to be activated.

The Master reached into the leather pouch at his side for sustenance. The worms were about a finger's length, and twice as thick. He shoved one into his mouth, biting off the head before it could let out its high-pitched squeal.

He knew that others of his ilk had been hired as well, each assassin ordered to observe those who were close to the Seraphim called Remy Chandler. But he was growing impatient. He listened to the sounds of the building, knowing that his target wasn't at home, tempted to leave his hiding place and explore the dwelling. Perhaps he would find another to satisfy his urge to kill.

This was his first assignment since reaching the level of Bone Master, and he was eager to show what he was capable of. The Liege Masters that had trained him in his art had warned against his immaturity, saying that he needed to control his impatience, and use the energy that it created in a more productive manner.

The Bone Master just wanted to kill something.

His weapon hummed eagerly in his grasp, and he reached out to pet the spiny ridge of bone that ran the length of its body. It, too, was eager to prove itself, to perform the task for which it was bred.

But he—*they*—had to wait for their final instructions from the one who had hired them, even though they were certain what those instructions would be.

*Why else would one go to the effort of hiring a Bone Master?*

Time passed ever so slowly, and the young Master entertained himself with thoughts of how he could eliminate his prey. Using his weapon was of course the ultimate choice, but there were times when the weapon could not be used.

He remembered his training, the feel of the lesser beings used for educational purposes dying in his grip. How many had he strangled? Bludgeoned? How many necks had he broken? All in the name of learning to be the perfect killer.

A perfect killer bored nearly out of his mind.

The young Master wanted to scream. He thought about eating some more worms, but that just made him all the more anxious.

He heard his prey returning before he saw him. From the sounds of the human's heavy breathing, the Master would be doing him a favor by taking his life.

The front door to the building opened, and his prey walked in, closing the door behind him. The Master smelled the sickly scent of alcohol, cigarettes, and fatty meat.

It was as if this human was begging to die.

The killer continued to listen as the man slowly climbed the stairs to his dwelling. He heard him take keys from his pocket, unlock the door, and step inside, closing it behind him.

The young Bone Master felt his every instinct come alive; here was his assigned prey ready for the killing.

And all that stood in his way was the designation of time.

It was not yet time for death to be delivered. He had not received his final order, even though he'd been told that it was inevitable.

He seethed in the shadows. Here was the perfect situation, the perfect opportunity to show the Seraphim Remy Chandler that no one was safe, that he and all that he cared for were targeted by the Bone Masters.

The young assassin doubted that the moment would ever be better.

And the killer made a decision that his trainers would have frowned upon, although it was not unheard of from more experienced Masters. He would act, taking down his quarry, to show off his superior skills.

It was decided—the Bone Master left his place in the shadows and silently climbed the stairs.

To at last perform the act of murder.

# CHAPTER NINETEEN

A good beating was often like a time machine.

And Francis was back in time with a front-row seat, watching as he screwed up on a monumental level.

But to be fair, at the time he really did believe the shit the Morningstar was shoveling; God didn't love them anymore, and they were going to be replaced by humanity.

That pretty much summed it up.

In hindsight, it was amazing how much damage was done because of this petty, selfish notion.

Francis saw himself as he'd been, adorned in armor stained with the blood of those who had not believed as he had—as Lucifer had—leading an army toward the Golden City to confront their Lord and Creator.

*Had the idea that Lucifer might have just been a jealous prick started to tickle his brain yet?* he wondered. He couldn't really remember.

It was painful to watch his own acts of war, the brothers who tried to fend off his advances cut down by his blistering sword of fire.

Francis found it interesting that on most days he couldn't remember what he'd had for breakfast, but he could still remember every single angel he had killed in the name of the Morningstar's mission. He saw their faces as they died, as enthralled with fighting for God as he had been about Lucifer's message.

*We will not be cast aside.*

But that's what happened anyway, for those who had opposed God's plan were sent away, imprisoned, banished to a world teeming with life deemed more worthy than theirs.

And maybe it was, but Fraciel—*Francis*—had been on that world a very long time now, and from what he could see humanity was just as fucked up as the angels were.

It made him wonder if the Lord of Lords had a plan after all, or was He making it up as He went along, flying by the seat of His oh-so-holy pants. It was certainly something worth considering, especially during times like this, when it looked as though shit was about to hit the fan big-time.

Francis saw himself taken down by a legion led by Dardariel. Remembering the pain of the event, he was glad it was over. He'd expected to die that day, to be executed for his betrayal of God, and if Dardariel and his armies had had their way, he would have.

But God had seen things differently.

Francis slowly awoke from the special presentation of *This Is Your Life*, wondering how He saw things now.

Did God realize how close they were to repeating the past? Did He even care?

It was something to consider.

Francis opened his eyes just in time to see the studded gauntlet descending, and felt it land squarely on the side of his face.

"Oh yeah," he slurred, his mouth filling with blood that began to spill from the side of his swollen mouth. "That's something I've really missed."

He was chained to a wall in the dungeon of an ancient Mesopotamian prison, one used by angels for questioning war criminals who had fled to Earth when Lucifer's rebellion had been struck down. It was a lovely old place of wet stone and mold that still stank of torture and divine bloodletting. As he dangled from his chains, he had to wonder if he wasn't the only one of late to be a guest in these ancient accommodations.

Dardariel flexed his muscled shoulders, his magnificent wings shining in the light of a burning brazier in the center of the room. He brought his gauntleted hand to his nose and sniffed Francis' blood.

"Your blood stinks of corruption," he said. "Not like the blood of one who was shown mercy by his Creator."

"I had an omelet with a shitload of garlic in it yesterday, maybe that's what you smell," Francis suggested, as he spit a wad of blood onto the dungeon floor.

Dardariel surged forward with a powerful flap of his wings, burying his metal-sheathed fist in Francis' stomach.

"I could never understand His mercy toward you." Dardariel was close to Francis' face, his breath smelling of something akin to cinnamon. "When so many others were cast down to Tartarus—it was as if He saw something in you."

Francis was about to crack wise, but Dardariel's words struck a note, and he again found himself thinking of what he had lost in Heaven, and how he could never get that back.

Even if he was to be as nice as pie, something cut right from the Disney mold, it would forevermore be denied to him.

For Heaven wasn't the same anymore.

"The Lord God showed you mercy and this is how you repay Him." Dardariel had backed off and was pacing before Francis.

"Why did you do it?" he asked suddenly.

"I know this will probably get me hit, but why did I do what?"

A wing lashed out and was followed by a fist. Francis felt as though his jaw had been ripped away and thrown across the room.

"I'm psychic, too," he mumbled, getting used to the taste of his own blood.

Dardariel stared, his eyes like two burning coals in the dimly lit dungeon.

"I'm serious," Francis tried again. "What did I do?"

The angel lunged forward, hands striking the stone wall on either side of him.

*Better the wall than me,* Francis thought.

"You murdered the general."

Francis looked directly into the angel's eyes. "I did not."

Dardariel could barely contain his rage, first striking the wall, then Francis, hitting him again and again.

"Beating me to a pulp can't change reality," Francis said, struggling to hold on to consciousness.

The angel dropped his hands to his sides and weapons from Heaven's armory took shape.

Francis blinked blood from his eyes as he tried to focus on them.

"Are those sais?" he asked, recognizing the Japanese martial arts weaponry. He had a fascination with ancient armaments, and kung fu films.

"Why yes they are," Dardariel said, just before jabbing one of the fiery metal batons into the former Guardian's chest.

For the briefest instant, Francis felt the fires of Heaven inside his accursed body.

But that was more than enough.

He wondered where all the noise was coming from before realizing that it was his own screams of agony.

"Now, tell me again how you had nothing to do with Aszrus' death. . . . I dare you."

It took a moment for Francis to compose himself, the feeling of God's divine fire still worming its way through every aspect of his being.

"You might as well take those pig stickers and shove them in my eyes. My answer isn't going to change," Francis snarled. "Your beloved general was already dead when I arrived on the scene."

Dardariel surged forward again, one of the flaming sais jabbing toward Francis' chest.

Anticipation made Francis scream.

The point of the sai stopped a mere hair from his chest. Francis looked down at the hovering point, and then up into Dardariel's unwavering gaze.

"And why would someone the likes of you arrive on the scene?"

Francis swallowed hard, feeling the heat from the weapon tickling the center of his chest.

"My employer heard a rumor," he explained. "Asked me to look into some things."

"Your employer," Dardariel said as if his mouth was filled with poison.

Francis said nothing, knowing that any answer he gave would likely result in pain.

"So somebody else was assigned the deed, and you were sent to make sure that the job was done."

Francis closed his eyes and sighed heavily. "Listen to me," he said. "I didn't have anything to do with killing your general. My employer knew how this murder would be perceived, and wanted to be certain that the right individuals got the blame."

Dardariel raised the sai's point to Francis' eye.

"Not to point fingers," Francis said quickly. "But one particular side has quite the itchy trigger finger and is just looking for an excuse to fire the starter's gun."

For a moment it was like all the air had been sucked from the room. Francis felt it, and from the look on Dardariel's face, the angel felt it as well.

"Are you implying that one of us wants a war, Fraciel?" asked a voice from somewhere in the darkness of the dungeon.

Dardariel turned, the sais disappearing in a flash of golden flame.

A powerful figure emerged into the light cast by the burning brazier.

It had been a long time since Francis had laid eyes on the Archangel.

"Hey, Mike," he said flippantly. "Long time no see."

The Archangel Michael was dressed to the nines, looking as though he'd just stepped off the fashion runway, though Francis couldn't be sure that he'd ever seen a seven-foot-tall warrior of Heaven, with skin like white marble and hair the color of pure gold, walk the runway before.

"Nice suit."

The Archangel stopped beside the brazier, his gold-flecked eyes glistening in the dance of the flames there.

"Even after all you've endured, you still have not learned to respect your superiors," Michael softly spoke. His voice was like a fine violin—a Stradivarius—expertly tuned. He reached into the brazier, careful not to catch his sleeve afire, and removed one of the blazing coals.

"The Lord God gave you a very special gift, Fraciel, and this is how you repay Him?"

Francis tensed, pulling on his chains. *Let me tell you about the Lord God's special gift,* he wanted to spit, but thought better of it.

God did not send him to the prison of Tartarus with the other traitors, but he'd been given over to the angelic host, the Thrones, to serve as their assassin—removing those they deemed a threat to the edicts of Heaven. It was a less than pleasant position, but one that he'd endured for millennia in pursuit of God's forgiveness.

Francis was still waiting.

"Just being polite," Francis said, holding back the bile that threatened to spill from his lips.

Michael moved without being seen, suddenly close enough to shove the burning coal against the prisoner's chest and hold it there.

Francis ground his teeth together and tossed his head back against this latest assault upon his senses; the sound of his flesh cooking, the sickly sweet smell of roasting meat, the feel of the coal—kept insanely hot by contact with the Archangel—as it tried to melt its way through his chest to his heart.

"We know that you are serving him again," Michael said. "And to say that the Almighty is disappointed—"

"Never . . . wanted to . . . disappoint," Francis managed, the pain threatening to take him someplace dark, and cool, and away from the perpetual agony. "Only trying . . . trying to keep the peace."

Much to his surprise, and relief, Michael took away the coal.

"Tell me, Fraciel," he said. "Is the act of murder how your master attempts to keep the peace?" The burning coal fell from the Archangel's hand to smolder upon the wet, stone floor.

Francis' head slumped to his chest. His breath came in pants, but he kept his eyes fixed upon the white-hot stone that gradually cooled on the ground in front of him. He imagined the coal as his pain, slowly—ever so slowly—being dialed back.

"As I told your handsome partner . . . ," Francis began, shifting his eyes briefly from the coal to Dardariel, who had stepped obediently aside when the big guns had shown up. He saw the angel tense, clearly wanting another crack at him.

*Shit, who wouldn't?*

"I had nothing to do with the general's untimely demise," Francis finished.

The Archangel strolled back to the brazier, helping himself to another of the burning coals. "Then, pray tell," he said, casually tossing the white-hot object up into the air and catching it, as somebody would with a pebble found on the beach. "How did his body come to be found in your dwelling?"

Francis tried to assemble the facts inside his head into some discernible order before speaking.

"My companions and I . . ." He suddenly remembered Montagin and Heath and wondered if they were being treated as well as he was. "How are my companions by the way?"

"Quite well," Michael answered. He was holding the coal between thumb and forefinger, blowing on it to make it glow all the hotter. "I just checked on them myself."

Francis didn't like the sound of that, but there was nothing he could do.

"We didn't want the general's body to be found," he explained. "So we brought it to my place for safekeeping."

"Safekeeping?" Michael repeated. He continued to toss the coal, and it appeared to be getting hotter each time it landed on the Archangel's palm.

"Somebody murdered General Aszrus. There isn't any doubt about that. But who actually did it, is where it gets tricky."

Michael listened, the coal going up, and then down.

"The situation between Heaven and . . . my employer is nothing short of volatile, and now that the general's death has been revealed, we're dancing on the cusp of what my companions and I feared would happen."

Dardariel must have been feeling brave, because he interrupted the grown-ups talking.

"He lies," the angel proclaimed. "This one was untruthful to the Lord God Himself; do you seriously believe that—"

Michael flicked the coal away, striking Dardariel in the forehead.

"Silence," the Archangel commanded.

Dardariel scowled, but he did as he was told.

"Your companions," Michael said to Francis. "The angel Montagin, the human sorcerer, Heath . . . Am I forgetting anyone?"

"There was a hobgoblin, but he had some things to do and couldn't stick around for all the fun."

"Anyone else?" Michael prompted.

Francis smiled, realizing what the Archangel was getting at.

"Yeah, Remy's involved in this," he said, watching as Michael's expression changed from bored to interested.

The Archangel stepped closer to Francis, his mere presence making him feel as though he was being crushed against the stone wall.

"What part does he play?"

Francis tried to suppress his smile, but he couldn't. He looked up into Michael's eyes. "The most important part of all: He's trying to keep it all from turning to shit."

Remy took point, moving down the corridor as quickly and as carefully as he could, Malatesta at his heels. His first instinct was to get the hell out of Dodge, but to come this far, with still so much unanswered, he decided that he was going to go for broke.

Besides, there was far too much at stake to stop now. For the briefest of moments, he imagined what the world would be like as Heaven went to war with Hell. It was all a little overwhelming.

He turned to make sure that the Vatican magick user was keeping up. "You with me?"

"Unfortunately," Malatesta said, leaning against a plaster wall.

They were in a lower part of the charnel house. It wasn't very fancy, and Remy guessed that this was some place the customers seldom saw.

He suddenly tensed as he heard the sound of multiple voices coming from somewhere farther down the corridor. He motioned for Malatesta to follow him and cautiously moved forward.

The voices were female, and they were coming from behind a heavy wooden door to their left. Remy stepped closer to the door, and listened. One of the voices was definitely the woman who had questioned him about Aszrus' photo.

The woman who still had answers that Remy wanted to hear.

"We're going in," Remy told Malatesta.

The magick user looked as though he was about to protest, but Remy was already turning the knob, and quickly darted inside.

The women stopped talking immediately, all five of them looking toward the door as Remy and Malatesta stepped in, closing the door behind them.

Remy recognized Natalia, who had gone off with Malatesta, Morgan, and the older woman.

"What the fuck are you doing here?" Morgan asked, a look of shock on her beautiful face.

"I'll call security," one of the others said, heading for an old-fashioned phone on the wall.

A blast of magickal energy struck the woman in the side, hurling her backward into the wall, where she dropped to the floor unconscious.

Remy turned to Malatesta, seeing his hand crackling with the residue of the spell he'd cast.

"No security," the magick user said, and Remy had to consider if it was the Larva or the man who was with them now.

"We don't want any trouble," Remy said, as much to Malatesta as the women. "We just need some answers."

"I'll give you answers," Natalia said, holding up her hand as the bright red fingernails began to grow longer.

"Knock it off, Nat," the older woman said.

Remy noticed then that older woman was still holding the baby photo in her hand.

"But, Bobbie . . . ," Natalia started to protest, before a cold look from the woman silenced her.

"I think this one might have some answers to our own questions," Bobbie said, shaking the photo.

Morgan snatched the picture from the woman and advanced on Remy.

Malatesta looked as though he might be getting ready to let loose again, when Remy turned to him.

"It's all right."

"Where did you get this?" Morgan demanded. Her eyes were shiny and wet, most likely from crying.

"I'm sure Bobbie already told you," Remy said.

"You tell me," she demanded.

"I found it in Aszrus' place. Hidden . . . as if he didn't want anybody to see it."

Morgan was staring at the image again.

"It means something to you." Remy stated the obvious.

Her moist eyes locked on his. "Yeah, you might say that."

"That's a picture of her child," Bobbie announced. "She'd know it anywhere. . . . I'd know it anywhere. . . ."

"I was told my baby died at birth," Morgan said, not taking her eyes from the photo. "Does this look like a dead baby to you?"

Remy shook his head. "No, it does not."

It was Natalia's turn now. "What's it mean?" she asked, her nails having receded back to their normal length. "We've all been knocked up by angels, given birth to corpse babies. . . .

"If this one is alive," Natalia said, reaching for the picture held by Morgan, "could my baby be alive, too?"

Morgan let Natalia have the photograph for a moment, but then quickly took it back.

"Do you know, angel?" Bobbie asked.

"All I know is that Aszrus is dead . . . murdered," Remy told them. "And I think whoever was responsible is somehow connected to this."

"Prosper said that he was fine after that business the other night," Bobbie said. "Which is why I wasn't surprised to hear that he'd shown up tonight."

"Prosper seemed pretty upset that we were here poking around," Remy said. "I don't know about you, but I think somebody might have a guilty conscience."

One of the other girls who'd been silent until then spoke up.

"He told me that my baby was dead," she said, holding back tears.

"Prosper?" Remy asked.

She nodded. "He held my hand, talking all sweet to me," she said, sounding as if she were there again. "He said that she was just like all the others, born dead—just too damn different to live."

They all seemed to be listening to the woman, as if they could feel her pain as well.

"What if he was lying?" she asked, her voice barely audible.

"I think we need to find out," Malatesta said, leaning against the door.

"Yeah," Remy agreed, looking at the women.

"So, who wants to take us to Prosper's office?"

The demon sat alone, at the far back of Methuselah's tavern indulging in its fourth libation of fermented basilisk blood and grain alcohol.

He exuded a cloud of menace, only the bravest of waitresses coming over sporadically to see if he wanted another of the foul drinks. Normally he would have had something to eat as well, but when he thought of his stomach, and what he could fill it with, it just made him remember how he had ended up this way.

The memory of how he'd lost face with his clan.

The incident had happened there, at Methuselah's. The day had been no different from multiple others, the demon locating a passage to the tavern to slake his thirst and fill his hungry belly.

He hadn't even noticed the Seraphim or his beast, and why should he? They were no matter to him.

That was how his species had managed to survive as long as they had: sticking to the shadows, keeping to themselves, drawing little attention to their actions.

It was a practice that would serve them well when their kind was ready to emerge and reclaim what had been stolen from them.

He had ordered a libation and an appetizer—something he had grown to love called a blooming onion. He had been about to take his first bite of the delicious, fried onion treat, when the angel's beast had approached his table. It had looked upon him hungrily, its eyes demanding food.

The demon had no intention of sharing, and had ordered the beast go away. However, it appeared to have no intention of leaving, and had demanded that he share the blooming onion.

The demon brought his drink to his mouth, taking gulps of the thick fermented blood, as he continued to recall that troubling evening.

He had insisted the beast go away as peaceably as he was able, but the black-furred animal remained.

Eventually bringing its master to the table.

The Seraphim appeared, the light of the divine nearly blinding the demon. He'd had no quarrel with the angel, and had attempted to shy away, but the Seraphim would not have it, belittling the demon in front of the tavern's patrons, causing him to lose face.

News of the event had traveled like the most virulent of plagues, and those of his tribe were aware of what had occurred within hours.

His entire reputation was destroyed in a matter of days.

Because of what the Seraphim had done to him, he was deemed unworthy, ostracized. Tribal law dictated that he should kill the Seraphim and his beast, but he knew it was an impossible task, his own hunger for survival canceling out any desire to attack the divine creature of light.

But in not slaying the angel, he was shunned by his kind, as if dead.

The demon had some more of his drink, mulling over the decision that he had made.

It had taken all the wealth that he'd squirrelled away to hire the assassins. But the Bone Masters were well worth the price, for once they had completed their task, he would be resurrected.

Reborn in the eyes of his people.

The demon raised a pale hand to summon a waitress. He was suddenly feeling a bit hungrier at that moment, and decided to take a chance on a blooming onion.

Before the moment of optimism could pass.

# CHAPTER TWENTY

Just being in the presence of the angel had made Prosper's hands begin to shake.

The owner of Rapture took a bottle of Kentucky bourbon from the bottom drawer of his desk and poured himself a glass. He'd been around all kinds of angels before—for fuck's sake he was one himself—but he hadn't been affected like this by any other.

Images sparked inside his brain, flashes of events that he hadn't thought about—*hadn't remembered*—in centuries. He didn't like this, didn't like it at all, and for making him suffer, he decided to make Remiel and his little friend suffer as well.

The thought of the indignities that would be heaped upon the Seraphim in the bowels of Rapture made Prosper smile as he leaned back in the leather chair behind his desk. Some of his customers were real sick fucks.

The memory came unbidden, like a rock thrown through a piece of frosted glass to reveal the images behind it. He saw a scene of war, and all the horrors it entailed. He had been part of the battle, fighting just as much for his life as for the cause of the Morningstar.

He hadn't yet become Prosper; his name was Puriel, and as his compatriots had died around him, he'd wanted nothing more than to run and hide until the madness abated.

Prosper steeled himself against the flood of memories, trying to keep them back. He didn't want to remember what had been.

How it used to be before . . .

He was attempting to get away, the air thick with an oily black smoke that rose from the burning bodies of his comrades. Puriel had been wrong in siding with the Son of the Morning, and just wanted this to stop . . . wanted it to be the way it had been.

Blindly he had leapt into the air, his tattered yellow wings carrying him over the battlefield. Something hissed as it sliced through the air, cutting into one of his wings and sending him spiraling down to the corpse-littered ground.

He landed upon an angel named Celiel, who had once boasted that he would tell the Lord God Almighty how wrong He had been about humanity, and if He didn't like it, he would spit in His eye. Celiel was now quite dead, blackened flesh showing through the gash in his armor that stretched from his neck down through his shoulder.

Rolling from atop the corpse, Puriel realized that he could no longer fly—a large portion of one of his wings having been cut away. He struggled to stand, eyes searching the roiling black smoke for a sign of the one that had struck him from the sky.

He remembered with sorrow how he had stood there, waiting for the inevitable.

Prosper let out a short scream, the glass of bourbon slipping from his hand and falling to the floor. The picture inside his head was as clear as day: an armored warrior of Heaven emerging from the billowing smoke, a sword of fire held tightly with purpose.

How could he ever have forgotten that face? The face of the one who spared him his life allowing him to be imprisoned in Tartarus.

The face of the angel Remiel.

"Son of a bitch," Prosper growled, leaning over to pick up the glass that he'd dropped. His hand was still shaking, and it took more than one try to finally snatch up the tumbler and place it on the corner of his desk.

Prosper stood, breathing heavily through his nose, attempting to calm himself. It was no wonder that he'd reacted in such a way to the angel.

Grabbing the bottle of bourbon, he began to pour himself another finger's worth. *Maybe I'll pay the angel a visit myself,* he considered, downing the drink in one huge gulp. It would be something special for Remiel to remember *his* face this time.

The door into his office swung open then, and Prosper turned to see Bobbie coming in.

"Don't you fucking knock?" he asked, his rage suddenly inflamed. Then he saw that she wasn't alone, and once again the glass fell from his hand, this time shattering as it hit the floor.

The angel Remiel came into his study.

"I think you and I need to have a little chat," the angel said.

It took all that Prosper had at that moment not to drop to his knees and pray for his life.

Remy saw Prosper begin a desperate dive for the phone on the corner of his desk, and met him halfway, knocking him to the floor with a solid slap across the face.

"Lock the door," Remy said to Malatesta, who had entered behind him. "We don't want anyone interrupting our discussion."

The magick user stepped away from the door and lifted his hands, muttering beneath his breath as he sealed the door with a spell.

Prosper scrabbled across the floor away from Remy. "Do you have any idea who I am?" he asked. "The forces that I could call down upon your sorry ass?"

"I know, I know," Remy said, humoring him. "You're a very important person." He casually sat on the corner of the desk.

"We can do this one of two ways," he began. "You can answer all of my questions, truthfully, or you can fight me every inch of the way and I will take a certain amount of pleasure in breaking every bone in your body, starting with your hands."

Prosper was now standing, moving toward the leather chair behind the desk. "Oh how the mighty have fallen," he said with an idiot's grin.

"What are you talking about?" Remy asked, confused.

"Look at you," Prosper said. "The champion of Heaven, now nothing but a fucking thug. Guess it can happen to the best of us, too."

Remy wasn't sure exactly what he was getting at, but he got a sense that it had something to do with the old days.

He chose to ignore the comment, instead asking, "So, what's it going to be?"

"I'm not telling you anything," Prosper declared with a cocky smile, leaning back in the chair, as if daring Remy to do something.

At one time Remy would have thought his own reaction troublesome, that the often violent angelic nature that he worked so hard to contain was getting stronger, and perhaps even out of control.

But now he looked at it as something that happened when he needed it to.

His wings were out in an instant, launching him over the desk, where he landed atop Prosper, sending them and the chair upon which they struggled backward onto the floor. His hand was around the fallen angel's throat.

Prosper was trying to scream, but Remy squeezed tightly, refusing to let anything out except a frightened-sounding squeak.

"You want to be a badass, you do it when the world isn't on the verge of being burned to a cinder."

Remy allowed a small amount of the divine fire that was so eager to come out into his hand, burning Prosper's throat. Then he released his grip, and loomed above the choking fallen angel.

"Now are you ready to talk to me?" he asked.

Prosper looked as though he might continue to fight, but appeared to think better of it when he touched the reddened flesh around his throat.

"Good boy," Remy said. "Tell me everything you know about this." He pulled the wrinkled photo from his shirt pocket, and tossed it into Prosper's lap.

The fallen angel picked it up, staring at it. "Cute," he said with a smirk just begging to be swatted from his face. "Isn't that how you're supposed to react to human offspring?" He tossed the photo at Remy with a flick of his wrist. "I don't know shit about it."

Remy's wing suddenly lashed out to savagely smack Prosper's hand as he drew it back.

The fallen angel cried out, grasping his injured wrist.

"Fucking hell!"

"Oh, I'm sorry," Remy said, feigning compassion. "Reflex action toward douche bags. Didn't even know I was going to do it."

He smiled. "Tell me about the picture."

"I told you," Prosper began again.

Remy advanced, wings fanned out around him threateningly. "If I have to ask again . . ."

Prosper cradled his arm to his chest, eyeing Remy fearfully. Remy was pretty sure that the fallen angel's wrist had been broken. There was no better an incentive than broken bones.

Remy sensed movement, and turned to see Bobbie darting toward him. He was about to act, lashing out again with his wings, when she avoided him, heading toward Rapture's owner.

"I'll get him to talk," she said, and that was when Remy noticed the short-bladed knife in her hand.

She was at the fallen angel in an instant, pressing the knife to his throat just beneath his chin.

"Enough of your fucking games, Prosper," she said, her voice trembling, eyes filled with tears. "Tell us what happened to the babies or I will cut your throat."

Prosper yelped as she pushed upon the blade, a trickle of scarlet running down his neck to stain the collar of his dress shirt.

"You're fucking done here," he told her, snarling. "You're over."

"I pretty much figured that out as soon as I saw the picture," she said. "Tell me about the children."

"Not a hell'uva lot to tell," Prosper said with a loud swallow. "What had once been nothing more than an accidental by-product of business suddenly was going to make me some money."

"A by-product!" she screeched, pushing on the blade, forcing Prosper to lean back. "They were our babies—our children—and you told us they were dead."

"How else were you going to give them up?" he asked. "The fact that lots of them did die gave me the perfect excuse. The babies died in birth. It was sad, but nobody gave it another thought."

Prosper made his move then, ducking his head beneath the blade and grabbing Bobbie, twisting the knife from her grasp, and bringing it to her chest.

"Another fucking step, any of you, and I'll open her up," he warned.

"You're a fucking monster," Bobbie said, spitting in the fallen angel's face. Prosper flinched, but didn't release her.

"I'll remember that when this is over," he told her.

"Since you've already started talking," Remy said, "why don't you keep it up so we're all on the same page?"

"Guy came to me out of the blue and said that the kids might be worth something down the line, and I asked him to make me an offer," Prosper said. "I like a guy with vision, so I started turning the kids over. We kept them safe and sound."

Remy attempted to find the angle, and could think of only one thing.

"For what?" he asked. "Blackmail?"

Prosper laughed. "Y'know, the blackmail angle was the first thing I thought of, too. But it turned out to be just the tip of the fucking iceberg."

Remy cocked his head inquisitively.

"This guy had a plan all right," Prosper continued. "Got to the point where I just did as I was told, and collected the money."

"Sounds like things were pretty good," Remy said.

"Yeah," Prosper agreed. "They were."

"Until Aszrus got murdered," Remy said. "Bet that threw a monkey wrench in the works."

Prosper's face looked as though somebody had stuck a handful of shit beneath it.

"I fucking told them to watch the kids," he said, shaking his head. "They were getting weirder."

His eyes focused specifically on Remy. "You're kind of the expert on living here," he said. "It's got something to do with being teenagers, right? Puberty, is it?"

Remy gave him nothing.

"Aszrus was coming around to Rapture more often, wanting to see them," Prosper continued. "I think the general was actually getting attached."

"One of the children did this," Remy stated. "One of these offspring killed a general in Heaven's army."

It was Prosper's turn not to answer.

"Doesn't that make you the littlest bit nervous?"

There came the sound of the doorknob rattling, and then a pounding on the door.

"Boss? It's me!" called a rumbling voice. "We just found Luke and Tony. The prisoners are—"

"They're in here!" Prosper screamed, and things went from zero to crazy in a matter of seconds.

Malatesta's magick did very little to hold back the zombies pounding on the other side of the door, and the flimsy wood shattered as the walking dead fought their way inside.

Remy heard the short scream, and looked away from the monstrous dead men to see Bobbie dropping to the floor, an expression of horror on her face as blood streamed from between her fingers, which she clutched to her stomach.

Prosper was already on the move, running to the back of the office. Thinking he had nowhere to go, Remy caught Bobbie as she fell.

"The children," she said softly. It looked as though she was having a hard time breathing. "You've got to do something. . . ."

Remy hadn't a clue what to do. He lowered her gently to the floor, and decided that handing out a vicious beating to Prosper would be a good start.

But the fallen angel was gone.

Remy stood, eyes darting around the back of the room searching for any sign of the charnel house owner, but he was nowhere to be found.

"Remy!" came a cry from behind him, and he turned to see that the zombies were fully inside the room now, and Malatesta was on the verge of being overwhelmed.

"I could use some help!"

The magick user's spells were driving the dead men back, but they quickly recovered, surging at Malatesta again.

From the looks of it, Malatesta wasn't going to last much longer, and besides, Remy had some serious frustration issues at the moment, and could certainly use an opportunity to blow off some steam.

He looked around the room for something that he could use, and saw that Prosper had dropped Bobbie's knife as he fled. Remy darted toward the blood-stained blade, calling forth his wings and the power of the Seraphim that waited patiently, knowing that in Remy's line of work these situations often had a tendency to arise.

Knife in hand, Remy took to the air, flying across the room. As he traveled, he willed the fire of Heaven down his arm and into the short, metal blade, transforming it from merely a knife, to a weapon of Heaven.

A short-bladed weapon of Heaven, but a weapon of Heaven nonetheless.

The zombies didn't know what hit them.

Malatesta had been driven back, and lay atop Prosper's desk, a shield of magick protecting him from the dead men's fists that were attempting to pound him into pulp.

Remy landed among them, distracting them from the magick user. He wasted no time lashing out at the first of the animated corpses, the enhanced knife blade passing through the putrid flesh and bone of a zombie's neck, severing the head from its body.

In one smooth move, Remy kicked that still thrashing body away, and acted upon the next of the undead attackers.

The burning knife-blade crackled as it cut through the air, before reaching its next target. The blade sliced down vertically through the chest, to the belly, allowing the no-longer-functioning internal workings to spill out onto the zombie's feet and floor.

The look upon the dead man's face seemed almost comical, as if he were embarrassed to have his innards exposed to the world.

Remy took away his embarrassment as he drove the burning knife into a waiting eye socket, igniting his head in glorious yellow flame. He looked like a jack-o'-lantern. The zombie's hands immediately went to his burning face, his feet going out from underneath him as he slipped on his own intestines, which were coiled upon the floor.

A rock-hard fist struck with powerful force at the back of Remy's head, knocking him down. The zombie wasn't going to wait until Remy recovered, delivering a solid kick to Remy's midsection and sending him hurtling across the room.

Using his wings, he sprang from where he'd fallen, shaking off the ringing in his ears, replacing it with his own scream of anger as he flung himself at the zombie that now charged at him. Remy smiled as he saw what the zombie was holding: a rusty machete, raised menacingly above his head.

A machete would be much more efficient than a small knife, Remy thought as he collided with the zombie's rock-solid midsection, the two of them now headed into the wall.

The plaster caved inward with the impact as the zombie, unfazed by the act, attempted to bury the machete blade in Remy's head. The short sword came down, but Remy captured the animated corpse's wrist, stopping its descent.

Remy smiled as he willed the fire inside him to climb, soon engulfing the zombie's hand as it traveled to the machete.

The zombie watched in awe as its appendage crumbled to ash, and Remy found himself with a new, divinely enhanced weapon.

"Nice," Remy said, admiring the flaming blade just before swinging it across, and cutting the zombie's head from its body with little resistance.

"And sharp, too."

There were more zombies spilling in from the hole broken in the office door, and Remy found himself tiring of the pointless battle. There were still important matters involving the safety of the world to be considered. He allowed himself to grow hotter, the divine fire radiating from his body. It was as if the zombies were drawn to it. The walking dead men charged at him with weapons of all kinds, one of them even spraying the office with an assault rifle in an attempt to take him down.

*Good luck with that,* Remy thought, throwing his burning body amidst them as the machete cut them down to little more than writhing torsos and severed limbs upon the office floor.

"I'm getting tired of this," Remy announced to Malatesta behind him.

"Any suggestions?" the magick user asked, casting a spell that pushed several zombies away with a deafening clap of displaced air.

Remy waded among the dead men, allowing himself to be surrounded. "Erect a bubble of magick around me and my playmates," he ordered.

Malatesta looked at him, hesitating.

"Just do it," Remy urged.

And the sorcerer did, weaving a spell of crackling white energy that encased the Seraphim and the zombies that threatened to bring him down in a sphere of magick.

Remy caught the magick user's eye and gave him a little nod, before he allowed his body to go completely nova.

It felt good to allow his body to shine as it once had in the presence of the Holy Father—an angel showed its true respect for the Almighty being that had created it by willing its body to glow like one of the stars in the sky.

Then he called the fire back, taking it within his body, allowing his flesh to cool and the human visage that he wore to heal. Since reconciling with his angelic nature, the regeneration process of his human skin and attire was much quicker, and certainly far less painful.

Remy was kneeling amidst piles of ash—all that remained of the animated dead men that had been trying to kill him. He looked toward Malatesta and nodded again, and the Vatican sorcerer opened the bubble of magick with a wave of his hands.

"It was getting stuffy in there," Remy said offhandedly, returning to a more human guise.

He walked past the open door, giving it a sideways glance. "Think you could maybe shut that for a bit longer?" he asked Malatesta.

Again the magick user did what was asked of him, using a spell of reassembly to make the door whole.

"What are we doing?" Malatesta asked. "Don't you think it would be wise to get out of here?"

Remy passed Bobbie as he strode to the back of the room where Prosper had disappeared. She was most certainly dead, and he made a silent promise to her that Prosper would be held accountable.

"He just disappeared," Remy said as the magick user joined him. "One minute he was here, and the next . . . gone." He searched for a sign of a secret door or passage that would have allowed the club owner to escape. "I can't see anything," he said, his frustration mounting.

Malatesta was running his hands along the wall as well, his eyes tightly closed. "It isn't supposed to be seen," he explained.

Remy looked over to him.

"What do you mean?"

"I'm sensing the use of magick here," Malatesta said. "Powerful stuff."

"What kind of magick?" Remy wanted to know, feeling himself growing excited.

"A spell of passage," Malatesta replied.

He opened his eyes and looked to Remy. The magick user still looked sick, and Remy couldn't help but feel a pang of guilt.

He quickly brushed it aside; there would be time for that when the threat of war wasn't breathing down their necks.

"Can you find the opening?" Remy asked.

Malatesta sighed, closing his eyes again. "I get a sense, but I don't have a key."

"Pick the lock," Remy suggested.

Malatesta looked at him.

"Pick the lock?"

"Yeah, if you call yourself a powerful sorcerer, pick the lock."

The man seemed flustered, stepping away from the wall.

"You don't understand what I've just been through," he said. "It's taking everything I have to keep it together . . . to keep what's inside me from—"

"Which won't matter at all if Heaven and Hell turn the planet into a battleground," Remy finished.

Malatesta glared at him for a few moments as Remy's words appeared to sink in.

"I'm not saying I can do this," he finally said.

"Sure you can," Remy urged. "I've got faith in you."

The magick user extended his arms, fingers splayed. He closed his eyes, and Remy watched as his expression turned to one of exertion and strain.

"Anything?" he asked, impatiently.

"Shut up," Malatesta commanded.

Remy continued to watch as a sheen of sweat broke out on the man's brow and upper lip.

"I'm not sure how much longer . . . ," Malatesta said, his voice shaking with exertion.

Remy could hear scuffling from the hall outside the office and doubted that they had much time before the next assault wave started.

"I don't know if you can hear that but . . ."

"Shut up!" Malatesta cried again, his hands moving in the air as if he were untying some huge, invisible knot.

The man suddenly went rigid, air exploding from his lungs as if punched.

"Constantin?" Remy questioned.

Malatesta was standing perfectly straight now, head bowed, hands by his sides.

"You all right?"

"I'm perfectly fine," said a voice that Remy recognized as belonging to the spirit entity. "Let's see what I can do."

Remy wasn't sure exactly how to react, and found himself simply watching as the possessed man again worked his hands in the air, sparks of magickal energy leaving glowing trails as they moved with incredible speed.

And then he stopped, taking a step backward with an enormous grin on his face.

There was pounding now on the office door behind them.

Remy glanced at it, then returned his attention to the possessed Malatesta. "Well?" he asked the evil spirit, again in control of its host.

"What do you think?" the Larva asked, still grinning.

The air before them was shimmering ever so slightly; images of another place were briefly visible on the other side.

The dark entity extended his hand, gesturing for Remy to pass through.

"You first," he said, grabbing Malatesta by the shoulders, pushing him into the passage.

Malatesta was gone from the office, and from what Remy could see, had made it to the other side without any mishaps.

The pounding on the door was growing more insistent, and cracks began to appear in the wood. It wouldn't be long now.

He took a deep breath, steeling himself, and then dove into the magickal passage toward the unknown, as the door crumbled behind him.

The demon Beleeze was worried.

Something was happening on the island. If he'd been braver he would have approached his master Simeon and told him that they should just find a safe place.

If he were braver.

The normally horrible weather on the Pacific island was suddenly worse, crackling bolts of a strange energy reaching up from somewhere within the ruins of the mining city to entice the storm's fury. The clouds grew darker, heavier, dropping closer to the rooftops, as the rain continued to fall in drenching sheets.

Beleeze watched his master standing at the end of the street, gazing up curiously at the odd atmospheric conditions.

He sensed a presence move closer and glanced over to see that Dorian had come to join him. He was tempted to place his arm around her shoulder in comfort, but he restrained himself. That was not behavior befitting a demon of his stature.

"What is he doing?" Dorian asked very quietly.

Beleeze was surprised that she had even uttered the words, but could certainly relate to her curiosity.

"It is not my place to ask," he answered, just as quietly.

Robert, who had once been called Tjernobog, paced back and forth, muttering beneath his breath. It was obvious that he could sense it as well.

Something was happening.

There came a terrific boom of thunder, so loud that it caused what little glass remained in a nearby building to shatter, falling to the street with the rain.

Beleeze advanced partway down the street, in case his master needed him, but Simeon appeared safe—for now.

The sky had become like night, the energy shooting up from the street beyond and striking the clouds, illuminating them eerily.

It was within that illumination that he saw them: human figures flying up into the storm, to be lost among the clouds.

"It's what I was afraid of," Simeon said, finally turning away from the view of the sky to look at Beleeze. "The murder of one's sire. It must have been a catalyst of sorts."

Simeon strode past the demon, his hands clasped behind his back.

"Now change is upon them."

Beleeze followed, as Simeon continued to speak.

"And they are becoming so much more than anyone could have ever dreamed."

Beleeze practically crashed into his master's back as Simeon came to an abrupt stop.

"A threat to one and all," he said.

And as if in response to his master's words, the sky shook, and just barely audible over the roar of thunder, Beleeze thought he heard the sound of laughter.

"A danger to both Heaven, and Hell," his master said.

Of that, the demon Beleeze had no doubt.

# CHAPTER TWENTY-ONE

Prosper stumbled from the passage into the freezing rainstorm.

He hated this fucking island more than anything, but it had been Simeon's choice, and who was he to argue with the mysterious figure.

A chill, surprisingly not caused by the rain dripping down the length of his spine, caused him to shudder.

First, it had been losing track of one of the kids and the chaos that followed. Now, it was the angel Remiel flipping over rocks and getting too close to their business. Prosper could already hear Simeon's words: *Why didn't you just kill them?*

It was a good question—one that he really didn't have the answer to at the moment. He was too fucking busy trying to keep himself alive.

Thunder boomed so loudly above him that he found himself recoiling from the intensity of the burst. "What the fuck?"

Prosper began to run, the rain falling so hard that it obscured most everything around him. It took him a moment to realize that there weren't any of the usual security teams present to meet him.

That just made him all the more angry.

The rain was falling harder now—if that was even possible—and Prosper stopped momentarily in the deluge to get his bearings. He placed a hand to his forehead, shielding his eyes from the severity of the storm. He couldn't remember ever feeling more miserable.

Something moved ahead of him, dark shapes behind a curtain of rain.

"You there!" Prosper called over the hissing downpour.

There was no response, and the fallen angel's ire rose to an unbridled level as he trudged ahead, hand still shielding his eyes from the heavy rain.

The sky was suddenly filled with a flash of unearthly light. At first he believed it to be lightning from the storm—what else could it be? But something didn't feel quite right.

Prosper stopped, scanning the tumultuous sky, seeing only fat, billowing storm clouds, like smoke. He waited, curious to see if the strange phenomenon would repeat itself.

Again it happened, the sky lighting up as a snaking tendril of raw, luminescent energy shot up from somewhere ahead of him, to illuminate the sky. Prosper was drawn to the source of the flash, but not before there came another explosion of thunder. The sky grew bright, as if lit up by multiple klieg lights, and for the briefest of moments, before his eyes were seared, he saw . . .

Prosper froze, averting his gaze, rubbing at his stinging eyes. To be sure of what he thought he saw, he again turned his vision skyward.

A figure floated in the air, gazing down at him. He recognized her; she was one of the children. Her name was Mavis.

"What—what are you doing?" he stammered, realizing how foolish the question sounded as it left his mouth.

The girl drifted closer, as if carried by invisible wings on the rain-swept winds.

He heard her laugh then. "Poor Prosper," she taunted. "Not even enough sense to come in out of the rain."

Before he had a chance to react, she flew at him like a bullet, snatched him up from the ground, and carried him into the sky—up into the storm.

Prosper saw that they were not alone.

And once again, he knew the power of fear.

\*     \*     \*

Francis had some difficulty opening his eyes.

He'd thought that he would avoid more beatings by mentioning Remy Chandler to Michael, but instead, the Archangel had simply left the dungeon, leaving him alone with Dardariel.

The cold stone floor actually felt good against his swollen face, but he decided to forgo the pleasure to assess his current situation.

He managed to push himself up along the stone wall into a sitting position. Through swollen, blood-encrusted eyes Francis saw that he wasn't alone.

"Well, look at that," Montagin said. "You're alive—your middle name must be Lazarus."

"You wouldn't have a couple of Advil on you, would you?" Francis asked, exhausted from the effort of righting himself.

He heard Montagin make a sound of disgust, not even bothering with a reply.

He caught sight of a larger shape huddled in the corner beside the angel, and guessed it was Heath. The sorcerer wasn't making any noise.

"How are you holding up there, Angus?" Francis asked.

Angus grunted, which at least told Francis that the magick user was still alive. Then Heath shifted his weight so the faint illumination from the lone skylight in the ceiling shone on his face.

Francis actually gasped at what he saw.

Heath's face was bloody and swollen, his lips sewn together with thick black thread.

To prevent him from uttering any spells, Francis gathered.

Heath's bloodshot gaze bore into his.

"That certainly doesn't look pleasant," Francis said.

Heath grunted, and leaned his bulk back against the wall.

Francis moved his arms, feeling the weight there, and hearing the rattle of chains. He looked down to see the golden manacles, etched with angelic sigils.

"Shit," he grumbled. "Anybody got a paper clip?"

"Could you really pick those locks if you had a paper clip?" Montagin asked.

"Probably not," Francis admitted. "But I've seen it done in movies lots of times. How hard could it be?"

"Idiot," Montagin grumbled.

"At least I had an idea," Francis retorted. "What have you got?"

"What does it matter?" the angel answered. "We're all as good as dead."

"That's the one thing I like about you," Francis said. "Your upbeat attitude."

It sounded as if Heath tried to laugh, but it turned to a moan.

"Sorry, Angus," Francis said.

Montagin continued to be a ray of sunshine. "I should never have gone to Chandler," he complained. "I should have gone right to Michael and shown him what had happened."

"And what good would have come of that?" Francis asked.

"I wouldn't have been tortured and thrown into a filthy jail cell with the likes of you two. I wouldn't be awaiting my inevitable demise for withholding information from the legions of Heaven."

"No, you'd be watching the earth being turned into a battleground, with humanity caught right in the fucking middle."

"That will happen anyway," Montagin said. "Right now we're only delaying the inevitable, and have signed our death warrants in addition."

Francis tried to get comfortable on the damp, stone floor, but no matter how he maneuvered, his body ached. "We did exactly what we were supposed to do."

"What, die?" Montagin demanded. "We were supposed to die? I don't remember volunteering to—"

"We needed to buy him time," Francis interrupted. "Let's just hope that Remy found what he needed to keep all the flaming swords in their sheaths."

They were silent for a bit, and Francis had begun to drift off when Montagin's voice called him back.

"Do you seriously believe it will matter?"

"What?" Francis asked. "What Chandler's doing? Yes . . . yes, I do."

Montagin chuckled. "You obviously haven't been around them—the soldiers and generals. They're just looking for an excuse. I'm surprised that Aszrus has actually managed to hold them off this long. He was as hawkish as any of them, but it was as if he was waiting for something, that one last thing that would say it's time."

Francis felt Montagin's gaze upon him.

"Maybe it was his own murder he was waiting for," Montagin continued, "and he just didn't know it."

"Or maybe it was the success of *Toddlers In Tiaras*," Francis suggested. The dungeon fell silent again, which was fine by him.

"I hate that show," Montagin said after a few minutes, and Francis could not help but laugh, which ended up being one of the most excruciating experiences that he'd endured in quite some time.

"Serves you right," Montagin added, which only made Francis laugh all the more.

The laughter eventually subsided, and then it was the wait for the pain to die down. The cell was silent, occasionally interrupted by the rattle of chains and moans of discomfort from Heath.

Francis was lost in pain-addled thought, wondering where they might go from there. They had no idea if Remy had been successful, and the former Guardian was sure that information wouldn't be shared by their captors. Angels could be real cocks when they wanted to be, and since they had them, why would they bother to let them go?

Especially since they had such a hard-on for his employer.

Francis thought about his current boss, and wondered if the Morningstar was fully aware of the situation. Lucifer knew that Azsrus was murdered, and that it could be used for political purposes, which was why he had put Francis on the case.

But Francis had to wonder how in the loop his boss actually was. He decided that it probably couldn't hurt to find out.

He shifted again, grunting in pain as his limbs made it known they didn't care to move in those specific directions.

"Can't you just die in your sleep or something?" Montagin asked. "I'm tired of hearing the two of you voicing your discomfort."

"I'm going to try something," Francis said, searching for a section of the cell where the darkness seemed almost liquid.

"What?" Montagin asked.

"I'm going to try to contact my boss," he said.

"You're what?" Montagin questioned. "Are you mad? Do you seriously believe that Lucifer Morningstar would intrude on a stronghold held by one of Heaven's legions?"

"You've forgotten how strong he is," Francis said, focusing on the darkness. "And if he can get us out of here, why the fuck not? Especially if we're all going to die anyway."

"I want nothing to do with this," Montagin said, and Francis could hear the angel trying to move as far away from him as possible, while Heath moaned about the the invasion of his space.

"Fine," Francis said. "I'll leave you here to rot, and Angus and I will take off. Right, Angus?"

Francis heard a noise that he took to be an affirmative answer.

He was concentrating on the darkness, reaching out with his mind to where he imagined the Morningstar would be. He had no idea if this would work, but he didn't see any other options.

"What are you doing?" Montagin demanded.

"I'm trying to contact him."

"Will that work?"

"We'll have to wait and see, won't we?"

"I wish you'd been beaten to death," the angel snapped.

"Sorry to disappoint you."

Francis suddenly felt the pull of the darkness on him. Concentrating all the harder, he attempted to follow the pool of shadow down to its source.

To a sea of bottomless black, and beyond that, to what he hoped would lead to his master's ear.

Something moved in the ebony pool, surging up from the inky gloom. His concentration momentarily broken, Francis sat back.

"Well?" Montagin questioned.

Francis wasn't sure how to respond.

"I don't know," he said, keeping his crusty eyes on the shadows.

The darkness undulated, as if something moved behind it.

"What have you done?" Montagin demanded. "If you've brought more ruin upon me, I will do everything in my power to—"

"Yeah, yeah, yeah," Francis said. "But before you get your panties in more of a bunch, why don't we make sure that I've actually done something, all right?"

The shadows grew denser, like oil, beginning to churn as whatever it was that was concealed beneath it moved closer.

Francis gazed quickly away from the moving patch to see Montagin staring, mesmerized, Heath leaning slowly forward, his eyes also drawn to the spot where something was about to appear.

He didn't know why he said it—he really didn't know why he said half the shit he did—but he just couldn't help himself.

"Thar she blows!" Francis cried as something pushed upon the veil of shadow, causing it to stretch outward as if made from rubber.

It actually made a kind of wet, ripping sound as the shape tore away from the liquid embrace, and landed upon the jail cell floor.

It took Francis a moment to realize that his call had not reached his intended, and that he had gotten the wrong number. "You're not Lucifer Morningstar," he said.

"No shit," Squire said, wiping oily drippings of concentrated darkness from his shirt and pants. "You haven't gotten any smarter in the month you've been gone."

"Month?" Francis exclaimed. "It's only been a day."

"Yes!" The hobgoblin pumped a fist in the air. "Thought I'd get here too late and find a big fucking crater or something."

"You've been looking for us for a month?"

Squire nodded. "Looks like it," he said, sitting down on the floor. He rubbed his stubby hand along the back of his neck. "The shadow paths can be pretty tricky, even for the experienced," the hobgoblin said. "Must've taken a wrong turn someplace."

"Tell me about it," Francis said. "How did you track us anyway?"

"Your blood," Squire said. "Fallen angel blood has a real distinct odor—can't miss it. Shot back to the apartment after you'd been taken, used an old sock to soak up some of your juice, and here I is."

"What's it smell like?"

"What? Your blood?" Squire asked. "You know those little sheets that you throw in the dryer to keep your clothes smelling fresh and the static cling away?"

"Yeah. It smells like that?"

"No," Squire said shaking his head. "Smells worse than shit, really."

Montagin cleared his throat.

"Hey, Mary! I didn't know you were here, too."

Heath leaned forward so Squire could see him.

"Angus . . ." The hobgoblin noticed what had been done to his sorcerer friend. "Holy shit, does that hurt?"

Heath tilted his head in a way that said, *What the fuck do you think?*

Squire reached into one of the pouches on his belt and withdrew a pair of scissors. He approached his friend carefully.

"Hold still," he said, and started to snip at the stitching that held the sorcerer's lips closed.

With each cut of the thread, Francis could not help but wince. Heath's lips had started to bleed again, blood running down from his face onto the T-shirt that he wore.

"How's that?" Squire asked as he cut the last of the threads.

"Better," Heath managed.

"So," Francis said, lifting the golden manacles that hung from his wrists. "You wouldn't happen to have a paper clip in that bag of tricks, would you?"

The rain was torrential. Remy unfurled his wings, extending them in such a way as to provide cover from the onslaught as he scanned his surroundings.

He saw that he was in a city of some kind, but from its dilapidated appearance, it had been abandoned for quite a long time. An electric chill passed down his spine, as he was reminded of a recent cable television program that tried to show what the world would be like after mankind had gone.

After humanity had died.

From what Remy could see, this was pretty damn close, and the bleak surroundings also reminded him that a fate even worse-looking than this could very well be waiting for the planet if he didn't get all the facts straight about a certain murdered angel general.

He took to the air, flying above the cracked and weed-covered streets, the vegetation pushing up defiantly through the asphalt. The air was rich with the smell of the ocean, and as he flew higher he saw that he was on an island in the middle of a choppy gray sea.

*Interesting*, he thought, gliding back down, still on the lookout for Malatesta and, if he was lucky, Prosper. Searching for something—a sign that would give him a clue as to where he was—he landed in front of what looked to be an administrative building. Sticking out from a clump of twisting vines beside the building, Remy found a rusted sign with what appeared to be Japanese characters on it. He brushed away some mud, and could just about make out the name: GUNKANJIMA.

"Gunkanjima," said a young voice over the pelting downpour. "Battleship Island."

Remy spun around, hiding his wings away.

"That's all right," the pale little girl in the tattered, pink Hello Kitty raincoat said. "I already know what you are—no sense in hiding it."

"Hi," Remy said, dropping the bent metal sign. "What is this place?"

She was wearing torn and faded blue jeans, and sneakers split at the sides, as if too small for her growing feet. "Used to be a coal-mining facility, but then it got turned into a prison during a big war . . . the second one . . . war number two."

"World War Two?" Remy helped her.

She nodded and he got a better look at her. The child couldn't have been any older than eight, but her skin was terribly pale and sickly looking.

"The Japanese kept Koreans here and forced them to work really, really hard," the little girl stated. She was poking around in the dirt with the toe of her sneaker. "A lot of people died here."

Remy moved a little closer.

"Do you live here?"

She stopped digging with her toe when she saw that he was getting closer. "Of course I do," she said, warily. "I live here with my brothers and sisters."

The little girl was Nephilim, of that he had no doubt. This was where they were kept, for what reason he had no idea.

But he was going to find out.

"I wouldn't come any closer if I was you," the child warned.

Remy stopped where he was. "I don't mean you any harm," he told her. "My name is Remy. . . . What's yours?"

"Kitty," she said, smiling simply. She pointed to the chubby white corporate symbol on her torn raincoat. "That's what they call me 'cause I always wear this coat."

"That's quite a coat, and a really nice name," Remy told her.

"Thanks," she said, kicking at the dirt in earnest.

"So you live here with your brothers and sisters?" Remy asked.

"Uh-huh," she answered. She squatted and began digging with her hands.

"Do you think that I might be able to meet them?"

Kitty stopped digging, turning her pale gaze toward him.

"I know what you're up to," she said.

Remy shook his head. "Not up to anything, Kitty."

"You're like that other angel," she said. "The one who was all nice and everything, but was really mean."

Remy could see that she was getting upset. He backed away a bit, hoping that if he kept his distance . . .

"Gareth said that you want to teach us to kill and stuff," she said suddenly. "To be an army . . . to fight a war . . . World War Three!"

"Is Gareth one of your brothers?" he asked, trying to calm her down.

"Yes, he's my oldest brother and he didn't want us to do any fighting for the angels so he ended up doing something really bad."

Remy knew what Gareth had done.

"He killed an angel, didn't he?" Remy said. "Gareth killed an angel called Aszrus."

She was picking at stuff in the dirt again, pulling things out, looking at them, and tossing them aside.

"Yes, he did," Kitty said. "And he got into really bad trouble . . . but that was before they knew he had powers."

Remy didn't quite understand. "Powers?" he asked. "What kind of powers?"

Kitty was still poking around in the mud. She shrugged her shoulders. "All kinds," she said. "We all got 'em now—well most of us. Some of the babies don't."

Remy felt that horrible feeling begin to form in his stomach, the horrible feeling that told him things were much worse than he thought.

"Do you have powers?" he asked, realizing as the words left his mouth that it might not have been the question to ask right then.

Kitty was looking at him again, and smiling.

"Uh-huh," she said. "Do you want to know how I know so much about this island?" she asked.

Remy didn't respond.

"All those people who died here a long time ago?" she asked. "They told me."

She poked at the things she'd been pulling from the mud and dirt.

"Here are some of their bones. If their bones are here, they're here, too."

Remy watched as a thick mist seemed to erupt from the muddy bones, growing in size to form a grayish cloud that transformed into multiple ghostly shapes with eerily burning yellow eyes.

"Guess what my power is?" Kitty asked, and then she started to giggle.

It didn't take a rocket scientist to know that something bad was about to happen.

"Kitty, you don't have to do this," Remy tried to persuade her. "I don't mean you, or your brothers and sisters any—"

"I control the ghosts!" she proclaimed. "And I can get them to do whatever I want."

"Kitty," he tried again, calling forth his wings because it might be necessary.

"Get 'im!" the child ordered.

The ghosts glided through the air, their mouths open in a disconcerting psychic scream that Remy could hear—*feel*—inside his head. He tried to evade them, flying up into the rain-filled sky, but the spirits clung to him, swarming around his body, filling him with the weight of their sorrow.

As hard as he tried to shake them, the ghosts held on, filling his thoughts with the pain and misery they had suffered there as prisoners of the Japanese. Remy was having a difficult time concentrating. He crashed into the side of a nearby building, breaking one of the few panes of glass that had managed to remain intact.

The ghosts wanted him to know them—their loves, their hates, what they so desperately missed. He knew it would be impossible to escape them, so he landed, dropping to his knees on the muddy ground. He wrapped himself in his wings and rocked to the psychic onslaught, experiencing each and every thing they wanted to him to know.

Remy could feel the heat of life slipping away from him, the spirits eagerly taking anything they could use to manifest themselves more strongly in the living world. He felt cold, and colder still as the ghosts of Gunkanjima grew more powerful.

It was time to make his move. Calling upon the divine power that resided within him, Remy communicated with the disembodied dead, telling them that it was time to move on.

The ghosts fought him at first, having been tormented for so long, bound to the island. But Remy showed them the light, and what it would mean if they let go.

And as he'd hoped, the spirits calmed, soothed by his message of eternal rest. Their torture would end. They would at last know peace, their ghostly energies finally able to travel on to join the stuff of the cosmos.

The stuff of creation.

"What's he doing to my ghosts?" Remy heard Kitty cry from somewhere far away. Before he could react, he was struck by a bolt of energy that picked him up from the ground and tossed him against the side of a building.

The ghosts were in a panic once more.

Remy crawled to his knees, raising his head, certain that he wasn't going to like what he was about to see.

And he was right.

Kitty had been joined by some of her brothers and sisters.

They were of various ages, some a little younger than Kitty, while others looked as though they were in their teens. The angels at Rapture had been busy.

"I don't . . . ," Remy started again, wanting them to know that he wasn't there to hurt them. But his words fell upon deaf ears.

One of the young teens approached him, a smile on his dirty, pimply face. His hands were outstretched, and from the tips of his fingers flowed streams of some kind of bioenergy. It was like being touched with a power cable, and Remy's body immediately convulsed.

The ghosts were back as well, their number growing by the second, and Remy's mind became so crowded with horror and misery that he could barely put his own thoughts together enough to stand.

"Please," he begged. He had no desire to hurt them, but if they kept this going . . .

The wind kicked up, and Remy felt as though he'd been clutched by a giant, elemental hand. He was picked up, his wings flapping uselessly, and tossed back to the ground by the invisible hand of some angry, and powerful godlike being—a godlike being controlled by a fourteen-year-old child in a torn Sex Pistols T-shirt, jeans, and scuffed-up cowboy boots.

Remy was about to plead with them again, but their eager faces told him they were having way too much fun. Instead, he decided he should consider getting the hell out of there before the sadistic brood ended his life for good.

The invisible hand had him again, this time by the legs, and whipped him savagely against the ground. He could hear the children's excited cheers as he was tossed aside like a rag doll, rolling to a stop in the center of a street now lush with vegetation. He lay there, playing dead, gathering his wits. No matter how badly his warrior nature railed inside him, he would not hurt children, no matter how bloodthirsty they appeared.

They were approaching him. He could hear their feet scuffing across the ground over the wailing of the dead still inside his mind. This was it.

Remy sank his fingers deep into the muddy ground, and willed the fire that churned inside of him forward. It exited his fingertips in an excited rush, pouring into the ground and causing the vegetation and anything else lying within it to explode in bright yellow flames.

The children began to scream, and Remy took to the sky, beating the rain-filled air unmercifully as he flew away from the angry tribe, maneuvering between the abandoned buildings as he sought a place to set down, to rest and gather his thoughts.

He hadn't been paying attention to the airspace in front of him until it was too late.

The teenage girl hung in the air as if floating in water, her hands held out on either side of her churning with some bizarre mutation of divine fire. As he grew closer, he saw her mouth twist in a grimace of exertion, and as he dropped from the sky in an attempt to escape, she tossed the flaming orbs of hissing fire where he'd just been.

Evading the fireballs, Remy twisted in the air above another street that had succumbed to the elements, and saw another gathering of children.

Almost as if they'd been waiting for him.

The wind picked up suddenly, savagely, and it took all that he had to stay aloft. A wall of air pushed down upon him, and Remy found himself striking the side of another building, his wings beating as hard as they could to keep him airborne as the screaming winds forced him back down to the street.

Twisted by the ferocity of the unnatural air, Remy was slammed down upon his back, the oxygen forced from his lungs in a wheezing explosion. Colors danced before his eyes, and he did everything he could to maintain his consciousness. He could only imagine the fate that awaited him if the children found him helpless.

A piece of pipe lay upon the ground, and Remy reached out to snatch it up. He needed a weapon, and if a sword or gun wasn't handy, then this would have to do. Willing some more of his inner fire into the body of the makeshift club, he watched as it began to glow.

By the light of the divine fire he saw something that took his breath away.

Malatesta and Prosper were tied to twin posts sticking up from the ground. The fallen angel was unconscious and looked as though he'd been beaten within an inch of his life, while the Vatican magick user, though bloody and bruised, at least was awake.

"I'd ask if you're all right, but you'd probably tell me to go fuck myself," Remy said, flaming pipe in hand.

"You're probably right," Malatesta answered weakly.

At least the sorcerer was in control again.

"Prosper?" Remy asked, keeping his eyes on the children, who were now coming closer.

"Alive," Malatesta said. "But just barely."

The teenage girl dropped down from the sky to land before Remy. Her hands blazed as if dunked in gasoline and lit on fire.

"Anything you can tell me that could help me out?" Remy asked.

"Not that I can think of at the moment," Malatesta said. "One of them seems to be able to broadcast directly into my head, making it rather difficult to think straight, never mind cast spells."

"So much for asking for a hand," Remy said.

He was watching the group, sensing power the likes of which he'd never encountered. Holding the flaming piece of metal out before him, Remy decided that fighting would lead to nothing good, and let the makeshift weapon clatter from his hands to the street.

"I don't mean any of you harm," he said, raising his hands in surrender, and allowing his wings to fold upon his back.

The teenage girl just laughed, and threw one of her balls of fire directly into Remy's chest. It exploded on impact, knocking him backward to the ground where he found that he no longer had the will—or the strength—to rise.

The children gathered around, staring down upon him—some with curiosity and the wonder of youth, others with distrust, fear, and hate.

He wanted to tell them again that he wasn't like the general, that he wasn't like Aszrus, but the girl's fireball had taken away everything he had left.

Suddenly, Remy noticed movement in the gathering and a murmur passed through the crowd. Then they moved aside, allowing another of their number to step forward.

He was an older boy, probably sixteen or so, and in his eyes Remy saw something that scared him.

In the young man's eyes were anger and defiance.

"He wanted to turn us into weapons," the young man said as he stared down upon Remy.

"I guess his wish has come true."

# CHAPTER TWENTY-TWO

In that bizarre state between waking and unconsciousness, Remy waited until he was able to pull enough of himself together to function again.

But in the cool, soothing darkness, he wasn't alone.

"You're really in a fix this time, Mr. Chandler," said a voice that he missed with every fiber of his being.

Madeline was sitting beside him, wearing that yellow sundress she'd worn one day on Nantucket during their honeymoon.

"Hey you," Remy said, forcing himself up to a sitting position. "Long time no see."

"Aww, did you miss me?" she asked, with a tilt of her head.

*If she only knew.*

"Always." He smiled at the woman who'd been gone from his life two years now.

"But you're doing so well," she said, leaning against him. "Personally, anyway."

"Yeah," he agreed, shrugging.

"I like her. She's tough. I think she can handle the nonsense you'll put her through."

It was odd to hear his dead wife talk about Linda, but also strangely comforting to have her approval, even though she was only a manifestation of his subconscious.

"I hope you're right," Remy said. "Although I'm not sure even I can handle my current situation."

"It is a bad one," Madeline agreed. "What are you going to do?"

Remy shrugged again. "My original plan was to find out who was responsible, and then turn him over to the legions to defuse the situation. But now . . ."

Remy recalled the pain and anger in the boy Gareth's voice as he talked about the angel that was his father. Gareth hated the Heavenly being, but at the same time, he seemed to hunger for his acknowledgement, to be recognized as his son.

Aszrus had finally begun to take an interest in Gareth and the other children. For a time, Gareth had actually started to believe he was something more than the forgotten by-product of an unholy union.

But then Aszrus had revealed his true motivation, his plan for the children to be used as weapons against the forces of Hell. Gareth's dreams of belonging suddenly came tumbling down, and the full extent of his unnatural power began to take shape.

"You can't turn them over," Madeline said, speaking his own thoughts.

"No, I can't." Remy shook his head. "Although they are extremely dangerous."

"Angry children," Madeline said. "Not the easiest creatures to reason with."

"Tell me about it." Remy had tried to calm Gareth and the others, which resulted in one of the children reaching into his skull and giving his brain a good squeeze to shut him up.

And that was why he was here, but at least he was in very good company.

"So where does that leave us?" Madeline asked.

"It leaves us in a pretty bad place," Remy admitted. "Gareth wants to lead his brothers and sisters from the island to confront the angels responsible for siring and abandoning them."

"That's probably something they've been wanting to do since they were old enough to know better," Madeline said. "A power fantasy—if they couldn't be loved by those who cast them away, then they would destroy them."

"That sums it up," Remy said.

They sat, silent in the cool darkness, each deep in thought.

"I can't let them be hurt any more," Remy finally said.

"Yeah, I figured you'd say something like that."

"Am I that predictable?" Remy asked.

"All in a good way." Madeline leaned over and kissed his cheek. "So what's the plan?"

"Really not much of one," he said. "I've got to convince Gareth not to attack, and then to stay hidden."

"That's it?"

"I told you it wasn't much."

"But it is a start." She kissed him again, only this time longer, pressing her lips firmly against his cheek. Remy turned in to the kiss, eager to feel her lips against his own.

Even if it was only a dream.


Water dribbled down his chin as a cup was pressed to his lips.

Remy drank, but started to cough, and the figure kneeling in front of him moved the cup away.

"Are you all right?" the figure asked.

It took Remy a moment to get his bearings. His eyes darted around the first floor of one of Gunkanjima's abandoned buildings. He could see Malatesta and Prosper sleeping to his right, both of them still tied up.

He remained bound as well, though not for much longer. He could already feel his strength returning, the interference in his brain that had laid him low no longer present.

"Who are you?" Remy asked.

The figure was tall, and quite thin, with a dull, sickly pallor.

"A friend," he said. "I was trying to look after them." His gaze turned toward the broken window. "But now . . . I'm afraid for them."

Remy tried to sit up, but the rope and thick knots around his wrists and ankles made it incredibly awkward. He concentrated on the fire inside him, allowing it to leak just enough from his pores to weaken his bonds. Then straining just a bit, he broke them, the pieces of rope dropping to smolder upon the floor.

"I know what you mean," Remy said. "Could I have some more water, please?"

"Certainly." The man handed the cup to Remy.

"They're not equipped to deal with the world outside," he continued, as Remy quenched his thirst. "To challenge the angels responsible for their abandonment . . ." The man shook his head sadly.

"I want to help them as well," Remy said. "But I'm afraid it might be too late. . . . They seem to have already made up their minds."

The man was quiet, eyes fixed upon a particular spot, deep in thought. He played with a silver ring that adorned a finger of his left hand, turning it around and around.

"If there was some way they could be taken from here," he said after a few moments. "Protected from harm. Taught to understand their abilities."

Remy suddenly remembered Malatesta's tale of being found by the Keepers, taken away, and taught how to deal with his affliction. Maybe there was a chance. . . .

"You look as though you might have an idea," the man said to him.

"Yeah," Remy answered slowly. He still didn't trust the Vatican, but perhaps they really were the only hope the children had.

He turned and crawled across the floor to Malatesta.

The sorcerer lay on his side, and Remy gripped his arm, preparing to awaken him. "Constantin," he said, knowing immediately that something was wrong.

Malatesta rolled onto his back, eyes wide and unblinking, his teeth clenched together in a rictus-like grin. His body twitched wildly, and Remy knew that there was nothing he could do right then.

There was a battle taking place inside the Vatican magick user—a battle for the soul of the sorcerer as the evil being within attempted to wrest away control.

Remy briefly turned his attention from the sorcerer to the man he'd just been talking with, but the stranger was gone.

Taking Malatesta's hand in his, Remy tried to lend him the strength he would need to defeat the darkness inside him.

It was a similar battle to one that Remy himself had fought many times.

Simeon left the building, allowing himself to be swallowed up in the sharp angles of darkness around the rotting structures.

"Are we leaving, master?" Beleeze asked, nearly invisible in the shadows.

Simeon was staring back toward where he had come from, and the angel he'd left behind. It had been a very long time since last he'd seen him.

The forever man had often wondered what became of the angel that led the siege against Ignatius Hallow's castle; and here he was, going by the name of Remy Chandler.

*Funny how things work out,* Simeon thought. It was this angel—this Remy Chandler—who had helped set him on the path to fulfilling his most heartfelt desire, and now the angel would assist him again.

The angel would never know that it was Simeon's idea that the Vatican might provide for the children's well-being. He would think it a solution that suddenly came to him, a bolt from the blue.

A chance for the children to survive.

Simeon frowned. *No, that wouldn't do at all.*

"Yes, we're going." Simeon turned his attention to the demon that had already begun to weave the arcane magicks of his kind to take them from this place. The two other demons that also served the forever man stepped closer.

"Where to?" Beleeze questioned.

"Rome," Simeon replied. "I need to speak with some old friends."

## Castle Hallow
### 1349

Simeon rose from where he'd been thrown, eyes unable to move from the scene unfolding before him.

The angel stood there in the gloom of Castle Hallow, his holy radiance burning as if a miniature sun had suddenly taken up residence in its shadow-filled halls.

"It is the time of your reckoning, necromancer," the angel's voice boomed.

Simeon could not take his eyes from the being; this was a servant of the God who had rejected him, and he wanted to remember every detail about him.

He would remember this one. He would remember all of them, and he would rejoice as they fell, their God unable to help them.

The angel advanced toward Simeon's ancient master. He was tempted to go and stand closer to him, but a brief glance from Hallow froze him where he stood.

As a being who believed nothing could harm him, there was a cockiness in the angel's stride. But Simeon knew that if nothing else, Ignatius Hallow was full of surprises.

The necromancer raised his hand, adorned with the sigil of Solomon, and called forth the demons that were compelled by the ring to serve him. They swarmed to their master's side and attacked en masse.

The angel was a sight to behold, his sword of fire cutting deadly swathes through the air as he battled the nightmare beasts. The demons fell dead at his feet, sometimes two and three at a time, but still they came, driven by the commands of their master. Simeon could not believe the number; most he had never laid eyes on. He imagined that they had been stored away somewhere deep beneath the castle, waiting for such a time as this.

The demons died one after the other, their wails of pain filling the cavernous entryway, as the angel advanced upon Hallow.

Simeon wanted to tell his ancient master to run, but Ignatius Hallow held his ground, arms extended, continuing to command the demonic beasts that were forced to serve his every whim, even if it meant their deaths. The angel did not slow, his golden armor stained black with the blood of his vanquished foes.

Simeon desperately wanted to go to the necromancer's aid, but he had been warned not to interfere. In fact, he had been ordered to escape the castle through one of the secret underground passages that had been tunneled by demonic hands. Still, the forever man could not turn away.

He had to witness the power that could strike down one such as Hallow. For it would be power such as this that he would face when his plans for the future reached fruition.

Through a wall of burning demons the angel exploded, the creatures' pathetic attempts at protecting their master failing horribly. Hallow still held his ground, staring defiantly into the face of the force that could so easily wipe him from the earth. The angel bore down upon him, but the necromancer did not flinch before the terrifying visage of the thing from Heaven.

"Do you know why you hate me, angel?" Hallow asked as the angel raised his mighty sword.

It took a moment, but the question seemed to permeate, the sword of fire hovering in the air.

More of the demonic surged into the entryway, and the angel spun toward them.

"Hold!" the necromancer commanded, and the demons did as they were told.

The angel looked back to him with eyes that burned with rage, but there was a question there as well.

"You are compelled to slay me, but I am certain that if you ask yourself the reason, you'll find nothing to justify such an insatiable hunger for my death."

The necromancer's words appeared to be having some physical effect upon the angel. He blinked rapidly, then tried to raise his fiery sword, only to have it drop harmlessly to his side.

"You are bewitched, angel," the necromancer stated, lifting his withered hand to show him the sigil ring upon it. "By the sibling of this very ring, created by the powerful magicks of Solomon."

Simeon could not believe what he was seeing. His master was actually having some success in taming the fiery power of Heaven sent to destroy him. He emerged from his hiding place, desperate to bear witness to the unimaginable events transpiring.

"My ring gives me sway over the demonic, while its sister—"

The lance pierced the oily smoke wafting up from the bodies of the burning demons. It impaled the necromancer through the chest, exiting from his back in a hissing spray of crimson.

"No!" Simeon cried, as his master these past years fell limply to one side. He ran out into the open, dropping to his knees on the stone floor beside the injured man.

Hallow was still alive, but barely, eyes fixed upon the angel of God, the churning smoke behind him, and the figures that now emerged.

"Where is it?" demanded a figure clothed in the elaborate garb of the Pope of Christendom. "Where is the ring?"

The Pope's cold, reptilian eyes touched upon the fallen necromancer. "Remiel," he growled. "Kill him for me."

The angel immediately rushed forward to do as he was bidden.

*But why?*

He did not stop, but continued to question his own actions as he advanced upon the prone body of his enemy. The necromancer had been trying to convince him that he was somehow not in control of his actions.

*But how?*

Wings of crackling, Heavenly fire spread wide upon his back, the angel Remiel loomed above the necromancer, preparing to strike him dead.

The man did not appear afraid.

A servant bravely leapt to his master's defense, standing between Remiel and his quarry.

"I curse you and all that you stand for," the young man pronounced. "There will come a day when I see you, your brethren, and Heaven itself fall into ruin."

"Do not waste my time!" Pope Tyranus commanded, eager for his Heavenly servant to complete his task.

*Servant?*

Remiel slapped the young man aside, feeling the bones in his face turn to paste with the ferocity of the blow.

"Kill him," Tyranus ordered. "Kill him now so I may claim my prize!"

Remiel reached for the dying man, who continued to cling to life, gazing up at him defiantly.

"This ring . . . this ring controls the demonic," the necromancer managed, rich arterial blood oozing up from his destroyed innards, flowing over the sides of his mouth. He plucked the ring from his finger, and strange wails rose up from the demons to echo through the castle halls.

Remiel reached down to close his burning hand around the man's throat, and began to squeeze.

"Its sister controls that of Heaven," the necromancer struggled.

"The angelic . . . A second ring controls the angelic."

The words sank in, permeating the thick fog that had seemed to encase Remiel's brain since . . . since first encountering the pope, Tyranus.

The old man was burning in the angel's grasp, skin bubbling to fluid-filled blisters.

"Take it," the necromancer croaked, pressing the ring against him. "Take it . . . take it and break the other's hold upon you."

"Kill him and allow me my prize!" Tyranus shouted from somewhere behind him.

Remiel continued to gaze into the necromancer's eyes as the life left him. He could feel the ring pressed against his own armored chestplate, as if it were attempting to melt through the metal forged in Heaven to the divine flesh beneath.

"Take it," were the last words uttered by the magick wielder called Hallow.

And again, Remiel did what was asked of him, taking the golden ring from the burned and crumbling hand as the necromancer's body fell away, breaking into smoldering pieces that hissed upon the floor.

The ring was like a piece of the harshest winter, yet at the same time it burned in the palm of his hand.

"Where is it?" the Pope demanded. "Give it to me."

Remiel saw the brother ring adorning the holy man's finger, as he closed his hand over what had been given to him by his dying enemy.

"Give it to me!" Pope Tyranus roared, extending his spidery hand greedily.

The angel Remiel's thoughts became suddenly clear, and he understood the magnitude of what had been done to him.

And he became very angry.


Remy placed his hands upon Malatesta, trying to keep the man from hurting himself as he convulsed on the ground.

He could feel the sorcerer's skin ripple, and saw the bones beneath his face distorting as he attempted to fight the evil that tried to usurp his control. From the looks of it, he wasn't doing too well.

The disturbing sound of popping joints and the elastic-band snap of tearing tendons filled the space, and all Remy could do was beg the man to fight.

Prosper was suddenly awake and beside Remy, begging the angel to show the man some mercy, and put him down—for his sake, and for the sake of the world.

For a moment Remy actually considered the request.

The demon peered out through the Vatican magick user's eyes, as he twisted and writhed on the floor, trying to escape the bonds that still held him. And then Remy noticed its gleeful expression change.

"Who is that?" the Larva asked, his struggles intensifying.

Remy turned to see a small shape standing just inside the door. It was one of the children.

"Hey," Remy said, trying not to scare the youth.

The little boy, who appeared no older than six, shuffled farther into the room, the cuffs of his overly long sweatpants practically covering up his shoes.

"That man has something bad in him," the child said, squatting down next to Remy, his gaze never leaving the panicking Malatesta.

"Keep him away," the Larva roared, eagerly trying to get his hands free.

"I can see it," the child said. "I did when he first got here, too."

"You can see the bad thing?" Remy asked.

The child nodded. "I can see the good . . . and the bad."

The child's eyes seemed to twinkle with an eerie incandescence as he looked at Remy. "You're a good guy," he said, smiling. He was missing his two front teeth.

"I like to think so," Remy replied.

Malatesta's hand broke free of his bonds then. His fingers were horribly distended, and adorned with razor-sharp claws. He grabbed at the boy, but Remy was faster, grasping the deformed arm of the possessed by the wrist.

"He doesn't like you," Remy said to the boy.

"Yeah," the child said, rubbing a filthy finger beneath his nose. "He knows I can see him hiding inside. . . . He knows what I can do."

Malatesta started screaming, his body writhing in the throes of agony.

"Get that fucker away from me!" the evil spirit screeched in a voice that was filled with fear.

"What can you do?" Remy asked the little boy, as he struggled to hold Malatesta down.

The little boy looked down at his hands, dirty palms up.

"I can make him so he ain't so strong," the child said. He looked up into Remy's eyes. "It's my gift, I guess," he added with a shrug.

It was then that Remy truly saw this child—these children—for what they were, for the potential they had, if they were allowed to survive long enough to show it.

"Would you use your gift to help my friend?" Remy asked.

"No!" the evil entity inside of Malatesta wailed. "No! No! Fucking no!"

"I never done it before," the little boy said, nervously.

Remy was curious. "Then how do you know . . ."

"We all got something special," the boy explained. "I just know what I can do." The child looked at Remy again. "Does that sound crazy?"

Remy shook his head. "Not at all."

The child smiled, then turned his attention to the man who lay upon the ground, violently twisting and turning. "That's enough outta you," he said, and placed his hands on Malatesta's chest.

Malatesta's neck stretched, and sharp teeth grew from his mouth as he tried to bite the child. Remy reached out, placing his palm against the man's fevered brow and shoving his head back.

"Go ahead," he urged the boy. "Do your thing."

The child leaned forward upon his hands, looking as though he was going to start to perform CPR. Malatesta's body went suddenly rigid, as if an electrical current was coursing through it. The Larva's screams became higher and higher pitched until his mouth remained cavernously open.

Remy heard a sudden buzzing, and a swarm of flies, their bodies fat, shiny, and green, flew out of Malatesta's gaping mouth. The sorcerer's body had gone suddenly still, and Remy noticed that it had returned to normal. Malatesta's eyes were fluttering now, about to open, as if coming up from a very deep sleep.

Remy looked to the boy, who was leaning back on his haunches.

"It's weaker now," the child said.

"It appears that way," Remy said, amazed at what he had just seen.

The child was staring at him again, as if waiting for something.

"You did a very good job," Remy told him, and the child beamed from ear to ear.

Malatesta awoke. "What . . . what happened?" he stammered. He sounded weak, but did not appear to be fighting the monstrous spirit that lived inside of him.

"This little guy here just saved you," Remy said, placing his hand upon the boy's shoulder. "And showed me that we need to do everything we can to help these kids."

Remy burned away Malatesta's bonds, and helped him to sit up.

"What can we do?" the sorcerer asked.

"We have to get them away from here—hide them," Remy said.

"And how do you suppose we do that?"

"We'll need some help," Remy said as he fixed Malatesta in a powerful stare.

"That's where your employer comes in."

# CHAPTER TWENTY-THREE

Remy emerged from the building to confront the gang of children who had been left there to guard him and the others. Malatesta and Prosper followed him, propping each other up.

The children leapt to their feet and advanced menacingly toward them, but Remy held his ground.

"I don't want to fight you," he said, infusing his voice with the power of Heaven. It boomed, echoing powerfully in the chasms created by the abandoned buildings around them.

"Then you should go back inside," a teenage boy said, the air around his body shimmering as if with incredible heat.

Remy shook his head. "I'm not going to do that. If I did, I couldn't help you."

"You're going to help us?" the flying girl who'd hit him with one of her fireballs asked with a smirk. "Who said we wanted your help?" She hovered a few feet off the ground, and Remy could see the beginnings of fireballs coalesce in the palms of her hands.

"You're all in incredible danger," Remy tried to explain. "There are forces out there, in the world, that will see what you are—what you can do—as an enormous threat."

The children looked at one another.

"You're talking about the angels, aren't you?" the girl who floated in the air asked him. "The angels responsible for us being born."

Remy nodded. "Yes."

"And what you are."

He nodded again.

"And what about you?" asked another voice.

Remy looked over to see the older boy, Gareth, strolling down the street toward them.

"Are you afraid of us?"

Remy knew that he couldn't lie. He couldn't take the chance.

"Yeah," he replied. "At least I was."

Gareth laughed boisterously. "You should be."

He looked to the children, who laughed along with him.

"But I'm not anymore," Remy added.

Another boy pushed through the crowd and slowly stepped toward Remy, the flesh of his hands transformed into two blades of solid bone.

"I'd say that's a big mistake," he said, slashing at the air.

Remy was ready to defend himself, but was hoping that he wouldn't have to.

"Stop," Gareth commanded.

The boy did as he was told, and turned toward his leader.

"Get back," Gareth said, motioning for the young man to return to the crowd.

The boy hesitated, and Remy saw the potential for a challenge, but then he returned to the group of children, his hands morphing back to normal.

"So you say you're not afraid of us anymore," Gareth stated. The son of Aszrus moved closer. "Why is that?"

"Don't get me wrong," Remy said. "I still think you're extremely dangerous, and in need of some serious guidance, but a little while ago I saw the good that you're capable of."

Remy's eyes found the little boy who had weakened the demonic spirit that had been attempting to take over Malatesta, but did not single him out, just in case there were repercussions.

"Good?" Gareth questioned. "You saw good?"

He strode toward Remy, stopping with his face mere inches from the angel's. Remy could feel the raw power emanating from the youth, and wondered at the extent of the teen's might.

"Do you see any good in me?" he asked, defiantly.

"I don't want to fight you," Remy said softly, so that only Gareth could hear. "And I don't want to see you hurt."

Gareth backed down slightly, but Remy could see the frustration that burned in his eyes.

"What makes you so different from the rest?"

"Let's just say I left their company a long time ago and leave it at that," Remy explained. "But I still understand them well enough to know what they'll do when they find out that something like you—*all of you*—exists."

"We'll fight them," Gareth said angrily.

"And you'll die," Remy told him as a matter of fact.

"If that's the way it has to be . . ." Gareth's voice trailed off. "We're all supposed to be dead anyway."

"But it doesn't have to be like that," Remy said. "You could live."

Gareth turned away, walking back to the gathering of children. He could see the anticipation on their faces, eagerly awaiting their leader's orders to take him down.

Remy continued to stand his ground, hoping Gareth was smarter than that.

"Do you know how much I wanted him to like—to love—me?" Gareth asked.

Thunder rumbled in the distance, another storm on its way to the island.

Remy remained silent.

"At first, when I realized what he was—who he was—all I wanted to do was kill him," Gareth said through gritted teeth. "But then something started to change inside of me and I realized the connection."

He stepped toward Remy again.

"I realized that I was part of something . . . *someone*. . . . I wasn't alone—*we* weren't alone. And for a moment . . . a very brief moment . . .

I thought that we were going to be accepted . . . that we were going to be part of a family."

Remy could hear the pain in the young man's voice and see the turmoil in his eyes. The poor kid just didn't understand the kind of creatures he was dealing with.

"But I was no more important to him than a really sharp knife, or a sword. He—they—were going to use us as weapons, to fight some sort of war they suspect is coming."

Gareth clenched his fists by his sides, and Remy suddenly felt the atmosphere around him begin to change, charged with a power the likes of which he was certain he'd never experienced before. And as if somehow picking up on the power he was broadcasting, the children behind him allowed their own new abilities to jump to life.

"They wanted weapons," Gareth stated. "Then so be it."

"They'll kill each and every one of you without a second thought," Remy stated flatly.

It looked as though Gareth was going to continue to rouse the crowd, but his speech was cut short by another voice.

"I don't want to die," said a small voice from within the gathering, and Remy watched as the little boy who had weakened the demon inside Malatesta pushed his way through the crowd, stopping before his leader.

"I don't want to die," he told Gareth again.

"You might not have a choice."

"But he says we don't have to." The child pointed at Remy.

And before Gareth could reply, Remy jumped in. "That's true. With his help," he pointed to Malatesta. "We could take you from the island to somewhere you'd be safe and cared for."

Remy glanced over to the sorcerer.

"The people who raised me—taught me—could do the same for you," Malatesta said, taking his cue.

"Personally, I think it's a whole lot better than dying," Remy added.

Gareth looked as though he was about to reiterate his defiance, when the child spoke again.

"We did just get our gifts," he said, holding his dirty hands up before his face. "It would be pretty sad for them to go away when we died."

Gareth looked out over the crowd of children. It wasn't hard to see that they were looking for some sort of guidance, and would follow whatever he decided.

The teen glanced back at Remy, and the angel could see there was still a struggle going on behind his eyes.

"What do we have to do?" he finally asked, forcing the words from his mouth.

## Rome

Patriarch Adolfi lay beneath the covers in a restless slumber.

As one of the leaders of the Keepers, he was made privy to more than any man should know, the unnatural just as much a part of his day-to-day as the normal.

Of late the unnatural was all he knew, for the fate of the world was dangling precariously at the edge of the abyss.

Tonight, as he had during many recent nights, the old priest dreamed of the end of the world. He saw the planet's greatest cities crumble, its citizenry swept up in waves of fire, and above it all God's winged messengers waged war with nary a thought for the innocent dying in the streets below.

Above the clashing swords of fire that rained hungry sparks down upon Earth and its inhabitants, who cowered in fear, Adolfi saw the shape of Heaven in all its glory.

And then he saw it was in ruin.

The old man awoke with a gasp, clutching his pillow in the dark and realizing that he had been crying. The images of the Celestial City floating dead in the sky above a dying world filled him with such terror and sadness.

The patriarch knew that it would be impossible to sleep anymore, and pushed himself up into a sitting position—to find that he was not alone.

Adolfi gasped, throwing his frail body back against the heavy oaken headboard, a cry poised upon his lips.

"Good morning, Adolfi," the intruder said calmly. "I didn't mean to frighten you."

The intruder sat in the patriarch's favorite reading chair, beside the window that looked out onto the garden. Three others, who wore the shadows of the room like cloaks, stood to the side and behind the chair.

It was then that Adolfi realized that he knew this one, although it had been many, many years since last he'd seen him.

"Is it you?" the priest asked, his voice old and brittle.

"Yes," the stranger replied. "It's me."

He stood, and silently glided across the room, stopping at the foot of Adolfi's bed. The patriarch stared in awe at the man with the pale, almost translucent flesh, and thick black hair.

He hadn't aged a day.

"Simeon?"

The man smiled. "I can't tell you how good it makes me feel that you remember."

"But how? You look no older than the last time we . . ."

"Ah yes, the good old days," Simeon spoke wistfully. "Perhaps later there will be time to reminisce, but now . . ."

Simeon gripped the wooden footboard and leaned forward, a look of urgency on his face.

"If the world is to survive, I need you to make some calls."

Another storm had found the island of Gunkanjima. But it did not deter Remy and his party as they headed for the passage that would take them back to Rapture.

Remy and Malatesta supported the injured Prosper, while the children eagerly swarmed around them, excited for what was about to happen.

Excited for their future.

"Are we close?" Remy asked Prosper.

The fallen angel grunted once, and the group stopped. Remy and Malatesta released the fallen angel and he swayed for a moment in the falling rain.

Then Prosper lifted a hand, his fingers bloody, some oddly twisted. He began to draw shapes in the air before him, shapes that suddenly came to glowing life, as the space before him began to shimmer.

Prosper turned his bloodied face to Remy.

"It's done," he said through split and swollen lips. "Now where does that leave me?"

Remy looked at him. "I don't think I'm following."

"You don't need me anymore," Prosper said. "So where does that leave me?" The fallen angel's eyes were darting from Remy to Malatesta, and then to the excited children milling about.

"We're taking you back to Rapture," Remy told him. "And maybe somebody there will take care of your sorry ass."

Prosper's stare was intense.

"You're not going to kill me?"

Remy stared back with equal intensity before answering.

"No," he said. "To tell you the truth, I've got bigger things to worry about right now than offing you."

The children were eyeing the fallen angel hungrily.

"If I wanted to be a real son of a bitch I'd leave you here with the kids," he said. "Let them show you how much they appreciate the life you've given them so far."

Prosper refused to look at them, hanging his head.

Gareth joined them, standing beside Remy.

"Are you sure this is the way?" he asked.

"It's the only thing I've got," Remy replied.

The air was filled with the hissing of the storm.

"And you think that's right?" Gareth asked. "That we should remain alive?"

"I do," Remy told him, hoping that what he was about to attempt would bring some semblance of peace and normalcy to these sad, pathetic creatures that were the product of divine lust.

With that said, Gareth turned, and walked away.

"Will you be back soon?" asked the little boy who had pushed Malatesta's demon deeper.

"Soon as we can," Remy reassured him.

"Will it be raining all the time where we're going?" the child asked.

"I bet it's going to be sunny a lot of the time there," Remy told the boy. "If that's all right," he added.

The boy nodded vigorously, and Remy reached out to ruffle his rain-soaked head.

Malatesta was holding Prosper up by the arm.

"Ready?" the sorcerer asked.

"Ready as I'll ever be," Remy answered.

Malatesta began to help Prosper through the passage, but Remy paused for a moment to give the children one final wave.

He caught sight of Gareth in the distance, watching with dark eyes filled with fear of what was to come.

A fear of the fate that might befall them all.


Morgan was sipping a pear martini and pretending that she gave a shit about her latest john's confession that he'd been responsible for at least two of the murders credited to Jack the Ripper, when she noticed the security staff moving en masse down the corridor toward Prosper's office.

She and the rest of the girls had been pretty much left in the dark not only as to the fate that had befallen their boss, but also what had really happened to the children they believed had died at birth.

She excused herself with a smile, and followed the walking dead men down the corridor. As she suspected, the door to Prosper's office was wide-open, and a strange humming sound that made her inner ear itch was coming from inside.

Security was on full alert, but she managed to maneuver herself through their obstructing bulk into Prosper's office. The air at the back of the room had begun to shimmer and blur, finally spitting out an all too familiar shape.

Prosper fell through the fluctuating passage to land on his knees in his office. He looked like someone had taken a hammer to him, and for a moment, Morgan was tempted to go to the angel.

But then she remembered what he had done to Bobbie, and what he had kept from them.

Prosper knelt for a moment, before falling forward to all fours. The passage behind him shimmered and blurred some more, before another shape emerged that Morgan recognized as the guy who'd been disguised as Aszrus. And then the angel Remiel stepped through behind him.

Morgan was pushed aside as the zombie security team surged forward.

"Stop!" Prosper croaked. "They're with me."

The zombies nearly fell over one another as they froze in their tracks. It was then that Morgan caught the angel's eye, and she couldn't help but feel a smile begin to tease at her lips.

"You wouldn't happen to have a phone we could use, would you?" Remy asked.

And she found herself reaching into the pocket of the silk jacket she wore to give the angel what he asked for.

Patriarch Adolfi could not stop staring at the man called Simeon. It had been at least thirty years since last they'd met, and the man didn't appear to have aged a day.

"How—," Adolfi began, only to have Simeon interrupt.

"There's no time for that now, Patriarch," Simeon said, raising the china cup to his mouth for a sip of coffee. "There are other more pressing matters."

Patriarch Adolfi reached for his own steaming beverage, trying to keep his ancient hands from trembling, but not having much luck.

"The jet will be fueled and waiting for us within the hour," Adolfi said.

"And when we reach Tokyo?"

"A helicopter will take us to the island."

"Very good," Simeon said, and the three figures that stayed in the shadows in the far corner of the room shifted.

"Are you certain that your . . . people . . . would not care for some refreshments?" Adolfi asked.

"They are not people, and merely being in the presence of one such as yourself is probably filling them with an overwhelming revulsion," Simeon snapped. "No offense, but I think it best they stay where they are."

The patriarch silently agreed, continuing the uncomfortable wait for the call that Simeon promised would be coming. The call that would summon them to duty.

The cell phone on the cherrywood table beside the patriarch's chair began to play the beginning strains of *Tocatta in D minor,* and he quickly picked it up.

"There we are," Simeon said, taking another sip of his coffee.

"Hello?" The patriarch listened to the voice on the other end with increasing interest.

"Why yes, Constantin," he said, looking to Simeon. "I've been expecting your call."

Francis wasn't about to leave with his tail tucked between his legs; he wouldn't allow himself, given the pain he was still feeling as a result of his questioning—*torture.*

He had some questions to ask Michael, and might even have a few for Dardariel, in between tearing off his wings and shoving them up his ass.

They climbed the dusty stone steps up from the bowels of the ancient prison. He was surprised that the others had all agreed to join him, albeit some begrudgingly, but they were still here.

Francis suspected their decision had more to do with them not feeling comfortable traveling the shadow paths with Squire, and less to do with wanting to have his back, but whatever the reason, they were there.

*Always good to have more bodies at your back,* he thought, imagining the fight that might soon ensue.

Francis thought of Remy, wondering if he had met with success. He couldn't imagine that the Seraphim hadn't, but then again there was always the chance—

Voices from the landing interrupted his thoughts, and he paused on the stairs.

"Are you sure about this?" Squire asked from beside him. "There's a nice patch of shadow we can crawl through at the bottom of the steps."

Francis glanced back to the others. "What do you think?"

Montagin still looked as though he had a stick shoved up his butt, but he held out his hand and called forth a pretty funky-looking sword that could probably do some serious damage. "Does this answer your question?" he asked.

Heath, whose lips looked as though he'd been intimate with the tailpipe of an eighteen-wheeler, extended his fingers and gave them a little wiggle. He said something that Francis couldn't quite make out because it sounded like the sorcerer had a mouthful of marbles, but he guessed that Heath was staying.

"All right," Squire said with a shrug. He reached into a pocket of his tool belt and produced two short-bladed knives that he held tightly in both pudgy hands. "Can't blame a guy for tryin'."

Seeing the others with weapons made Francis realize how naked he was. He closed his eyes and envisioned the Pitiless pistol and the scalpel-like blade taken from the dead hand of one of the architects of creation. He missed his weapons, his deadly friends.

"How much longer do you plan on skulking there upon the staircase?" asked a voice he recognized as belonging to the Archangel Michael.

Francis glanced to the others, seeing the beginnings of panic in their eyes as he climbed the rest of the way to the landing. So much for surprise.

He was met at the top of the stairs by the angel Dardariel, and immediately tensed. But Dardariel just stood there, holding out his hands to present Francis with the most unexpected of things.

In one palm rested his knife, and in the other the Pitiless pistol.

At first Francis thought it was some sort of joke, but he sensed from the weapons themselves that they were the real deal, and were anxious to be back in his possession.

He took them, first the knife and then the gun.

"I haven't forgotten about our little conversation downstairs," Francis said, dropping the knife into his pocket. He hefted the pistol. It felt good in his hand, which suggested to him that he was spending a little bit too much time with the gun.

Then again, maybe it wasn't enough.

"Of course not," Dardariel said, and gestured for them to follow. "They're waiting for you on the roof."

Francis looked to the others.

"Who is waiting?" Montagin asked.

Squire and Heath shrugged.

"Only one way to find out," Francis said. He continued down the corridor, following Dardariel up another small flight of stone steps that led onto the prison rooftop.

He really had no idea what to expect. A catered lunch would have been nice, but he was completely taken aback by the sight that awaited him.

It was a gathering of angels.

Everywhere he looked stood a soldier of Heaven, and as Francis emerged onto the rooftop, every eye turned to him. The Pitiless grew warm in his hand, excited by the prospect of violence, but Francis knew it would be hopeless.

Sure, he could take a bunch of the peacocks down, but eventually one of them would reach him, and that would be all she wrote.

Still, not a single weapon of fire was called upon. The angels simply stood and stared, as if waiting for something.

"Ah, there you are," the Archangel Michael said, moving away from the crowd. "Now we can go."

Montagin was standing beside Francis, and the former Guardian could sense Heath and Squire at his back. They all seemed just as confused as he was.

"Go where?" Francis asked.

"There has been a cessation of hostilities," the Archangel stated as he spread his wings.

All the other angels opened their wings as well.

"A conference has been called."

Angel soldiers appeared behind Francis and his group. They were incredibly close—close enough to take them inside their winged embrace, and transport them away.

"And we must answer the summons."

# CHAPTER TWENTY-FOUR

Remy stopped in the doorway of Prosper's room, a steaming mug of coffee in hand.

A few of the female staff were seeing to the fallen angel's needs—changing bandages, fluffing pillows. Remy noticed that none of the Nephilim that Prosper employed were present. He figured that the lie about the death of their children was just too much for them to forgive.

"You wanted to see me?" Remy asked.

"Yeah," Prosper said, shifting his weight upon the bed. He dismissed the girls with a wave of his hand, and they passed Remy with a smile as they went out the door.

"I wanted to thank you," the fallen angel said, playing with the corner of his bedsheet.

"For what, not killing you?"

"Yeah, there's that," Prosper answered. "But also for getting me out of there."

The fallen angel looked at Remy. His eyes were still bloodshot, his face swollen and bruised in places.

"I have no doubt in my mind that they would have killed me if . . ."

Remy took a sip from his coffee mug.

"And you would have deserved it."

Prosper shrugged. "Maybe, but it's also because of me that they're still alive."

Remy silently considered that.

"They would have been tossed in the trash, whether they were dead or alive."

"So you think of yourself as some kind of savior? That they owe you?"

"No, nothing like that," Prosper said.

Remy drank some more coffee, watching the fallen angel.

"You did me a solid, so I wanted to do the same for you," Prosper continued.

"And what are you going to do for me?"

"I called off the hit," Prosper said. "You don't have to look over your shoulder for the Black Choir anymore."

"Until they come for me again."

"Yeah, but it won't have anything to do with me."

"What about the others?" Remy asked. "The Bone Masters."

Prosper looked at him strangely. "Bone Masters?"

"The other assassins you sicced on me—the guys with the freaky guns that shoot teeth."

Prosper stared, then slowly shook his head.

"I only hired the Choir," the fallen angel said. "I don't know anything about any Bone—"

Malatesta appeared behind Remy.

"We should probably head back," he said, his voice low. "The Keepers should be there within the half hour."

Remy nodded, and looked back to Prosper.

"You be sure," Prosper said, hands flitting nervously over his bedclothes as Remy prepared to go.

"Sure about what?"

"That you're doing the right thing," Prosper said. "That it's okay for those things—children, if you want to call them that—to remain alive."

"Of course I'm sure," Remy said, disgusted at the notion that the children of Gunkanjima should be denied the right to exist.

He left the fallen angel and followed Malatesta back to Prosper's office. Some of Prosper's girls were there already, bags packed and stacked beside them.

"What's this?" Remy asked as he came into the room.

"They want to be with their children," Malatesta explained.

"How could we not be with them now that we know they're alive?" Natalia asked.

"What kind of mothers would we be?" asked Morgan.

It all sounded perfectly reasonable to Remy. He simply nodded as Malatesta reopened the passage to Gunkanjima.

The microwave beeped, announcing that Mulvehill's Hungry-Man Salisbury steak dinner was done. He went to the oven on the counter and pulled open the door, reaching in to withdraw his meal.

"Shit!" he swore, as he burned his fingers on the hot packaging.

He dropped the dinner on the counter, and blew on his fingertips as he went to the fridge for a bottle of water. He'd already had a glass of Irish whiskey to relax after a particularly insane day, and would probably have a second before calling it a night, but he preferred some water with his meal.

Twisting the cap off the water, Mulvehill took a long drink, then returned to his dinner on the counter. Cautiously, he peeled back the plastic covering, careful not to get too close to the cloud of steam that billowed out from underneath. He tossed the damp, plastic covering in the trash, then placed the still-hot plate on a dish towel for easy carrying. Retrieving his water, he took his meal toward the living room, hoping there would be something worthwhile to watch on television.

As he left the kitchen on his way to the living room, Mulvehill happened to glance down the hallway and saw that his door was partially open, moving ever so slightly in the phantom breezes that passed through the old Somerville apartment building.

*I could'a sworn I locked that,* he thought. He placed his dinner atop the towel on the coffee table, then went back to the door. He pulled it open first, looking up and down the corridor outside the apartment, before closing it firmly, and sliding the bolt in place.

His mother referred to this feeling as somebody walking over your grave, that strangely electric sensation that ran down one's spine for no apparent reason. Mulvehill could never understand how somebody could be walking on his grave when he wasn't dead yet, but he still thought of his mother every time he had that feeling.

Steven Mulvehill was thinking of her now.

He wasn't sure why he moved when he did. Perhaps it was that strange, grave-walking chill that caused him to suddenly twitch, convulsing to one side, or maybe it was that sixth sense that cops often develop after so many years on the street, that sense that tells them that something is about to happen.

Whatever it was, Mulvehill moved, just before he heard the noise—like somebody blowing air through a hollow tube—and the wood to the right of the doorframe exploded into splinters.

Pure instinct kicked in then as he dove back into the kitchen where he knew he'd left his gun on the kitchen table along with his car keys. He heard that noise twice more, followed by breaking glass and the sound of something punching through the metal body of the stove, before he was able to retrieve the Glock from its holster.

Mulvehill crouched near the wall of the kitchen, flicking off the safety on his weapon. He was just about to peer around the corner into the living room, when everything went dark.

*Son of a bitch.* His mind raced as he tried to calculate his next step. His eyes went to the phone cradle hanging on the wall beside the fridge, and he saw that there was no phone there. Most likely it was in the living room, where he'd used it last. His cell phone was in the bedroom, charging. He remembered how proud he had been for actually remembering to charge his phone. Normally he would have left it on the kitchen table with his gun and keys, almost dead.

But at least then he could have made a call. He cursed his unusual efficiency and pledged never to charge his phone again until it was completely dead, and he clutched his gun, tilted his head toward the living room, and listened. Something was moving in the darkness, waiting for him.

Panic started to set in and he was immediately transported back to the day when he was first made painfully aware that the world in which he lived wasn't at all what it had seemed, and that his best friend, Remy Chandler, was the one who had left the door open for all the weirdness to come inside.

And that was what this was. He was certain of it. Sure, it could have been a run-of-the-mill break-in—there wasn't a shortage of junkies in the area—but something told him otherwise. He could feel it in the pit of his stomach, a sensation like no other.

He guessed it was a variation on that cop's sixth sense that he had; it had become more finely attuned of late, almost as if it were picking up a brand-new channel. It was the *weird shit* channel, and alarm bells were going off inside his head now.

His body had become drenched with a cold sweat, and he could smell the aroma of his Hungry-Man dinner cooling in the living room on the coffee table. He'd been really hungry when he set that meal down.

Like he didn't have enough to be pissed off about.

Mulvehill had faced things in the dark before and had survived. In fact, he was starting to become really good at it. With each new exposure he gained a certain amount of knowledge that he could apply to the next time that something from Stephen King's closet tried to kill him.

He slowly stood, zeroing in on a sound like that of rustling fabric, and he fired the gun once.

*Yeah, weird shit,* he thought, charging into the darkness of the living room to confront who knew what.

*You can fucking keep it.*

It had stopped raining on Gunkanjima Island.

Remy stood off to the side, watching as the children gathered up their meager belongings to take with them to their new home. A pile of things that would have been discarded as trash by most had formed in the center court area of the mining settlement.

"I doubt they'll be able to take all that with them," Malatesta said, coming from the building where Prosper had kept his office. The Vatican sorcerer was carrying two steaming mugs of coffee.

"Well, I'll be," Remy said, taking the offered cup. "All the comforts of home."

The two drank their coffee silently, watching the children interacting with the women from Prosper's charnel house. There was no precise way for them to know which child was theirs, but somehow, they seemed to know. And they also seemed to be taking to their new role as mothers quite easily, jumping right in to help the children gather up their things.

"Any idea where they're going?" Remy asked Malatesta.

"The Keepers have many places of learning around the world," Malatesta said. "I'm sure one of them will be the perfect fit."

Remy still had mixed feelings about handing the children over to the Keepers, but he had very few options. He just couldn't imagine them out there on their own.

"I'll be keeping close tabs on them," Remy said, eyes still staring at the scene before him.

"I'm sure you will," Malatesta responded.

"Do you think your bosses are aware of that?"

"I think it foolish to say that they wouldn't be."

"And your problem?" Remy said. He looked to the sorcerer. "How's that?"

Malatesta took a drink from his mug before replying. "The child's touch helped me to regain control, but it doesn't mean the Larva spirit isn't still there, struggling to take it away. It got a taste of freedom, and liked it. It won't take much for it to be free again."

Remy felt bad for his part in all of that, but again, there hadn't been a hell of a lot of choices.

He caught sight of Gareth then, standing alone near his quarters, watching his brothers and sisters. There was a certain look in the teen's eyes that Remy understood only too well. He was questioning his own actions, wondering whether he had done the right thing.

Remy approached the boy cautiously, not wanting to rile him. The level of power in this teen was quite awesome, if not a little frightening.

"I think they'll be all right," he said to the young man.

"I hope you're right," Gareth said. "My father talked about a war and the part we would play." The young man grew quiet, continuing to stare ahead at the children who looked to him as leader.

"That war is still coming," he finally said quietly.

Remy was about to reassure the youth, but he never got the chance.

The sound came from across the water, multiple rotor blades spinning with blinding speed as a helicopter drew closer.

"This is it," Gareth stated, and then sighed, his eyes turning toward the gunmetal-colored sky, before looking directly at Remy.

"The beginning of the end."

# CHAPTER TWENTY-FIVE

In an area of the island that had once been set aside for the children of miners, was a park, now overgrown with a thick, tall grass that bent in the artificial winds created by the Chinook helicopter as it slowly descended from a darkening sky.

The copter touched down, back end pointed toward Remy and the collected children. There was a high-pitched whine of hydraulics, and the back of the large craft began to open; a loading ramp slowly lowered to the weed-covered lot.

Malatesta left the gathering, running across the grassy expanse toward the helicopter, shielding his eyes from the debris kicked up by the craft's slowing rotor blades.

"Am I going in that?"

Remy looked down at the child who had temporarily repressed the sorcerer's demon. He'd learned that the boy's name was Apple, because he liked apples. "Yeah," he said. "You all are. It's going to take you to your new home."

Remy was watching Malatesta standing before the loading ramp, waiting for his superior, when he felt the tiny hand find its way into his. He glanced back at Apple to see him staring up at him, a smile that was almost blinding on his dirty features.

"Thank you," the little boy said, and all Remy could do was smile back, and give his small hand a gentle squeeze of assurance.

An old man, dressed in a black cassock, a golden crucifix about his neck, carefully descended from the loading ramp. He extended his hand toward Malatesta, who bowed his head and kissed the man's ring.

The two talked as the rotors spun above them, and Malatesta briefly looked back in Remy's direction. The sorcerer's body language seemed to be trying to tell him something.

"Are we leaving now?" Apple asked, hand still in Remy's.

"Not quite yet," Remy said as several other men, also dressed in the robes of their faith, began to exit the belly of the mighty Chinook and spread out.

The angel let go of the boy's hand, and walked toward them. Malatesta turned and Remy caught sight of the look on his face. Immediately he knew they were in trouble.

The Keepers acted as one, suddenly raising their hands and uttering an ancient spell in some long-forgotten language. The atmosphere became instantly charged with unnatural energy, calling forth another storm.

"What's going on?" Remy demanded, still heading for Malatesta.

The Vatican sorcerer extended his hand, gesturing for Remy to stop. The old man standing beside him glared at the angel, and Remy saw a glimmer of something he'd seen long ago in the eyes of their church's leader—the cold detachment of an act of betrayal.

The magickal force erupting from the hands of the Keepers wove a canopy over their heads, an undulating dome of supernatural energies hovering above the overgrown playground.

Remy stopped cold, as the magick turned the gray sky to a blood red.

*How appropriate.*

His wings came on reflex, and the fires of Heaven raced from where they churned in his chest to pool in his hands. But he had no opportunity to act, for Malatesta's magick lashed out like the tail of a whip, wrapping itself around his neck as he attempted to take to the sky. The power coursing through him was overwhelming. He struggled to flap his mighty wings, but they were no longer in sync, and floundering he dropped to the ground, the tendril of humming magick still wrapped about his throat.

Remy dug his fingers beneath the band of preternatural force, desperately trying to rip it from his neck, but it seared his fingers, leaching away his strength even as he fought.

"I'm sorry Remy," he heard Malatesta say, realizing that the sorcerer was controlling the leash of magickal energy that was attempting to strangle him. "For the good of us all it must be this way."

Remy thrashed upon the ground, turning toward the children. The Keepers had used their spells to corral the children, and they cried out in surprise—and fear.

Another group of Vatican agents had separated the mothers from their children, moving them away, toward the transport chopper.

"What are you doing?" Remy managed, his voice rough and full of rage.

The old priest from the chopper walked over to stand above Remy. "Calm yourself, soldier of Heaven," he said.

"I'm nobody's soldier," Remy rasped. "What are you doing to those kids?"

The priest closed his old, watery eyes. "The appearance of innocence is deceiving."

"What are you talking about?" Remy fought to stand, his wings beating the wet ground as he struggled to his feet.

The priest stepped back.

"They are not as they appear," he said. "And they must be dealt with before . . ."

An icy claw gripped at Remy's chest.

"What do you mean dealt with?" he demanded. "What are you thinking of . . ."

"To keep peace and strengthen the covenant," the old man continued. "Decisive action must be taken." He turned and walked away.

"Don't you dare walk away from me!" Remy screamed. "What are you going to do? Keep the peace between who? Tell me!"

The old priest stopped, and turned ever so slightly.

"Without our intervention, there would be war," he said. "The threat to this fragile peace must be eliminated; the truce must remain strong."

The horror of the situation suddenly sank in. The children were being offered up as a sacrifice to prevent two opposing factions from going to war.

"Please," Remy begged the old man. "There has to be another way. . . . They're just kids; they have no idea of what—"

"It is not for me to decide their fate," the priest announced, looking past Remy as there came the crashing of thunder and flashes of lightning followed by what he knew at once to be the flapping of wings.

So many wings.

Two groups of angels appeared, one on each side of the dilapidated playground—one side representing God's Heaven, the other Lucifer Morningstar's Hell.

And between them both cowered the frightened children brought into the world through no choice of their own.

Malatesta and the old priest walked toward the gatherings, dragging Remy behind them by sorcerous tether.

"Who shall speak for Heaven and who shall speak for Hell?" the priest asked the two sides.

"You can't let this happen," Remy cried out to Malatesta.

The sorcerer continued to stare straight ahead, as the representatives from each side came forth. "There is nothing we can do," he said. "It's all too big, and there's far too much at stake."

Remy was about to argue, but his eyes were drawn to the powerful form of the Archangel Michael as he approached the priest.

The warrior angel was clad in his armaments of war, a fiery spear clutched in one hand as he came to tower before the ancient priest.

"I stand for Heaven," the Archangel announced.

The priest bowed, then looked toward the other angelic crowd.

"And who shall stand for Hell?" he asked.

There was silence among their numbers, and Remy watched for a sign of the one who would take on the mantle.

There was a sudden commotion at the far back of the gathering, and a figure began moving through the ominous-looking shapes clad in the heavy armor of war. The angels of Hell moved aside as their delegate stepped forward.

Remy felt his knees give out as the figure left the crowd to stand before the priest.

"I guess I am," Francis said, his gaze briefly landing upon Remy before quickly fixing on the priest.

"I suppose I'm representing Hell."

## Castle Hallow
## 1349

The angel Remiel's rage was matched in size only by the level of the Pope's betrayal.

Tyranus had used sorceries ancient and powerful, imbued within a ring of silver, to bend the angel to his commands. Only by clutching its sister ring to his armored breast had Remiel seen the truth of the situation.

"How dare you?" the Seraphim roared.

"Now, now," the Pope fretted. "Remember it is God's work that I do here upon this world and—"

"Blasphemer!" Remiel shouted. "This ring has shown me your true colors!" The angel shook his divine fist.

Pope Tyranus did not back away, fixing Remiel in an icy stare.

"You will do as I have commanded," he stated. "You will hand over the ring at once."

The magick of the Pope's ring pulled at the angel, ancient magicks once bestowed upon Solomon by powers greater than any here on Earth, moving to influence him. Though the sister ring helped him to see things more clearly, it did not completely block the ring's influence over creatures of the divine.

Remiel struggled against the Holy Father's command, waves of excruciating pain traveling through his form as he fought to hold on to control.

But the ring was too strong.

Remiel watched as his arm seemed to lift of its own accord, his hand extending toward the Pontiff.

"That's right," the Pope hissed. "For the sake of the world, the power over the demonic and the divine shall be controlled by one."

Just the idea of such strength being given to one person—this vile person before him—filled the Seraphim with a blinding rage, and he resumed his fight for control over his actions.

"You will not have it!" Remiel proclaimed, igniting his fist so it glowed like the molten core of Earth, forcing Tyranus and his soldiers to step back.

"It is only a matter of time, soldier of Heaven," the Pope said calmly. "Only a matter of time before you succumb to a power greater than you."

Remiel knew that the holy man was right, but it did not prevent him from trying.

From the corner of his eye, peering out from the darkness of the castle's many passages, he saw the eyes of the demonic, twinkling there—watching his struggle.

The angel thought of them, thought of their number, and how they had served the necromancer and felt the ring writhe within his clutches. Without realizing what he had done, the demons came forth, called by the angel's silent command.

It was the most excruciating thing he had ever experienced, the very essence of his being touched by the coldest fingers of purest darkness.

But the demons responded to his fury.

Pope Tyranus seemed taken aback. "How fascinating," the holy man said, playing with the ring upon his finger. "You're actually fighting my commands."

Remiel was bent over in agony.

The demons encircled him, chattering, spitting, and hissing, and he saw in their multitude of eyes an intelligence—an awareness that told him they were as repulsed by his control of their actions as he was of being in control.

The Pope drew nearer, only to leap back as the demons lunged.

"Give it to me," he commanded once more.

Remiel squeezed the ring all the firmer as the demons tightened their circle, as if protecting him.

"You would die to defy me?" Pope Tyranus asked.

Remiel lifted his head to fix the holy man in his gaze. "I defy you, and all that you stand for," he proclaimed. "Power such as this does not belong in the hands of one."

"You are wrong," the Pope declared. "Only I am strong enough to prevent the world from plunging into chaos."

Tyranus stepped closer, hiking up his priestly robes to squat before Remiel. He held out his hand.

"The ring," he demanded.

Remiel could feel himself dying, the darkness of possessing the second of Solomon's rings surging through his body like a poison. Eyes affixed to the ground, he watched in horror as feathers dropped from his wings like leaves from a dying tree. His flesh was turning gray, and the heat of the fire at his breast was dwindling; all this because of the ring he held in his fist.

The demons drew closer, like a freezing person drawn to the heat of a fire.

He didn't want to look, but his eyes were pulled upward as if attached to invisible strings. He stared at the Pope's beckoning hand—compelling him to surrender what he believed to be rightfully his.

But even though he was dying, Remiel could not do it.

"It won't be long now," the Pope cajoled. "Your flesh will wither. The divine spark will be extinguished, leaving behind the remains of a once-holy creation determined to keep something of great power from its predetermined owner."

Remy lifted his face toward Pope Tyranus. The demons were snuggled even closer now, as if stealing away his life force.

"Last chance," the Pope said, bringing his beckoning hand all the closer.

It took almost all the strength that Remiel had remaining not to do as the Pope instructed him, but the sight of something—someone—moving from the darkness behind the holy man was more than enough of a distraction to hold on.

The Pope did not see that Hallow's servant, the young man who swore to see Heaven in ruins someday, was coming up behind the un-suspecting Pontiff.

Remiel lifted his shriveled hand. He could see genuine excitement in the Pope's eyes, believing he was about to receive what he most de-sired in all the world.

"Here, give it to me," the servant demanded.

Tyranus turned toward the voice, a feral snarl more demonic than divine escaping his lips as Remiel did the unthinkable.

Summoning all that he had left to give, he lifted his arm, opening his creaking fingers to release the ring.

It was as if time had become transformed by alchemy into some form of viscous liquid, the ring of Solomon slowly tumbling through the air toward its new owner.

The necromancer's servant lunged, fingers splayed, before closing upon the prize. Pope Tyranus leapt as well, colliding with the man and sending them both sprawling to the floor of the castle.

Remiel lay upon the stone floor, still surrounded by the demonic creatures. He was dying, and all he could contribute was to lay there as the spectacle unfolded before his failing sight.

The Pope and Hallow's servant desperately struggled for the ring. There was a sudden cry of elation and the servant raised his scuffed and bloody hand—adorned with the silver sigil ring of Solomon.

The one that controlled the demonic.

Remiel's eyes fell heavily shut, but he could still hear the servant's commands to the demonic hordes assembled there.

"Take him, and be sure that he suffers."

And in the darkness, all the Seraphim could hear were screams.

Of terror and elation.

The holy and the wicked.

One no easier to discern than the other.

The sky above the island of Gunkanjima raged, as if offended by the heinous acts going on below it. Rain pelted the magickal barrier erected by the Keepers, hissing and sputtering like grease in a frying pan.

Remy could only watch as it all unfolded. He'd thought the Vatican would be the children's savior, that the Keepers would protect the innocent offspring of angels and Nephilim.

But he had been wrong—so very, very wrong. The Keepers had come, not as saviors, but as conciliators to prevent the breakout of war, to mediate a truce between two warring sides.

With the innocents trapped somewhere in the middle.

"Before you are the creatures responsible for the most heinous of acts," the old priest began. He gestured toward the children tightly corralled in another sphere of crackling magickal force.

Some stared defiantly, while others wailed in terror.

Remy wanted to go to them, to tell them that everything was going to be all right, but he knew that it wasn't. Things couldn't have been any worse. Again he tried to remove the magickal leash entwined about his neck, but he'd only grown weaker since the last attempt, and it hurt him all the more.

"A patriarch of Heaven was murdered," the priest announced. "His life brutally stolen from him."

The Keeper first looked to his left, at those gathered under the banner of Hell, and then to the right, and those representing Heaven.

"Suspicions were inflamed, and two mighty forces grew closer to conflict."

The Heavens roared in the thrall of the storm, almost as if something—someone—was giving their two cents, but Remy knew that was the furthest thing from the truth. Be they God, or monster, neither could watch the travesty going on before them now and not be forced to act.

But it was allowed to continue.

"Heaven and Hell were at the brink, and an unsuspecting world slumbered between them, unaware of the dangers they would soon face."

The old man slowly turned, presenting Remy with a flourish.

"But there was one, a being once of Heaven, who now walks the Earth, living among God's sheep, who would see the destructive potential of the murderous act and seek to quell the growing fires of discord.

Remy struggled to stand, but all it did was make him cry out.

"Stay down," Malatesta hissed. "You're only making it worse for yourself."

Francis, the Archangel Michael, and all the other angelic were staring at Remy as the Keeper continued his pitch.

"This one saw that it was not the act of one side against the other, but another force at work—a force that sought to ignite a war."

Against his better judgment, Remy let his opinion be heard.

"That isn't true!"

And he suffered for it.

The tendril of magick around his neck became tighter, sending pulsing waves of agony into his body. He fell to the ground again, where he grunted and thrashed in the throes of pain.

"Seduced by the visage of innocence . . . ," the old priest continued.

"Not true?" the Archangel Michael asked, interrupting the old priest's roll. The soldier of Heaven clutched his flaming staff all the tighter as he turned his full attention to the Seraphim that twitched pathetically on the ground before him. "Tell us of this lie."

Remy's eyes darted to Malatesta, still holding the other end of the magickal leash.

Michael then looked to the Keeper. "I wish him to speak."

The Keeper nodded, and Remy felt the hold upon him begin to loosen. He surged up to his feet, wings flapping powerfully, and considered his few options.

"The actions of these children were not premeditated," Remy began. "They didn't sit around on this cesspool of an island planning ways to turn the armies of Heaven and Hell against each other." He paused for a moment. "And if you believe that they did, you're just being fucking stupid," he finished.

A shock wave went through the crowd—barely perceptible, but it was there. He had their attention.

"Look at them," Remy said, motioning toward the children. "They're just kids, scared kids with no knowledge of the heritage they were carrying inside them."

The Archangel's gaze grew more intense, like a hawk zeroing in on a rabbit hiding just beneath a bush. Remy wasn't in the least bit intimidated. After all, what did he have to lose?

"The offspring of angel and Nephilim," he continued. "Who even thought that was possible?"

Remy watched the crowd, not sure what he hoped to see, but seeing nothing.

"I think you should leave them alone," he finished. "Let the Vatican look out for them . . . teach them, like they said they would."

Remy fixed the Keeper in a bruising stare. He would remember this one, and the Keeper would remember him.

"But the act of murder has been committed," the old man stated. "And the balance must be restored in order to keep peace."

Francis was staring intently at Remy, but he couldn't bring himself to make eye contact. Remy had suspected Francis' new allegiance, but never realized it would go to this extreme.

Instead, he focused on the gatherings of angels and stated simply, "I believe the murder was justified."

Multiple gasps went through the crowd of those serving Heaven, while those serving Hell seemed strangely amused.

Michael puffed out his chest, his wings slowly flapping, fanning the fires of his rage.

"You speak blasphemy, Seraphim," he growled.

"No," Remy stated. "I speak the truth."

He caught a glimpse of Francis, the look upon the former Guardian angel's face saying, *What the fuck are you up to now, Chandler?*

It was a good question, and one Remy hoped he had an answer for.

"General Aszrus was father to at least one of these children," Remy explained. "He was also the one to begin to see their potential."

"Potential," Michael repeated. "In what way would—"

"He wanted to use them as weapons," Remy interrupted.

The legions of Hell immediately perked up.

Michael tensed, advancing toward Remy. The old Keeper stepped between them, reaching out a hand to stop the archangel.

"Explain yourself, Seraphim," the Keeper stated.

"I was about to," Remy said. "These children were born different . . .

very different, with special abilities hidden inside them just waiting to blossom. Aszrus saw that in some of these children, and foresaw their use in a potential conflict."

"This is insanity," the Archangel Michael scoffed. "If the general was planning something like that, I would have known."

"Just like his assistant would have known?" Remy suggested. "Somebody who spent countless hours by his side?"

"Of course," the Archangel agreed.

Remy searched the crowd for Montagin, hoping that he was there, and finding him on the periphery of the Army of Heaven; Squire and Heath were also present beside him.

"Did you know of this, Montagin?" Remy asked.

"I knew nothing of what you speak," the angel said, under the watchful eyes of everyone there. "The General was quite adept at keeping secrets."

Remy nodded, giving Montagin a wink of thanks. "Our general was beyond adept, as evidenced by them." The Seraphim directed their attention back to the children huddled in the bubble of crackling, supernatural energy.

"You speak of Aszrus' nefarious plans," the Archangel stated. "Of how these poor creatures were to be used as weaponry in a war that does not even exist."

"Yet," Remy stated. "C'mon, Mike, don't bullshit a bullshitter."

The Keeper looked annoyed at Remy's comment. "Where is your proof?" he demanded. "You talk of the general's plans, but with him murdered . . ."

There was a commotion in the distance, and Remy saw Gareth step forward, close to the magickal barrier.

"I am that proof," the young man stated. "I killed my father for what he wanted to turn me, and my brothers and sisters, into."

Remy began to move toward the children, but a wave of debilitating magickal energy coursed through his body, bending him over at the waist. He could feel Malatesta's eyes on him again, warning him to stay in his place.

The Archangel strode toward the corral.

"It was you?" the angel warrior asked. "You were the one to slay the general?"

"Yes, I killed my father," Gareth admitted.

Michael paced before the young man, cold, black eyes unwavering. "Look at you," the angel pronounced. "How could something so . . . small, be a danger to beings such as us." The Archangel looked to the gathering of angels.

"We are not a danger," Gareth announced. "All we want is a chance to exist like everybody else."

"But you are a danger, boy," Michael stated. "You killed one of the most respected of the Lord God's generals."

"I did it in defense of my brothers and sisters," Gareth said. "We want to live, but not as things . . . not as weapons."

Michael stared at the boy, but Remy could see that the Archangel was seeing much more. He strode back to the gathering.

"I have seen enough," the Archangel announced.

The old Keeper bowed, turning his attention to Francis.

"And have you, spokesman of Hell?" he asked.

Francis seemed taken aback by the title. "Yeah," he said, glancing briefly at Remy. "I think I've got it."

Remy then noticed the Pitiless pistol had appeared in his friend's hand, and a sick feeling began to churn in the pit of his stomach.

"We have been presented with the facts," the Keeper announced. "And in these facts we have found what is to be considered the truth." He considered both sides, from left to right. "And this truth has halted the escalation of war."

The Keeper priest folded his hands before him, turning his attention to the children.

"And now, the question remains: What is to be done with this truth?"

Thunder above the island boomed as if for dramatic effect. Remy looked first to Michael, who studied Gareth and the children huddled behind him with an unwavering eye, then to Francis, who held the golden pistol up to his ear, as if on the phone, receiving a call from a higher authority.

It was Gareth who decided the moment.

"I offer myself up for the crime I committed," the boy announced in a voice heard above the hissing of the rain. "I was responsible for the act that led to this, so it is I who must pay the price."

"Gareth, no," Remy called out.

"Silence!" the Keeper commanded.

Remy felt the tendril of magick again grow tighter against the flesh of his throat.

"The guilty has offered himself up as sacrifice for his sin," the Keeper proclaimed, throwing his hands in the air. "How say you all?"

"It's good," Francis said, lowering the gun from his ear.

Michael nodded as well. "I accept this."

"Bring the guilty forward," the Keeper announced, motioning for two other sorcerers to bring the boy from the corral.

One created an opening in the enclosure, while the other stood ready to act. But there was nothing to be done, as Gareth calmly left the others, putting their fears at ease with a reassuring glance.

*Something's not right,* Remy thought. Where was the fighter? The one who was going to strike against those who had abandoned them at birth.

No, something didn't feel right at all.

"Halt!" the old priest's voice boomed, and the youth did as he was told.

"Restrain him," the Keeper ordered, and tendrils of magickal energy similar to the ones that held Remy wrapped around Gareth, making him cry out.

"The guilty is now ready to receive punishment," the Keeper proclaimed to all in attendance.

Remy could now hear the other children crying out, calling their brother's name in pitiful sobs. And the storm continued to grow more intense over the island.

"Come forward." The priest motioned at Francis and the Archangel Michael.

Francis moved as Michael did, but the former Guardian turned to look at Remy. Remy had seen that look before, and it chilled him to the bone, for it was a look that said it was nothing personal, just part of the cost of doing business.

It still felt wrong to Remy. He could feel something invisible, yet dangerous, gradually building up, just waiting to explode.

The women from Rapture began to cry out, but were held back by the Keeper sorcerers. The old priest looked in their direction, annoyance on his wizened face, before returning his full attention to the guilty before him.

"Do you have anything to say before judgment is passed?" he asked Gareth.

Gareth slowly raised his head, and Remy thought he saw a flash of something in his eyes. He tensed, ready for anything, but nothing happened.

"Only that I am not sorry, but accept this punishment to absolve my brothers and sisters of any wrongdoing." He lowered his head and fell silent.

"Is there anything that either of you wish to say?" the priest asked.

"Nothing personal," Francis said, cocking the weapon forged with the power of the Morningstar.

Michael clutched his flaming spear in both hands, its tip turning white-hot. "I speak for the Almighty when I say that you are nothing more than a mistake," the Archangel said. "And you are to be erased." And with those biting words, the angel raised his spear.

"So be it," the Keeper said, stepping away from the youth. "Let the punishment fall."

Remy held his breath as Francis extended his arm and took aim, and Michael drew back his spear and brought the fiery point down.

Both weapons delivered their payload at exactly the same moment, the report of a single gunshot emanating from within an explosion of blinding light.

Remy looked away instinctively, but then forced himself to look into the diminishing brilliance. Francis and Michael stood over the prostrate form of Gareth, his punishment delivered, his penance done.

The old man returned solemnly to inspect the body. A fine, gray smoke now drifted up from the young man's clothing.

"I believe we are done here," the Keeper announced, addressing both sides. There were children's mournful cries in the background, accompanied by shrieking winds and rumbles of thunder that sounded like the approach of a mighty army on horseback.

And Remy still felt that something was horribly, horribly wrong.

Francis had turned from the body, the golden pistol sliding back inside the waist of his pants, when the Archangel spoke.

His voice was like the blast of a trumpet. "We are not yet done."

The angel spread his wings and leapt into the air, landing before the corral and the young within. A sword of crackling fire appeared in his hand, and he directed its point at the frightened children.

"We are not done, until they are no more."

Remy knew at once what the Archangel was up to.

"No," he screamed, not as man, but as a Seraphim, his own voice projecting across the island. "The boy made a deal for the safety of his brothers and sisters."

Michael turned his attentions back to Remy, now a fearful visage of God's wrath.

"And that compact will now be broken," Michael spoke with grim finality. "For there will always be a danger to Heaven . . . Hell . . . and the Earth itself if these creatures are to live."

The children began to panic, pushing against the magickal bands that kept them captive. The spell of containment bit back, painfully repelling those who tested the strength of the bonds.

"They should not be," Michael proclaimed. "They are freaks of nature . . . abominations, and a harsh reminder that we were not ever meant to be part of this mortal world."

Michael looked directly at Remy, and the Seraphim stared back defiantly.

"So, because of your weakness, innocent lives will be taken," Remy said.

Michael did not respond, but Remy was sure that he'd heard him. The Archangel looked to the children again, cowering behind a fence of magickal force.

"Nobody likes to be reminded of their imperfections," the Archangel spoke. "And every time I look at them . . ."

Michael quickly turned away, his mind made up.

"Put them down," he commanded, striding toward his soldiers. As he walked he looked toward Lucifer's men. "Feel free to join us if you care; they could be as much your problem as ours."

Remy watched helplessly as the nightmare continued.

Angels of Heaven and Hell setting themselves upon the captive children. The Keepers dropped the magickal barriers to let the slaughterers in.

It was more than Remy could stand to see, but he felt compelled to watch, to see it all in every grisly detail.

To remember every horrible thing.

The children tried to fight back, to use their newly given abilities, but against the combined armies of Heaven and Hell, there was very little they could do.

It was bad enough that he felt compelled to watch, but to hear their cries was even worse. Again Remy fought against the magick that restrained him, but only managed to cause himself more pain.

Maybe it was some sort of safety mechanism: If he caused himself enough pain he would be rendered unconscious, and then he would no longer see them dying, or hear their pitiful cries.

But oblivion chose not to come for him, and he was forced to witness the atrocities as they unfolded.

Remy managed to rip his gaze away momentarily to see that Malatesta had turned his back to the carnage.

"Don't you dare look away," he cried, reaching up to yank upon the tendril of magickal energy entwined around his neck.

The sorcerer stumbled forward. "Please, Remy," he begged. "It's for the better."

"Turn around," Remy screamed, his anger beyond measure. "Turn around and see what's happening . . . then tell me it's for the better."

He suddenly realized that the screaming had stopped, and found this even more disturbing, for it meant the act was done. There was nothing more he could do.

He watched the shapes of angels flying in circles above the mound of dead, like carrion birds. The bodies were burning, thick oily smoke snaking up to collect against the magickal barrier that still covered the old playground. The storm had subsided, the patter of rain and the faint roll of thunder now a ways off in the distance.

"Release him," Remy heard Michael command, and turned toward the Archangel who now stood before him.

"Is there something you wish to say, angel?" Michael asked.

Remy's thoughts raced, but he could not find the words. There had always been a part of him that believed someday he would return to where he had begun, that the deep psychological wounds he'd received during the Great War would eventually fade, and that he would be able to go back to the joy he remembered in the presence of God.

But now he saw that the poison he'd first recognized during the war had continued to flow through the veins of Paradise, killing what he had known, and making it impossible for him to ever return.

"It's a sad day," Remy managed, something suddenly missing inside of him.

The Archangel looked toward the smoking pyre. "Think of it as an act of mercy," he said. "Something released from its suffering."

Remy could only stare in horror at the being from Heaven.

"Come now, Remiel," the Archangel spoke. "Do you seriously believe there was a place for creatures such as they?"

Remy's gaze fell upon the pyre. He could just about make out the shapes of things that had once been alive, now reduced to smoke, charred bone, and ash.

"I used to think there was," he said, remembering a time that was gone now, never to return. "But now . . ."

He walked away from the angel, not wanting to be in the presence of something so foul. He watched as two of Hell's soldiers swooped down from the sky, each grabbing one of Gareth's ankles, hauling his corpse toward the still-burning mound comprised of his brothers and sisters.

"I had no idea," said a familiar voice.

Remy didn't want to talk to him, but Francis forced the issue.

"I didn't even know where we were going, and suddenly I'm here and being told that I'm representing."

"I promised them that they'd be safe," Remy said, trying to keep his anger in check.

"I had no idea what I would be doing," Francis said again.

Remy turned to stare at his friend.

"But you did it," he said, eyes dropping to the golden pistol shoved in the waist of his pants.

"Didn't have a choice," Francis said. "Part of the deal I made. He says jump, and I ask how high."

"Exactly how high can you jump, Francis?" Remy asked.

Francis touched the butt of his weapon.

"Guess we'll just have to wait and see," the former Guardian angel said, walking away, heading back into the abandoned mining city of Gunkanjima.

The roar of the transport Chinook's engines filled the air, and Remy watched as Malatesta walked behind the old Keeper and the other sorcerers, up into the belly of the craft, as the loading platform began to rise behind them.

*Their work here is done,* Remy thought, wondering what the next atrocity they would preside over would be.

He watched as the helicopter lifted off from the ground, but he was distracted by the angels who still flew above the island city now that the magickal barrier had fallen.

One by one Remy watched as they disappeared, not sure if they were legions of Heaven, or Hell.

And finding that he didn't really care. They were all the same to him now.

The Archangel Michael remained, standing beside the still-blazing pyre. Spreading his wings, he pushed off from the ground to hover aloft, above the site of the massacre.

"You might consider leaving now," the angel Montagin said, walking past Remy.

Squire, Heath, and the mothers of the slain children were with him. Remy could feel the pain of the mothers as they passed, and wanted to tell them how sorry he was, but knew that if the shoe were on the other foot, he wouldn't have wanted to hear another word from the likes of him.

He looked back to the sky, and to the Archangel that still hung there. There seemed to be something forming around him, a whirlwind of flame.

"What's he doing?" Remy asked Montagin.

"He needs to be sure," the angel said.

"Sure of what?"

"That there isn't any trace of them remaining. That they're all dead."

The flames around the Archangel were growing, swirling, creating a vortex of divine fire that had begun to reach down to the island below.

"Are you coming?" Montagin asked.

Remy looked over to see that the angel and the women were waiting, Squire having opened a passage in the shadow thrown by the shell of a concrete storage shed.

"C'mon, Remy," Squire said. "Ain't nothing good gonna come from you sticking around here."

Remy looked back to the sky. An enormous tail of writhing fire snaked down from the body of the whirlpool to spear the ground where the bodies of the children smoldered.

"Go on," Remy told them. "I think I need to see this."

He could hear the hobgoblin begin to protest, but Remy ignored him, shedding his human visage as he walked in the midst of fire.

He didn't know why he wanted to stay, but he felt that he should, to show in some way how sorry he was that this had happened.

The fire swirled around him with hurricane force, and he watched as the buildings that had stood upon the island since it was a coal-mining facility and prison camp began to crumble and were soon scoured from the earth.

"I knew that he would betray me," said a voice beside him within the fire.

Remy turned in disbelief to see the forms of Gareth and the children, standing there, untouched by the Archangel's cleansing fires.

"But I'd hoped that he wouldn't," Gareth said.

"Are you real?" Remy asked, knowing how stupid the question was, but still needing to know.

"Yeah," Gareth replied.

"Are you ghosts?"

The young man shook his head. "They really didn't kill me; I just made them all think that they did. . . . I wanted to see if the angel would keep his part of the bargain."

"He didn't," Remy said. "And come to think of it, neither did I."

"What are you talking about?" Gareth asked.

"I promised to keep you safe," Remy said.

The boy shrugged, the fire swirling around him and the kids, but doing no damage.

"You did what you could."

"It wasn't enough."

He shrugged again. "It was more than most did for us."

The air became full of flying pieces of concrete and other debris that were eventually reduced to powder by the intensity of Michael's divine maelstrom.

"So you're not ghosts," Remy said. "And you're all fine?"

"The kids are a little spooked, but they'll be all right."

"You did this?" Remy asked. "You made the angels think that they slaughtered you and the children?"

"Yeah," Gareth said. "Give them what they want and they'll leave you alone."

"You can't ever let them know that you're still alive," Remy stressed.

"That's the intention," Gareth answered.

"Good," Remy said as the fires of Heaven swirled around them. "Any idea where you'll go?"

"No," Gareth answered. "But I'm sure we'll know when we find it."

The firestorm appeared to be dying, the island city of Gunkanjima leveled to the scorched and now-barren ground.

"You should get out of here," Remy stated as the fires died down. "Wouldn't want all your efforts to go to waste."

Gareth moved closer to the children.

"You're not like the others, are you?"

Remy shook his head. "No . . . no, I'm not." Now more than ever before.

"That's a good thing," Gareth stated, lifting his arms as if to embrace his brothers and sisters. "But it's also dangerous."

Remy understood exactly what Gareth meant, his final words echoing in the dwindling fire as the children left their past, on a journey to their future.

"You be careful, Remy Chandler," Gareth warned. " 'Cause there might come a day when they'll come for you."

The fires eventually died, and Remy stood alone on the barren surface of the place once called Battleship Island.

Nothing remained standing—nothing was left alive.

The island had been scoured of life.

For a brief instant he wondered what people would say when the condition of the island was discovered. How would they explain it? Bizarre atmospheric conditions resulting in multiple lightning strikes? A hidden pocket of methane gas beneath the surface of the former coal-mining facility suddenly igniting as a result of a particularly brutal storm?

The wrath of God?

Remy looked to the sky to see that the Archangel was still there, hovering over what he had wrought, looking down at Remy standing among the ashen remains.

Their eyes touched and Remy once again heard Gareth's words.

*"You be careful, Remy Chandler. . . ."*

And then the Archangel was gone, leaving behind only a distant rumble of thunder.

A hint of a storm in the distance.

A hint of a storm to come.

# CHAPTER TWENTY-SIX

The early morning sun found its way beneath the drawn window shades, chasing away the darkness, gradually revealing the carnage that had occurred overnight.

Mulvehill was propped against the living room wall, afraid to move, not sure of the extent of his injuries, fearing that even the slightest movement might reveal something he wasn't prepared to deal with.

He cautiously turned his head to the right to look at the still form that lay there as he searched for signs of movement—anything to show that his attacker might be alive.

The body remained unnaturally still, but these days he could never be sure.

The rising sun was slowly drawing back the curtains of night. He could see now that there was blood everywhere, spattering the walls and furniture.

Covering his hands.

Staccato images of the violence he'd been a part of appeared inside his head, causing him to gasp. He'd dove into the darkness of his living room, the muzzle flashes from his gun giving him an idea of where his target was.

And what it was that he was facing.

The light of dawn gave him the courage to look down again. His hands were black with blood, the foul coppery scent surprisingly enough to make his stomach rumble noisily as it wafted up into his nostrils. It seemed like forever since he'd pulled the Hungry-Man dinner from the microwave.

Mulvehill carefully moved his fingers, waiting for pain but feeling only minor discomfort, and a tightening of the flesh where the dark blood had dried.

The monster's blood.

In the blasts from his weapon he'd seen it: a pale-skinned monster dressed in a hooded cloak that seemed to be made from the darkness that filled the apartment. It had been coming toward him, closer and closer in the staccato flashes of gunfire. In one of its hands it was holding something, a weapon of some kind that appeared to be made from yellowed bone.

And the monster had pointed it directly at him.

Mulvehill felt his heart race, his breaths coming in short gasps. He forced himself to move. His shirt was covered in blood, both his own and foreign. He could feel the scratches on his arms, recalling with increasing clarity how the fight with his attacker had evolved.

He'd fired his weapon more, but the monster had managed a shot or two at him.

Mulvehill could still hear the odd sound, like a loud cough, as something spat at him.

At full speed he had thrown himself to where he thought his attacker would be. He'd connected with the coffee table, sending himself sprawling to the floor and his firearm flying from his hand.

He looked around to the patches of sunlight and saw the Glock where it had landed on the floor in the corner, beside the overturned coffee table.

He was tempted to go for it, as he eyed the body that remained so very still beside him.

Just in case.

He remembered the feel of the rough fabric of the monster's cloak as his fingers had closed around it. Holding on for dear life, he had pulled upon the clothing, dragging himself up on top of the monster, even as it had tried to escape him. He remembered the sound of the strange weapon, the blasts of fetid air that struck the walls of the living room with a force very much like the snap of a bullwhip.

The monster had struggled to throw him off, but Mulvehill had known that to relinquish his hold was to give up his life. It was as simple as that.

And he'd fought too hard of late to give up this life now.

Mulvehill counted to three before tensing his muscles and sliding up the wall to stand upon trembling legs. He almost laughed aloud with relief when he realized that he was all right. Every inch of him ached and burned, but that was just his body reminding him that he was still alive.

That he had survived.

His eyes fell to the floor, and he saw that there were yellow pieces of bonelike material scattered about—the remains of his attacker's weapon.

There had been nothing graceful about their fight. It was a fight to the death, and it was ugly.

The monster had been strong. Any pretense that Mulvehill had of being civilized was quickly thrown aside, and he allowed his survival instincts to usurp any civility. There was nothing he wouldn't do to take his opponent down, and he did just that, arms and fists flying, never letting up.

Things had become lost in a red haze, and he'd continued to deliver blow after blow, even long after his foe had ceased to move.

Mulvehill looked down at his hands, flexing them to make a fist, and remembering the feeling as he'd pummeled the creature that had invaded his home—the feeling of its flesh ripping as he rained down blow after blow.

The monster lay upon its stomach, its face hidden from him. He remembered the thing's face in the flashes from his firing gun, and bent over with a moan of pain. His back was killing him.

Grabbing a handful of its robe, Mulvehill turned the body over to look upon his attacker.

Its appearance was even more disturbing in the light of morning.

Nothing could look this way and not be a killer of some kind. Its flesh was pale and gray, the teeth jagged like a shark's. It wore an expression of surprise, almost as if it could not believe that it had died by his hands.

But it had.

Hate bubbled up inside him as Mulvehill looked upon the thing that had wrecked his evening. Bringing up something thick and nasty from his throat, he spat upon the corpse.

The beginning of a question sparked in his tired brain.

*Why? Why me?*

There was no reason other than the obvious: It had something to do with Remy.

The monster had fallen upon the landline phone, and Mulvehill reached down to pick it up from the floor. He hit the preprogrammed number for Remy's cell.

"This is Remy Chandler," the message began.

Mulvehill waited for the beep, then started to unload.

"I don't know what the hell you've gotten me involved with now, Chandler, but something just tried to fucking kill me," he said, feeling more tired than he had felt in his entire life.

He leaned back against the wall for support.

"It didn't succeed, just in case you're interested."

Remy walked through the doors of Rapture out onto the steps of the abandoned Prometheus Arms in Connecticut.

He turned back, watching the slight shimmering of the air as the charnel house left him where he'd first arrived.

He'd returned to Rapture from Gunkanjima to find Squire and Montagin saddled up to the bar, and the women who had left their jobs to be with their children already back to work as if nothing had happened.

"Buy you a drink?" Squire had asked as he passed them.

"No."

"I want to thank you," Montagin began from behind him.

Remy turned to look at the angel.

"For all you did in trying to determine who killed the general," Montagin finished, and raised his glass of scotch in a toast.

It wasn't much, but at least it was something to show that a creature such as Montagin could muster some gratitude. At this point, Remy would take whatever he could get.

"See how much you feel like toasting me after you get your bill," he said, continuing on across the bar to a table in the corner where a healing Prosper sat.

"Remiel," the angel said nervously. His face was still bandaged and bruised, but he appeared to be on the mend. "What can I do for you? Anything you want . . . on the house of course."

"How about a ride home?"

The charnel house gone on to who knows where, he walked down the steps from the abandoned arms factory to where he remembered leaving Aszrus' Ferrari.

Remy was glad to see that the car was still where he'd left it. Fishing the key from his pocket, he unlocked the door, and leaned inside to flip open the glove compartment where he'd left his phone. Leaning atop the hood of the sports car, he checked his messages. Linda had called three times, and he listened to each of them. Hearing her voice made him smile. She'd just wanted to say hi, and ended each call by telling him that Marlowe was looking forward to him getting home, and that she loved him.

Hearing something like that after all that he'd been through made all the difference in the world. It gave him a reason to go on; a reason to fight if indeed they ever did come for him.

Remy was going to call Linda back, but saw the time and decided he might give her another hour or so to sleep before disturbing her. Mulvehill had left a message not long ago, so he hit the keypad to listen.

His blood froze in his veins; the sound of his friend's voice was chilling. Remy flexed the muscles in his shoulders, calling forth his wings, and was about to travel to Steven's Somerville apartment when the last of his friend's message struck a very specific chord.

*"Not sure who the hell you pissed off this time, but if they're coming for me to get back at you . . ."*

The words slowly turned, and burrowed into Remy's gray matter.

*"Ugly son of a bitch in a hooded cloak . . . used some kind of gun that looked like it was made from bones."*

A Bone Master, Remy realized. He was confused for a moment, recalling that Prosper had called off the contract, but then he remembered.

Prosper said that he hadn't hired them.

The Bone Masters were attempting to fulfill another contract, one that appeared to include his friends as well.

And if they'd gone after Mulvehill . . .

Complete panic almost overtook him, but he realized that he had to remain calm. Calling upon his wings, he wrapped himself within a cloak of feathers, picturing inside his head where he wanted to go.

Where he needed to be.

Remy appeared in the tiny backyard of his Pinckney Street brownstone, already on the move toward the back door. The door was locked, but that was not a worry. He destroyed the lock as he tore the door open and forced his way into the house.

"Linda!" he called out, hoping that he'd find her terrified by the abruptness of his arrival, but safe. He could make up something to explain his worry later; he was good at things like that.

But neither she nor Marlowe were there, and his panic started to grow. He raced around the home, searching for any signs that something might have . . .

Remy forced the thought from his head.

He reached into his pocket for his phone, and was about to call Linda's cell when he heard sounds from the foyer. He dropped the phone and rushed to the door, opening it in time to see Linda and Marlowe coming into the entryway with a bag of groceries.

"Hey you," she said with a smile that nearly took his breath away. "Have you checked the mail?"

She was turning toward the mailbox, Marlowe excitedly trying to get to him but restrained by his leash.

"No. I just got in myself," Remy answered. He was coming toward them when his eyes caught the hint of movement behind her. Something had entered with her, something that moved in such a way that normal eyes did not—could not—focus upon it.

Something that moved silently, and with a deadly purpose.

A shift in the makeup of his eyes made it possible for him to see the hooded Bone Master assassin as he flowed into the foyer, one arm disappearing within the folds of his cloak to emerge holding the yellowed, skeleton weapon that had once lived, but now delivered death.

Marlowe reacted as Remy did, spinning toward the closing door as the Master took aim. Linda was still oblivious, opening the mailbox as death loomed behind her.

She was Remy's first concern. She needed to be out of harm's way.

But that would mean . . .

There wasn't any time for thought. If he was going to be successful, it had to happen. It was the only way.

Remy's wings exploded from his back as he leapt, carrying him over Linda and Marlowe to land directly in front of the assassin. He grabbed hold of the assassin's wrist and twisted it violently to one side, causing the weapon to fire into the wall.

"Get into the house!" Remy roared, allowing his voice to take on the characteristics of the divine. Some had described it as sounding like getting a message from God Himself.

He could see the look in her eyes, first of awe, and then of fear. He could imagine the little explosions cascading across the surface of her brain as her perceptions of the world were brought to ruin.

Remy didn't want to be rough, but couldn't risk her being hurt. He spun away from the attacker, grabbing her firmly by the shoulders and throwing her backward toward the still-open door to the brownstone. Her mouth was open in a scream, but no sound came out as he watched her fly through the air. The grocery bags tore in the scuffle, the contents spilling over the tile floor of the entryway.

Marlowe's bark boomed in the small confines, warning Remy that there was an intruder and that he would protect him.

"Go be with Linda," he managed to get out as he turned back

toward the assassin, ready to rend the killer limb from limb for daring to put those he loved at risk.

Divine fire formed in the palm of his hand, and he thrust it toward the Bone Master, who ducked, slipping beneath his arm, and worming his way around Remy. Remy lashed out with his wings, slashing the feathered appendages across the front of the Bone Master as he attempted to aim his weapon.

*Phutt! Phutt! Phutt!* went the weapon of bone, projectiles of poisoned teeth hurtling their way toward their intended target. But Remy did not slow down, thrusting off with his wings and colliding with the Master's midsection as the two of them hurtled back toward the open door into his home.

The Bone Master was smashed with incredible force against the wall inside, the sound of broken plaster crumbling to the floor accompanying a grunt of pain.

Lashing out, the assassin smashed the bony weapon across the bridge of Remy's nose. His eyes filled with tears as he reared back and away.

The Bone Master used the opportunity to dart to the side, flowing into the living room as he again took aim.

Wiping the running fluids from his eyes to clear his vision, Remy attempted to take flight, but the low ceilings in the entryway limited his distance, and he found himself dropping back down as the assassin prepared to fire.

There was a flash of black across the Bone Master's path, and an ear-piercing cry sounded, the shot going astray.

Remy saw in horror that Marlowe had attacked the assassin, taking hold of the would-be killer's wrist in his powerful jaws, causing the assassin to lose his hold upon the weapon.

Driven nearly insane by the attack upon his master, Marlowe held on to the demon's limb, growling and shaking it savagely in all his animalistic fury. The Bone Master continued to cry out, withdrawing a nasty-looking blade from the folds of his cloak with his free hand.

Remy was there, taking the demon's wrist in a fiery grip.

"I've got this, boy," Remy told the dog, and Marlowe listened, releasing the assassin with a bark and stepping back to make sure that Linda, who cowered in the corner of the room, was all right.

Remy didn't want her to see this, but it wasn't a time to be gentle.

The demon fought against his hold even as his pale flesh caught fire, and the serrated dagger dropped from his grasp.

But the Bone Master was not finished, driving his knee up into Remy's stomach as he wriggled from the Seraphim's clutches. Remy was surprised at the Master's strength as the wind wheezed from his lungs.

Dropping to the floor, the demon crawled upon all fours like some hideous insect toward where his bone gun had dropped.

With a hand charred black from divine fire the Bone Master reached for the weapon, only to pull it back with a quick snap as a foot came down upon the gun, crushing it against the hardwood floor.

Remy saw that Linda had left the safety of her hiding place to assist him, her eyes briefly touching his as she ground the weapon beneath the heel of her shoe.

The Bone Master screamed as if in great physical pain. And still screaming, the demon grabbed Linda's ankle, yanking her foot out from beneath her and sending her to the floor, her head bouncing off the hardwood, stunning her.

The killer crawled atop her with a snarl, going for the knife that he'd dropped when his hand was set aflame. The weapon still burned, but that did not stop the assassin, as he retrieved the smoldering blade and prepared to cut the woman's throat.

Remy pounced, reaching out to haul the Bone Master from atop her.

The assassin was wild, thrashing in his clutches, and Remy grabbed hold of the demon's pale, gaunt face, forcing the assassin to look into his eyes.

"You'll never hurt anyone ever again," Remy stated flatly, dispassionately, willing his hands afire.

The assassin continued to fight him, even as the divine flames began to hungrily consume the flesh of his face, his eyes bubbling and popping from their sockets before the flames spread onto his skull.

The Bone Master screamed for far longer than Remy would have imagined he could.

When he finally fell silent, Remy let the body slip from his grasp. The fire continued to burn, jumping to the assassin's robes and the flesh beneath. If allowed to spread, there would be nothing left to show that the assassin had even been there.

All except for the physical and mental damage the demon had inflicted in his wake.

Marlowe came to Remy, leaping up on his chest, stretching his neck to eagerly kiss his face. Remy found it suddenly difficult to remain standing, and dropped down to his knees, giving the dog ample opportunity to display his rampant affections.

As Marlowe frantically licked his face, Remy looked to see Linda staring at him from where she sat perfectly motionless upon the floor. He wanted to tell her to remain calm, that he would explain everything to her, but he found that the words would not come.

The look of fear in her eyes freezing them in his throat as he tried to speak.

"I believe," he started, the words for some reason so difficult to pry from his mouth. "I believe I owe you an explanation."

Remy heard himself, the words sounding strangely slurred, and wondered what could be the cause when he came to realize that his entire body was growing increasingly cold. He could not feel his limbs, and found himself suddenly toppling over onto the floor.

Marlowe yelped in panic as he fell, and Linda was at his side, leaning over him, tears in her eyes, her face racked with the beginnings of panic.

"You're bleeding," he heard her say, though strangely muffled, and he was able to lift his body and tilt his head in such a way to see that yes, he was indeed bleeding; a cold realization came to him.

The assassin's bullets had found their target, the venom-infused teeth sending a powerful poison coursing through his veins.

Remy attempted to react, to alter his internal chemistry in such a way as to burn the poison away before . . .

Nothing happened, and the cold continued to permeate his every fiber; he was finding it harder and harder to remain there—to remain with Linda and Marlowe.

Marlowe cried pathetically, pacing back and forth in front of them. Linda was holding him now, gripping him tightly in her arms and begging for him to stay with her.

"Remy, what should I do?" she pleaded, hoping that he would help her, but it was so difficult for him to speak.

"I . . . I'm so sorry," he managed to squeak out. "Didn't want . . . to lie."

She was hysterical, and he wanted to hold her, to tell her that he would be fine, but he could no longer move his arms, and now that everything had been revealed, he did not want to begin another lie.

"Remy," she pleaded, tears raining down upon his face; tears that he could not feel.

He tried to stay with her, but his eyes had grown so heavy, and he could no longer hold them open. *Maybe if I close them for just a moment,* he told himself.

*To rest.*

Marlowe was howling now, his cries reverberating through the lobby. Remy thought it was the saddest sound he had ever heard as he felt himself begin to succumb.

His eyes closed, and darkness fell, but there was fire in the midst of shadow; a struggling flame fighting to stay alight in the encroaching gloom.

But the fire grew dim, smaller by the passing moment, until it was but a faintly glowing ember, and it could fight no more, giving in to the dark.

The last thought Remy had before he, too, succumbed:

*Is this what it's like to die?*

# EPILOGUE

*Romania*

Simeon stood on the outskirts of the ancient cemetery, watching the burial from a distance, and trying to remember how it felt to die.

With each shovelful of dirt upon the wooden coffin, he imagined himself deep within the ground, lovingly held in the earthen embrace, waiting for the moment when he would at last pass from life.

But the Earth, and Heaven, would not have him.

The forever man's thoughts drifted back to a time that seemed not so long ago. But what was time for one who would breathe forever?

Castle Hallow had fallen, and the sorcerous might of the Pope named Tyranus had been unleashed as death had taken him. In his fury, Simeon had commanded the demon legions to attack, their number proving too great for the holy man. But as he succumbed, the Pope let flow his vast reserves of supernatural power, laying the castle low.

The fortress of the necromancer crumbled and sank beneath the moor, Simeon's body weighed down by pieces of heavy wall that took him deeper and deeper beneath the mire.

And that was when he experienced the vision.

In a moment of death—which was all that he was ever given—Simeon saw the way in which his desires could finally come true.

And in the time of death allotted, before he was wrenched back to wretched existence, he saw how it could all be made possible.

The rings. The two rings of Solomon.

With one ring already adorning his finger, Simeon had searched for the other, dying again and again while looking for the corpse of the Pope called Tyranus deep beneath the gripping marshland.

A woman's cry tore Simeon from his memory.

He watched as a group of men supported an older woman in a veil, and dressed entirely in black, holding her up as they escorted her from the new grave. Eyes drawn to the freshly turned earth, Simeon again remembered how it had been.

Now possessing both of Solomon's rings, he'd pulled himself up from the mire, a new purpose burning in his chest where a soul used to be.

He'd cried out his victory to the Heavens as he emerged from the mud, desperate for them to hear him, and to know that he would be the one to bring them down.

As usual, Heaven and all who lived within its glory chose to ignore him.

But that slight would come at a cost most severe.

He wondered if the angel that stood upon the ground where the necromancer's castle had once been would be returning to Heaven.

The angel turned to watch his struggles as he withdrew himself from the grip of the moor. A sword of fire glowed powerfully in his grasp as he observed him.

Simeon was tempted to share his vision with the divine creature, but he decided against it, believing that it was best that the Almighty and all who served Him be unaware as to what was coming sometime in the future.

The angel had asked who he was, and how he came to be alive, but Simeon did not have time for questions, raising his hands and feeling the power of the rings tingling upon his fingers.

"I'm nobody," he had told the angel. "And nothing worth remembering."

And the angel had agreed, spreading his wings and taking to the sky.

He'd often wondered in the passing years what had happened to that angel, and if he would ever see him again.

Simeon thought of the angel, now called Remy Chandler, and smiled. *There's something about that one,* he thought, turning to walk the path from the cemetery, his demonic minions walking respectfully behind him, as they had since he pulled himself from the mud and ruins of Castle Hallow.

Something to be watched, and if possible, cultivated.

This Remy Chandler could be exactly what was needed to move things along. It was something to consider, but there was another matter that needed attending to.

Another need to be filled.

It wasn't all that difficult to locate the one he'd been searching for. Simeon and his demonic lackeys stood outside the run-down stone building located just behind the bakery. The aroma of freshly baked bread wafted in the air as the forever man searched for the entrance.

The door whined like a hungry feline as he pushed it open and proceeded inside. His demons attempted to follow, but Simeon did not believe they would be necessary.

"Wait for me here," he told them, turning to climb the creaking wooden steps up to the top floor of the ancient tenement. The air was thick with the residue of the many Romanian meals that had been cooked there through the centuries the structure had stood. Simeon could just imagine the lives lived here.

The lives, and the deaths.

It hadn't been all that difficult to locate the one Simeon sought, no matter how hard he tried to hide himself. Purchases of baubles to ward off evil from a local Romani clan, thefts of holy relics from churches close by, reports of a strange man who openly wept when a story about an environmental calamity on a deserted Japanese island was reported on a news broadcast at the village tavern.

All were like a map to one such as the forever man; a map that pointed to the location of one who could be beneficial to his work.

Simeon could feel the presence of something unnatural—*preternatural*—as he reached the heavy, wooden door at the top of the stairs. It was obvious to him that he had come to the right place.

"Who's . . . who's there?" asked a weak voice from inside.

"I've come with a proposition," Simeon said to the closed door, listening for sounds of movement on the other side. "May I come in?"

There came a chilling laugh behind the door. "Oh yes, please do," said a voice unlike the one he'd first heard. This one sounded strong, confident. "We would truly enjoy hearing what you have to propose to us."

Simeon took hold of the metal knob and turned it, pushing open the door. The atmosphere inside was immediately oppressive, as if there was a storm about to rage within the tiny confines.

Closing the door behind him, Simeon took in the appearance of the place: the walls covered with pages of religious texts, strange symbols painted in blood upon any surface that had remained untouched, magickal talismans hanging from the ceiling, candles burning before makeshift shrines to gods and saints known, and long forgotten.

And in the center of the room, sitting in the middle of a circle of protection drawn upon the rough wood floor, sat the shadow of a man.

Simeon was surprised at how bad he looked, the incident on Gunkanjima having far more of a devastating effect on him than the forever man would have imagined.

"Do I know you?" the man asked, his voice soft with weakness.

"We met briefly," Simeon said. "On the island."

The man's eyes grew wide and filled with tears, before his expression changed and the evil spirit that resided within him reared its ugliness.

"Oh to be there again," the evil spoke in a voice horrible and rough. "To be part of all that death—glorious; but I do not remember you."

The man turned his body in the circle to face him.

"Come closer," the spirit said, motioning with a finger that had become like a claw. "Maybe if I was to taste you . . ."

Simeon crossed his arms, unfazed by the evil entity's teasing.

"You do not remember, for I chose that you not," Simeon said. He showed the entity possessing the man the rings adorning his hands.

The spirit gasped at the sight of the two rings.

"But I know you, Constantin Malatesta," Simeon said. "As well as the ancient thing that resides inside of you."

Malatesta closed his eyes, his face lined from incredible strain.

"Please," he begged. "You must leave at once; you're not safe. Even with all this protection . . ." His eyes darted about the room. "I don't know how much longer I can keep it contained."

Simeon smiled.

"Contained?" he asked. "And why would you want to do that?"

Malatesta looked horrified. "Why have you sought me out?"

"I come with an offer," Simeon said, picking up a piece of religious statuary from a nearby table. "I require someone with your skills."

"Skills?" Malatesta repeated with a shiver, still attempting to keep the entity inside him from regaining control.

"A sorcerer," Simeon said. "I have need of a sorcerer."